Raiding Forces Series:

Those Who Dare

Dead Eagles

Blood Wings

Roman Candle

Guerrilla Command

Necessary Force

Private Army

Visit **www.raidingforces.com** and **www.facebook.com/raidingforces**
to read more about the Raiding Forces Series.

BOOK SIX IN THE RAIDING FORCES SERIES

NECESSARY FORCE

PHIL WARD

This book is a work of fiction. Names, characters, businesses, organizations, places, events, and incidents are either a product of the author's imagination or are used fictitiously. Any resemblance to actual persons, living or dead, events, or locales is entirely coincidental.

ISBN: 978-0-9860771-0-4
LCCN: 013943059
Published by Military Publishers LLC
Austin, Texas
www.raidingforces.com

Distributed by Military Publishers LLC

For ordering information or special discounts for bulk purchases, please contact Military Publishers LLC at 8871 Tallwood, Austin, TX 78759, 512.346.2132.

DEDICATION

DEDICATED TO LT. COL. CHARLES HARDIN

In early June 1968 then Captain Hardin took command of A/2/39. The timing could have hardly been worse. The company had been decimated in the Battle of the Plain of Reeds...thirty-seven men flying out after the four day running battle. The officer he replaced had been killed, there were only two platoon leaders and virtually no NCO's. Never the less the mission continued with no time to stand down to allow him to reorganize his new command.

A/2/39 was engaged in intensive combat operations...160 air assault missions in one four month period. Captain Hardin provided a steady hand at a time when that was exactly what was needed. He was quick to adapt to rapidly changing missions that could come out of nowhere at any hour of the day or night, cool under fire, made commanding a hard fighting airmobile rifle company look easy and I never saw him make a tactical error.

It does not get much better than that.

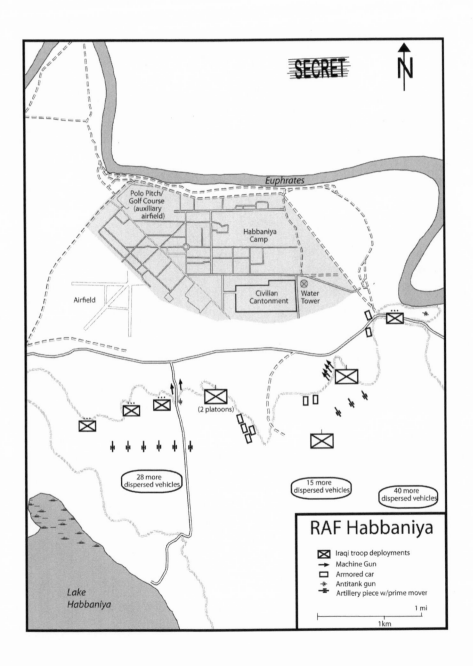

N

Euphrates

Polo Pitch/
Golf Course
(auxiliary
airfield)

Habbaniya
Camp

Airfield

Civilian
Cantonment

Water
Tower

(2 platoons)

28 more
dispersed vehicles

15 more
dispersed vehicles

40 more
dispersed vehicles

Lake
Habbaniya

RAF Habbaniya

⊠ Iraqi troop deployments
→ Machine Gun
▢ Armored car
⊹ Antitank gun
⊨ Artillery piece w/prime mover

1 mi

1km

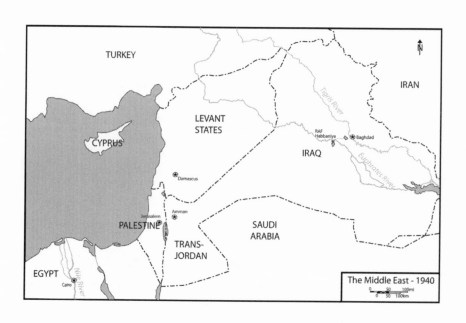

TURKEY

CYPRUS

LEVANT
STATES

IRAN

Tigris River

RAF
Habbaniya

Baghdad

IRAQ

Euphrates River

Damascus

Jerusalem

Amman

PALESTINE

SAUDI
ARABIA

TRANS-
JORDAN

EGYPT

Nile River

Cairo

The Middle East - 1940

0   50   100mi
0   50   100km

1

GOLDEN SQUARE

THE WOMAN CAME INTO THE ROOM. SHE WAS CARRYING A big knife with a curved blade. Maj. John Randal, DSO, MC, was not as sound asleep as he appeared. His fingers tickled the ivory grip of his Colt .38 Super under the covers next to his leg.

A shadow appeared behind the woman. From the dock where the Nile houseboat was moored, a lamp beamed through the porthole, creating a yellow glow into which materialized the distinctive slim silhouette of a pistol barrel. The question in Major Randal's mind: which one should he shoot?

Quick as a cat, the woman turned and stabbed the person behind her. Major Randal's Colt .38 Super spoke two times.

Flashlights came on. Armed policemen swarmed the boat. Someone blew a whistle. A sawed-off police captain with a toothbrush mustache, wearing an ill-fitting off-white linen suit, shouted, "Are you OK, Major?"

"What took you so long, Sansom?" Major Randal said as he swung out of bed, pulling on his pants and Blood's slip-on boots.

"Events did not go strictly according to plan," Capt. A.W. "Sammy" Sansom said. "Not anticipating a second party to show up."

"Well, neither was I."

"Fatima is, or I should say *was*, an operative for the Golden Circle—that much we know. The man she knifed is an unknown—Abwehr, Muslim Brotherhood or perchance a freelance ... who is to say?"

"You're supposed to know the players."

"I spy spies; I don't read crystal balls," the policeman said. "If you had been a little quicker on the trigger and shot the miscreant before Fatima went for him, maybe she wouldn't have felt compelled to kill you too."

"Right," Major Randal said. "If I had, he'd have turned out to be one of *your* boys."

"Had we wanted Fatima dead, Major, we could have killed her ourselves. The plan was for you to pass out. Then, as the lady in question photographed the classified documents about the Abyssinian guerrilla operation contained in your briefcase, we break in and nab her red-handed. Couldn't stick to the script, eh, lover boy?"

"One thing led to another," Major Randal said.

"Have to give it to you Major, you make first-rate bait."

"I've had practice."

"So we hear," said the chief of Cairo's Counterintelligence Department. "Remember, you were not here tonight. This never happened."

"Tell that," Major Randal said, "to the sporting set at the Kit-Kat Club."

"Quite right," Captain Sansom said. "You shot the best belly dancer in Egypt."

MAJ. JOHN RANDAL WAS LYING ON A LOUNGE CHAIR AT THE pool of the Gezira Club soaking up sun next to the leggy brunette Lt. Penelope Honeycutt-Parker, RM. Her husband, Capt. Lionel Honeycutt-Parker, was inside making reservations for dinner.

"Hot date last night?" Lieutenant Honeycutt-Parker asked. "You look tired, John."

"No," Major Randal said. Not that he would tell her if he'd had one.

She was a longtime friend of Capt. the Lady Jane Seaborn, OBE, RM—worked for her in the Raiding Forces Women's Royal Marine detachment.

The truth was, there had not been any dates. Last time he had been in Cairo, women were literally throwing themselves at him. It had helped to have Special Operations Executive supplying female operatives to sleep with him to see if he would reveal military secrets.

This trip, women would not come anywhere near him, except Fatima—and she had an agenda.

No books had been published about his latest military adventures this time around, either. In fact, Major Randal never heard the Abyssinian campaign mentioned at all. It was as if it had never happened. All the talk in the spring of 1941 was about the calamity in Greece, the threatened invasion of Crete and the German general named Rommel in Libya.

Except for the Honeycutt-Parkers, he knew hardly anyone in Cairo.

Captain Lady Seaborn was away in England. Her dead husband, Lt. Cdr. Mallory Seaborn, RN, had turned out not to be so dead when Major Randal rescued him on the first MI-9 mission to the Continent, before coming to Africa. Since Major Randal had been engaged to Lady Jane at the time, to say that his love life was complicated would be a major understatement.

When Force N, meaning Major Randal and Lt. Butch "Headhunter" Hoolihan, went missing in Abyssinia, Captain Lady Seaborn had abandoned her husband to travel to Africa to help organize a rescue operation. She stayed for the entire campaign, which did nothing to untangle their relationship.

Rita Hayworth and Lana Turner, the slave girls he had liberated in Abyssinia, had returned to England with Captain Lady Seaborn as members of her Royal Marine detachment. The girls were scheduled for complete medicals, and then who knew what Lady Jane had in store for them. Major Randal was surprised at how much he missed Rita and Lana, who had been his constant companions and shared every danger he had faced for the past six months. He wondered what the two Zar priestesses were up to.

Lieutenant Hoolihan was off on a course in England, attending a school designed to initiate him into the mysteries of being a Royal Marine officer. Captain Lady Seaborn had mentioned a visit to Chatterley's Military Tailors for the young Royal Marine lieutenant, who was her pet project.

Major Randal had been Lady Jane's pet project once upon a time. It was good to be her pet project.

Maj. Sir Terry "Zorro" Stone, KBE, MC, was home on leave too. His exact rank was in question (he had been an acting colonel). He was no longer commanding officer of the Lancelot Lancer Yeomanry Regiment, *aka* Lounge Lizards; his brother had resumed command in Addis Ababa following the conclusion of the Abyssinian Campaign. Major Stone had led the longest, fastest, most successful armored cavalry advance in modern history—over 1,700 miles. Nothing the Germans had done on any of their blitzkriegs had even come close. Only his father, the Duke, had wanted his eldest son, Reginald, to command—and it *was* the family regiment.

Maj. Jack Merritt, MC, MM, was staying in command of No. 9 Motor Machine Gun Company, Sudan Defense Force. Major Merritt had been nominated for an immediate Distinguished Service Order for his brilliant leadership during the run-up to the Battle of Kern and then the race to the strategic Port of Massawa on the Red Sea. There was a rumor the Free French also had plans to award him the Legion of Honor. No. 9 MMG Co. was being detached from the Sudan Defense Force to be trained by the Long Range Desert Group in deep desert operations. The plan was that it then be assigned to Raiding Forces, Middle East.

Mule Raiding Battalion commanders Capt. Taylor Corrigan, MC, Capt. Jeb Pelham-Davies, MC, and Capt. Pyro "Percy" Stirling, MC, were on home leave.

Lt. Randy "Hornblower" Seaborn, DSC, RN, had returned to Seaborn House with the naval contingent that had traveled with Lounge Lizard Force to operate the three-pound fast firers for the Lancelot Lancer Yeomanry. His boat, MGB 345, was back from its refit.

Capt. Mike "March or Die" Mikkalis, DSM, MM, had gone on leave somewhere in Africa. He had informed Major Randal that his temporary rank was only temporary as he did not intend to remain an officer. The job he wanted was Sergeant Major of Raiding Forces, Middle East.

Lt. Pamala Plum-Martin, OBE, RM, was away going to flight school. Major Randal was not sure exactly where, but it was in the Middle East somewhere. Because she had amassed so many hours flying combat missions for Psychological Warfare Executive (PWE) over Abyssinia in a Supermarine Walrus, she was going to be able to place out of most of the training. There was a possibility the aviatrix might be awarded her wings and the Distinguished Flying Cross on the same day.

Sqn. Ldr. Paddy Wilcox, DSO, OBE, MC, DFC, had gone along with Lieutenant Plum-Martin to be available to tutor her on the finer points of the written examinations. He had taught her to fly at Seaborn House, and it had been his idea to allow her to fly combat missions over Abyssinia. The Canadian pilot wanted to make sure the Vargas Girl-looking Royal Marine received her wings.

Brandy Seaborn was with her husband, Cdre. Richard "Dickey the Pirate" Seaborn, VC, OBE. Commodore Seaborn was going to get his wish at long last, command of a capital ship—a cruiser. Brandy had originally come out to Egypt to serve with Col. Dudley Clarke in A-Force, but now was thinking about doing something with Raiding Forces, Middle East, instead. She and Major Randal had always been very close.

One thing was certain—she was not going to be a Royal Marine. Brandy marched to her own drum.

Missing were Capt. "Geronimo" Joe McKoy, Waldo Treywick and ex-U.S. Marine Frank Polanski. The three had stayed behind to carry out a private enterprise the day Force N flew out of Abyssinia. No word of their whereabouts had turned up yet.

Major Randal was growing bored in Cairo. He was ready to go to work reorganizing Raiding Forces. He had been in talks with Captain Honeycutt-Parker. The Royal Dragoons officer had proven to be a superb organizer and was either going to take command of Raiding Forces, Europe, located at Seaborn House, or become deputy to Major Randal. There were a lot of possibilities for raiding to be had—he simply had to put the pieces of the puzzle together.

A blonde in a two-piece swimsuit that appeared to be made out of three Band-Aids and a couple of bootlaces strolled over to where Major

Randal and Lieutenant Honeycutt-Parker lay sunning. The woman was tanned pure gold and had white platinum hair the color of ice (even paler than Lieutenant Plum-Martin's, if that could be possible). It was pulled straight back in a long ponytail. There were a dozen thin gold bangles on her left wrist.

She looked vaguely familiar.

"Are you Major Randal?" the woman asked with a slight accent. She could not avoid staring at the scars on his chest, which were the result of being mauled by a lion.

"That would be me," Major Randal said. "Who might you be?"

Lieutenant Honeycutt-Parker raised her sunglasses to check out the golden girl.

"Rikke Runborg. My friends call me Rocky."

"Nice to meet you, ah, Rocky."

Actually we *have* met, Major." Rocky had an impressive set of white teeth when she smiled ... which it seemed like she did a lot. She was very supple.

"Really?"

"I was with Mallory," Rocky said, "the night you saved us. Never had the opportunity to thank you properly—things happened so quickly after the gun battle and the mad dash to the boat."

"Didn't recognize you," Major Randal said, "with your clothes on."

"Mallory failed to mention he was married," Rocky said. "When I discovered the truth, I came to Cairo to work with the Norwegian Legation. Call me."

"Fascinating," Lieutenant Honeycutt-Parker said as she watched Rocky ripple her way back to her lounge. "I would not make that telephone call if I were you, John."

"No?"

"Have you noticed women avoiding you?"

"As a matter of fact, Parker ..." Major Randal said.

"Before she flew out, Jane passed the word over the 'old girl network' you had spent the last six months behind the lines in Abyssinia," Lieutenant Honeycutt-Parker said. "Every woman in Cairo knows the

VD rate there is 80 percent or better. Get the picture, hero?"

"I hope you're making that up."

CAPT. LIONEL HONEYCUTT-PARKER RETURNED TO THE POOL area. "Who was that?"

"Mallory's ex-girlfriend," Lt. Penelope Honeycutt-Parker said. "John rescued her from the Nazis."

"Vichy French Police," Maj. John Randal said.

"She wants him to phone her."

"I would advise against that call," Captain Honeycutt-Parker said. "Mallory has damned fine taste in women, credit him that."

Jim "Baldie" Taylor walked out to the pool. "Who was that smasher you and John were chatting with, Parker?"

"Rikke Runborg, friends call her Rocky. She was with Mallory the night John brought the two of them out of France for Norman Crockett's MI-9—dropped by to ask him to call her so she can thank him properly."

"I am going to do you a favor, Major," Jim said. "We can take off this afternoon for the RAF base at Habbaniya. Pam is graduating from the flying school there in a couple of days. Let's fly up to see her awarded her wings.

"Take along a couple of those long-range Springfield 7mm-06s you brought back from Abyssinia. Get in some white oryx hunting. The place is a paradise in the desert."

"Am I invited?" Lieutenant Honeycutt-Parker asked. "Lionel is leaving for England to check on Raiding Forces operations at Seaborn House. I am at loose ends."

"Absolutely," Jim said. "Habbaniya is the home of RAF No. 4 Service Flying Training School. It's a man-made oasis where they send pilots who need rest. Said to have the best swimming pool in the service, golf, polo, riding … you name it. Have ourselves a nice quiet holiday.

"Besides, Major, you do not want to place *that* phone call."

2

OASIS

MAJ. JOHN RANDAL WAS SITTING IN THE CO-PILOT'S CHAIR of the Hudson, winging his way to No. 4 Service Flying Training School (SFTS) located at RAF Habbaniya, Iraq. Lt. Penelope Honeycutt-Parker was sitting in one of the few remaining theatre seats in the back, reading a stack of movie star journals. The publications were written in three different languages.

She could read them all.

Originally, the converted bomber was FM Sir Archibald Wavell's personal plane. He had loaned it to Capt. the Lady Jane Seaborn for the duration of the Abyssinian Campaign. That's why most of the plush carpets and theatre seats were missing. The plane had served as a paratroop dropper and freight hauler to 1 Guerrilla Corps (Parachute), Force N.

Unfortunately, the Hudson had crashed somewhere in Abyssinia.

At least that's what was recorded in the official record. In fact, the airplane (with a new tail number) was now part of a small Most Secret private air force belonging to MI-6, British Secret Intelligence Service (SIS)—though that information was classified. The Hudson that no longer officially existed belonged to Raiding Forces if anyone with a Most Secret clearance who thought they possessed a "Need to Know" inquired. No one outside SIS, including Major Randal, knew who really owned it.

"The Golden Square," Major Randal said. "What's the story?"

Jim Taylor, in the left seat, gave him a sideways look. "How do you know about the Golden Square?"

"Came up in conversation."

"I bet it did," Taylor said. The MI-6 operative was masquerading as a high-ranking Special Operations Executive (SOE) official—which would have been news to SOE, as they thought he worked for them. "The Golden Square is a fairly recent development in Iraq. You do not have a 'Need to Know,' Major, but since we are on our way to Iraq I'm going to give you an unauthorized briefing. We are not having this conversation."

"What conversation?"

"Now that the Italians are out of the Red Sea, Iraq is arguably the most strategic piece of real estate the British Empire controls. Typically His Majesty's government is treating the place as if it has no value at all."

"What makes the place so important?" Major Randal asked.

"Two things that are really three. It's the crossroads of the air link between Great Britain and India. Iraq has massive deposits of oil in the north around Mosul, Kirkuk and Khanaqin. And the final fifty-mile stretch of the Shatt el Arab, where the Tigris and the Euphrates merge to flow into the Persian Gulf, is the conduit for the export of oil from Southern Persia. In the event the UK was to be cut off from oil from the United States it would have to have Iraq oil."

"How might that happen?"

"The U-boats could win the battle for the North Atlantic sea lanes— you were briefed on that probability during OPERATION LOUNGE LIZARD," Jim said.

"Roger."

"For the interested military observer, what makes Iraq so vital is that it produces enough oil to supply *all* of Germany's annual military needs.

The Nazis have a treaty with the Russians that allows them overland access to Iraq. Get the picture, Major?"

"Loud and clear, sir."

"Don't call me 'sir,'" Jim said. "King Faisal was our friend, but he died in 1933. His twenty-something son Ghazi took the Iraqi throne. He lacked prestige, character, and courage. He was disinclined to cooperate with us and liked the Nazis—but he was conveniently killed in a car crash in 1939."

Major Randal said, "Where were you at the time, Jim?"

"The military success the Nazis achieved when they overran most of Europe and are now having in the Balkans has greatly impressed the peoples of Iraq and others in the Middle East," Jim said, ignoring the question. "The Germans appear as winners, and we look to be weak."

"I can see how we would," Major Randal said. "What's the Golden Square have to do with anything?"

"The new Prime Minister of Iraq, Rashid Ali al-Gaylani, is in the pay of the Abwehr—making him a *de facto* Nazi agent. He is supported by a cabal of four colonels, Salah al-Din al-Sabbagh, Kamal Shabib, Fahmi Said and Mahmud Salman—the *Golden Square.*"

"Four Iraqi colonels," Major Randal said, "who think they're golden— that's got to end bad."

"You're right about that. The Golden Square are supported in their pro-Axis stance by the Grand Mufti who fled Palestine for sanctuary in Baghdad, where he is churning out inflammatory, anti-British propaganda," Jim said. "Local public opinion is running against us. The region is a tinderbox. All it's going to take is a spark."

"What's the plan, Jim?" Major Randal asked. "You always have a plan."

"Not this time, Major. Our side has almost no military assets available in or anywhere near Iraq should we have to resort to arms," Jim said. "Worse, we do not have any way to send in troops in any reasonable amount of time in an emergency—if we were able to organize a military expedition."

"The Germans have to want the oil," Major Randal said.

"They do."

"YOU AND PARKER ARE GETTING OFF. I HAVE TO FLY ON TO Baghdad—it's only about sixty miles," Jim Taylor said. "Check into your quarters, head to the pool and enjoy your dinner tonight. Expect me back midmorning tomorrow—then I can start my leave. Looking forward to it.

"Take your carry-ons. The rest of your luggage will be delivered to your quarters while the plane is refueled. When I get back, we'll go bag a couple of trophy white oryx."

The Hudson flew over Lake Habbaniyah past the Royal Air Force Base. Jim came around to land on the airdrome built just inside the south side of the fence surrounding the RAF station. Coming in, Maj. John Randal saw at a glance RAF Habbaniya had not been designed for defense. Air bases rarely are.

Having raided quite a few of them, he tended to view airfields with a jaundiced eye. This one, Major Randal noted with detached professional interest, was one of the least defendable he had ever seen.

The lush, green 500-acre cantonment backed up to a bend in the Euphrates River on the north side. Two miles to the south was Lake Habbaniyah, which boasted the yacht club and a commercial flying boat port for BOAC Airlines. A couple of hundred yards or so out the front gate, between the RAF base and the lake, was a 150- to 250-foot high escarpment. Troops were conducting maneuvers on the high ground when the Hudson flew over.

The escarpment was commanding terrain—dominating the base.

A ten-foot tall fence ran for seven miles around RAF Habbaniya with blockhouses studded at 300-yard intervals all around the perimeter.

The airstrip was located *outside* the fence.

The most prominent feature of the man-made oasis was its water tower. At least the water well was inside the wire.

RAF Habbaniya was a backwater. Life traveled at a leisurely, prewar pace, undisturbed by outside world events. The fighting, for those fortunate enough to be stationed here, was far away. The base had a dual purpose: to train pilots and aircrew and to serve as a quiet tour for jaded combat pilots who were in need of getting their nerves back.

RAF Habbaniya seemed the perfect getaway to spend a couple of weeks relaxing and unwinding from an intense guerrilla campaign before going back to the frenetic pace of Cairo. Major Randal was looking forward to it. This trip was a good idea.

"Keep your eye on the Major, Parker," Jim advised as the Hudson rolled to a halt. "A lot of unattached women on this post. With the unrest in Baghdad, nonessential personnel at the Embassy were evacuated to RAF Habbaniya."

"Not me, what happens in another country does not count," Lt. Penelope Honeycutt-Parker drawled as she looked up from her magazine. "You know that, Jim."

"No idea you did—my three ex-wives never grasped the concept."

Sqn. Ldr. Paddy Wilcox and Lt. Pamala Plum-Martin were waiting when Major Randal and Lieutenant Honeycutt-Parker exited the Hudson. The Royal Marine officer threw her arms around Major Randal, exclaiming, "I am so glad you could come, John."

"Wouldn't miss seeing you get your wings, Pam."

Major Randal and Lieutenant Plum-Martin had a long history. She had been Lady Jane's driver in the early days when Raiding Forces was being organized—though that was only a cover for her intelligence activities. The Royal Marine had gone with him on an unauthorized raid on a pub in France called the "Gunfight at the Blue Duck." When he was passing through Istanbul, she was on a Special Operations Executive team that was attempting to rattrap the new Abwehr chief-of-station.

And, she had parachuted behind the lines in Abyssinia to serve with Force N before Major Randal eventually sent her back to fly psychological warfare missions against the Italians. She had serenaded their lonely troops with opera music at night from a Supermarine Walrus to make them homesick.

"We had to get John out of Cairo," Lieutenant Honeycutt-Parker said. "Mallory's friend turned up working for the Norwegian Legation."

"The Norwegian blonde?" Lieutenant Plum-Martin gasped. "The one with Mallory the night Raiding Forces spirited him out of France? I *have* to hear this story, Parker."

"Wanted John to call her so she could thank him properly—looked strikingly like you, Pam."

"Never, ever make that call, John," Lieutenant Plum-Martin said.

"Rocky Runborg doesn't hold a candle to you or Parker," Major Randal said.

He was immediately rewarded with a pair of insincere, million dollar smiles.

Squadron Leader Wilcox went aboard the Hudson. The aircraft was taxiing by the time Major Randal and the two women settled into the car sent by the Officers' Club.

"This place is a hidden jewel in the desert," Lieutenant Plum-Martin said. "A lost paradise that time has passed by."

"Never heard of Habbaniya," Lieutenant Parker said. "Located it on the map. The notation said 'featureless desert' with a little dot for the airbase."

"The Royal Air Force has turned this place into the Garden of Eden," Lieutenant Plum-Martin said.

Major Randal felt the accumulated stress of months behind enemy lines fighting a guerrilla war start to melt away. For the first time in a long time, he began to relax. You could not do that in Cairo—the pace was too fast.

THE SWIMMING POOL AT THE CLUB LIVED UP TO ITS advance billing. There were only a few people there, it being a workday. Major Randal was napping on a lounge chair while the two girls floated on rafts. For the first time in a long time, nothing was trying to kill him or eat him.

A captain in battle dress wearing the regimental badges of the Assyrian Levies arrived in the pool area.

"Hello, David," Lieutenant Plum-Martin called.

"Pam."

He walked over to Major Randal.

"Sir, Colonel Brawn, the ground commander here at Habbaniya, sends his compliments," Capt. David Lancaster said. "The Colonel requests your presence straight away for a courtesy briefing on the military situation."

"Situation?"

"Colonel Brawn will explain, sir."

"Roger, let me change into uniform."

"Pam has a tennis match in an hour," Lieutenant Honeycutt-Parker said, "mind if I tag along, John?"

"My military aide," Major Randal said. "Veteran of Abyssinia—behind the lines—but that's classified. Any problem if she sits in? She has clearance."

"Quite all right, I'm sure, sir," the Levies officer said. "Nothing we cover is going to be a secret for long.

"I must say, sir, you have exquisite taste in aides."

"Don't tell anyone, but *Mrs.* Parker is actually my minder."

"Major, I read your book, *Jump on Bela.* You *need* a chaperone, sir."

3

GUNS ON THE HEIGHTS

CAPT. DAVID LANCASTER CHATTED UP LT. PENELOPE Honeycutt-Parker in the car on the way to the hangar at the edge of the airfield where the briefing was to be held. Maj. John Randal noted that there was a sentry outside the building. However, he seemed to be more on watch than on guard.

Major Randal clicked on immediately.

The sentry slid the door to the hangar open to let them in. Major Randal and Lieutenant Honeycutt-Parker were escorted to an office in the back. Inside, a number of officers were gathered. Not present was the base commander AVM Harry "Reggie" Smart, OBE, DFC, AFC.

The senior RAF flight officer in the room and former officer-in-charge of the Royal Iraqi Training School, Wg. Cdr. John Hawtrey, made the introductions.

"Wing Commander Paul Holder, the Senior Administrative officer.

"Major Edward 'Ted' Everett, 10th Indian Division, in command of the 400-man detachment of the 1st Battalion King's Own flown in to reinforce Habbaniya two days ago.

"Lieutenant Colonel Alistair Brawn, Assyrian Levies commander.

"Squadron Leader Tony Dudgeon—our resident bomb-throwing rabble-rouser—does not suffer fools lightly. Tread lightly around Tony.

"And Captain Lancaster, you know. Wing Commander Ling is on the flight line and unable to be present."

"Lieutenant Honeycutt-Parker," Major Randal said. "Parker crewed on a private houseboat that made several trips rescuing troops at Dunkirk, went a thousand miles with the Lancelot Lancers Yeomanry chasing Italians across Abyssinia, then spent a month behind the lines on a classified guerrilla operation coordinating the disposition of Italian female dependents of surrendering POWs."

Several of the men cleared their throats. Lieutenant Honeycutt-Parker had seen more action than all of them put together.

"Mind if I smoke?" Lieutenant Honeycutt-Parker asked, as she took a Player's out of her silver cigarette case.

"By all means," Wing Commander Hawtrey replied, as every man in the room produced a light to offer her.

"Thank you," Lieutenant Honeycutt-Parker smiled, as she lit her cigarette from three different lighters.

"Major," Wing Commander Hawtrey began, "we asked you here to bring you up to speed on the military situation as we understand it exists at Habbaniya since your arrival."

"Only got here today, sir."

"Quite a lot has occurred in that time, I am afraid," Wing Commander Hawtrey said. "Squadron Leader Wilcox, whom we have come to respect rather highly, recommended we bring you into the picture when he learned that you would be coming to Habbaniya. Lieutenant Plum-Martin has entertained us with tales of your exploits over cocktails many evenings at the club.

"Your reputation, as they say, has preceded you."

"I see," said Major Randal, which meant he did not have a clue.

"Why not let me start at the top? This is an informal, off-the-record briefing, so feel free to pop in to comment or ask something at any point. No need to hold your questions until the end, as is normal protocol."

"Roger," Major Randal said. "Does that mean we're not having this conversation?"

"That shall become painfully evident," Wing Commander Hawtrey said.

"Habbaniya is a self-contained Royal Air Force cantonment built on the Indian model. Everything the inhabitants need is located right here on base—500 acres surrounded by a high, supposedly unclimbable, fence and guarded by Assyrian Levies. No one has to venture outside the wire unless, of course, they want to go to the Yacht Club located on Lake Habbaniyah.

"Amenities include fields for football, hockey and rugger. Unfortunately, our polo field and golf course were recently bulldozed to create an auxiliary landing strip. Habbaniya has fifty-six tennis courts. We have the Royal Exodus Hunt for those who like to ride to the hounds. Our swimming pool is the best in the service.

"Stationed on the base are No. 4 Service Flying Training School (SFTS), and the Iraqi Communications Flight. Previously we hosted the Royal Iraqi Training School, which I commanded, but those activities were curtailed a month ago due to unrest in Baghdad.

"While we have eighty-nine aircraft of a wide variety on station, none can be considered modern, many are not airworthy and some are unarmed trainers painted bright yellow. We have a total of thirty-nine qualified pilots, of which one is your Lieutenant Plum-Martin. Might have had a few more, but among those unfortunates who washed out, more than one or two claimed they were unable to fully concentrate with her in the class."

"Had the exact same problem in high school," Major Randal said. "One of my teachers was Miss UCLA."

"On the military side we have the Assyrian Levies commanded by Lieutenant Colonel Brawn. They consist of an HQ Wing, Composite Company, four 125-man Assyrian companies numbered 1-4, and one Kurdish Company, No. 8.

"The Composite Company is the heavy weapons unit with a machine gun section, a three-inch mortar section and one .55-caliber Boys Anti-Tank Rifle.

"The six companies are staffed by seventeen British officers, three British non-commissioned officers, three surgeons, fifty Assyrian officers and 1,134 other ranks.

"The RAF has No.1 Armored Car Company with eighteen Rolls Royce Silver Spirits and two ancient tanks named—for some odd reason lost to history –'Walrus and Seal.'

"Two days ago the contingent from the King's Own commanded by Major Everett flew in.

"Our only artillery consists of two inert 4.5-inch ceremonial guns—decorations.

"On 30 April we received information that 6,000 Iraqi troops and thirty pieces of field artillery had departed Baghdad en route to Habbaniya. They occupied the escarpment between the base and Lake Habbaniyah. Claimed to be on training exercises. When the Iraqi Army arrived, Air Vice Marshal Smart sounded the general alarm at 0400 hours, but since no one knew what the siren was about because the base had never run any drills ... everyone ignored it."

"Those aren't your troops up on the bluff?" Major Randal said.

"Negative. Yesterday the Iraqi Army grew to 9,000 troops, fifty field pieces with twelve armored cars confirmed.

"This morning at 0630 an Iraqi field grade officer presented himself at the front gate. He claimed the Iraqis were on a training mission. However, he made a demand—we are to stop all incoming and outgoing flights, no armored vehicles are to leave the base. If any do they will be shelled by the Iraqi artillery—the Iraqis will not be responsible."

Major Randal said, "A *live* fire training exercise—staring down at your base from point blank range?"

"So the Iraqis assert."

"I don't think you should take their word for that, Wing Commander."

"Prudent advice," Wing Commander Hawtrey said. "At 1100 hours the Iraqi envoy returned. This time he demanded all training flights be suspended—essentially an act of war since it violates a long-standing treaty. That gave Reggie ... ah... Air Vice Marshal Smart and the staff something to think about."

"After deliberation, the Air Vice Marshal wired for permission to launch a preemptive air strike. The response came back in record time directly from Prime Minister Churchill, who had to be consulted because to attack would be an act of war against a country we are not officially at war with. The PM ordered us to strike only if we had no other option. But if we felt compelled to attack to do so with 'All Necessary Force.'"

"Churchill said that?"

"Affirmative," Wing Commander Hawtrey said. "Questions, Major?"

"Total Iraqi forces?"

"Four divisions and an independent mechanized brigade deployed within fifty miles of Habbaniya. The Royal Iraqi Air Force has 116 modern aircraft of German, Italian, American and British manufacture."

"How many British personnel are here on Habbaniya?" Major Randal asked.

"All up, mostly civilian—approximately 9,000 people."

"How many days' rations do you have laid in?"

Wing Commander Hawtrey's eyes flickered, "Four days for civilians—twelve days for military."

"Why'd you ask me here?"

"Two reasons, basically. We have it on good authority that you are an expert at attacking airfields. We would appreciate if you would take the time to survey our defenses. Make recommendations on how we can improve our base security plan."

"No problem, sir."

"Without question you are the most experienced ground combat officer on Habbaniya, Major. We would be interested to hear your assessment of the overall situation."

"What's the part you're not telling me?"

"This cannot leave the room," Wing Commander Hawtrey said. "Create a panic among the civilians if they find out.

"The Iraqis blew the dikes protecting the road behind them after they deployed here. The resulting floodwaters from the Euphrates turned the road into a quagmire—quicksand. Arab invaders for centuries have called the combination of water and sand in Iraq the "Arab Mud Bath.'"

"What does that mean exactly, sir?"

"There will not be any relief column from the direction of Baghdad coming to save us, and the other way is open desert for 500 miles to our nearest friendly outpost in Palestine."

"Attack immediately," Major Randal said. "Work the Iraqis over with air strikes for two or three days, set up a strike force to ambush and raid the Iraqi positions at night, then go in with your ground troops. You've got to win this thing quickly."

"We have to man the defenses—seven miles of perimeter," Lieutenant Colonel Brawn said. "At most we could spare one company from the Levies to form an offensive strike force. In addition to, say, one company from the King's Own."

Major Everett nodded in agreement.

"Then they better be damn good men," Major Randal said.

"We would be able to attach the RAF No.1 Company Armored Cars to this 'strike force' you propose, provided it takes on the mission of providing mobile counterattack response," Wing Commander Hawtrey said. "Also, the two tanks—not that they will be much help."

"There is this one other issue—Squadron Leader..."

Squadron Leader Dudgeon said, "Air Vice Marshal Smart is a nice enough chap—decorated veteran of the last war—but he did not need this emergency at the end of his career. The Air Officer Commanding made the right decision to request permission for a preemptive air attack.

"But what the AOC *really* wants is to stall for time in hopes the Iraqis will go away. Reggie wants things to get back to normal here at Habbaniya, which means comfortable."

Major Randal said, "You don't have any time."

"We are all in agreement about that here in this room, but it is not clear what the AOC will do next. The staff at Habbaniya was selected because of their proven ability to carry out mundane training tasks—cranking out pilots, bombardiers and air-gunners. The staff officers are mostly all over the hill—well past their prime. Quite a number are qualified pilots but refuse to fly.

"When we first learned about the pro-Nazi activities of the Golden Square, it was suggested modifying our Audex trainers to carry bombs in event of an emergency. The AOC rejected the idea. 'Not an authorized alteration'—we do things by the book at Habbaniya. The staff obsessively hides behind regulations. No one ever takes a risk.

"In secret, Wing Commander Ling and I fitted the bomb racks

anyway. Forced to do the same with a couple of other similar projects. The only thing we have been able to get the AOC to agree to has been turning the polo pitch and golf course into an auxiliary airstrip.

"Air Vice Marshal Smart has a policy: 'Abide by the Kings Regulation. Don't make waves.'"

Wing Commander Holder said, "Habbaniya has a small intelligence section—totally worthless. They gave no warning that this situation was going to develop. Reggie was blindsided.

"When I learned of the *coup* by the Golden Square, I suggested we could snuff it out with no air operations, nor any loss of life, by simply warning Rashid Ali and his henchmen that we could have Messrs. Waterlow in Britain, the printers of currency for many countries including Iraq, do a special, high-volume run for us. Unless the Golden Square did our bidding we would fly over Baghdad and the other major cities and drop tons of it, flooding the market. Instant runaway inflation that would devalue all the money the Golden Colonels are stashing away in Swiss banks as fast as they can with both hands."

"Capital idea," Wing Commander Hawley commented. "Guaranteed to work."

"What'd he say?" Major Randal asked, lighting a Player's with his battered U.S. 26th Cavalry Regiment Zippo.

"'Not be cricket'—direct quote, Major."

Lieutenant Colonel Brawn added, "When you make your defense assessment, Major, you are going to advise roving patrols all around the perimeter day and night. I have already recommended them, but the AOC forbade it—wants to avoid a mistake in the dark resulting in a friendly fire incident.

"The AOC claims the fence is impenetrable," Wing Commander Hawley said.

"Of the thirty-nine pilots we have on station to fly against the Iraqis," Squadron Leader Dudgeon said, "a number are recent graduates of the school—meaning they are green pilots with only a handful of flying hours flying Tiger Moth trainers. Others are worn out from flying combat—sent here for a rest cure while still others are here because their commanders did not think them suitable to fly in an operational squadron."

Lieutenant Colonel Brawn said, "As briefed, the majority of our ground troops are the Assyrian Levies. We are not entirely confident how reliable they are. Could very well desert, or worse, turn on their British officers."

"What's the good news?" Major Randal said.

"The only positive development since I have been on base, Randal," Major Everett said, "is that you arrived out of the blue and magnanimously volunteered to organize and command the Habbaniya Commando Strike Force."

"I'm on vacation."

"Major, to put the situation into terms an American like you might appreciate, this is 1836 and you just checked in to the Hotel Alamo," Wing Commander Hawtrey said. "The odds against us are approximately the same."

"General Slim told a story about the battle of Gallabat at a dining-in one night before we deployed here from India," Major Everett said. "Claimed you saved his life. Said it was the neatest piece of work he ever saw."

"Slim?" Major Randal said. "I thought he got shot in the ass!"

"Fully recovered," Major Everett said. "Except for a little hurt pride and a scar he's not able to show anyone at cocktail parties. Plans are for him to take command of my division, the 10th Indian, in the near future when it arrives in Iraq.

"Is it true, Randal—you saved the General?"

"I was saving myself," Major Randal said. "Slim just happened to be standing there."

MAJ. JOHN RANDAL AND LT. PENELOPE HONEYCUTT-PARKER walked their ponies out the front gate of Habbaniya. Then they made a hard left and, staying near the fence, rode slowly toward the Euphrates River. They could see the Iraqis up on the escarpment. One of them waved at them.

They waved back.

"What are we doing, John?" Lieutenant Honeycutt-Parker asked.

"This seems a little over the top—riding out in front of the Iraqi positions in broad daylight... even for you."

"Inspecting the base defenses, Parker—Iraqis are on a training exercise. They don't care if we go for a ride."

"A perimeter road runs around the entire 500 acres of Habbaniya—shows it on the brochure you had me bring from the lobby of the club, John. We could have inspected the defenses from inside the fence."

"Need to see it from the opposition's perspective—ingress and egress," Major Randal said. "What does that pamphlet say about the base's flora and fauna?"

"Habbaniya has been compared to Eden," Lieutenant Honeycutt-Parker read as they rode. "Laid out by the Knightsbridge contractor, Messrs. Humphries & Co., it boasts casuarinas, pepper and eucalyptus tree-lined boulevards, manicured lawns, roses, sweet peas, bougainvillea, hibiscus and oleander ..."

"There you go," Major Randal said.

"John, we are surrounded by a horde of bloodthirsty Iraqi savages, outnumbered nearly ten to one in fighting men, only have enough food for four days before the women and children start starving to death and you are interested in the foliage of Habbaniya?"

"You don't think the Iraqis are going to come down off that bluff and attack the base's fortified positions, do you, Parker?" Major Randal said. "Probably attempt to infiltrate at night so we want to make sure that's not easy. They'll try to starve us out, but they're exposed to air attack up on that escarpment."

"Sounds like the Siege of Cawnpore to me—every man, woman and child slaughtered, almost," Lieutenant Honeycutt-Parker said. "Some vacation Jim brought us on."

"The Iraqis do have us in a corner," Major Randal said.

"The Alamo, wasn't that the place the Mexican Army surrounded a group of Texans, overran their fortress and put them to the sword?"

"Yeah, but there's a difference—they didn't have a swimming pool," Major Randal said. "Here at Habbaniya we're sitting behind wire with the Euphrates River on three sides, surrounded by a million miles of desert.

"The Iraqis, on the other hand, are out in the desert with us in front and the flooded road to Baghdad to their rear—which *they* blew."

"I did not come away from that briefing with the slightest impression anyone else sees the situation even remotely the same way, John," Lieutenant Honeycutt-Parker said. "My takeaway was that Habbaniya is laid to siege in desperate peril—I am in no mood to be despoiled."

"The Iraqis," Major Randal lied, "are the ones in trouble."

"Fascinating," Lieutenant Honeycutt-Parker said. "If I had not spent a month in Abyssinia with Force N, I should think you quite mad right about now."

"Whoa, here we go," Major Randal said, reining in his pony.

"John, those are wild goat droppings ... we rode out here for a trail of goat scat?"

"Yeah, it's headed straight as an arrow for those rose beds, sweet peas and all the other Garden of Eden stuff. If you were a wild goat, Parker, would you try to scratch out a living in the desert or would you go for the hibiscuses come nightfall?"

"The botanical garden, naturally," Lieutenant Honeycutt-Parker said.

"How do you think the goats are going to get into Habbaniya?"

"Not about to scale the fence," Lieutenant Honeycutt-Parker said.

"Roger that," Major Randal said. "Goats have a place already dug out they'll wiggle right under ... it's their MO."

"And why do we care that wild goats are going to crawl under the fence?" Lieutenant Honeycutt-Parker asked.

"Because that's exactly what the Iraqi infiltrators are going to do. They'll follow the goat droppings and slip under the wire some dark night."

"Pretty sneaky."

"Mark this spot on your brochure," Major Randal ordered. "We'll find trails like this all the way around the wire. We want to ambush the places *inside* the fence where the goats cross."

"Fascinating ..."

"Parker, probably not a good idea to mention our earlier conversation."

"You mean about our having the Iraqi Army right where we want it?"

"Roger," Major Randal said. "We wouldn't want anyone to get overconfident—you can tell Pam.

4

DEFENSE

AVM HARRY "REGGIE" SMART SAID, "WHAT WAS THAT cheering?"

"Major Randal, sir," Wg. Cdr. John Hawtrey said. "Colonel Brawn assigned him No. 4 Company of the Assyrian Levies, and Major Everett gave him A Company of the King's Own to form a provisional strike force. Randal will conduct raids and ambushes and serve as the commander of the base mobile counterattack group. I have attached No. 1 Armored Car Company and the two tanks for additional firepower.

"Still, not very much, sir—for what we require."

"Randal, the American Commando chap?"

"He arrived this morning for Lieutenant Plum-Martin's graduation," Wing Commander Hawtrey said. "Had no idea the Iraqis have risen."

"Why the cheering?"

"Major Randal marched the Strike Force troops outside the gate, pointed to the escarpment and said, 'There is your enemy, baking in the sun while we rest in the cool shade. They cannot run away. We shall kill as many of them as we can and chase the rest back to Baghdad ... or words to that effect, sir."

"That is a provocation," Air Vice Marshal Smart protested. "This Randal may be a bad influence."

"Got off to a fast start, sir," Wing Commander Hawtrey said.

"In what way?"

"Ordered the King's Own and Assyrian Companies to assemble at the pistol range. Put on a shooting demonstration—stuck up two 12-inch tin squares and shot a 'KO' in one and a '4' in the other with his pistols, rapid fire. The troops went wild, sir. The men think he's a regular Wild West gunfighter."

"Keep your eye on the man, Wing Commander. The decision has not been made to commence hostilities," Air Vice Marshal Smart said. "Still may be able to work out a diplomatic solution. Would not do for this Special Forces fellow to bolt the starting gun."

"Sir!"

"Do you believe Major Randal actually said, 'Kill them all and let Allah sort them out?'"

"That is what Captain Lancaster tells me, sir—I have yet to read Randal's book."

"What is the man doing now?"

"I believe, sir, he and Mrs. Parker are laying out taking the sun by the pool at the Officer's Club."

LT. PENELOPE HONEYCUTT-PARKER WAS SITTING BY THE pool in her valentine-shaped black swimsuit. She was taking notes on a legal pad. Maj. John Randal was lying on the lounge next to hers dictating instructions.

"Have three large sand table terrain maps constructed. One goes in the empty hangar assigned to Strike Force at the primary airstrip; we need to find a location to put another at the alternate strip built on the golf course; and one goes here."

"I shall have the club erect one of their party pavilions on the secondary landing ground," Lieutenant Honeycutt-Parker said.

"I want every pilot returning from a mission to go in and make adjustments to the maps as a part of their debriefing. Special emphasis on artillery positions, Parker—so we can go after 'em come night."

"*Papier-mâché* model miniatures for the table," Lieutenant Honeycutt-Parker said. "I shall organize a team of women from the dependents to make them."

"We'll make the O Club the Strike Force Headquarters," Major Randal said. "From now on this place is off-limits to anyone not involved with our operations. Have Lancaster post a guard at the gate. Tell management to evict anyone staying here who is not involved with our operations.

"Put up a tent out here by the pool for the sand table where I can conduct briefings. In fact, set up an Operations Center out here with a Command Post tent for me to sleep in."

"I shall arrange to have people stationed at the primary and alternate airfields to make notes on the changes to the Iraqi positions as the pilots report them. Then repair here hourly and keep our master terrain map updated so we always have the latest intelligence," Lieutenant Honeycutt-Parker said.

"Good," Major Randal said. "Did you get the list of clubs and organizations?"

"Yes," Lieutenant Honeycutt-Parker said, as she handed him a piece of paper.

"Find out how many parachutes the RAF has."

"Matter if they are classified serviceable or not?"

"No."

Capt. David Lancaster arrived. "Colonel Brawn turned down your request for additional troops from the Levies to ambush the goat trails, sir. He does not have the men to spare—seven miles of wire to secure. Likes the idea, though; says you should use your own men to do it."

"Strike Force personnel are going to be working outside the wire," Major Randal said, scanning the list of clubs.

"How do you put the word out on the base about something when it needs to be done quickly?"

"Habbaniya has its own radio station. We also have a sound truck that can drive around making public announcements," Captain Lancaster said. "If need be, I can arrange to have people go door to door."

"I want the President of the Rod and Gun Club and the Boy Scout troop leader here in the next fifteen minutes," Major Randal ordered.

"Let's not use the radio yet, but get the sound truck going. Have volunteers for the Habbaniya Home Guard report here to the pool area in one hour. Hunters and long-distance shooters needed—age irrespective. Women can serve—anyone over fifteen who wants a job."

"Yes, sir!"

"We're taking over the Club," Major Randal said. "Get yourself a room here, Captain. You're going to be busy for the duration."

Capt. Valentine Fabian, commander of A Company, King's Own Royal Regiment, accompanied by Capt. John Smith, commander of No. 4 Company, Assyrian Levies arrived poolside. They were the two senior infantry troop commanders of the Strike Force. Sqn. Ldr. John Page, commanding No. 1 RAF Armored Car Company (ACC), came right behind them.

"We don't have very much time to get to know each other," Major Randal said. "I want you and your junior officers to move in here so we can spend as much time around each other as we can," Major Randal said.

"My guess is the Strike Force will be out tonight. Make your plans as if we will be—if not, we will be going out tomorrow night. What I have in mind, initially, is a series of ambushes along the front of the Iraqi positions and probing reconnaissance patrols round the flanks. Nothing heavy, but I want intelligence, and I want to kill bad guys. The idea is to give the Iraqis something to think about come sundown.

"Second night it will be raids based on the intelligence you bring back and what the pilots give us. We're going to be operating all night, every night, until this is over.

"For starters, to keep it simple, we'll draw a line down the middle of the escarpment from the front gate to the lake—King's Own will be on the right and No. 4 Levies on the left. Squadron Leader Page, No. 1 ACC will be the mobile reserve on call twenty-four hours a day.

"What are your questions?"

None of the officers said a word. The ground commanders had just been issued the simplest orders they had ever been given. The captains would have never admitted it, but they were staggered by Major Randal's nonchalance.

"We are going to war—this is how we are going to do it. Move out.

"Squadron Leader Page, I'll spend some time with you later working up a plan to employ your armored cars. Initially, have one platoon driving the perimeter road beginning at sundown."

"Yes, sir."

"What's your recommendation for the two tanks?"

"I would suggest keeping them near the front gate," Squadron Leader Page said. "If the Iraqis deploy their armor they will be in a position to sally forth—they are so old as to be almost immobile, Major."

"Roger, do it. In the future, I'm open to suggestions," Major Randal said. "My experience with cavalry lately has been limited to mules in Abyssinia."

"My pleasure, sir," Squadron Leader Page said. "Afraid the Walrus and the Seal are terribly obsolete, as are my eighteen Rolls Royce Silver Spirit armored cars—veterans of the last war."

"Captain Lancaster, you and Captain Smith pick me out an Assyrian striker," Major Randal said, "I'll be going out tonight."

MAJ. JOHN RANDAL HAD CHANGED INTO HIS FADED GREEN battle dress. He was wearing both of his ivory-gripped Colt .38 Supers, and the High Standard .22 was in its chest holster with his Fairbairn Fighting Knife laced to it. He was conducting an inspection of a troop of Boy Scouts drawn up in formation.

The Scoutmaster was a tubby, middle-aged man whose day job was base plumber.

Cpl. Basil James, King's Own Royal Regiment, had been detailed by Capt. Valentine Fabian, to fill Major Randal's request for a junior NCO to take command of the troop. The Corporal was doing his best imitation of a regimental sergeant major, conducting a formal parade mount inspection—hard as nails. The Scouts were quivering as the trio worked their way slowly through their ranks.

Major Randal took his time, stopping to chat with each boy. The Scouts were aged thirteen to fifteen, with a handful of ex-Scouts aged sixteen and seventeen who had been recalled to the colors. Younger members of the troop had been excluded from the formation.

"Men," said Major Randal when he completed his inspection, "I have a mission for you."

No one had ever called any of the Scouts "men" before, and the news that they were getting a real, live combat assignment sent a thrill like an electric spark through the group of eager youngsters.

"Corporal James will be taking command of your troop, which has been given the designation Scout Strike Force. The SSF will be reorganized into three patrols. Your task will be to conduct night ambushes inside the perimeter of Habbaniya at selected positions along the wire.

"According to your Scoutmaster, you have spent time on the rifle range, and most of you are hunters. You will be authorized to carry your own rifle or shotgun. If you do not have one, a .22 from the base Rod and Gun Club will be provided.

"For those of you under the age of fifteen, a letter signed by one of your parents is a requirement of service. Any of you who do not feel up to the job, see your Scoutmaster immediately following this formation—volunteers only.

"Good luck and good hunting," Major Randal said. "Corporal James, take charge of your troops—carry on."

A meeting with the Habbaniya Rod and Gun Club was next. The president of the club had rounded up civilian rifle shooters. There were eighteen of them. Some were on the club's Big Bore Rifle Team (BBRT); others were hunters, not competitive marksmen, but all had experience with big bore rifles. The men ranged in age from fifty to seventy-eight, and they were waiting in the bar.

Major Randal said, "Gentlemen, as you all know by now, a large formation of the Iraqi Army has occupied the escarpment outside the RAF Habbaniya front gate. Certain demands have been made, and those have been rejected. The most likely scenario is hostilities commencing as early as this afternoon—tomorrow at the latest.

"I command the newly organized base Strike Force. We will perform a variety of missions. My intention is to inflict casualties on the Iraqis to cause them to lose the will to fight. To that end, I intend to organize a group of two-man sniper teams to take up positions along the wire and start inflicting those casualties the first instant we are cleared to engage.

"Age is not a prohibiting factor," Major Randal said. "What I need are good, long-distance rifle shots who will not hesitate to kill an enemy soldier.

"Volunteers, see Lieutenant Parker. Sign on and pair off into two-man teams of your own choosing. Return home, secure your weapon, ammunition, binoculars, spotting scopes, etc., and report back here as soon as possible.

"You will be taken to your hide positions later today."

As he was leaving the room, a stout man in his sixties introduced himself, "Walter Stanberry, Major. I am the captain of the BBRT. We fire military Enfields and shoot the equivalent of the Wimbledon course out to 1,000-yard targets."

"What can I do for you, Mr. Stanberry?"

"Major, you are going to need someone to organize your Strike Force snipers. Carry out the logistics of keeping them fed and fit on the firing line. No need to detail one of your men. I can handle that assignment for you."

"Consider yourself hired," Major Randal said. "You report directly to me—if I'm not around, see Lieutenant Parker. She is very capable."

"Someone has to make sure the lads take their pills," Mr. Stanberry said. "That said, Major, these old men can shoot. You shall see for yourself right enough.

"Those Iraqis are in for a bloody rough go."

"I'm going to hold you to that," Major Randal said. "Stack 'em up for me."

LT. PENELOPE HONEYCUTT-PARKER SAID, "YOU ARE NOT going to be able to ambush all the goat entry points in the wire with the Boy Scouts alone."

"That's a fact."

"The Habbaniya Women's Skeet Club is here to see you, John."

"Really?"

"They are in the billiard room."

"How many?"

"Fifteen women."

"Well, let's go talk to them."

Unlike the men from the Rod and Gun Club, the women showed up with gun cases. The ladies were prepared to demonstrate their shooting ability. Apparently, like Lieutenant Honeycutt-Parker, the members of the Women's Skeet Club were in no mood to be despoiled either.

"My name is Major Randal. I understand you ladies have volunteered for the … ah … armed Women's Home Guard."

The women in the room ranged in age from their early twenties to late sixties. They were paying rapt attention. No one smiled.

"We need volunteers to conduct night ambushes at certain preselected locations inside the fence of the base. There is a good possibility Iraqi infiltrators will attempt to penetrate Habbaniya. Lieutenant Parker and I have identified a number of likely points.

"Those skeet guns of yours will do good execution—could be dangerous work and it's all night, every night, from now on, if you're interested."

"Major," one of the older women said, "our club came here prepared to do our duty for God, King and Country. We thought you might simply need extra bodies to stand sentry duty.

"Give us a chance to have a real crack at the Iraqis and you will not regret the decision."

"See Lieutenant Parker," Maj. John Randal said. "We'll call you the Annie Oakleys."

The women were instructed to link up with the Boy Scouts so they could practice ambush drill under the gentle tutelage of Cpl. Basil James until another NCO could be assigned.

As they were leaving the billiard room, Lieutenant Honeycutt-Parker said, "Since we know where the goat trails cross the wire, the ambush sites will be permanent. Why not have the Habbaniya Phone Company string a line from the nearest pole to each one. The Scouts and the Annie Oakleys can be in direct phone communications with No. 1 ACC for a really quick response if it is needed."

"Very good, Parker. Corporal James can command and control all the ambushes from here at the O Club," Major Randal said. "Tie the phone net in with the Ready Reaction Team out of our Operations Center."

A woman with a clearly distraught youngster was waiting in the lobby.

"Major Randal," the woman said. "My son, Charles, desperately wants to be on the Scout Strike Force, but he is only twelve. Will you make an exception if I write a permission slip?

"Charles is an expert marksman."

"No problem," Major Randal said. "Welcome to the Strike Force, stud—we can use a shooter."

5

AIR POWER, OR LACK OF

WHEN MAJ. JOHN RANDAL ARRIVED AT THE AIRFIELD, SLIT trenches were being dug in anticipation of shelling by the Iraqis. He met privately with Wg. Cdr. Larry Ling and Sqn. Ldr. Tony Dudgeon. It was immediately apparent the three men shared a common view of war fighting: Do what needs to be done, do it right now, with what you have available. Don't let anything stand in the way.

Squadron Leader Dudgeon had cut his teeth as a pilot in India, where no one ever went by the book when regulations did not suit the exigencies of the situation. Running his own show, he had operated out of a dirt strip landing ground with one airplane and one mechanic, ferrying supplies to isolated frontier outposts. That sort of flying fosters a great deal of independence in a pilot officer, which makes it difficult to conform to restrictive conventional duties later.

It also creates world-class combat leaders.

Wing Commander Ling was a like-minded officer not afraid to buck the system. When the threat of Iraqi rebellion first surfaced, he and

Squadron Leader Dudgeon had worked out multiple plans to increase the striking power of the fleet of obsolete aircraft stationed at RAF Habbaniya. Then Wing Commander Ling had presented those ideas to upper management, only to have them shot down if they did not conform to Royal Air Force specifications or regulations.

Day after day, Wing Commander Ling had done battle with Grp. Capt. William "Butcher" Saville and his hidebound air staff. There was a disconnect between the senior officers, who were determined to maintain the status quo—following the book no matter how senseless the regulations when applied to the situation, and the flying officers who would have to lead the fight if it came down to conflict with the Iraqi rebels.

Over drinks at the Club, Wing Commander Ling and Squadron Leader Dudgeon schemed and plotted and fumed in frustration. Night after night they managed to come up with some creative way to carry out their plans. The military should not be like that. But when talented officers can see the troops under their command are in peril, and the senior men present cannot make independent decisions for fear of risking their careers, sometimes rules have to be broken ... or at least bent.

The firm of Ling and Dudgeon became champion regulation benders.

"What I'd like," Major Randal said, "is for you to bring me up to speed on air operations at Habbaniya."

The two Royal Air Force officers looked at each other, "Where would you like us to start?" Wing Commander Ling asked.

"Why don't you tell me everything you think I need to know?"

"I flew out of makeshift airfields in India for four years until the war broke out," Squadron Leader Dudgeon said. "Assigned initially to Singapore, then diverted to Cairo, where I was given command of No. 55 Bomber Squadron. After fifty missions, the doctors ordered me here for the rest. I was, they claimed, burned out, and possibly... maybe ... it was true.

"Wing Commander Ling is my immediate boss. Above him in the chain-of-command is Group Captain Saville, who is known as the "Butcher" because he slavishly adheres to the rules, insists on petty, mind-numbing discipline and washes out students for the most minor of misdemeanors.

"Group Captain Saville reports to Air Vice Marshal Smart, the Air Officer Commanding Habbaniya—you were briefed about Smart earlier."

"Roger."

"I flew in approximately a month ago. My arrival coincided with reports of a possible rebellion in Baghdad. However, everyone from the AOC down continued with business as usual, blissfully ignoring the growing troubles. Nothing was going to be allowed to disrupt the comfortable flow of the daily training regime, then off to the Club for a swim in the afternoon, tennis or a round of golf."

"When Tony arrived," Wing Commander Ling said, "he and I began to take a serious look at various war-fighting scenarios—what might happen if and when. We knew the Iraqis possessed an army and an air force. I helped trained them.

"Started with the question of what would the situation be if the base was besieged by a mob of unruly rebels. Straight off, there would not be any way to fly off the airfield. It lay outside the perimeter fence, though the hangars are inside the wire."

"I noticed that," Major Randal said.

"Too expensive to enclose back in the day when the base was built," Wing Commander Ling explained.

"What we needed was a secure aircraft parking area. We were not able to improvise using the road network—the eucalyptus trees lining them prevented taxiing or towing. The obvious solution was to bulldoze the polo pitch and golf course to make a small, secondary airfield where we could park the aircraft out of sight. The Butcher took the idea to Smart, and he signed off on it straight away, giving us false hope that the AOC was open to war planning.

"Our air force consists of three Gladiator biplane fighters used as officers' runabouts, plus six more that flew in from Egypt two weeks ago. In our inventory are thirty Hawker Audaxes, seven Fairy Gordon biplane bombers, twenty-seven twin-engine Oxford smoke bomb droppers used to train bombardiers, and twenty-five Hawker Harts. Finally, we have twenty-four Hart trainers. The heaviest bomb load any of our planes were capable of carrying was eight twenty-pounders in the Audaxes. More than half the school's aircraft are not capable of carrying any bombs at all.

"We started with the Gordons," Squadron Leader Dudgeon said. "They are so out of date we only use them to tow targets—fly about 80 mph. The students shoot at the flag they pull on a cable.

"However, back in the stone ages, the Gordon had been designed as a bomber. We had universal bomb racks we could fit, and *bingo*, we had seven aircraft—each capable of carrying two 250-pound bombs—off to a roaring start."

"Next we turned to the Gladiators," Wing Commander Ling said. "As I mentioned, we had three of our own and then six more flew in. Each is armed, or I should say *can be* armed, with four .303-caliber machine guns. We had the guns for our three in storage, and the other six came with theirs mounted, ready to fight."

"Except," Squadron Leader Dudgeon said, "the school did not have any belted ammunition in storage."

"That's a problem," Major Randal said.

"The station armory had a strange and wonderful device like a mincing machine—worked by cranking a big handle," Wing Commander Ling said. "You feed a cartridge into a metal clip, turn the handle once and it pokes the bullet into the clip; feed in a second bullet, turn the handle again and there is round number two; again and again and again. Pretty soon a complete belt of machine gun ammunition is coming out. Not difficult, but a painfully slow business."

"One needs to be careful," Squadron Leader Dudgeon added, "not to get fingers in the works—go in easy enough, but the ends would be a hindrance to the machine gun later."

"Roger that," Major Randal said.

"We have teams of extremely bored pupils cranking out the belts around the clock," Wing Commander Ling said. "There are four guns on a Gladiator. A ten-second burst fires up an hours' worth of manpower."

"Sounds like you men are improvising and adapting," Major Randal said as he lit a Player's with his battered U.S. 26th Cavalry Regiment Zippo.

"We were on a roll," Squadron Leader Dudgeon said, "until it came to the bulk of our planes—the thirty Audaxes and twenty-five Hart bombers. In the late '20s, Hawker designed a single-engine, two-seater, multipurpose aircraft that came to be called by a number of different names. As a day bomber, it was called a Hart—carried a pair of 250-pound bombs. Made an awful noise because the plane was not equipped with a muffler. Harts were so easy to fly, some were equipped with dual controls to be used as trainers, but those had no hard point fittings for weapons or machine gun mountings.

"When the Hart was used in the Army co-operation role, it was called the Audax. The Army model had a muffler because the pilot needed to be able to hear the radio. The Audax carried eight small, twenty-pound bombs designed for antipersonnel harassment.

"We have Harts and Audaxes at the training school. They are both the same airframe, the only difference being the muffler. Between the two, we have fifty-five of them. Wing Commander Ling said to me, 'How can we increase their striking power?'

"I recommended we simply bolt on universal bomb racks, which we have in storage, in addition to the light-series racks already on the aircraft," Squadron Leader Dudgeon said. "The UBR allowed our Harts and Audaxes to carry a pair of 250-pound bombs, plus their eight twenty-pound bombs. Problem solved."

"I took the idea to the Butcher," Wing Commander Ling said. "He pulled out a technical manual, thumbed through it and said, 'Not an authorized bomb load'—interview over.

"When I pressed the issue, citing Tony's experience in India doing what we proposed, Group Captain Saville insisted that Tony had never flown *our* bombers with those loads. It would be a violation of RAF regulations not to stay strictly within the ordnance guidelines as laid down in the technical manuals.

"After going 'round and 'round, the Butcher finally kicked the buck up one level to the engineer officers in Headquarters in order to get me out of his office.

"The engineers proved even more intractable. What Tony proposed was not an authorized modification, and if we had an accident the chap who said 'go ahead' might be held responsible. No engineer was going to stick his neck out *that* far.

"I demanded the question be sent up another level to Smart's operational air-staff for resolution. There was a war to be won—agreed.

"The air-staff granted they could see the advantage of heavier bomb loads but as far as sanctioning a trial flight to determine if it could be done—rejected—too dangerous.

"At this point, I was not in any mood for taking no for an answer, so the air-staff reluctantly agreed to allow the engineer officers to send a cable to the Air Ministry in Whitehall, London. The engineers carefully crafted the wording of the request and sent a wire that asked, 'What is the bomb load of an Audax?' The response came back, 'The stated bomb load of an Audax is eight twenty-pound bombs'—which we already knew—that was in the manual.

"Point, game, set, match—the engineers smugly told me to 'go away,'" Wing Commander Ling said.

"I was confident the load was safe," Squadron Leader Dudgeon said. "So, over drinks, Larry and I decided to fit the racks and go ahead and run the test anyway without permission.

"And that is what we did. After my successful test flight, everyone in the chain-of-command, from Smart on down, to include the bloody closed-minded engineers, commended Larry on a useful innovation. And that was that."

"How'd you know it was going to work, Tony," Major Randal asked. "For sure?"

"I regularly carried double the weight of the bomb load Larry and I tested out on the Northwest Frontier," Squadron Leader Dudgeon said, "flying in our liquor."

"Cheated," Major Randal said.

"Finally, we needed to do something about the Oxfords," Wing Commander Ling said. "We have twenty-seven of them. The problem was this plane started life as a civilian transport, later adopted for use by the RAF. But the Oxford was never, ever considered as an operational war-fighting machine. What it *could* do was carry eight practice bombs mounted on a cut-out recess *below* the cabin floor—which could be problematic for real live bombs if you had to land with them."

"Yeah," said Major Randal, "I could see how it would."

"In the Habbaniya Air Headquarters Air Plan, Oxfords were written in as being capable of photography, machine-gunning and making swoops showing the flag."

"My experience on the Northwest Frontier," Squadron Leader Dudgeon said, "had been to spend a lot of my time trying to work out how on earth to screw on, bolt, fasten, glue or fix two—or better yet four—universal bomb racks to anything that flew. Knowing the intended passenger load of eight—plus luggage—the Oxford should be able to easily carry four of our 250-pound bombs.

"How to make it happen? There was no bomb bay, and the planes sat too low to the ground for bomb trolleys to get underneath to load bombs. So in the end we were limited to hanging eight of the twenty-pound bombs on the wings.

"Even that was easier said than done. But finally I designed two small, simple metal fittings that could be bolted on the smoke bomb racks. We could continue training as usual, and then if war broke out, we'd screw on the fitting, hang on the antipersonnel bangers, and we'd have an attack aircraft—twenty-seven of them."

"I was tickled pink—thought Tony was a genius," Wing Commander Ling said. "Dead simple, easy to produce, worked like a charm. Off I went to the machine shop to have the 100-plus fittings produced.

"Workshop went bananas, flung up their hands in horror, ran around in circles. The barrage of objections are too numerous to list. They refused to make those little pieces of metal, unless the engineering staff signed off on the modification, waiving responsibility should they be used and something untoward occur.

"Engineers went berserk. What we proposed was an 'unauthorized modification.' To go forward, the Air Ministry would have to enter discussions with the designers and makers of the aircraft. No way could we get drawings, descriptions and reasons for the needed changes to the Air Ministry for a decision to be made and get the answer back here in time to be of any value.

"AOC *did* send a telegram describing Tony's idea, but he worded it to say only that the purpose of the proposed modification was for 'prudent local preparations within our normal training routine.' The Air Ministry's reply was indecisive. That sealed it—Smart nixed the idea, and he, in fact, ordered me not to proceed. *Written* orders, no less. I was to be 'arrested' if I disobeyed. No unauthorized flight this time."

"Back to the Mess Bar," Squadron Leader Dudgeon said. "We decided to do a Nelson, turn a blind eye to the orders. The story would be that I was unaware of them.

"I went to work on a borrowed workbench with drill, bits, files, saws, etc., and my original drawing. Happily doing something positive, I looked up to see myself surrounded at a distance by shop workmen, student pilots and mechanics—all pretending not to see what was happening.

"Naturally the word got out and eventually worked its way to Air Headquarters. Larry was summoned to a meeting with the AOC, who had the Butcher present as a witness. Reggie was apoplectic at this 'Gross Breach of Good Conduct and Order.'

"Smart was going to hang Larry if this experiment proceeded against written orders—or maybe give him a firing squad.

"Meantime, while all this was going on, I fitted my handmade devices, stuck on the bombs—perfect fit—and took off. Worked like a charm."

"Fortunately," Wing Commander Ling said. "Smart and the Butcher were only concerned about the loss of a valuable aircraft—no mention of Tony. Since the plane did not crash, all was well—carry on."

"Larry was back in everyone's good graces," Squadron Leader Dudgeon said. "Workshop was ordered to make the devices required, and we had twenty-seven bombers we did not have before."

"Last were the Hart trainers," Wing Commander Ling said. "Nothing worked—not even fitting machine guns."

"I need three for the Strike Force," Major Randal said. "Why not use the rest to drop hand grenades—probably not do much damage, but it'll give the bad guys something to think about."

"We should have thought of that," Wing Commander Ling said. "Tony, dispatch a plane to Basra to fly in a hearty supply of grenades."

"Wilco."

"What do you need three Oxfords for?"

"Sleep interdiction," Major Randal said. "Fly at night in shifts, drop flares and hand grenades to keep the Iraqis awake."

"Tony is our only pilot with any night flying experience, and it's limited," Wing Commander Ling said.

"Not possible to simply assign pilots to fly at night as part of the duty rotation. Shooting landings in the dark is not for the faint of heart or the inexperienced aviator."

"Pam has a lot of hours flying at night in Abyssinia," Major Randal said. "So do Paddy and Jim Taylor when they get back."

"You can have the Hart trainers—only no pilots," Wing Commander Ling said. "We shall be delighted to service them for you—if we can ..."

"What does that mean, exactly?" Major Randal said. "If you can?"

"Never got around to the bad news," Wing Commander Ling said. Air Vice Marshal Smart was artillery in the last war. When the Iraqis showed up, he reverted to First World War thinking. Ordered us to have everyone at the school start digging WWI-style slit trenches and man machine gun posts."

"I saw that," Major Randal said, "on the way over."

"We appealed to the AOC that we needed the school's highly-skilled ground personnel released from digging to start servicing and arming our aircraft. The response was 'keep digging.' Which means once we get the clearance to "GO," it will take us hours to launch our first strike instead of minutes—if we can get it off at all."

"Pull your key people out of the trenches," Major Randal said. "I'll send someone to dig in their place. My Strike Force will take over responsibility for your MG positions—marksmen from the Rod and Gun Club are on the way too, to back the Iraqis off your exposed perimeter."

"You're a lifesaver, Major," Wing Commander Ling said.

"What else can I do for you men?" Major Randal said.

"How about giving a pep talk to our civilian staff? Our nonmilitary employees have not been overly cooperative since this Golden Square business began. They are essential to our operations. Maybe you can motivate them to work harder."

"Love to."

ALL NONMILITARY PERSONNEL OF NO. 4 SERVICE FLYING Training School were assembled in a hangar. The crowd was in a surly mood. The civilian workers did not like the situation they found themselves in. What the men wanted was to be airlifted out immediately. They had been informed that this was not an option.

"My name is Randal. I make my living attacking airfields," Maj. John Randal said. "You men need to know that not one thing can stop the Iraqi Army from walking down that hill and overrunning Habbaniya. If they do, they'll detain all military personnel but consider civilian contractors as mercenaries and kill every one of you.

"Have a nice day."

6

RED

BEFORE MAJ. JOHN RANDAL LEFT THE AIRFIELD FACILITY, A bedraggled Iraqi civilian arrived and engaged in an animated conversation with Wg. Cdr. Larry Ling and Sqn. Ldr. Tony Dudgeon. The man, who was gesturing with his hands, appeared exhausted and emotional.

The men were joined by Wg. Cdr. John Hawtrey.

Major Randal heard Squadron Leader Dudgeon say, "Damn, what a waste!"

"I thought they got off," Wing Commander Ling said.

"Is there a problem?" Major Randal asked.

"Ahmed works for BOAC," Wing Commander Ling explained. "Two of their flying boats were on an overnight stopover at Lake Habbaniyah station when the Iraqis occupied the escarpment. The planes loaded their passengers and all the British personnel early and managed to get away, but one of the female aircrew was left behind in the rush.

"The Iraqi BOAC employees were allowed to leave, but the rebels are holding the stewardess."

"I thought it was Imperial Airlines," Major Randal said.

"Was," Squadron Leader Dudgeon said. "BOAC recently took them over. That stewardess was one good-looking redhead—things will definitely not be pleasant for her. Use your wildest imagination, then multiply that by three. Iraqis are no respecters of women prisoners."

"Redhead?"

"That's what she goes by ... Red," Squadron Leader Dudgeon said. "A real knockout—what a waste."

"Tony is our local lady-killer," Wing Commander Ling said. "Never stood a chance with Red, however. She has a boyfriend."

"Tiny mole right about here?" Major Randal pointed to the left side of his upper lip.

"How did you know that?" Squadron Leader Dudgeon asked.

"I need to know everything Ahmed can tell me about the location where Red is being held."

"He says she is being held in the BOAC office on Lake Habbaniyah."

Have you got a map of the lake area?" Major Randal asked.

"Better than that," Wing Commander Ling said. "Tony has been up taking aerial photos of the Iraqi positions all morning. We have a wall-sized mosaic pictomap made up of 8 by 10 photographs. The Butcher asked us to put it together for operational planning in his office. Shows the BOAC facility."

"Anything you *don't* do, Tony?" Major Randal asked as they walked to the map room.

"I routinely flew aerial photo missions in addition to being a bootlegger," Squadron Leader Dudgeon said. "Jack-of-all-trades, that's me—had to be on the Northwest Frontier."

Lake Habbaniyah was a large, 100-square mile lake in the desert. The BOAC amphibious air station was located on the shore nearest the RAF base, approximately two miles away over the escarpment. There was a floating passenger loading/unloading dock, fuel tank farm, a hostel for passengers to stay overnight, and the air terminal where the passengers assembled prior to boarding.

The black-and-white photographs did not show the Iraqis occupying the place in force.

"OK, Ahmed," Major Randal said, "Start at the top and walk me through exactly what happened."

The Iraqi looked at Wing Commander Ling, who nodded, "Tell the Major everything you know."

"When we were notified the rebels of the Golden Square were coming early this morning before the sun came up, a great haste was made to get the passengers loaded. Also, all British persons boarded, leaving only the Iraqi staff behind to maintain the station.

"After everyone flew away, Miss Red was discovered asleep in her room. Since she was not a member of either crew—only passing through to some other distant place as she does from time to time—in the hurry, no one accounted for her. A most unfortunate oversight with terrible consequences for her, I am very sorry to report, sir."

"When the soldiers showed up, Ahmed," Major Randal said, "how many were there?"

"Half a dozen, sir."

"What did they do with Red?"

"Placed her in the terminal office, sir."

"Where are the soldiers?"

"Two men were stationed on guard at the front of the terminal building. The officer, a captain I believe, sir, and the other three men were inside at the time I was allowed to leave."

"How'd you get here?"

"Walked, sir."

"When you left the station how far did you travel before you came to the Iraqi positions?" Major Randal pointed to the pictomap. "Show me."

"More than half a mile, sir," Ahmed said. "The army positions are very wide, as far as the eye can see in either direction between the Euphrates. However, from when I first entered their lines, sir, until I walked out at the top of the escarpment in front of the RAF base, it was only a mile."

"Draw me a diagram of the inside of the terminal building," Major Randal ordered.

"That is easy, sir, only the three rooms," Ahmed said as he drew a sketch. "Passenger check-in/check-out station, baggage room and passenger waiting area."

"Exactly right," Wing Commander Ling confirmed.

"I'm going to need an amphibious airplane and driver," Major Randal said, holding the diagram as he studied the pictomap.

"We do not have any amphibious airplanes stationed here," Squadron Leader Dudgeon said. "Even if we did, there are no amphibious-qualified pilots on staff."

"There is the Seagull," Wing Commander Hawtrey said, "still in its shipping crates. We never assembled it."

"A Seagull is the same as a Walrus, right?" Major Randal said.

"That is correct."

"I need that airplane put together and ready to fly as soon as possible," Major Randal said, "if not sooner."

"The mechanics will not be able to assist with the rearming, which is my top priority, if I do," Wing Commander Ling said.

"Get that Seagull put together, serviced and ready to fly," Major Randal ordered. "Has to be airborne a half hour before sundown—I don't care what you have to do to make it happen."

"I can arrange for the airplane to be assembled," Wing Commander Ling said. "Hope you can fly it—or better yet, land it. No one else can."

"When you trained the Iraqi Royal Air Force, did the student pilots live here on base?" Major Randal asked.

"On base," Wing Commander Hawtrey said.

"Where'd they stay?"

"Same place you do, Major. The Officer's Club."

"Mind if I use your phone?"

While Major Randal was waiting for the operator to connect him to the Strike Force switchboard in the gazebo out by the pool, he said to Squadron Leader Dudgeon, "I want one of these pictomaps with updates set up in the Strike Force Command Post. When you develop the photos after every recon flight, make me a copy. There will be someone here to pick them up."

"Wilco."

Wing Commander Hawtrey asked, "Is it true, Randal, during the Battle of Britain that you learned there was a bar on the French coast where German fighter pilots gathered at the end of the day's flying, put a couple of pistols in your coat pocket, jumped in a motor boat, went across the Channel one night and walked in the bar and shot them?"

MAJ. JOHN RANDAL SAID, "WHEN THE SENIOR IRAQI OFFICERS stayed here, did they leave uniforms behind so they would not have to pack for every visit?"

Mr. Howsham, the Bachelor Officers' Quarters (BOQ) manager, said, "That was their practice, Major."

Capt. David Lancaster walked into the lobby. He was followed by a powerful-looking man dressed in khaki who was sporting a 9mm Browning P-35 automatic. Also on his pistol belt was a long knife with an iron beaded grip. He was not wearing any insignia of rank. The man had a bushy mustache, pockmarked face and a scar running down his cheek.

"I want to see those Iraqi uniforms," Major Randal said to Mr. Howsham.

"Major, they are in a suite of rooms under contract to the Iraqi Air Force," Mr. Howsham protested. He was more than a little put off by Major Randal—evicting guests, setting up camp in the pool area, giving orders with no visible authorization to do so. Several of the dispossessed officers outranked him, and they were less than pleased.

"Mr. Howsham, the Iraqi Army is outside the main gate aiming cannons at us right now," Major Randal said. "Cancel that contract. Go get the keys."

The manager squawked like a startled chicken and rushed off.

"Major Randal, this is Mr. Zargo," Captain Lancaster said, "our chief of security. You asked for a striker."

"Chief of security?"

"Vets all the volunteers in the Levies," Captain Lancaster said. "Has certain other duties."

"Are you Iraqi, Mr. Zargo?" Lt. Penelope Honeycutt-Parker inquired. Straight from the pool, she was clad in short shorts, halter top and three-inch wedge sandals.

"No, ma'am."

Mr. Howsham returned and called, "Right this way, gentlemen." He led the group to a stairway, where they descended into what appeared to be the basement.

"Lots of people are wondering," Captain Lancaster said as they were walking down the stairs, "whether the Iraqi Levies are going to fight against the Iraqi Army surrounding Habbaniya. The thing about Iraq most people do not realize is that the Iraqis hate other Iraqis more than almost anyone else.

"Mr. Zargo is neither an Arab or a Muslim. The reason he works for us is because he murdered his last employer, a rich sheik of some sort or the other. Hates everybody."

"How do you feel about Americans?" Major Randal asked.

"The United States is the Great Satan," Mr. Zargo said.

"Really? I didn't know that," Major Randal said.

"Why'd you kill your last employer?" Lieutenant Honeycutt-Parker asked.

"He deserved it."

"Make a note, Parker," Major Randal said. "Mr. Zargo said the man needed killing."

"Seems like a perfectly reasonable explanation," Lieutenant Honeycutt-Parker said.

"How'd you get your scar?" Major Randal asked as they came to a double set of heavy metal doors.

"Cut myself shaving," Mr. Zargo said. "You?"

"Shaving," Major Randal said.

"I have explicit instructions not to enter the premises unless the Air Marshal or one of his designated representatives is present," Mr. Howsham protested, "You will have to assume responsibility for this, Major. I shall require that in writing."

"Open the door, Howsham."

Inside was a scene out of *One Thousand and One Nights*—wilder than anything a Hollywood set designer could have dreamed up.

"The Air Marshal used to entertain here," Mr. Howsham said, red-faced. "The establishment is not a party to nor do we assume any culpability for the illicit nature of any activities that may or may not have transpired in this apartment. Under the terms of the lease it is—or *was*—considered sovereign Iraqi territory."

The place was a four-bedroom bordello. It contained a well-stocked bar with a tiny, elevated dancing platform surrounded by mirrors. There was a movie projector with a screen mounted on one wall. The place smelled of musky perfume tinged with a faint trace of hashish.

"Uniforms are in the closets in the bedrooms," Mr. Howsham said. "The Air Marshal allowed his senior officers to stay here from time to time when he was not in residence."

"I thought Muslims did not drink alcohol," Lieutenant Honeycutt-Parker said as she studied the erotic oil paintings in baroque golden frames on the walls. "Or, allow art that depicted animals or humans."

"You would be surprised what these religious gentlemen do, ma'am, when no one is around to see them at play," Mr. Zargo said.

"Possibly not—father was a Lancer."

"There a safe?" Major Randal asked.

"In the closet in the master bedroom."

"They keep anything in your safety deposit boxes?"

"No, sir."

"OK," Major Randal ordered, "the Strike Force is requisitioning this space and everything in it. Get a locksmith to drill the safe. Parker has scheduled people to meet with me in the gazebo by the pool. Have someone direct them down here instead."

"Major ..."

"Move out, Mr. Howsham. From now on, have one of your staff posted at the top of the stairs. No unauthorized visitors—meaning no unannounced visitors—get past. Clear?"

"Captain Lancaster, there are going to be people arriving shortly. Take charge outside. I want to see the tailor, and the head of the road works or the water department immediately, whoever gets here first. Send in the tailor the minute he arrives."

"Sir!"

"Mr. Zargo, toss the joint," Major Randal ordered.

"What am I looking for, Major?"

"Everything, anything ... who knows?" Major Randal said. "Find the safe Howsham doesn't know about. Then pick out a senior officer's uniform that fits."

Mr. Zargo raised a bushy eyebrow.

"How would you like to go with me to pay a call on the Iraqis about sundown?" Major Randal asked

"Social call?"

"Not exactly; they're holding a friend of mine in the BOAC terminal on the lake—Clipper Girl named Red."

Lieutenant Honeycutt-Parker gasped, "Red's captured?"

"We'll drop by the BOAC terminal about dark and ask them to let us have her back," Major Randal said. "I can do it by myself but I thought …"

"Can we kill these Iraqis holding the woman?"

"Only the ones we don't want to deceive."

"I am at your service, sir."

There was a knock on the door. "Tailor's here, and the saddle maker from the Hunt Club."

"Send them in," Major Randal ordered. "Parker, would you go to my room and get my High Standard .22 out of the locker under my bed—don't forget the silencer.

"Now, Mr. Zargo, you'll be dressed as a senior Iraqi officer. I can go as the Air Marshal—I'd do it the other way around, but I don't speak the language, and the senior man can get by without talking."

"Major, there is a possibility that the Iraqis at the terminal would recognize the Air Marshal," Mr. Zargo said, taking out a short, straight cherrywood pipe and clenching it in his teeth. If you arrive as a civilian, you can be Rashid Ali for all they will know—or possibly the Chief of the Secret Security Police—even better.

"No one would ever recognize him," Major Randal said. "Pretty good, Mr. Zargo, I may get to like you."

When Lieutenant Honeycutt-Parker returned with the pistol, she found Major Randal in his swimsuit, standing barefoot and shirtless on the stage, looking in the mirrors as the tailor was measuring him.

"I need you to modify my holster," Major Randal said to the saddle maker as he was screwing the silencer on the barrel of the High Standard

Military Model D. "This one fits on my chest and I need it to be under my shoulder concealed by a lightweight suit jacket. And I need to be able to get to it in a hurry."

They were interrupted by a knock on the door, and two of Mr. Howsham's staff came in lugging a sewing machine.

"Set that up in the adjoining room," Major Randal ordered, standing with his arms outstretched as the saddle maker measured with his tape and adjusted the holster.

"I can have you a brand new holster by tomorrow, sir."

"No good," Major Randal said. "I need it right now."

Captain Lancaster announced, "Mr. Smyth, the superintendent of the Road Works Department, sir."

"Anyone contacted you with orders," Major Randal asked Mr. Smyth, "about what to do when the war starts?"

"I have received no instructions from anyone."

"You understand the situation?"

"Not entirely, Major."

"There are approximately 10,000 Iraqis up on the escarpment with fifty or so field pieces," Major Randal said. "Sometime in the immediate future they will open on Habbaniya. The airplanes on the primary and secondary airstrips will be the only thing that can keep them off us if they try to launch a ground attack.

"I command the base Strike Force. Once the siege begins, my mobile reaction troops will need the roads in good repair to react quickly to emergencies."

"I served in the last one, Major," Mr. Smyth said in a distinctly Australian accent. "What do you require from me and my crews?"

"Send every man and every piece of earth-moving equipment you can scrape up to the airfields. Build revetments for the airplanes, throw up as many sandbags around the hangars as you can and dig slit trenches for the airfield personnel," Major Randal said.

"Once the incoming starts, have your crews prepositioned around Habbaniya at strategic locations to rush in and repair artillery or bomb damage to the roads."

"You can count on my boys, Major," Mr. Smyth promised. "Couldn't help but notice you're setting up a Command Post out by the pool. If it's all right with you, either me or one of my foremen will be there twenty-four hours a day from now on to monitor the situation so that we can react faster."

"That's the spirit," Major Randal said.

"Mr. Whitehead of the Habbaniya Water Works, sir," Captain Lancaster announced.

"Hold up, Mr. Smyth," Major Randal ordered. "Mr. Whitehead, do you have a backup well if anything happens to your primary?"

"Habbaniya has only the one well, sir."

"Get with Mr. Smyth, he'll explain the military situation to you. Better start figuring out what to do if the well gets knocked out.

"If there's any other construction crews on Habbaniya, Mr. Smyth, tell Captain Lancaster. We'll mobilize 'em and put them under your supervision."

"More battles have been won with picks and shovels than bayonets," Mr. Smyth said. "But, that stipulated, you'd better go to work and knock off as many of those bloody Iraqis as you possibly can, Major.

"They've got us outnumbered fair dinkum."

7

PONY EXPRESS

"AMANDA," CAPT. DAVID LANCASTER ANNOUNCED.

Maj. John Randal was standing on the tiny elevated dancing platform in khaki army-issue swimsuit, no shirt, and a beautiful, pale gray, raw silk suit coat. The tailor was stabbing the coat with pins and marking adjustments to be made by his seamstress in the room next door. Major Randal looked over at Lt. Penelope Honeycutt-Parker reclining on a plush, violet, velour love seat in short-shorts, halter top and cork wedge sandals.

She glanced at the clipboard in her lap and said, "Captain of the youth equestrian team."

A slim, mahogany-haired girl in jodhpurs and riding boots came into the room.

"Wow, is this place for real? Never realized Habbaniya actually had its own cathouse," she said.

"We're just borrowing it," Major Randal said.

"You sent for me? Mandy Paige?"

"Roger that," Major Randal said. "My name's John, and that's Penelope. She's a lieutenant in the Royal Marines."

"Love the uniform," Mandy quipped.

"*Mrs.* Honeycutt-Parker's husband is one of my officers. Call her Parker—everyone else does," Major Randal said. "She's a horsewoman too—rode in the Grand Nationals when she was seventeen."

"Excellent!" Mandy said.

The tailor ducked out of the room just as Mr. Zargo came in, carrying a large tray he had pulled out of a giant-sized jewelry box. It contained a collection of expensive men's watches running to gold and precious stones. "You'll need one of these, Major, the gaudier the better. A gold chain too, sir—wear them both on the same wrist, loose."

"Really? Which watch do you like, Mandy? Parker picked my tie," Major Randal said. "The pale gray one over the chair with the tiny white dots."

"I like your Rolex," Mandy said. "Parker's tie is perfect for that beautiful suit. The watches—going to a masquerade ball?"

"Something like that—pick one out. Make it a sparkler."

"The Patek Philippe with the diamond-encrusted *pavé* face on the heavy gold link watchband is the tawdriest."

"Good choice, Miss Paige," Mr. Zargo said.

The locksmith arrived with his tools and was ushered into the closet where the safe was located. He came out and reported, "Piece of cake, Major. It's a cheap model. May be able to do it by touch."

Mr. Zargo brought in a tray of men's sunglasses, then went back to searching the apartment.

Major Randal tried on a huge pair with tortoise shell frames.

"That's so you, John," Lieutenant Honeycutt-Parker drawled.

The two women broke up laughing.

"How many girls on your squad, Mandy?" Lieutenant Honeycutt-Parker asked.

"Eight," Mandy said, "not counting me."

"What age?" Major Randal said.

"Sixteen to twenty—I'm the oldest."

"So Mandy, why are you at Habbaniya?" Lieutenant Parker asked.

"My father is on Air Vice Marshal Smart's staff after a dreadful tour with Bomber Command. I was supposed to be at school, but the war broke out. Switzerland has a common border with Germany. Father thought it safer if I should come out to Habbaniya—oh well."

"Parker and I are here on vacation," Major Randal said.

"Some holiday; welcome to Custer's last stand—saw the movie. *Love* Errol Flynn."

The tailor returned and took off Major Randal's suit jacket, gingerly avoiding the carefully placed pins as he headed back to the seamstress. The saddle maker appeared to help Major Randal out of the shoulder holster, to take it to his shop to make the final stitches on his heavy machine.

"Oooooh," Mandy said when she saw the scars on Major Randal's chest. "Hot date? Mother warned me about men like you!"

"Kitty-cat."

"Scratched your cheek too?"

"Manager of the base club bar system, sir," Captain Lancaster announced.

Turning to the manager, Major Randal said, "I'm going to need a couple hundred empty beer bottles to start with, then another hundred every day. In egg-type cardboard crates so the bottles don't bounce around and make contact with each other."

"No problem providing the bottles, Major," the manager said. "Have to produce the crates. When do you need them?"

"Any time in the next hour will be fine."

"I understand, sir, right away, sir."

"Whatever are you going to do with empty beer bottles?" Lieutenant Honeycutt-Parker asked after the manager left.

"Drop 'em on the Iraqis."

"You are planning to drop empty beer bottles on the Iraqi Army? Fascinating."

Lt. Pamala Plum-Martin arrived in tennis whites. "Hi, Mandy," she said.

"You know each other?" Major Randal asked, holding his arms out for the tailor, who had silently reappeared with the coat. He slipped the jacket back on, and the tailor brushed out stray wrinkles with his hands before disappearing again.

"Mandy is the local heartthrob," Lieutenant Plum-Martin said.

"Pam," Mandy said, "you know it's you the pilots are crazy about. The failure rate went up 20 percent at the school after you arrived."

"What is this place?" Lieutenant Plum-Martin asked. "Dance platform barely large enough for one person, mirrors everywhere, movie projector ... anyone want to wager on the *genre*?"

"Private quarters of the Air Marshal commanding the Iraqi Royal Air Force." Lieutenant Honeycutt-Parker said. "Sovereign Iraqi territory until about twenty minutes ago, when John commandeered it."

"You've never been down here, Pam?" Major Randal asked.

"I was invited—by the Marshal."

"Right," Major Randal said. "Get your flying gear on. The RAF is assembling a Seagull at the airstrip. About sundown we're going over to the BOAC terminal."

"Why would we want to do something like that? The Iraqis occupy the terminal."

"Red is being held there," Major Randal said. "Mr. Zargo and I are going after her—we need you to fly us in."

"Mr. Zargo?"

"My new best friend," Major Randal said.

"Killed his last boss," Lieutenant Honeycutt-Parker said. "He deserved it, though."

Mr. Zargo nodded from across the room, where he was tapping on the wall with his knuckles.

"Bet he's not as much fun as Rita and Lana," Lieutenant Plum-Martin said. "Had a date to be at the Lake Habbaniyah Sailing Club today until the Iraqi Army showed up and ruined our plans. We can put down at the floating dock easy enough, John. I know the place well."

"Meet you at the airfield at 1800 hours," Major Randal said. "Have 'em paint Iraqi colors on the Seagull."

"*Ciao,*" Lieutenant Plum-Martin said.

"Red captured—how horrible," Mandy said. "Do you have any idea the dreadful things those Iraqis do to women prisoners?"

"You know Red too?" Major Randal asked.

"Absolutely. She rode with the club on layovers," Mandy said. "Promised to help me arrange a flight attendant position with BOAC after I do my National Service. You have to rescue Red."

"Director of Habbaniya Base Civil Operations, Mr. Twinning," Captain Lancaster announced.

"What can I do for you, Mr. Twinning?" Major Randal asked.

"For your information, Major, I happen to be the equivalent of town manager here at Habbaniya," Mr. Twinning fumed. "Who gave you authorization to go issuing orders to my department heads, Major?"

"I'm here on vacation," Major Randal said. The tailor slipped past the irritated director of civil operations, handed the major the pants to his suit, and slipped out again.

"Found out the Iraqi Army had surrounded the place while I was out at the pool this morning—what steps have you taken to defend Habbaniya, Mr. Twinning?"

"Steps?"

"Not one person has mentioned the base's minefield—would you be in charge of maintaining it?"

"Minefield?" Mr. Twinning said. "There is no minefield. We have a fence—no reason to kill the odd goat herder."

"War is going to break out with the Iraqis later this afternoon or tomorrow morning at the latest," Major Randal said, slipping on the gray pants while trying not to fall off the small stage. "How long would it take to put one in?"

"No idea," Mr. Twinning said. "Installation of minefields is a job for military engineers, of which the base has virtually none. My guess is it would take thousands of man hours."

"How long is that in days?"

"Several weeks, if not months, Major."

"We are toast," Lieutenant Honeycutt-Parker said.

"You need to get your street sign people painting signs that say "DANGER—MINES" in English and several other local languages. Then, tonight when no one can see you, stick 'em up all around the perimeter of the fence three or four hundred yards out."

"Not a bad idea. We could do that easy enough," Mr. Twinning said. "Not across the front, though. The escarpment is closer than that on the far side of the airfield."

"I'll take care of the signs in 'No Man's Land,'" Major Randal said. "I want one every hundred yards, so you do the math on how many it'll take. Put a skull and cross bones on 'em."

"Have the signs for you later this afternoon," Mr. Twinning said.

"Hoarding," Major Randal said. "If I were the city manager, I'd have crews going door to door confiscating canned goods. Wouldn't you be responsible for feeding the civilian population in the event of a siege?"

"The subject has never come up," Mr. Twinning admitted. "Habbaniya was not designed to withstand an attack by a conventional army—unruly tribes were what was envisioned when the base was built in 1936."

"Well, you're under one now," Major Randal said. "Are you retired RAF?"

"I am."

"The AOC has ordered the ground crew, mechanics and armors at No. 4 Service Flying Training School to dig trenches," Major Randal said.

"Oh dear," Mr. Twinning said. "They need to be servicing the base's airplanes, not digging ditches."

"I told Mr. Smyth to round up every piece of earth-moving equipment and every construction crew on base and get to work at the airfields. I'd make sure he had all the support he can get to carry that mission out if I were you."

"He shall have it," Mr. Twinning said. "Needs to harden the electric generator plant, too. Disastrous if it were to be knocked out. Habbaniya has only the one.

"For the record, Major, no one has actually authorized you ..."

"Negative," Major Randal said. "Like I said, I'm here on R&R and was asked to take command of an improvised Strike Force to carry out offensive patrols and quick reaction counterattacks. I'm trying to take steps to make sure I can."

"Quite right. Count on me, Major," Mr. Twinning said. "The people of Habbaniya stand ready to their duty—someone simply needs to tell us what that is. I have yet to receive a single instruction from the AOC."

"My impression, Mr. Twinning, is that you're on your own, The chain of command around here seems to be frozen like deer in the headlights."

"Unfortunately, Major, I suspect you are correct. We shall start implementing our own plans. In the future, I would appreciate it if you would pay me the courtesy of going through my office before issuing orders to my department heads, if at all possible."

"My apologies, sir," Major Randal said. "No offense intended. Mr. Smyth is going to post one of his men in my command post here. Why don't you do the same—you'll be in the loop about everything we're doing."

"I will, Major. No one else has made that offer."

As the Director of Civil Operations was leaving, Captain Lancaster said, "Major Everett to see you, sir."

Maj. Edward "Ted" Everett, commander of the 1st Battalion, King's Own Royal Regiment, came in. "I thought the maharajas at my last duty station were the world beaters in decadent interior design. Your new digs, Randal?"

"Could be," Major Randal said. "Mandy's promised to recruit teenage dancing girls, so we'll be good to go."

"Now a good time?" Major Everett asked.

"As any," Major Randal said. "You've met Parker, and Mandy is the daughter of a serving officer on the staff—shoot."

The tailor was at Major Randal's elbow with an impeccably pressed shirt.

"When we flew in, we brought a consignment of Thompson submachine guns with us from Basra. Intended for issue to the Iraqi Army out from Great Britain, but we put paid to that when we discovered them."

"Thompsons—you can't be serious?"

"Can you believe it? The Iraqis have Bren guns and every other modern implement of war my battalion has only dreamed of."

"Actually, no," Major Randal said. "Ranchers in the U.S. had to donate privately-owned Tommy guns when my outfit, Raiding Forces, was formed. In Abyssinia we had to use captured Italian Breda machine guns to augment our unreliable Hotchkiss guns—a little hard to believe about the Brens."

"Our problem," Major Everett said, "is that no one knows how to unload the submachine guns. The troops have resorted to simply firing off the entire magazine."

"Have hand-picked men from every platoon out by the pool in one hour," Major Randal said. "I'll give 'em a quick class.

"When we landed here," Major Everett said, "I brought Group Captain Saville a message that a consignment of forty Triumph motorcycles had arrived in Baghdad for sale to the Iranian Army. The dealer wanted instructions on what to do with them now that the rebellion had started.

"The Group Captain got on the horn and bought the lot, sent a DC-2 to pick them up, arrived today. He gave them to the King's Own. What am I supposed to do with that many motorcycles?"

"Check with Colonel Brawn, he might need a few to communicate with his bunkers around the perimeter," Major Randal said. "Strike Force can use five—maybe more."

"The Butcher went to a lot of trouble for not much to show for it. Typical of the kind of command decisions being made," Major Everett said as he was preparing to leave. "The RAF people stationed here do not seem to have their priorities straight."

"What Father says," Mandy said. "Do not quote me."

"One last thing—a couple of American contract mechanics in the pay of the Royal Iraqi Air Force hitched a ride to Habbaniya with the King's Own. From here they hopped a BOAC flight, getting out ahead of the revolution.

"The last thing they said to me, while laughing their heads off, was, 'there's probably more sand in the Royal Iraqi Air Force planes than out in the desert.'"

"Really," Major Randal said.

"Is that some sort of Americanism?" Major Everett asked. "What did they mean by that?"

"We're not having this conversation," Major Randal said. "This does not leave the room—those two mechanics sabotaged the Iraqi Air Force."

"And why do we want to keep that a secret?"

"The RAF pilots will be fighting for their lives. No reason for false hope or bad intelligence," Major Randal said. "We have no idea exactly what those mechanics meant."

"Whatever, those two cowboy mechanics thought it was hilarious," Major Everett said.

"I need a Boys Anti-Tank Rifle," Major Randal said, walking Major Everett to the door, "and an Omnibus general purpose tripod."

"The King's Own can spare you the Boys, but we do not have the tripod. I shall have it delivered within the hour."

"Good."

"Major Randal," the locksmith called. "Safe's open."

At almost that same instant, Captain Lancaster ushered in two carpenters carrying tools. Mr. Zargo came out of a back room and said, "Come this way, gentlemen."

"Why don't you step outside and take a smoke break," Major Randal said to the locksmith. "We may need you for another job."

Lieutenant Honeycutt-Parker and Mandy crowded in to see what was in the safe when Major Randal opened it. Inside was drawer after drawer of expensive women's jewelry. There was an ornately engraved Saur 38 (H) 7.65 with pearl grips—a trinket from Field Marshal Hermann Goering.

There was not much else.

Major Randal slipped the pistol in his pants pocket.

"A king's ransom in diamonds and pearls," Lieutenant Honeycutt-Parker said.

"Excellent," Mandy exclaimed. "The pot at the end of the rainbow!"

"Sir," Mr. Zargo called from another bedroom.

In one of the large walk-in closets, the carpenters had pulled down the wall.

"Most likely there's a secret switch to open the concealed door hidden somewhere," Mr. Zargo said. "But I was unable to locate it."

Behind the wall was a secret room containing racks of 9 mm Bergmann MP-18 machine pistols. There was an open crate containing brand new 9 mm Luger P-08 pistols. There were several more crates, possibly containing other side arms. Metal ammunition containers were stacked to the ceiling.

"My, my," Major Randal said.

"You realize what Bergmann MP-18s suggest, sir?"

"Why don't you tell me, Mr. Zargo?"

"No. 800 Special Purpose Training and Construction Company," Mr. Zargo said, clenching his is pipe in his teeth. "Brandenburger Commandos, Germany's clandestine warrior elite."

"I had a run-in with one in Istanbul a while back—big guy," Major Randal said. "What do you think it means?"

"Nazis advising the Golden Square," Mr. Zargo said. "Brandenburgers slip in ahead of the arrival of regular troops to arm and train the locals, then lead them in battle. Then the Germans reinforce them with airborne troops."

"Let's keep that thought to ourselves," Major Randal said. "We don't have any proof that Brandenburgers are on the ground—I doubt they are, Mr. Zargo."

"What leads you to say that, Major?"

"Because if Brandenburgers were here, the Iraqis would have marched down that hill and killed everyone on this base by now," Major Randal said. "But that doesn't mean they aren't on the way—probably are."

"Could be right, sir."

"I'll have Captain Lancaster get people in here to clear out this room. Set up an arms bunker out by our command post. We'll put these MP-18s to good use with the Strike Force.

"Keep searching—you may not have uncovered everything yet. Should be another safe. We haven't found what the Marshal didn't want found yet—besides this room."

"I will find it if it's here, sir."

"Mr. Zargo, you see something you take a fancy to, it's yours," Major Randal said. "Spoils of war. Just let me know what it is."

"Thank you, sir."

Back in the main room, Lieutenant Honeycutt-Parker and Mandy were trying on the jewelry.

"Mandy," Major Randal said. "I have a mission for you—if you accept."

"Like what, John?"

"We need to mobilize your equestrian team as a mounted messenger service. The Iraqis will shell the base," Major Randal said. "Telephone lines are vulnerable to artillery. Also, I'm going to need photos and after-action reports delivered to the Operations Center from the airfields as soon as they're ready."

"Excellent," Mandy said. "My girls know every inch of Habbaniya base, and they can ride like the wind."

"Dangerous assignment," Major Randal said. "Out on horseback during incoming fire."

"Nothing," Mandy said, "could be more hazardous to my girls than being taken by Iraqis."

"Right," Major Randal said. "We'll call your team the Pony Express. Have your girls bunk in here. This underground suite should be the safest place on post once the action starts.

"You're in charge—report to Parker."

"Does that mean I get the big bedroom," Mandy said, "with the mirror on the ceiling?"

8

GETTING READY

OUTSIDE THE FRONT GATE OF RAF HABBANIYA, POINTING vaguely in the direction of Great Britain, was a sign that said, "London 3,287 miles." It might as well have been on the moon as far as sending any help. Three brigades of Iraqis were now ensconced on the escarpment, approximately 300 yards or so on the far side of the airstrip, which, as a cost-cutting measure, had been constructed outside of the 10-foot perimeter fence running around the installation.

The bureaucrats had saved money, but now the inhabitants of the base were trapped in a defenseless man-made oasis.

RAF Habbaniya was virtually impossible to defend against direct ground attack. The base was dominated by the escarpment between it and the lake it was named after. It was not protected by a minefield. There were no bombproof shelters, no antiaircraft positions, not a single redoubt nor any antitank obstacles. The post was defended in most part by Assyrian Levies commanded by British officers who were not certain that their troops were reliable.

There were fourteen two-story concrete block machine-gun bunkers constructed every 300 yards running around the 7-mile fence surrounding the lush 500-acre post. The bunkers were impressive-looking, but after the sun went down, they were ineffective against infiltrators. On most nights it was not possible to see 30 feet, much less 300 yards.

The Euphrates River bordered RAF Habbaniya on three sides. The military architect who designed the base thought it a clever way to have a moat without building one. The protection was an illusion—in fact, it was a trap. The river kept the Iraqis from crossing in force, but it did not prevent them from occupying the far bank and firing into the encampment.

The Euphrates did keep the occupants of the RAF base from breaking out in any direction except the front gate.

AVM Harry "Reggie" Smart had taken to sleeping in his office on a camp bed. He was a man in turmoil. What had been one of the most idyllic berths in the service had turned out to be the best stateroom on the Titanic.

The AOC found himself in a crossfire of recommendations, recriminations, finger-pointing, dissembling and outright lying by military/political personalities far above his pay grade, all who had their own agenda. Air Vice Marshal Smart loathed FM Sir Archibald Wavell, who he blamed for leaving RAF Habbaniya twisting in the breeze. He wandered around his HQ complaining incessantly to anyone on his staff who he could pigeonhole, letting them know that the Field Marshal had abandoned them.

Staff had passed the point of trying not to be drawn into lengthy conversations with him. Now they tried to avoid the AOC altogether.

The Royal Iraqi Air Force badly outnumbered his primordial fleet of training aircraft; the Iraqis possessed fairly modern attack planes, and their pilots were competent. Air Vice Marshal Smart knew their capabilities. He had trained them.

The Iraqi Army outnumbered his ground troops more than ten to one, and they had over fifty pieces of artillery by the latest count, while he had two inert ceremonial cannons that had fired their last shots against the Turks in the Great War.

Field Marshal Wavell did not want to support military operations in Iraq. He claimed he did not have any spare troops to send. He recommended a diplomatic solution. PM Winston Churchill ranked Iraq as "last" in priorities—Libya, Crete and Greece taking precedence, in that order.

Now a copy of a communiqué from Sir Kinahan "Ken" Cornwallis, the Ambassador to Iraq, arrived. The wire, which he had sent to the Foreign Office, claimed that the AOC Royal Air Force Habbaniya had disregarded his order to attack the Iraqis that morning.

Ambassador Cornwallis was a lifelong politician, virtually all his time in government spent in the Middle East. He was a self-described "Arabist." The instructions referenced in the communiqué that the Ambassador had wired RAF Habbaniya were so self-servingly ambiguous that no one could have interpreted them as an order to do anything—the AOC's staff had spent hours that morning trying to. What they did say was the decision to attack or not to attack was his call—Air Vice Marshal Smart was responsible.

To complicate the situation, AM Sir Arthur Longmore, Air Officer Commanding Middle East, had weighed in with the recommendation that instead of bombing the Iraqi Army on the escarpment, Air Vice Marshal Smart should dispatch his aircraft to bomb the Iraqi government buildings in Baghdad—a recommendation so divorced from reality that it gave cause to doubt the judgment of the senior commander of the Royal Air Force in the theatre.

Air Vice Marshal Smart's boss wanted him to raid distant nonmilitary targets that posed no direct threat with a menagerie of aircraft so obsolete they could only be used for training purposes. His pilots were incompetents, or men burned out from battle, inexperienced student aviators and over-age staffers who had not kept their flying status current. Many of his attack aircraft were dangerously overloaded, armed with bombs bolted on in improvised nonregulation racks.

To comply with Sir Arthur was militarily insane. Air Vice Marshal Smart felt like he was standing on the gallows with a rope around his neck. Surely he was going to wake up from this nightmare and start laughing.

The Iraqis had sent an envoy, Maj. Hassain Najib, demanding that all training flights cease or they would be fired on. That was a violation of treaty, which left Air Vice Marshal Smart with but one option under standing orders that had long been in place—to attack. He knew his only hope was to strike first.

His idea had been to attack at dawn this morning so he would have a full day of flying fighting light. His tiny air force had no, as in zero, night-flying capabilities. Darkness favored the Iraqis—they could shell the base with impunity with no fear of retaliation because RAF Habbaniya had no artillery.

The problem was that Air Vice Marshal Smart had to get clearance because a state of war did not exist between Great Britain and Iraq. Then he had to respond to the Iraqi demand. After that, the AOC had to give the rebels reasonable time to reply, which burned up precious daylight.

So, he had stood by, hoping for clear instructions from someone above him in the military/political chain of command. And then when he had given up hope, a message arrived, signed by the Prime Minister: "Our position at RAF Habbaniya must be restored."

Which meant that Air Vice Marshal Smart had to act. But by now he had wasted half a day's flying light waiting. And the communiqué still did not tell him *how* to restore the British position. He had his orders— but what to do?

The AOC knew—bomb the Iraqis threatening his base. Strike first, hit them hard with everything RAF Habbaniya had, exploiting the element of surprise. There was no other option left.

The attack would go in at first light tomorrow.

MAJ. JOHN RANDAL WAS IN THE RED-AND-WHITE-STRIPED tent designated as his Command Post. Mr. Twinning had dispatched a team of telephone operators from the post phone exchange to operate his switchboard, which a crew of engineers was installing next door in the larger Operations Center tent. The women would be on duty around the clock in shifts.

"Mr. Fleming to see you," Lt. Penelope Honeycutt-Parker said.

"President of the Habbaniya Photography Club."

"Can you develop your own photos?" Major Randal asked.

"Yes, sir," Mr. Fleming said. "We have members who are proficient in all the photographic skills."

"I want to station a team at the airfield to make copies of the aerial photos the recon pilots take of the Iraqi positions. In the heat of battle the RAF may not have time to produce copies for us, and I need them immediately," Major Randal said. "Can your people handle that?"

"If the RAF will allow us access to the negatives," Mr. Fleming said. "My members will set up their own dark room in one of the hangars, and you shall have your photos in a jiffy, Major."

"Going to be dangerous," Major Randal said. "The airfield is sure to come under artillery fire."

"The club will do its duty, sir."

"Good man; coordinate with Squadron Leader Dudgeon at the airfield," Major Randal said. "Mandy Paige will have a rider waiting to deliver the photos here the instant they're developed."

"You shall have them, Major."

"Mr. Thymes," Lieutenant Honeycutt-Parker announced, "publishes the post newspaper."

"I need you to print up copies of my "Rules for Raiding.""

"When would you like them, Major?"

"Next thirty minutes or so," Major Randal said. "And, we're going to need some psychological warfare leaflets to drop on the Iraqis. You must have some bright lights on your staff that can come up with ideas."

"How about surrender leaflets," Mandy quipped as she walked by with a clipboard. "Need stick figures for those stupid Iraqis—to show them how."

"We shall go to work on the project immediately," Mr. Thymes said. "Play tricks with reader's minds ... my lads are good at that sort of devilry. Mandy may not have a bad idea—surrender now while you still can. We shall see what we can come up with, Major."

"Cpl. Melluish," Lieutenant Honeycutt-Parker said, "the base armorer."

"Corporal, I need an Omnibus General Purpose Tripod to mount a

Boys Anti-Tank Rifle on," Major Randal said. "And I need you to install a No. 32 scope on the Boys—I'll give you the scope and mountings."

"Sir!"

Major Randal continued, "Need you to improvise a ring mount of the type on a Valentia bomber that will allow me to attach the Boys to the handrail on the water tower."

"You intend to shoot off of the tower, sir?"

"Roger that."

"I shall have to go up and inspect the rail," Corporal Melluish said. "You will be wanting to bolt the Boys down solid to tame recoil, I presume, sir, then shift the weapon rapidly as needed?"

"That's the idea."

"What is my deadline, sir?"

"The Boys needs to be on that water tower locked and loaded with a hefty supply of ammunition laid in when the sun comes up tomorrow morning—I'll be manning it."

"As long as you permit me to come up on my work breaks," Corporal Melluish said. "Love to take a crack at the bloody Iraqis, sir."

"Anytime, Corporal."

The Boy Scout Leader came into the tent.

"I'm going to be busy this evening until around 1830 hours," Major Randal said. "Have your Scouts here at that time, armed and ready to move out to their assigned ambush sites. I plan to do a short briefing followed by an inspection. We'll make a practice of that every evening for the duration."

"Yes, sir, Major. Does that mean we will be setting up tonight?"

"It does," Major Randal said. "The war hasn't started yet, but the bad guys could jump the gun."

"The Scouts shall be standing tall, 6:30 sharp."

"I might be running a little late," Major Randal said. "Corporal James will probably want to perform his own inspection. Let him. You report to James—he reports to me."

"Understood, sir."

"Platoon Commanders, John," Mandy said. She had taken over for Lieutenant Penelope Honeycutt-Parker, who was off on some mission.

The six lieutenants from both the King's Own Company and No. 4 Levies Company assigned to the Strike Force were assembled in the Operations Center tent. None of them had ever been called to a platoon commander's conference before, except those held by their company commanders. This was a novel experience.

When Major Randal walked into the tent, one of the young officers jumped up and called, "Attention!"

"As you were," Major Randal ordered immediately.

"I thought you gentlemen might want to hear my thoughts on the way the upcoming battle is going to shape up for the Strike Force."

There was a hush in the tent. Not one officer present, with the exception of Major Randal, had ever heard a shot fired in anger. Several of them were inexperienced Territorials recently assigned to the King's Own. The Levies lieutenants were commanding native troops they were not totally confident in. They were all aware the cantonment was besieged by an enemy force that outnumbered them ten to one.

"This is going to be a platoon leader's fight—you're going to have a lot more responsibility and independence than officers of your grade normally do," Major Randal said. "Any man who does not feel up to the challenge can leave. Better now than later once the battle is joined.

"You fail me then, and I won't be so forgiving."

Mandy was standing by the side of the tent. Though she had grown up in the military, never had she seen a group of officers so riveted. Major Randal had cast a spell over them.

No one moved. The six lieutenants were barely breathing. This was the day they had all been anticipating for a long time but did not think was ever going to arrive. Going to war.

"All right then, you had your chance," Major Randal said.

"I just wound up a campaign in Italian East Africa where the odds stacked against us were worse than we're facing here at Habbaniya.

"Don't let being surrounded bother you—simplifies things."

The officers laughed.

"I understand the Iraqis follow the Arab proverb, 'The day is for fighting, the night is for sleeping.' If that's true, we'll make 'em pay for it.

"As soon as this briefing is over, hit the rack. Starting now, you sleep by day, operate at night—same for your troops. Don't let anyone try to put your men on some work detail. The only thing I want Strike Force personnel doing is resting, preparing to go on patrol and going on patrols. Is that clear?"

"CLEAR, SIR!"

"Each of your platoons in the Strike Force will operate as a stand-alone independent command. Instead of squads, I want you to reorganize into a HQ patrol and three raiding patrols. Pick your most talented men as patrol leaders, regardless of rank. The best man leads. Patrol Leader becomes a rank—they're the studs.

"We're going to carry out pinprick raids. The idea is to move by stealth under cover of darkness, utilizing the element of surprise and to execute our operations with speed coupled with extreme violence—come at the Iraqis from all directions.

"Your mission is to kill as many bad guys as you can," Major Randal said. "It doesn't get any better than this—small unit raiding leading from the front. It's why you became officers. I'll be going out with you every night—I wouldn't miss it for the world.

"Be here with your handpicked patrol leaders for a Warning Order at 1900 hours—move out."

The platoon commanders stood up in a state of disbelief. The only place they had ever heard a briefing like Major Randal just gave was in the movies. In their wildest imagination, they had never expected to be the recipient of an assignment like the one he had laid out.

The chance to be a part of something like the Strike Force mission was the reason they had joined the Army and become officers.

Mandy escorted the two infantry company commanders, Capt. Valentine Fabian, A Company, King's Own Royal Regiment, and Capt. John Smith, No. 4 Company Assyrian Levies, in next. The captains were apprehensive. Neither officer had ever had his authority usurped by their platoon commanders meeting with the CO before they did. And they were wondering why the exiting platoon leaders had been so excited.

Being trapped in an indefensible position by an enemy who occupied the high ground equipped with fifty field pieces staring down at point-blank range was not something one would normally cheer about.

Maj. Ted Everett arrived, asking, "Do you object if I sit in?"

"Be my guest," Major Randal said.

"Starting right now, you two captains need to think of yourselves as battalion commanders. Your platoon commanders have been ordered to break their platoons down into a HQ and three raiding patrols per platoon. That means you will each have up to twelve patrols out every night conducting pinprick raids. The idea is to hit hard and run."

Mandy thought she heard a sigh of disbelief. Neither company commander had ever commanded in battle. Now their role in the upcoming battle was being expanded. Planning and coordinating a dozen night patrols was a complex military undertaking.

"In practice, you'll function as my Strike Force operations officers," Major Randal said. "As new intelligence information on enemy positions comes in from photo recon and the pilot's after-action reports, you'll be evaluating it and selecting the night's targets for your patrols to raid. Every day you will prepare a target list within your individual AO and recommend the patrol you think best qualified to handle each mission.

"I'll sign off on your recommendations, make changes or add new targets. I'll either select or announce the target that my personal patrol will raid at that time.

"You'll brief your platoon leaders on their target list for the night. The platoon leaders will brief their patrol leaders.

"Patrol leaders will plan their scheme of maneuver, brief their patrol and conduct rehearsals.

"I'll conduct a final briefing for all patrol leaders. Then we'll go do it.

"What are your questions?"

Captain Fabian asked, "Will we be working out of your Operations Center here, sir?"

"Roger, Mandy's Pony Express girls will be delivering new photos of the Iraqi positions as they're developed at the airfield. They'll also bring updated reports on Iraqi dispositions as the pilots are debriefed after each mission.

"You're my war planners. Your job will be to keep our terrain map current, change out the photos on the pictomap as the new ones arrive and work up your target list for the night's raids as the situation develops during the day's action. You'll quickly develop an operational rhythm tied to the flow of intelligence.

"We have the RAF armored car company for our local reaction force so you don't have any responsibility to plan for anything but the night's patrols. However, special tasks may come up unexpectedly from time to time," Major Randal said.

"And, when the Iraqis do throw in the towel and retreat, you'll have to shift gears, plan the pursuit phase and then lead it. So be prepared to be flexible when that happens."

The two captains glanced at each other, thinking, "How could Major Randal be so confident?"

"The RAF fancies they're going to be fighting this battle all by themselves—theirs to win or lose. Not going to happen like that.

"Battles are won by boots on the ground, and you're the two studs who are going to craft the strategy that'll make the Iraqis wish to be anywhere on planet Earth but outside our wire during the hours of darkness. That, gentlemen, is how we're going to win this thing.

"I want the maximum number of patrols operating against point type targets every night," Major Randal said. "Is that clear?"

"CLEAR, SIR!"

"MANDY," MAJ. JOHN RANDAL ORDERED, "I WANT EVERY twelve-gauge semi-automatic or pump shotgun on the installation, except those used by the Scouts or the Annie Oakleys, commandeered immediately. No double barrels or over and unders—only repeaters.

"Start the sound truck on the rounds. Have the radio station start putting out public service announcements every ten minutes. Have teams going door to door to collect them.

"Notify Cpl. Melluish we'll need the shotgun barrels shortened."

"Excellent," Mandy said. "Open season on Iraqis.

"What's the bag limit, John?"

9

GOOD TO HAVE A PLAN B

MAJ. JOHN RANDAL INVITED LT. COL. ALISTAIR BRAWN and Maj. Ted Everett into the striped tent. This was the first time the three senior ground commanders had had a chance to meet privately. The clock was ticking, war was coming and what the three officers determined at this meeting might decide the fate of the cantonment.

Lieutenant Colonel Brawn went first. "Neither Ted nor I have ever been in combat, much less commanded in a situation like we face here. We understand that you held the rank of Brigadier in Abyssinia. If you agree, we will ask to have you reappointed to take over command of ground operations."

"I never used the rank," Major Randal said. "It was more to impress the natives than anything else. I'm going to have my hands full with the Strike Force—speaks well of you two men to make the offer, though."

Lieutenant Colonel Brawn glanced at Major Everett, "We were hoping you would accept."

"The ground commander's going to have to deal with administration," Major Randal said. "I won't have time."

"The offer stands," Lieutenant Colonel Brawn said. "But, you are correct. There would definitely be administrative duties. Someone needs to coordinate with the RAF. We are not getting guidance or even much information out of the AOC's office. It appears as if the RAF will be fighting one battle, while the Levies and King's Own fights another. Smart has left the land forces campaign to its own devices."

"Can you give me a rundown on the defense plan?" Major Randal said. "The only thing I know at this point is the base has a fence around it—no minefield."

"It is a joint undertaking by the Levies, the King's Own and No.1 RAF Armored Company," Lieutenant Colonel Brawn said. "Until you showed up, the idea was for the Levies to be responsible for the perimeter defense and the KO and the ACC to provide the mobile reserve.

"I divided the camp into three sections—each one defended by a company of the Levies. The blockhouses around the seven-mile perimeter will be manned by two NCOs and six troopers armed with Mark III Lee-Enfields and a Hotchkiss light machine gun. One company is in reserve, and we have a composite weapons company. Total strength all up is 750 men.

"The Assyrians in companies No. 1 through No. 4 are Christians and have suffered at the hands of the Iraqis in the recent past. We hope they will be reliable, but we have no way to know that until they are put to the acid test.

"One of our companies, No. 8, consists of Kurds, who—while Muslim—are not Arabs. They *hate* the Iraqis. Virtually been in a constant state of conflict with them since the country of Iraq was formed at the end of the last war."

Major Everett said, "The King's Own have 400 officers and men present for duty with more scheduled to be flown in. I have only been the CO for a few weeks. Prior to our deployment by air to Iraq, everyone had to pass a physical, and the Colonel was ruled medically unfit.

"Acting on Colonel Brawn's orders upon arrival at Habbaniya, I developed a plan to divide the King's Own into two elements. Half to be deployed in point defense of positions like the water system, electrical plant, hospital, etc. The other half will join the Levies mobile reserve."

Lieutenant Colonel Brawn said, "Now that you have taken command of the mobile Strike Force, Major, you may want to modify those plans."

Major Randal said, "The RAF have thirty-four Lewis guns for defense on the air strip, and they recently found four more in a warehouse, according to Tony Dudgeon. They don't know anything about using machine guns in the ground role—they're aerial gunners.

"We have a rule in Raiding Forces—'Right Man, Right Job.' I'd comb the Levies and the KO, to include the two companies you sent me, for machine gunners and put professionals on those Lewis guns."

"Makes perfect sense," Lieutenant Colonel Brawn said. "Now that I think about it, it's probably better to concentrate on defending the exposed airfield than to tie up troops securing point-type targets in the interior of the base. Those installations are safe as safe can be in a situation like this during daytime. We can detail troops to guard them at night. I shall provide as many of my Lewis gunners as the Levies can spare," Lieutenant Colonel Brawn said. "We should be able to deliver thirty-eight qualified men."

Major Everett said, "I agree, transfer the troops on interior guard duty to the airfield to harden it."

"Tell me about your mortars," Major Randal said.

"Each of our six companies has a section of 3-inch mortars commanded by a warrant officer III, which we call a sergeant major," Lieutenant Colonel Brawn said. "The Levies are organized under the old establishment, meaning we only have two tubes. But we have a lot of 3-inch ammunition laid in since we seldom fire the mortars and the section is automatically resupplied every month."

"Ted?" Major Randal said.

"Same for us," Major Everett said. "We are authorized eight tubes per company but only have the two. We flew in a basic load of ammunition when we arrived. I am afraid the state of our mortar section is not what it should be.

"Over the last year the King's Own has lost a high percentage of our prewar professionals as they have been posted out to more active battalions. For the most part, replacements have been untrained militia. To be frank, the battalion is only a shadow of its former self. Our mortar crews are probably incapable of hitting the broad side of a barn."

"Not a problem," Major Randal said, lighting a Player's with his battered Zippo with the U.S. 26th Cavalry Regimental crest engraved on the front. "Having a lot of ammunition—that's the main thing."

"Our mortar sections are proficient—at least in their drill," Lieutenant Colonel Brawn said. "But as I mentioned, they are seldom allowed to practice live fire. The AOC does not want mortars interfering with flight training because of their high angle of fire and it would not do to upset the chance migrant sheepherder who might wander onto our mortar range. Public relations, what!"

"Yeah, that's a bad thing," Major Randal said. "Disturbing nomads."

"Air Vice Marshal Smart thinks so."

"Here's what I propose," Major Randal said. "Set up a combined mortar battery under central control. Keep it masked during the day. But fire H&I missions all night."

"The AOC could not possibly have any objections to that plan," Lieutenant Colonel Brawn said. "The RAF is going to be fighting over the Iraqi position on the escarpment, an area no larger than a medium-sized golf course.

"The flight pattern over the battle area is going to be extraordinarily congested. The pilots would not much enjoy mortar shells raining down through it—on top of being shot at from the ground while dodging each other, dropping bombs and shooting it out with the RIAF.

"Night firing, that's another story. Our pilots, I have been informed, do not fly during the hours of darkness. I am all for it, Major."

"Harassment and interdiction, just the ticket for my people," Major Everett said. The plan, I take it, is merely to cause the Iraqis to stay awake?"

"Always good to have sleepy opposition," Major Randal said. "Nothing raises the spirits of the home team more than listening to the other side getting hammered."

"We'll need to coordinate the fires with the raiding patrols," Lieutenant Colonel Brawn said. "Simple enough. Who knows, we might actually hit something. Inflict material damage. One can always hope."

"If you do," Major Randal said, "the RAF will claim it."

THE FIRST THING MAJ. JOHN RANDAL DID AFTER THE TWO senior ground commanders departed was to simplify the mobile part of the defense plan. When the King's Own Royal Regiment had been given the assignment, they commandeered every vehicle capable of transporting troops—military and civilian and including a school bus—they could lay hands on. The result was an oddball gypsy caravan … but it worked.

The problem was finding qualified drivers. Very few men in the King's Own knew how to drive a truck. Under the circumstances, any man who had so much as cast eyes on one was designated a driver. Driving practice was initiated immediately.

RAF Habbaniya was surrounded on three sides by the Euphrates, which would make it difficult for the Iraqis to cross in force quickly. If they did make the attempt at a river crossing, there would be advance warning from the RAF or the blockhouses guarding the perimeter. Troops would then have time to be assembled and moved to counter the threat.

Should the Iraqis attack in force down the escarpment, all the counterattack troops on the cantonment would not be able to stop them.

That being the case, there was no good reason to keep a full infantry company on standby at all times. The men would be of more use to Maj. Ted Everett defending the airfield. The company on alert was reduced to one platoon designated the "Ready Reaction Platoon," and the rest returned to the King's Own.

However, the drivers needed to transport a full company were retained to stay with their assigned vehicles and continue driving practice.

Neither the Levies nor the King's Own had a use for all the motorcycles recently purchased by Grp. Capt. William "Butcher" Saville, so Major Randal decided to take the surplus and form a "Motorcycle Patrol." It would be assigned to cruise around the twenty-eight miles of road inside the cantonment during the day showing the flag.

The Patrol could reinforce the Ready Reaction Platoon in an emergency, but their primary mission would be to make a show of force to buck up civilian morale. Twenty-five Triumph motorcycles rumbling in formation making a slow speed thunder run on a base three by one and one-half miles in size would sound like a powerful military deterrent.

Even though it was not.

A call went out for volunteers. To qualify, a man had to know how to ride and not have any other unique military proficiency. The patrol was for show. It could not be allowed to siphon off men with specialist military skills.

Major Randal knew there were not enough experienced riders who could be released from their duties to fill the ranks of the Motorcycle Patrol.

Mandy said, "We have a motorcycle crowd on Habbaniya. Possibly some of them could serve?"

"I didn't see a club on the list."

"Some older boys and men get together to work on their bikes. Ride them in the desert. I doubt it's a formal organization. Fun, though!"

"Have 'em report to the commander of No.1 Armored Car Company," Major Randal ordered. "Squadron Leader Page will be in charge of the Motorcycle Patrol.

"By the way, where's Parker?"

"She and Mr. Zargo are down in my new bedroom. He came looking for you while you were in your meeting with Colonel Brawn and Major Everett. Parker went to see something he found."

One of the female civilian switchboard operators hurried in. "Wing Commander Ling is on the line for you, sir. He has been ordered to make a flight over the Iraqi positions and would like to know if you care to accompany him. The Commander is departing in half an hour."

"Roger that, I'll be at the airfield in thirty minutes," Major Randal ordered, "Tell him if I'm running late not to take off until I get there."

"Yes, sir."

"I am reasonably certain," Mandy said, "Wing Commander outranks Major."

MR. TWINNING JOINED MAJ. JOHN RANDAL AS HE WAS walking into the BOQ to check on what Mr. Zargo had found in Mandy's bedroom.

"Understand you are intending to shoot off my water tower."

"I'm having a scope-mounted Boys .55 placed up there," Major Randal said. "In Abyssinia we got hits on targets using one like it out to a range of one mile."

"You are going to draw fire to my water tank," Mr. Twinning said. "The Iraqis will blast their bloody great cannons at you once you engage, Major."

"You might as well paint a red bull's-eye on the water tank, Mr. Twinning. The Iraqis are going to shoot at the tower no matter what. If I were you, I'd write it off right now before the battle gets started."

"Quite right, most likely," Mr. Twinning said. "I have developed a contingency plan in the event the tank gets holed."

"It's an irresistible target," Major Randal said.

"A .55-caliber antitank round is a big, heavy bullet," Mr. Twinning said. "You will need some way to haul ammunition up the sixty-foot tower. I shall have my engineering department install a winch up top to make your resupply task more manageable."

"Good idea, Mr. Twinning," Major Randal said. "Now, if you will excuse me, sir."

MR. ZARGO AND LT. PENELOPE HONEYCUTT-PARKER WERE in the master bedroom with the mirror on the ceiling. The super-king-sized bed was pulled out into the middle of the floor. The massive headboard sported an impressive assortment of black metal rings conveniently studded in it. When in place, the bed concealed another false wall. Behind the false wall was a walk-in closet.

Sturdy-looking leather luggage trunks were stacked to the ceiling along the walls. A small safe was embedded in the concrete floor. The door was slightly ajar. Apparently the locksmith had been at it.

"Elephant skin luggage," Mr. Zargo said. "Toughest material in the world."

"Take a look in one of the valises, John," Lieutenant Honeycutt-Parker said.

Maj. John Randal flipped the lid back on a trunk. Inside were gold bars. There were a lot of them.

"Anyone know?"

"Only the three of us," Lieutenant Honeycutt-Parker said. "We intentionally did not break them open until the carpenters and the locksmith departed."

"What's in the safe?"

"Several different passports in various names with the Air Marshal's photo on all of them," Mr. Zargo said, clenching his pipe in his teeth. "Bank documents to access his private Swiss accounts—the man had a Plan B."

"It's 'Good to Have a Plan B,'" Major Randal said, quoting from Raiding Forces Rules. "Except now we have it."

"Oh, and there is this," Mr. Zargo tossed Major Randal another engraved 7.65 mm Saur 38 (H). "Second half of a matched pair."

Major Randal checked it. Like its twin, it was loaded. The Air Marshal liked to keep a little insurance in his safes.

"Put the bed back and seal this closet off." Major Randal ordered.

"You do not wish to report the find to the AOC?" Mr. Zargo asked, lighting his pipe.

"Negative," Major Randal said. "Sooner or later Lady Jane Seaborn will arrive at Habbaniya. In the event that anything should happen to Parker or me before she does, Mr. Zargo, inform her privately of what is in the trunks—use the word *frogspawn* to identify yourself. Tell no one else. Is that clear?"

"You can depend on me to carry out your orders," Mr. Zargo said. "How will I recognize this Lady Seaborn?"

"Jane's a captain in the Royal Marines. You won't be able to miss her," Major Randal said. "She'll find you."

10

BRANDY

SQN. LDR. TONY DUDGEON GAVE MAJ. JOHN RANDAL A QUICK briefing before he and Wg. Cdr. Larry Ling took off on their flight over the Iraqi positions on what was unofficially called a "provocation patrol." The idea, coming from AVM Harry "Reggie" Smart, was to fly over the escarpment and see if they could draw fire. If the Iraqis opened on them, then that signaled hostilities had commenced.

At this point, it was deemed desirable that a state of war exist. Because tomorrow morning when the sun came up, the Royal Air Force was going to bomb the Iraqis outside RAF Habbaniya. Hostilities or not, the decision had been made—the balloon was going up.

"One twenty-pound bomb carries as much explosive as a six-inch shell," Squadron Leader Dudgeon said. "We now have twenty-seven Oxford trainers modified, which in total can carry 216 of them. Adds up to nearly two tons of bombs, total. Better than zero, which is what they could carry before Larry and I did our unauthorized field-expedient modifications.

"We only have one bomb-aimer and two air-gunners on our school staff, so we began crash courses—no pun intended—in both those skills. Better to have a partially trained bomb-aimer or air-gunner than a complete ignoramus when we go to war for real!"

"You're planning a precision bombing campaign against point-type targets with bombardiers who have never dropped a bomb?" Major Randal said.

"One of them has."

"How many bombers can you put up?"

"Twelve Audaxes and seven Gordons able to carry two 250-pound bombs each. Nine Audaxes and the twenty-seven Oxfords armed with eight twenty-pound bombs."

"One experienced bombardier," Major Randal said, "for your entire air fleet?"

"Less than optimal, huh?"

Major Randal said, "It doesn't sound good."

Wing Commander Ling arrived. "Ready, Randal?"

The two walked out to a waiting Audax that had its motor idling, having been warmed up by its crew chief for the Wing Commander. The aircraft was still wearing its yellow training colors. The two officers climbed aboard, taxied out and took off.

Major Randal could see the Iraqi positions stretched out between the banks of the Euphrates. The river looped around behind the RAF base and then cut back toward Lake Habbaniyah. It marked both the boundaries of the enemy's flanks. Wing Commander Ling flew low over the escarpment. Down below were Iraqi soldiers setting up. Infantry had been estimated at nine to ten thousand. Armored cars, field pieces and thin-skinned vehicles too numerous to count were parked as if on parade. Tents dotted the desert.

No one paid the Audax the slightest attention. Wing Commander Ling flew out over the china-blue lake, came around and flew low over the BOAC dock and terminal building complex. The place seemed deserted. There were no Iraqi troop units positioned anywhere near the lake. Not within a mile. Major Randal looked down at the terminal building through his Zeiss binoculars and could see two sentries posted outside, but no other activity.

Having drawn no fire, the Audax returned to base and landed.

"See what you needed to see, Major?" Wing Commander Ling asked.

"I did," Major Randal said. "How about you, sir?"

"Afraid not; Reggie is on the sharp end all on his own," Wing Commander Ling laughed. "No joy from the Iraqis. A pity for the AOC we were not shot down—not even fired on."

MAJ. JOHN RANDAL SPENT THE NEXT HOUR TOURING THE defenses along the perimeter of the airfield. He was escorted on his inspection by Mr. Walter Stanberry, captain of the Rod and Gun Club's Big Bore Rifle Team. The civilian riflemen were preparing firing positions at places of their own choosing.

Many were located on top of sandbag bunkers protecting Lewis gun teams. A point was being established on top of each of the concrete bunkers built every 300 yards. Three were positioned on top of hangars. The men, mostly sportsmen in their fifties and sixties, were methodically going about the business of preparing for the upcoming battle as if preparing for a rifle match.

Each two-man team was equipped with a high-power spotting scope borrowed from the club rifle range. The shooters were armed with their personal weapons ranging in caliber from a 220 Swift Winchester to a Rigby 375 H&H magnum. The men had selected their rifle they shot the best, not necessarily the one they fired in competition. All the rifles were scoped.

Hunting in the desert was done at long range, about the same distances they would be firing on the Iraqi positions.

Since the terrain surrounding RAF Habbaniya was desert or marshland, and having wisely chosen to locate next to the MGs on the bunkers or the top of hangars, every position had a good field of fire. Iraqi soldiers were in plain sight everywhere. The enemy did not seem concerned about concealing their positions, and they were not digging in or camouflaging their vehicles. The desert in front of the airfield was a "target-rich environment."

The rebel troops acted like they were on a camping trip.

"Have your people ready to go at sunrise," Major Randal ordered. "I'll be out to brief you later this evening, but as things stand now, starting at first light, take down every man standing on the other side of the wire."

"You can count on us, Major."

"Back those Iraqis off out there, Mr. Stanberry."

"We shall make things hot for them."

"Your signal to execute will be the RAF air attack," Major Randal said. "When the first bomb explodes, you men go to work."

"Simple enough," Mr. Stanberry said. "My lads may be over-age for field service, but they can shoot the lights out. Those rebel gentlemen over there are in for quite a jolt when we commence."

"How're you fixed for ammunition?"

"Every rifle has a minimum of 200 rounds," Mr. Stanberry said. "Hand-load our own. Our plan is to go home nights and reload the brass we fire each day. The club is well stocked with components."

"Outstanding," Major Randal said. "The airstrip's the most critical location, but you do have other teams positioned along the rest of the front fence?"

"I do, sir."

"Perfect, I'll try to come out tomorrow and troop the line," Major Randal said. "I have a wildcat 7 mm-06 converted 1903 A-1 Springfield with an 8X Zeiss Zielacht scope we used in Abyssinia.

"Get in a little work."

"Look forward to it, Major."

LT. PENELOPE HONEYCUTT-PARKER AND MANDY WERE outside Wg. Cdr. Larry Ling's Ready Room when Maj. John Randal concluded his inspection of the civilian rifle club shooters. The two were there attempting to coordinate where to station the Pony Express messenger girls and how to manage obtaining access to the pilot debriefings. The RAF battle plan called for the bombers to land after every mission and either the pilot or a crewman would dash over to Grp. Capt. William "Butcher" Saville's office and report on the mission.

The Butcher planned to keep an operations map in his office and develop an updated target list from the mission debrief information. The Group Captain was a qualified pilot, but he was going to sit this one out. He had no intention of flying combat missions.

"Grp. Capt. Saville has chosen not to be accommodative," Lieutenant Honeycutt-Parker said. "Refuses us permission to sit in on his debriefings."

"Not in King's regulations," Mandy said. "The Butcher strictly adheres to the book. Claims nothing in it authorizes female military officers or their designated civilian representatives like me to observe RAF operational briefings and take notes."

"We're going to need a Plan B," Major Randal said. "Besides, if Saville is expecting pilots or crew to fly combat, land and then run all the way over here on foot from the new strip on the polo grounds to make a situation report, then run back and fly another mission—he's dreaming."

"That is the Butcher's plan," Lieutenant Honeycutt-Parker said.

"Pilots won't do it," Major Randal said. "If we expected them to and only collected our information from here, we wouldn't be getting access to all the intelligence we need."

"I shall think about it," Lieutenant Honeycutt-Parker said. "Possibly you could station Captain Lancaster here to work with Group Captain Saville man-to-man. We will simply have to find someone else to gather reports from the pilots at the alternate airstrip when they return from a sortie."

"I could do it."

"Negative," Major Randal said. "I need you running the show at the Operations Center. Find somebody else, Parker."

"David might not be suitable either," Mandy said. "He's army, so Group Captain Saville may not work with him—inter-service rivalry and all that silliness."

A courier plane landed and taxied to near where they were standing. The door of the plane opened, and folding steps came down. Mrs. Brandy Seaborn climbed out, holding a tennis racket.

"Brandy," Major Randal said, "what the hell are you doing here?"

"Hitched a ride when I learned you and Parker came up to see Pam awarded her wings," Brandy said. "Dickie's gone to sea in his new cruiser.

I was bored and alone in Cairo."

"You won't be bored here," Major Randal said.

"May not be alone either," Lt. Honeycutt-Parker said.

"According to the brochure put out by the Royal Air Force, Habbaniya is a lost paradise with fifty-six tennis courts. Best swimming pool in the service."

"Brandy," Parker drawled, "Habbaniya is under siege by the Iraqi Army … completely surrounded. War starts tomorrow. The cantonment is virtually defenseless. You arrived in time for the rapine and debasement phase."

"Those troops on the ridge we flew over are rebels?" Brandy said. "Uh-oh!"

"Pool's fabulous," Mandy said. "No polo or golf though."

MAJ. JOHN RANDAL PULLED MR. ZARGO ASIDE. "WHEN I FLEW over Lake Habbaniyah, there were quite a few sailboats at anchor out in the middle. What's the story?"

"Yachts owned by wealthy European expatriates who work in Baghdad or Fallujah. A few belong to senior Iraqi military officers. They leave them out in the middle of the lake because the yachts are safe out there."

"How do the owners get out to 'em?"

"Commute by motor launch from the Yacht Club."

"The motorboats at the club all looked like they had been sunk in shallow water along the shore," Major Randal said. "That means there isn't any way to reach the yachts."

"The Iraqis most likely immobilized them when they occupied the escarpment," Mr. Zargo said.

"Those boats may provide us an opportunity," Major Randal said. "We need to infiltrate around the Iraqi's flanks. The problem is the Euphrates. In order to get in the enemy rear, conduct a raid and return, a patrol launched from here will have to cross the river four times. River crossings are complicated, dangerous and take up a lot of time. Besides, we don't have small, easily man-transportable boats to make the crossings."

"The Euphrates is a double-edged sword," Mr. Zargo said.

"If we could station a patrol out on one of those yachts they could slip ashore under cover of darkness," Major Randal said. "Hit the bad guys from behind. Then disappear back into the middle of the lake."

"You need English soldiers for that kind of operation, sir," Mr. Zargo said. "Neither the Assyrians or Kurds will want to be a part of such an undertaking. They would not care for being on the water."

"Understood—what do you think of the concept?"

"No Iraqi is going to anticipate a raid coming from the lake," Mr. Zargo said. "The element of surprise is a given, sir."

"I'm going to need five good men for my personal fighting patrol, Mr. Zargo," Major Randal said. "We'll be going out every night. Can you find me operators who like quiet work in the dark?"

"My pleasure, Major."

"SMART HAS CALLED A BRIEFING FOR 2000 HOURS," LT. Penelope Honeycutt-Parker informed Maj. John Randal. "Your presence has been requested."

"I have an 1800 hour inspection of the Boy Scouts," Major Randal said. "Need to do the same for the Annie Oakleys—set that up for 1830 hours. Tell them I could be running late."

Brandy came into the striped tent, wearing shorts and a crop top. She was a sparkler, a happy girl, always laughing—fun to be around. It was hard to believe she was the mother of 19-year-old Lt. Randy "Hornblower" Seaborn—Raiding Forces senior naval officer.

During OPERATION DYNAMO, the evacuation from Dunkirk, she and Lieutenant Honeycutt-Parker had taken the Seaborn family houseboat on a number of rescue runs to the beaches of France to bring home troops. During the Abyssinian Campaign, the two adventuresses had traveled with the Lancelot Lancers Yeomanry aka Lounge Lizards, an armored car regiment, on the southern advance by East Africa Force until it reached the central highland region where Force N, under the command of Major Randal, was operating. Then she and Lieutenant Honeycutt-Parker had traded their Rolls Royce Silver Spirit armored car for a pair of mules and joined 1 Guerrilla Corps (Parachute), Force N behind the Italian lines for over a month to organize the surrender of enemy female dependents.

Brandy and Major Randal were particularly close.

"How many men could a thirty-foot yacht sleep for four or five days, Brandy?" Major Randal asked.

"Comfortably?"

"Military operation," Major Randal said. "Troops will have to stay below deck during daylight hours."

"Depends on the interior configuration of the boat," Brandy said. "Six armed men minimum."

"Can you handle a sailboat that large?"

Brandy flashed a beautiful smile, laughing, "You *are* joking?"

"Right," Major Randal said. "What could I have been thinking?"

Mandy came into the striped tent, "Pam says she will be here in the next twenty minutes, John, per your request."

"Ask Captain Fabian to step over here for a moment," Major Randal said. "Then get Major Everett on the horn for me."

Outside on the street, motorcycles began rumbling to life. The hastily-formed Habbaniya Motorcycle Patrol (HMP) was preparing to make its debut thunder run. Twenty-five Triumphs in symphony made an impressive roar. And that was the idea.

Rest easy, folks—the HMP is on patrol.

Major Randal was also considering using the HMP as the initial quick response unit when the Boy Scouts or the Annie Oakleys initiated an ambush. There were two problems with that idea. RAF Habbaniya would most likely go to full blackout restriction once hostilities commenced. The pitch dark would make it problematic for a platoon of motorcycles racing hell-for-leather to the scene of a contact.

And, not all the HMP members were in the service. About a third were civilian motorbike enthusiasts with no military training. Their proficiency with firearms was unproven.

Capt. Valentine Fabian arrived. "You wished to see me, sir?"

"A special assignment has come up. Give me the name of the best infantry lieutenant in the King's Own," Major Randal said. "I need a hunter—a reliable man who can operate independently. Skill with small boats is a plus. He'll be working deep behind the Iraqi lines. You'll be planning and briefing the missions, which will be classified."

"You mean a lieutenant in addition to my three platoon commanders already assigned to the Strike Force, sir?"

"Unless one of your officers happens to be the best man for this assignment," Major Randal said, taking out a Player's and lighting it with his Zippo. "In that case, we'll have to bring in a replacement for him."

"Roy Kidd, sir," Captain Fabian said. "He would be my recommendation."

"Why?"

"India Command takes generous annual leaves," Captain Fabian said. "Lieutenant Kidd spends his leave sport hunting. He is a man who likes dangerous game. Tigers are his favorite—though he will go after leopard when there is a problem."

"Problem?"

"Leopards kill livestock and take to man-eating occasionally in the district where the KORR is stationed," Captain Fabian said. "When that happens, sir, the civil authorities contact the battalion to request that Roy be detailed to resolve the issue.

"He's a regular Jim Corbett, Major."

"Jim Corbett?"

"The man-eater exterminator *extraordinaire*—wrote a series of true life books, sir," Captain Fabian said. "Though none of Roy's cats have been as famous or run up as many kills as those Corbett stalked."

Mandy came in, carrying a phone on a long extension cord. "Major Everett on the line for you, John."

Major Randal took the handset from Mandy, "Ted, I'd like to interview a lieutenant of yours for a special assignment—Roy Kidd. OK, thanks.

"Major Everett didn't sound like he wanted to release him," Major Randal said, "but he agreed."

"Roy is not the most popular officer in the battalion, sir," Captain Fabian said. "Keeps to himself, but when it comes to infantry skills and field craft he is the best we have."

Lt. Pamala Plum-Martin arrived.

"Brandy, what are you doing here?"

"Came to see you graduate," Brandy laughed. "Swim, sun, and play tennis. No one informed me the place was under siege."

"Give me a report, Pam," Major Randal said, "on the status of your Seagull."

"Assembled, topped off and ready for a test flight," Lieutenant Plum-Martin said. "I was making final preparations to take off when Mandy called."

"Go make your test flight," Major Randal ordered. "Take Brandy with you. When you lift off, bank out behind the cantonment, loop far out into the desert, staying out of sight of the Iraqi Army, then swing around and come back over Lake Habbaniyah from the far shore. Check out the sailboats anchored out in the middle of the lake. Then turn around and come back home the same way—don't want you flying over the escarpment."

"Can do, John."

"Let Brandy pick out a yacht—make it a good one," Major Randal said. "We'll fly out later tonight and commandeer it for her.

"Any questions?"

"You want to hijack a yacht for Brandy," Lieutenant Plum-Martin said, "with a shooting war ready to break out at any moment?"

"It's the least I can do."

Mandy said, "Wow!"

11

RESCUING RED

MAJ. JOHN RANDAL WAS IN THE COMMAND POST TENT, briefing his Strike Force's six platoon commanders and the eighteen patrol leaders. Capt. John Smith and Capt. Valentine Fabian were present. Maj. Edward "Ted" Everett was also in attendance, accompanied by a young officer, Lt. Roy Kidd.

"The Patrols will be named from left to right A-X. Mr. Zargo and his men will be designated as my personal 'Z Patrol.'

"The Patrol Leader will issue a Patrol Order. What we call in the Commandos a 'frag order,' meaning a fragment of an order. Your frag order will focus primarily on the mission, with most emphasis placed on the concept-of-the-operation paragraph," Major Randal said. He was pointing at the chalkboard on a tripod that had the elements of the frag order listed on it, which he had explained in detail.

"Mandy is passing out copies of 'Raiding Forces Rules for Raiding.' Use these simple guidelines when planning your patrols and writing your frag order. When you issue your order, always keep it short and simple.

Some say *KISS* stands for 'keep it short and simple' and others say it's for 'keep it simple, stupid.' Take your choice."

The men in the tent all laughed. This was a serious briefing—there was no horseplay. However, Major Randal had the knack for explaining a military subject in a way that was both easy to understand and interesting. The officers and other ranks patrol leaders were enjoying the lecture, knowing they would be putting what he was teaching into practice in the immediate future.

"My regiment, The Rangers, was originally trained in America by Maj. Robert Rogers during the French and Indian War—he laid down his 1st Standing Order: "Don't Forget Nothing.""

The group laughed again.

"That's not one of our rules in Raiding Forces but we say it a lot," Major Randal said. "Don't any of you forget nothing—is that clear?"

"CLEAR, SIR!"

"Keep in mind," Major Randal said, "Attack is the easiest form of warfare. You men are going to attack, attack, attack and then you're going to attack some more. I want you thinking offense all the time.

"Last thing," Major Randal said. "'Patrol Leader' is a rank in the Strike Force.

"Mandy is passing out a pair of violet strips made of velvet cloth—like the ones I'm wearing—to each of you who'll be Patrol Leaders—put 'em on your epaulettes. Badges of honor, they're to identify you as a stud.

"Questions?"

"Does that mean, sir," a corporal in the King's Own Royal Regiment asked, "you will be leading patrols—in person like?"

"Roger that," Major Randal said. "Every night."

MAJ. JOHN RANDAL INVITED LT. ROY KIDD INTO THE RED and white striped tent that he was using as his Command Post. The slim young lieutenant was not what you might expect of a man-killer killer or the officer said to be the best infantry expert in the King's Own Royal Regiment. Lieutenant Kidd was wearing a heavy 9 mm Mauser C-96 "Bolo" automatic in a chest holster.

It was rumored in the regiment that he never went unarmed.

"Tell me about yourself," Major Randal said.

"My father was a JAG officer on Pershing's staff in London during the last war, sir. He met and married my mother while he was stationed there. Lost his money during the crash of '29, then his job in the Great Depression, sir.

"When he died, my mother and I moved back to England, where she had family. Mother's people had connections and land but were cash poor. My prospects did not look good, sir, and I didn't care for living in the wet, foggy UK, so when the opportunity for a commission in the Indian Army came up, I jumped at it.

"Then the war broke out, the King's Own lost a third of their officers and men reassigned to battalions in England. I was transferred in from the 114th Mahrattas Light Infantry to help make up the loss."

"What's your opinion of the KO?" Major Randal asked.

"An ancient regiment with a glorious past, fallen on hard times," Lieutenant Kidd said. "Major Everett is an excellent CO, sir—the troops call him 'Daddy.'"

"You're a hunter, I understand?"

"Yes, sir," Lieutenant Kidd said. "I like to hunt."

"Leopards," Major Randal said, "never went after them myself—understand they're tricky."

"You have to pay attention to what you're doing when you're out after spotted tabby, sir," Lieutenant Kidd said, "Especially the ones who've taken to dining on the locals. Want to make sure who's hunting who."

"I heard man-eating leopard are strictly for professionals," Major Randal said.

"I've heard that too, sir."

"How do you like your C-96?"

"Bulky for my tastes, sir," Lieutenant Kidd said. "Mauser's the best pistol I've been able to get my hands on. More firepower than my issue Webly service revolver."

"Let's step over to our arms locker, Lieutenant," Major Randal said. "Maybe we can find something you'd like as an upgrade."

"Love to, Major," Lieutenant Kidd said.

The two strolled over to the sandbagged tent Mr. Zargo had set up to store the weapons found in the Iraqis' basement suite. Inside were racks of submachine guns. Trunks contained a variety of pistols.

Lieutenant Kidd's eyes lit up when he saw the weapons. "Makes the KO's arms room look like a museum, sir."

"Those are Bergman MP-18s," Major Randal said. "Made by the Swiss firm SIG under license. Pick yourself out one—German Special Operations troops swear by 'em. Unless you prefer one of the Thompson SMGs the KO flew in—gave the Strike Force a dozen."

"Thank you, sir," Lieutenant Kidd said. "I'm not familiar with the MP-18. Sure has a mean, nasty look. Magazine on the side—take a little getting used to. I like it."

"Some say it's the best submachine gun ever designed," Major Randal said.

"Now this is my idea of the perfect sidearm," Lieutenant Kidd said, admiring a 4-inch Luger P-08. "Magnificent—9 mm Parabellum, beautifully balanced. Always wanted one."

"It's yours," Major Randal said. "Take two, you might need a backup."

"Thanks for the toys, Major," Lieutenant Kidd said, sliding the weapon into his chest holster and another around back under his belt. "You don't strike me as Santa Claus, sir."

"Roy," Major Randal said, "Strike Force has an opening. Go get your gear and move into the BOQ—you're one of us now."

"Yes, sir," Lieutenant Kidd said. "There a problem cat you need me to take care of?"

"More like a tiger by the tail—need you to twist it."

"Be back in zero five, sir."

"Who was that?" Mandy asked, arriving just as Lieutenant Kidd walked out.

"Lieutenant Roy Kidd."

"Interesting."

"Yes he is."

THE BOY SCOUT TROOP HAD FALLEN IN BY THE SWIMMING pool. The boys were quivering in anticipation, though they could not help being distracted by Mandy standing off to the side with a clipboard. Maj. John Randal took the salute from Cpl. Basil James. Then he conducted a rifle inspection of the Scouts in their ranks. He was accompanied by Corporal James, the Boy Scout Leader, and Mr. Zargo, who lent a sobering air to the proceedings.

Major Randal took his time. When he came to each boy, he slapped the .22 rifle out of his hands, racked the bolt to make sure it was unloaded, did a quick professional examination of the weapon, then handed it back. Unlike real inspections, he made it a point *not* to find any deficiencies. The rifles were well-maintained, and the boys had spent the morning cleaning them.

"What's your name, Scout?"

"Uh, William, sir."

"Are you ready, William?"

"SIR!"

"Outstanding—light up a bad guy for me."

When the inspection was concluded, Major Randal returned to the front of the formation. "Men, you will be conducting your first night ambush in a few hours. Kill anything that comes though the wire. Good luck and good hunting.

"Corporal James, take charge of your troops and move them to their Release Point."

The inspection of the Annie Oakleys was completely informal, conducted indoors. The women were assembled in the Officer's Club banquet room with their shotguns. Cpl. Jeffery Jeffers, a hand-picked NCO seconded from the King's Own Royal Regiment, had been working with them all day on ambush tactics and a few simple immediate action drills in the event of an emergency.

"Corporal Jeffers," Major Randal ordered. "Make sure there are no emergencies."

The women were eager but apprehensive and deadly serious in their preparations. Prior to this morning, none of them had ever imagined they would be getting ready to go out on a night ambush.

No one called "Attention!" but the women stood up when Major Randal walked in.

"As you were," Major Randal ordered immediately.

"Shortly, you ladies will be moving into your prepared sites for the night. When you do, understand this: you are there to fire up anything that moves in the zone of your ambush. You've all practiced the drill … know what to do.

"You see something, notify your team leader. She'll give the signal to commence. Fire discipline is very important. Work together as a team. Aim low. Keep shooting until your weapon runs dry. Reload immediately, stay in place—do not move out of your position until full daylight.

"I don't want anyone going out to check to see what was hit—clear?"

The women nodded. A few said, "Clear."

"Anything coming through the wire is either a goat wanting to eat your flowers or a bad guy with evil intentions—either way, let 'em have it."

The Annie Oakleys laughed. Tension ratcheted down. Major Randal made a perfectly crazy enterprise sound reasonable. Well, almost reasonable.

"You can do it," Major Randal said. "Don't take any prisoners."

WHEN MAJ. JOHN RANDAL AND MANDY WALKED OUT OF THE banquet room, Mr. Zargo was waiting in the lobby of the BOQ with five hard men in faded uniforms with no rank insignia showing. They were older than the average soldier, early- to mid-30s. There was no way to determine the men's nationality at a glance. All were dark-skinned or deeply tanned, with dark hair and dark eyes.

A lot like Mr. Zargo.

Major Randal guessed the men to be professional soldiers, mercenaries or ex-Foreign Legion. The five looked dangerous, and when grown men look dangerous, they usually are. Each of the five men had a playing card pinned to his pocket. That seemed strange.

"Your Z Patrol, sir," Mr. Zargo said. "Subject to approval, naturally. All capable, every man speaks English fluently.

"Time is short, you might possibly have trouble pronouncing their names and they might not be real names anyway. We will simply use *nom de plumes*—Ace, King, Queen, Jack and Joker."

"You men have any problem working for an American?" Major Randal asked. "I'm from California. We have a lot of sand too, but it's mostly on the beach."

No one said anything. It took the men a few moments to figure out what that meant. Then they realized it did not mean anything at all.

Everyone relaxed.

"Heard about your shooting skills, Major," Mr. Zargo said.

Major Randal said, "Seeing is believing."

He led the group outside and around the pool to the sandbagged firing range Mr. Twinning had built on the edge of the grounds for the Strike Force. It was for test firing weapons prior to patrols, so only twenty-five feet in length.

Having anticipated a moment like this would come sooner or later, Major Randal already had a square of tin nailed up on a piece of plywood leaning against the sandbags at the end of the range. Without fanfare, he produced the ivory-stocked 9 mm Browning P-35 from the skeletal holster around the back of his pants under his bush jacket and commenced firing. Then he reloaded and holstered the pistol.

When the group strolled down to the sandbags they saw a ragged "Z" in bullet holes.

Mandy said, "Unbelievable!"

"Any questions?" Major Randal said. "No? OK—let's step over to the Strike Force arms locker and get you men armed."

The team acted like kids in a candy store when they saw the array of weapons, a sign that the men were true professionals. Racks of various models of shotguns with barrels shortened had recently been added to the small armory. The men took their time examining different makes and models of the modified civilian shotguns, but in the end each of them selected a 9 mm Bergmann MP-18.

Not one chose a .45-caliber Thompson submachine gun. The mercs preferred the MP-18's lighter weight and the ability to carry more 9mm ammunition.

"Major," Mr. Zargo said, "the team needs single-barreled 12-gauge guns."

"What for?"

"Patrolling," Mr. Zargo said. "Saw the stock off at the pistol grip and the barrel just past the end of the shell in the chamber. Hook them to our webbing like this."

Mr. Zargo demonstrated, placing his right hand on his chest and swiveling it up like a pistol, "Fire it in an emergency while still hooked on. To break contact."

"Do it, Mandy," Major Randal said. "I want enough single-barreled shotguns to cut down for every man in the Strike Force—make it happen."

"Done."

"Have the men move into the BOQ, Mr. Zargo," Major Randal said. "We're going to spend every available minute rehearsing our patrolling techniques."

"Yes, sir."

MAJ. JOHN RANDAL WAS DRESSED IN HIS TAILORED GRAY silk suit. He was wearing the gaudy gold diamond pavé watch with a heavy, 18-karat gold chain bracelet buckled next to it. His ivory-stocked High Standard Military Model D .22 w/suppressor was strapped under the beautiful jacket in its new holster.

The tortoise shell sunglasses were in his breast pocket.

Lt. Penelope Honeycutt-Parker drove one of the BOQ's Humblers. Brandy, Mandy, Mr. Zargo (wearing a Royal Iraqi Air Force uniform with the rank insignia of a colonel) and Lt. Roy Kidd were in the car with Major Randal. They arrived at the airfield just as the sun was beginning to sink into the desert.

When the red ball went down, it was going to get dark fast.

Lt. Pamala Plum-Martin was standing by the Seagull when they arrived. The airplane's motor was ticking over. Several officers, student pilots and aircrew gathered, curious to see what was taking place. Elsewhere around the airfield, feverish preparations were underway to ready the motley collection of bombers for the air attack to be launched at sunrise.

No. 4 Service Flying Training School was going to war.

Servicing of aircraft, construction of air raid shelters, digging of slit trenches and the sandbagging of buildings and hangars would continue all through the night.

"You understand the flight plan, Pam?"

"Loop around the cantonment and come in from the far side of the lake, staying down low coming across the water and put down at the dock by the BOAC station," Lieutenant Plum-Martin said. "Sure you do not want me to come with you, John, when you go in to retrieve Red?"

"Stay with the Seagull, and if we're not back in fifteen minutes you take off and fly back here—clear?"

"I understand," Lieutenant Plum-Martin said, realizing she sounded as unhappy as Brandy had when Major Randal had given her similar orders in the motorboat offshore Enemy Occupied France just prior to the "Gunfight at the Blue Duck"—a night that seemed like a hundred years ago.

"Let's do this," Major Randal said.

Mandy was sobbing; Brandy looked anxious and Lieutenant Honeycutt-Parker angry—she wanted to go.

The party boarded the little pusher amphibian, and Lieutenant Plum-Martin prepared for takeoff. The Seagull taxied out on the strip, made a short run and lifted into the air.

"If anyone had known a Seagull was capable of carrying bombs," Sqn. Ldr. Tony Dudgeon said as the plane flew out of sight, "we never would have agreed to assign it to Major Randal for his Strike Force.

Brandy said, "In Italian East Africa, Pam used to serenade one Italian camp at night with opera music, and then bomb another on the way home."

"Mandy, will you quit crying," Lieutenant Honeycutt-Parker ordered.

"John is going to be fine," Brandy said, sounding like she had a lump in her own throat. "He will be back in twenty minutes with Red. Watch and see."

"What if he's not?" Mandy sobbed. "There are 10,000 bloodthirsty Iraqis over there."

On board the Seagull, Major Randal said, "You know what you're supposed to do?"

Mr. Zargo took out a pair of handcuffs and locked one on Lieutenant Kidd's left wrist and put the other bracelet on his right wrist but did not lock it.

"I stay outside and interrogate the two guards while you and Lieutenant Kidd go into the building and bring out the lady," Mr. Zargo said. "When we leave, I order the two guards not to allow anyone into the building until daylight tomorrow—those inside are under house arrest for detaining Miss Red without authorization."

"And who am I?"

"Chief of the Royal Iraqi Secret Police."

"Lieutenant Kidd?"

"A prisoner—he provided you with the information that your lady friend, Miss Red, was being detained against her will."

"Doesn't make a lot of sense," Major Randal said. "Ought to confuse two guards ... confuses me."

"The Iraqis will believe anything if we manage to convince them you are Secret Police," Mr. Zargo said.

The Seagull purred through the saffron sky, came in low off the desert and skimmed over the lake. Fed by the Euphrates, Lake Habbaniyah covered 100 square miles. Seemed strange to fly in off the desert and find such a huge body of water.

"That's Brandy's yacht," Lieutenant Plum-Martin said as they skimmed across the lake.

"She picked a big one—larger than thirty feet," Major Randal said, craning his neck. "A lot."

"Good choice," Mr. Zargo said. "That yacht belonged to the Iraqi Air Marshal whose suit you are wearing, Major. No one will ever dare go on board to inspect it."

"The Marshal's?" Major Randal said. "How do you know that?"

"I have been aboard," Mr. Zargo said. "Nearly 100 feet—96 feet, I believe they told me."

"Your new home, Roy," Major Randal said. "You'll be staging your raids off her."

"I hope Mrs. Seaborn can handle something that size," Lieutenant Kidd said. "I sure can't."

"Brandy can sail anything afloat," Lieutenant Plum-Martin said.

"Bad news is," Mr. Zargo said, "we have to expect security on board when we first go on board."

"Always something," Major Randal said.

"BOAC airport, dead ahead," Lieutenant Plum-Martin announced. "Three minutes until splashdown."

The amphibian purred straight ahead and glided in short of the floating dock. Lieutenant Plum-Martin taxied up close and then made a U-turn before docking so the Seagull was facing out toward open water—ready to make a quick takeoff.

Mr. Zargo was off first, pulling Lieutenant Kidd with him, then they waited on the dock for Major Randal to exit the aircraft. Not hesitating a moment, with Major Randal in the lead, they strode up the floating dock toward the BOAC terminal, walking with a purpose. The two sentries out front had been sitting in chairs, but now they stood up.

The guards did not like the look of things. The man in the suit was coming at them fast. In the Iraqi Army, high-ranking civilians moving with a purpose generally meant bad news for someone. This one had his own airplane and as they came closer the guards could see that the man in the uniform bringing up the rear was a colonel—the civilian was clearly the ranking member of the party.

The Colonel was escorting a prisoner in handcuffs.

Before the guards had a chance to decide what they should do, the three men on the dock had arrived.

Mr. Zargo barked an order.

Ignoring the sentries, Major Randal walked past the guards who were now at the ramrod position of attention and went inside the station building. Lieutenant Kidd followed him in. The BOAC air terminal was laid out exactly as it had been diagrammed.

An Iraqi captain was sitting in the lobby area. A sergeant was talking on the phone. Two privates were leaning against the wall.

Red was sitting next to the captain.

Major Randal had no idea who the sergeant was talking to, but he could not afford to take a chance. The silenced High Standard .22 appeared in his hand, *Whiiiiicccccch*. A bullet hole appeared just above the sergeant's left eye.

Whiiiiiccccch. Whiiiiiccccch. The two privates went down with bullets to the head. *Whiiiiiccccch. Whiiiiiccccch. Whiiiiiccccch.* Three rounds caused tufts to puff on the captain's chest, center of mass.

"John, is that you?" Red cried. "I did not recognize you with those sunglasses on—what are you doing?"

"Rescuing you," Major Randal said. "Let's get the hell out of Dodge, Red."

"Rescue?"

"Time to go," Major Randal said. "We're out of here—move out."

Lieutenant Kidd had his Luger in his hand, "Damn, that was fast."

He put his pistol up under his khaki bush jacket and started dragging the dead men into the baggage area behind a counter where they could not be seen through a window.

"Act calm, Red," Major Randal ordered. "We don't want the guards at the door to know what happened in here."

"Get my luggage," she said, Clipper Girl cool. An experienced traveler, Red was not about to leave her suitcases behind.

"Grab her bags, Roy," Major Randal said, as he helped finish moving the bodies. "Let's go."

The trio walked outside without a word, past Mr. Zargo, who gave a final order to the guards. Then they were walking down the floating dock and climbing into the Seagull.

Lieutenant Plum-Martin said, "You OK, Red?"

"Maybe a little in shock—what just happened?"

"Buckle up," Pam said. "Prepare for takeoff."

The Seagull lifted into the darkening sky and looped around through the desert to the RAF base. Within minutes Lieutenant Plum-Martin was lining up her approach back at the RAF Habbaniya airfield.

"A curious thing, Major," Mr. Zargo said. "The guards are not aware that a state of hostilities exists between Iraq and England. The two had been issued live ammunition, which was confusing to them, but the men told me they thought they were on a training exercise."

"What the hell were they doing with Red?"

"Protective custody—safeguarding her in the event a mob of civilian rebels showed up to loot the installation after it had been abandoned by the BOAC staff."

"You mean," Major Randal said, "I shot four Iraqis who didn't know they were enemy combatants?"

"Appears to be the case," Mr. Zargo said.

Lieutenant Kidd said, "You sure looked good doing it, sir."

12
MILITARY GENIUS

AVM HARRY "REGGIE" SMART CALLED A MEETING OF ALL commanding officers and department heads at 2000 hours in the Air Force Headquarters (AFH) briefing room. The officers were all present in their seats five minutes early. Maj. John Randal was last to arrive, having barely had time to change out of his gray silk suit.

Air Vice Marshal Smart gave the Strike Force commander a look as the Commando slipped in at the last minute. The Air Officer Commanding was a stickler for promptness. He had no idea what Major Randal had been up to in the previous hour, which was probably best since the operation to rescue the Clipper Girl had not been authorized for the simple reason that it had not been submitted for approval.

Most of the others in the room did know what Major Randal had been up to in the previous hour. Small salutes, approving winks and *V* for Victory signs flashed from all quarters as the officers turned to stare when Major Randal slid into his chair. Apparently a large percentage of the men present knew Red.

The AOC was having the wildest roller coaster day of his career. Earlier in the morning he had been in the depths of depression, convinced the defenseless RAF base would be overrun and everyone, including his own family, murdered or violated. By briefing time tonight, Air Vice Marshal Smart had managed to convince himself he could win this battle—in record time.

Not one thing had changed during the day except more Iraqi reinforcements had arrived on the escarpment.

"The aerial bombing attack will begin precisely at 0500 hours tomorrow morning," Air Vice Marshal Smart announced. "Ten Wellington heavy bombers out of Shaiba will be flying in support of our operation. They will be on station at that time to rendezvous with our bombers to commence the air attack.

"Concentrated bombing, without warning, will be very demoralizing for the rebels. It won't last long. The Iraqis should be in full flight within about three hours. Do the best you can. Have every aircraft in the air before light and start bombing as soon as you can distinguish targets on the ground—0500 hours.

"Colonel Ouvry Roberts, Chief-of-Staff, 10th Indian Division, flew in today to inspect the King's Own, and I have prevailed upon him to stay and take command of all ground forces on the base.

"Dismissed."

The officers stood up uncomfortably as Air Vice Marshal Smart marched out. No one present actually believed the Iraqis were going to capitulate after being subjected to a short air attack. Not one land army in the history of armed conflict had ever been defeated in the field by an air force conducting an aerial bombing campaign, and the officers all knew it—they had studied air operations all their professional lives.

There was no reason to think the Iraqi Army would be the first.

COL. OUVRY ROBERTS PULLED MAJ. JOHN RANDAL ASIDE. "Major, let's you, Ted Everett and me go somewhere private so we can discuss your Strike Force."

"Why don't you come to my CP," Major Randal said. "You can see for yourself what we're doing, and I'll give you a detailed briefing ..."

Mandy burst into the room, "John, Scout Team 2 is in contact—I brought you a pony."

"Meet you at the BOQ in thirty minutes, sir. You'll want to hear a report on this," Major Randal said to Colonel Roberts. "We may have infiltrators in the wire."

He ran outside where Mandy was already mounted. She tossed him the reins to the horse she was holding. As he was in the act of catching them, the girl was off at a gallop. Major Randal made a wild flying leap onto the back of the pony, and the little Arab was away in a flash.

Mandy knew where she was going, and she could ride like a Cossack. Major Randal never had any chance of catching her. They pounded down the road, passing Cpl. Basil James who was sprinting toward Scout Team 2's ambush location.

The adult volunteer (one accompanied each Scout ambush team) was waiting by the perimeter road at the private phone that had been installed for the ambush. Mandy reined in. Major Randal finally caught up with her. He pitched her the reins and slid off his pony as Corporal James ran up.

The volunteer was smoking a cigarette and pacing back and forth nervously.

"Put that bloody fag out, you fool," Corporal James barked. "Give me a report, Wilson."

"Five minutes ago, the Scouts engaged a target," Wilson said. "The boys did exactly as ordered. Emptied their weapons, then stayed in place and reloaded. I moved forward at that time to question the Senior Patrol Leader. He informed me the ambush party had observed movement and he gave the command to commence firing."

"Any of the boys hurt?" Major Randal asked, immediately regretting the question, realizing it could be interpreted as interfering with Corporal James in the execution of his duties.

"No, sir, everyone is fine."

"Nice job," Major Randal said. "Carry on, Corporal. I can see you have things well in hand.

"Let's go, Mandy."

"Are we simply going to ride away," Mandy protested, "before discovering what was out there?"

"Corporal James will give us a report in the morning," Major Randal said as they walked their ponies back to the Command Post. "Standing orders call for all personnel to stay in position any time an ambush is initiated and wait for daylight to investigate.

"Who knows, something else might try to come through the wire here tonight."

"Bloody Iraqis trying to sneak in and molest some innocent person," Mandy said. "Hope they shot him where it hurt."

"My guess is," Major Randal said, "we'll find out the boys dusted a hungry goat."

Colonel Roberts and Maj. Edward "Ted" Everett were in the Strike Force Operations Center when Major Randal arrived. Lt. Penelope Honeycutt-Parker was giving them the tour. They were talking to Mr. Twinning, who had relocated his office along with the chief of police, the fire chief and a number of other department heads to the small tent city on the grounds of the Bachelor Officers Quarters.

"No one from the AOC's office was providing current information or communicating with me at all, to be blunt," Mr. Twinning said as Major Randal joined the group. "The Strike Force has been very accommodating. I decided to set up shop here with my key people to be able to provide a quick response to the community based on what Major Randal's people were willing to provide."

"If you ever feel like you are not getting the big picture, feel free to contact me any time, Mr. Twinning," Colonel Roberts said. "It is imperative that civil affairs be accorded highest priority. Particularly once hostilities commence."

"Bear that in mind, Colonel," Mr. Twinning said. "My staff is more than satisfied with the level of cooperation since Major Randal appeared on the scene."

Colonel Roberts, Major Everett and Major Randal repaired to his red-striped CP tent for a private discussion.

"Ted informed me you turned down the suggestion of being reinstated as brigadier and taking command of ground forces at Habbaniya,"

Colonel Roberts said. "I want to put that offer back on the table. Air Vice Marshal asked me—no, he *begged* me—to stay on here when I flew in this afternoon for what I intended to be no more than a short inspection of 10th Indian Division troops.

"Will you reconsider?"

"No, sir."

"Why not, pray tell?" Colonel Roberts asked. "You are the most experienced combat officer in the cantonment; the situation is critical, and I have pressing duties back at division—change of command with your old friend General Slim is in the offing."

"The only reason I'm here is to see one of my officers graduate flight school, sir," Major Randal said. "Almost as soon as we arrived, certain senior people invited me to join a mutiny..."

"That true, Ted?" Colonel Roberts asked.

"Yes, sir. I was present," Major Everett said. "Air Vice Marshal Smart has lost the confidence of his officers who will have to fight this campaign. Some find him obstructive to their efforts to defend the cantonment because of a slavish obsession with following regulations."

"That bad?" Colonel Roberts asked.

"Bad enough, sir. Senior RAF officers are making, and in some cases putting in place, battle plans without informing the AOC," Major Everett said.

"The RAF is planning to conduct a private war, sir," Major Randal said. "The Levies have been left to their own devices. The King's Own was earmarked to be the 'mobile reserve,' then had companies detached to carry out other duties—like guarding the improvised airstrip on the polo pitch."

"Exactly," Major Everett said. "Neutered my mobile reserve."

"I agreed to organize a Strike Force out of a company from the Levies and one from the KO plus RAF No.1 Armored Car Company," Major Randal said. "Being short-handed, the Strike Force is supported by the girl's equestrian team, a troop of Boy Scouts, the photography club and the women's skeet team.

"The Rod and Gun Club will be providing marksmen from its Big Bore Rifle Team to act as snipers along the perimeter fence.

"The Scouts executed an ambush inside the perimeter fifteen minutes ago—body count not available until daylight."

"Oh, my," Colonel Roberts said, "*Armed* Boy Scouts?"

"Strike Force is planning to have patrols in the field every night, starting tomorrow night, to go after the Iraqis on the escarpment.

"Later tonight we're conducting a cutting-out operation of a yacht on Lake Habbaniyah to use as a floating patrol base to launch raids against the Iraqi rear areas.

"For a guy on R&R, I'm pretty busy. The idea of the additional duties of coordinating with a dysfunctional command structure seems like a nonstarter, sir," Major Randal said. "We have a rule in Raiding Forces— 'Right Man, Right Job.'"

"Point made," Colonel Roberts said. "You seem to be getting on famously here. Is any of this authorized?"

"Negative, sir."

"Thought not," Colonel Roberts said, "Can you arrange a liaison officer to keep me current on your activities? I will make it my business to ensure that no one interferes with your activities."

"Capt. David Lancaster has been performing that role between Strike Force and No. 4 SFTS," Major Randal said. "I'll have him report to you—you may have other use for him as well, sir."

"What do you make of our chances, Major?" Colonel Roberts asked. "Best estimate."

"The RAF is over at the airfield right now putting a pencil to it," Major Randal said. "Drop X number of tons of bombs, we should win."

"Does that work," Major Everett asked, "in real life?"

"Didn't for the Italians in East Africa, and the Regia Aeronautica had total air supremacy with highly-trained, combat-experienced pilots and aircrew," Major Randal said.

"No. 4 SFTS only has one qualified bombardier—the rest are volunteers. The bombers are the school's trainers with bomb racks bolted on. Only thirty-nine pilots are available, counting burnt-out combat flyers, men unsuitable for operational duty, staff officers who haven't been a line pilot in years and recent graduates who qualified on an accelerated program.

"They aren't going to hit anything."

Colonel Roberts said, "I failed to appreciate that the situation is that desperate. The AOC's staff clearly neglected to give me the full accounting."

Major Everett said, "I was aware the school does not have a single combat-experienced officer who is both current *and* classified medically fit to fly operations."

Lighting a Player's with his hard-service U.S. 26th Cavalry Zippo, Major Randal said, "One of the burnt-out pilots sent here for a rest cure is going to be commanding one of the attack squadrons. He told me there are only four part-time rear air-gunners."

"What in the bloody hell is a *part-time* rear air-gunner?" Colonel Roberts blurted.

"The nearest British force to relieve Habbaniya is 500 miles away in Palestine, and the rescue column has not been assembled yet—so that's out," Major Randal said. "Only four days' rations for the civilians.

"The insurgents can overrun the base any time they want to. The RAF can't prevent it; the Levies can't keep 'em out—lightly armed as they are—there's no minefield."

"Pretty grim, Major," Colonel Roberts said.

"The only chance Habbaniya has is for the Iraqi Army to go away, sir," Major Randal said, "We need to make that happen."

"Do you have any thoughts on a plan?"

"Working on it, sir," Major Randal said. "Has anyone given you a detailed breakdown of the enemy forces?"

"No," Colonel Roberts said. "All Air Vice Marshal Smart informed me was the enemy forces consisted of an infantry brigade, a mechanized brigade and a brigade of artillery."

"Three brigades equals a division," Major Randal said. "Any idea which one, sir?"

"Not the foggiest," Colonel Roberts said. "The AOC's intelligence staff has no idea—I inquired.

"But, what does it matter, Major?"

"Three independent brigades with no one in charge would be good for us, sir—lacks cohesion."

"That is true," Colonel Roberts said.

"On the other hand, if there was an Iraqi division commander," Major Randal said, "I could pay him a visit."

"MANDY," MAJ. JOHN RANDAL SAID, "CALL THE NEWSPAPER publisher. I need to see him in the next fifteen minutes."

"In the middle of the night?"

"Make it happen."

"Calling now, John."

"Parker," Major Randal said, "Step into my office. We need to talk."

The two walked over to the red-striped tent where they could have a private conversation.

"Roy and I are going out tonight to take down a sailboat," Major Randal said. "Lieutenant Kidd's going to station a patrol on it to operate against the Iraqi rear areas nights."

"I am aware of that, John," Lt. Penelope Honeycutt-Parker said.

"What you don't know is that Brandy and Pam flew out and picked out a really big boat—100 footer. Looks like Roosevelt's Presidential Yacht. So here's the situation—I don't want Brandy out there alone while the troops are away."

"What are you going to do, John?"

"My options are—send Red with Brandy, find some woman or women from the Yacht Club to volunteer as crew," Major Randal said, "or you can go—it's your call."

"You know I want to be with Brandy, if that is a possibility," Lieutenant Honeycutt-Parker said.

"Yeah, I know," Major Randal said. "Red will have to take over for you here."

"She can step right in," Lieutenant Honeycutt-Parker said, "and not miss a beat. Red is very capable."

"We'll see," Major Randal said. "Hard to replace you, Parker. You may be a better deputy than your husband, Lionel—and he's good."

"Thanks, John," Lieutenant Honeycutt-Parker said. "I shall start bringing Red up to speed immediately. Mandy's a treasure; she can take on added responsibility, too."

Major Randal said, "kind of reminds me of …"

"We know who Mandy reminds you of," Lieutenant Penelope Honeycutt-Parker drawled.

Lt. Roy Kidd arrived. One of the 9 mm P-08 Lugers was riding in his chest holster, and the other was buckled up high around his waist on his right side, like he knew how to use it. He tossed his pack in the corner of the tent and leaned his newly-acquired Bergmann 9 mm MP-18 against it.

"Ready when you are, sir."

"Selected your team?" Major Randal asked.

"Yes, sir," Lieutenant Kidd said. "Six picked men—two corporals and me—that's my patrol. One of the corporals came over to the KO from my old battalion, sir.

"Oh, I brought my batman along to be my No. 2—he backs me on my hunting expeditions," Lieutenant Kidd said. "Never go anywhere without Pan."

"Take a look at this," Major Randal said, handing him one of the chopped single-barrel shotguns cut down to pistol size with a lanyard ring mounted on the grip.

"Snap it to your webbing at the shoulder so that it rides shoulder level. In the event of a meeting engagement at close range in the dark, reach up, cock the hammer, swivel it and touch her off—handy way to break contact."

"Variation of the Howdah pistols maharajas used in the last century to keep wounded tigers off the elephants they were hunting from," Lieutenant Kidd said. "Anything in front when this cannon goes off will be deaf, blind, wounded or dead—bet its murder on both ends, sir."

"No doubt."

"This mine?"

"It is," Major Randal said. "We have more for your men. Move your patrol over to the arms locker and get 'em armed and equipped with the weapons of their choice. We'll be departing within the hour."

"Yes, sir."

"Mr. Thymes is here," Mandy announced.

The publisher came into the tent. "You wanted to see me, Major?"

"Sorry to get you out so late, Mr. Thymes," Major Randal said. "But I couldn't discuss this over the phone. What was it Mandy suggested for a propaganda leaflet you liked so much?"

"Surrender cards."

"Scratch that idea," Major Randal said. "The thing to remember about propaganda and/or misinformation, Mr. Thymes—the idea is to make the opposition *do* something ... not *think* something."

"We do not want the Iraqis to surrender?" Mr. Thymes said.

"We'd have 10,000 of 'em inside our wire if they did," Major Randal said. "That's an old trick—shifta bandits used it in Abyssinia."

"What is it we *do* want the Iraqis to do, Major?"

"We want them to go away," Major Randal said.

"Go away," Mr. Thymes said. "How do we accomplish that?"

"That's your job," Major Randal said. "Think of something."

When they walked outside, Lieutenant Kidd asked Mandy, "The Major always delegate simple tasks like that?"

"Absolutely," Mandy said. "John's a military genius."

13

NIGHT MOVES

MAJ. JOHN RANDAL HAD LT. ROY KIDD'S PATROL, CAPT. Fabian Valentine, Lt. Pamala Plum-Martin, Brandy Seaborn and Mandy Paige assembled, sitting in folding metal chairs in his CP tent. Mr. Zargo was standing in the back with his pipe clamped in his teeth. Mr. Twinning had ordered the chief of police to assign one of his policemen to be with the Strike Force commander at all times on the base.

Flanigan, the policeman, was on duty outside the tent making sure no one could eavesdrop on the proceedings. The operation to station a patrol on board a yacht in the middle of Lake Habbaniyah was classified "Need to Know." No one not directly involved had any need to know.

Loose lips sink ships.

They were not going to sink Brandy's.

"*MISSION,*" Major Randal began.

"Lieutenant Kidd and a picked patrol of ten men total, designated Lake Patrol, will be afloat in a yacht/mother ship under the command of Mrs. Brandy Seaborn, who will be the captain of the vessel and addressed as either Mrs. Seaborn, Captain, or Skipper. The patrol will operate as a single unit or be broken down into two elements, each led by a corporal. Patrols will operate in the Iraqi rear with the primary responsibility of killing enemy personnel and causing material damage to Iraqi equipment with priority given to destroying artillery.

"*EXECUTION.*"

"The mother ship will remain out of sight of land during the day. Troops will stay below deck resting, cleaning weapons and preparing for their next patrol. Nightly, under cover of darkness, Mrs. Seaborn will sail the mother ship to within a mile of shore, immediately behind the Iraqi Army. The patrol, or patrols, depending on the night's mission, will board inflatable Air/Sea Rescue rafts navigated by Mrs. Seaborn and/or Lt. Penelope Honeycutt-Parker and paddle ashore.

"All missions have to be completed, with personnel back on board the mother ship, by 0300 hours—that's three o'clock in the morning for you Territorials."

Everyone laughed.

"*CONCEPT OF THE OPERATION,*" Major Randal said.

"This is a kill mission. Lake Patrol is to move by stealth through the enemy's rear areas, inflicting as many casualties as possible without becoming committed to a prolonged firefight. Enemy equipment is to be destroyed by the use of prepared explosive devices with timed fuses.

"Admin/logistics and command and signal will be briefed by Lieutenant Kidd once you have established your patrol base on board the mother ship.

"This concludes my briefing. Lieutenant Kidd, turn your troops over to Lieutenant Plum-Martin in order for her to run them through loading and unloading drills for the Seagull aircraft."

"Yes, sir."

"Mandy, you're in charge of setting up the landing flares on the polo pitch in accordance with written instructions Lt. Plum-Martin has provided you."

"Mr. Twinning is working with me on that project, John."

"Perfect."

"Lake Patrol," Major Randal said to the troops in a relaxed

conversational tone as he lit a cigarette, "is small in scale but it's a very sophisticated combined operation requiring detailed intelligence, thorough planning, and complex logistics, with land, air and waterborne elements all working together like a Swiss watch. The patrol has to slip ashore in the dark of night behind enemy lines, execute their mission, exfiltrate back to the mother ship and sail over the horizon.

"Then do it again the next night.

"When it's over, Raiding Forces is always looking for a few good men—those of you who think you might want to be Commandos can consider this a tryout."

"Brandy, if you will stand by, I would like a word with you. Fall out."

"BRANDY," MAJ. JOHN RANDAL SAID AS HE LIT HER cigarette with his battered U.S. 26th Cavalry Regiment Zippo, "I have written orders for you in this envelope. I'm going to go ahead and tell you what they are. In the event that anything happens to me or the cantonment is being overrun, Pam is to immediately fly out and pick up you and Parker. She will have Mandy and Red on board.

"Pam's orders, which I will also deliver to her in writing, are to transport the four of you to the safest British base as far away from Iraq as her Seagull can reach.

"You and Parker's orders are to drop what you're doing and board the airplane—is that clear?"

Brandy looked at Major Randal. The two had a very special relationship—close from the moment of their first introduction. Brandy had been on a raid to France with him, extracted him after another from a private island in the Red Sea and worked behind the Italian lines with Force N in Abyssinia.

Tonight was the first time she had ever seen him this cold-blooded serious. It scared her a little. Not much frightened Brandy Seaborn.

"Crystal clear; you know I will comply if those are your orders, John," Brandy said. "Is the situation quite so desperate?"

"Pam lands the Seagull on Lake Habbaniyah in broad daylight," Major Randal said, "get on the airplane."

MAJ. JOHN RANDAL AND LT. ROY KIDD READIED THEIR personal gear. Mandy stuck her head in the tent. "Truck is here, John."

"Tell Mr. Zargo to get his men mounted up," Major Randal ordered.

"Then find out who's in charge of the base laundry and have them report to you tonight—conduct a laundry call. Order every man assigned to Strike Force to turn in one pair of their khaki battle dress—get Roy's and his men's while they're still here."

"OK," Mandy said. "Clean uniforms for the troops."

"Negative, dye 'em black," Major Randal said. "Khaki won't do for night patrolling."

Mandy wrote on her pad, "John wants ninja suits."

"While you're at it, does Habbaniya have a drama club?"

"It does."

"Commandeer their theatrical makeup," Major Randal ordered. "Makes good face camo."

"OK," Mandy said, "have it here within the hour."

"Where were we?" Major Randal said to Lieutenant Kidd. "The problem with a Seagull or Walrus, which as far as I can tell is the same aircraft, is they can't carry many passengers—which makes 'em rotten Air/Sea Rescue craft since they can't pick up the entire crew of some planes. We will have to ferry your people out in two lifts tonight.

"Mr. Zargo says we have to expect security on the yacht."

"That's what he told me, sir," Lieutenant Kidd said. "Said there might be two men, maybe three."

"When the Seagull lands," Major Randal said, "if there is security aboard they'll be expecting the Air Marshal or at the least a very senior Royal Iraqi Air Force officer, so we should have the element of surprise working for us.

"Kill anyone you see, Roy. No hesitation—just do it."

"Roger," Lieutenant Kidd said.

"I'm handing you a difficult assignment," Major Randal said. "Can't give you much in the way of support. This is about the only thing I've got that might be of use."

He dragged out the metal trunk under the cot in the CP tent, opened it and extracted a holstered handgun.

"High Standard Military Model D, .22-caliber—has a silencer attached," Major Randal said, tossing it to Lieutenant Kidd. "Twin to the one I used at the BOAC station when we went for Red. This is my spare.

"I want it back when this is over—unless you decide to sign on with Raiding Forces permanently, then you can keep it."

"Thanks, sir," Lieutenant Kidd said, examining the weapon. "Used to have a Colt Woodsman .22 when I was growing up in the States. I may like this High Standard better—exposed hammer, very nice."

"As briefed, we're going to do the takedown tonight with part of my Z patrol, plus you," Major Randal said. "When the yacht is secure, Pam will shuttle Brandy, Parker and your men out to you on the mother ship, then bring me and my people back here.

"After that, you're on your own."

"I understand, sir."

"Captain Fabian will be flying out nightly to bring you your new mission. You may develop intelligence during your patrols you want to exploit—you get to make the call on which target to go after once Fabian briefs you."

"Outstanding, sir."

"That is, Roy," Major Randal said, "unless he says *frogspawn*, then you do the mission the Captain briefs—no questions asked. Clear?"

"*Frogspawn*," Lieutenant Kidd said. "Got it, sir."

"In fact," Major Randal said, "if anyone should ever say *frogspawn* to you, drop what you're doing and comply immediately."

"Understood, sir," Lieutenant Kidd said, "loud and clear."

"Particularly if it's a good-looking female Royal Marine captain," Major Randal said.

"You mean Lady Seaborn, sir?" Lieutenant Kidd asked. "Pam and Parker both have advised me to expect her to arrive sooner rather than later. Claim she's drop-dead gorgeous."

"When Jane shows up," Major Randal said, "life as we know it will cease to exist."

MAJ. JOHN RANDAL LOOKED AT HIS BLACK-FACED ROLEX. The lime green digits said 0130 hours. The watch had been a present from Capt. the Lady Jane Seaborn, his married former fiancée. Every time he checked the time he thought about her. Major Randal had it on good authority that this was why she had given him the watch.

Women are smart like that.

It did not simplify matters that the Rolex had originally been ordered as a birthday present for Lady Jane's husband. Major Randal's love life could best be described as "complicated."

When the truck arrived, the auxiliary airfield built on the polo field and golf course was a busy place, even at this hour. While pilots and aircrew were catching a few fitful hours of sleep before their scheduled 0500 attack on the Iraqi Army, ground crewmen and students of No. 4 Service Flying Training School were servicing the oddball collection of bombers that would be flying the morning air strike.

There were only thirty-nine RAF pilots, and they would all be taking part. The plan was to fly the first combat mission, return to base, rearm, refuel, and immediately take off for another mission—over and over again until the Iraqis were defeated or they were all shot down.

Considering that the Royal Iraqi Air Force had close to a hundred modern aircraft purchased from the United States, Great Britain, Italy and Germany, being flown by men chosen for their skills, while No. 4 Service Flying Training School was flying museum piece trainers with unauthorized, improvised bomb racks bolted on them, being piloted by a motley crew of aviators, it did not seem like much of a plan to Major Randal.

The auxiliary airfield created out of the polo pitch and golf course offered two advantages over the primary airfield for tonight's mission. The landing strip was inside the perimeter fence of RAF Habbaniyah, and it was obscured from view of the Iraqis on the escarpment by a stand of eucalyptus trees. The second reason was why Lt. Pamala Plum-Martin had chosen to use it.

The snow-blond aviatrix was going to have to make several trips out to the yacht tonight, and she did not want the Iraqis to see her doing it. Even though she would be flying in pitch dark, the trees would still help screen her takeoffs and landings.

Mandy was already at the field when Major Randal and the raiding party arrived.

On the advice of Lt. Penelope Honeycutt-Parker, Mandy, Mr. Twinning and a road repair crew had placed fifty-five-gallon barrel steel drums, each one-fourth full of diesel fuel and kerosene, every fifty yards down the landing strip. Lieutenant Honeycutt-Parker's advice had come from her first-hand experience with clandestine nocturnal air operations operating off improvised landing strips while in Abyssinia with Force N.

When the Seagull made a low-level pass over the strip on Lieutenant Plum-Martin's return flight, the fuel would be ignited inside the steel barrels. The directional landing lights created by the flames in the bottom of the barrels could only be seen from directly above. The lights would outline the landing strip. The amphibian would racetrack and touch down on the second pass.

The second lift of troops to go out to the boat would quickly load on board, and Lieutenant Plum-Martin would take off again.

"Let's go," Major Randal ordered. He trotted out to the waiting Seagull, followed by Lt. Roy Kidd, Mr. Zargo and two members of his Z patrol, Joker and Jack. Everyone was armed with a 9 mm Bergmann MP-18 except Major Randal, who was carrying his favorite 9 mm Beretta-M38 from Force N.

All of the Z patrol, with the exception of Major Randal, who was in his rubber-soled, canvas-topped raiding boots, were wearing army-issue athletic gym shoes with canvas leggings laced over them for a sure purchase on the deck of the yacht when they went aboard.

The men boarded the aircraft, and Lieutenant Plum-Martin immediately taxied for takeoff. The little plane rolled down the auxiliary strip, then lifted into the night, curling out behind the base across the gleaming Euphrates River headed into the desert. When they were far enough away, the Seagull came around back to a point where the river could barely be seen off the right wing tip and flew along, guiding on it until the giant lake swam into view.

In no time, Lieutenant Plum-Martin banked again, coming over the lake and dropping down until the little pusher aircraft was skimming across the surface. To everyone on board it seemed as if they were screaming across the lake. In fact, the Seagull was flying about 85 mph.

"Target in sight," Lieutenant Plum-Martin announced, "dead ahead."

"Lock and load," Major Randal ordered over his shoulder. The four men in the back seat immediately charged their weapons.

The drill for the assault on the yacht was simple. There was an inflated Air/Sea Rescue raft strapped on the floats outside the right door. Major Randal, riding in the front right seat, would step outside and, being the most experienced small boat handler, launch it as soon as the Seagull taxied up as close to the yacht as possible. The troops in the back seat would exit one at a time from the right side of the airplane, led by Lieutenant Kidd, and climb into the raft.

Mr. Zargo, armed with Lt. Plum-Martin's .22 High Standard Military Model D, would be stationed in the front of the raft with Joker and Jack. Lieutenant Kidd and Major Randal would be in the stern paddling.

The men had rehearsed the drill all afternoon.

The Seagull splashed down. Lieutenant Plum-Martin was a veteran amphibian pilot. She had landed on Lake Rudolph night after night at Camp Croc in northern Kenya after flying missions in support of Force N in central Abyssinia.

The three Z Patrol operators in the back seat were professionals. Lieutenant Kidd was clearly competent. They checked their equipment— something each man had done individually fifty or more times on the short flight. Major Randal glanced over his shoulder when he heard the rattle.

Lieutenant Kidd gave him a thumbs up. He looked like a lost lamb sitting wedged in next to Mr. Zargo's two killers. Joker and Jack grinned.

Not a pretty sight.

Major Randal said, "Let's do this!"

He stepped out on the float, cut the rope with his razor-sharp Fairbairn Commando Knife, toppled the raft over and stepped aboard. Lieutenant Kidd came out the back and slid into the raft; Joker and Jack followed. Right behind him Mr. Zargo was in the bow.

"Give way together," Major Randal said softly. He and Lieutenant Kidd began paddling. The yacht was only fifty feet away. From the raft, the target looked like a battle ship.

Major Randal's heart was in his throat. Tonight reminded him of the raid on Rio Bonita, only not so crazy. Nothing was happening, and that is always a tension-builder when going in on a mission. Everyone settles down once the action starts—it's the waiting that's hard.

Maybe the yacht was empty.

The Air/Sea rescue raft bumped against the boarding ladder. Major Randal and Lieutenant Kidd shipped their oars. Mr. Zargo had to holster the silenced High Standard Military Model D he had been holding in both hands to tie it off. A face appeared over the railing.

Major Randal fired two shots from his silenced High Standard .22. *Whiiich. Whiiich.* The twin match-striking sound was followed by two *thumps* one after the other, like someone had thumped a watermelon.

Nothing happened. Lieutenant Kidd shoved the High Standard .22 back down into his chest holster. He had not had time to get it all the way out. Then the man on the deck toppled over the rail, hanging with his head down and arms outstretched.

The two Z operators shot past Mr. Zargo and went up the ladder without seeming to touch it with their hands. A short burst of submachine gun fire up above was followed quickly by two more.

Mr. Zargo and Lieutenant Kidd were next up, with Major Randal trailing. By the time he arrived it was all over. Two dead Iraqis were sprawled on the deck.

"Good work, men," Major Randal said. "Lieutenant Kidd, take charge and clear the rest of the boat.

"Mr. Zargo, make a quick inspection to see if there's anything of intelligence value I can take back with me right now."

Major Randal took the hook-nosed flashlight off his webbing. It was fitted with a red lens. He blinked it three times at the Seagull to signal that the boat was secure.

Shortly, Jack came up on deck carrying three .45-caliber Thompson submachine guns by their canvas slings.

"Lieutenant Kidd sends his compliments, sir. The craft is clear of enemy personnel."

"Bring those weapons when you extract," Major Randal ordered. "Strike Force can use 'em."

"Yes, sir."

Lieutenant Kidd appeared, "Nothing much of interest below, sir, mostly clothes. Do a detailed search when the sun comes up. Mr. Zargo asked me to inform you that he has drawn a blank so far—still looking."

"The war starts in three hours," Major Randal said, glancing at the lime green hands on his Rolex. He started down the boarding ladder to the raft. "You know what to do, Roy."

"Roger that, sir," Lieutenant Kidd said with a straight face. "Kill 'em all and let Allah sort 'em out."

"I never said that," Major Randal said.

"Mandy told me it was your personal motto, sir."

"You make it yours, Roy—'til this is over," Major Randal said.

"Good luck and good hunting."

14

PREDAWN

MAJ. JOHN RANDAL WAS IN HIS ROOM IN THE BOQ SHAVING. There was a knock on the door. Since it was 0400 hours, he was not expecting visitors.

"Come on in."

Mr. Zargo entered the room with three canvas web pistol belts slung over his shoulder. He pitched them on the bed after withdrawing one of the automatics from its holster.

"Ever see one of these before, Major?"

Turning from the mirror, Major Randal said, "Browning design— looks a lot like a 1911. Never saw one like it."

"Vis 35 Radom pistol," Mr. Zargo said. "Polish Eagle, only this one does not have the eagle. Some claim this to be the finest military sidearm manufactured today. A cross between the Browning 1911/Hi-Power design."

"Really?" Major Randal said, wiping off the shaving cream and taking the pistol from Mr. Zargo.

"Nine mm, eight rounds in the magazine," Mr. Zargo said. "Nine total if you top it off."

"Get these off the three dead security men on the yacht?" Major Randal asked, racking back the slide on the pistol.

"Yes."

"Polish Eagle—no eagle," Major Randal said. "What's that mean, exactly?"

"The Germans continued to manufacture the Vis 35 after they overran Poland," Mr. Zargo said. "Nazi intelligence services occasionally issue this weapon to security units when they have a need to be armed with a full-sized pistol."

"You think those Iraqis on the yacht got these pistols from the Brandenburg 800th Special Purpose Unit you were concerned about earlier?"

"Thought you should see for yourself, Major," Mr. Zargo said. "Draw your own conclusion. I believe it is a possibility."

Major Randal admired the art deco triangular-shaped grips and round burr hammer. He checked again to make sure the weapon was empty and snapped the trigger. "Pretty nice—mind if I keep these?"

"Certainly," Mr. Zargo said.

"Let's hope a Brandenburger team slipped in, passed out a few presents and went back home," Major Randal said. "Bad enough to know they're encouraging the rebels. We don't need German Special Warfare people here advising 'em as well."

"There is a safe on the yacht, Major."

"Thought there might be," Major Randal said, buckling on his own Colt .38 Super automatics. "Have the locksmith be at my CP tonight before we fly out to link up with Lieutenant Kidd—take him with us to crack the safe."

"We will be returning to the mother ship?" Mr. Zargo said.

"Roger," Major Randal said. "Interesting night ahead of us. I'll explain it later when I have the details worked out."

"During the course of our brief association, Major," Mr. Zargo said, "I have come to appreciate the true meaning of the word *interesting*."

Major Randal said, "Is that a good thing?"

SQN. LDR. TONY DUDGEON HAD BEEN ABLE TO GRAB ONLY A couple hours sleep. He had attended AVM Harry "Reggie" Smart's wildly optimistic briefing, then spent the next four hours trying to get his mongrel squadron ready for the 0500 hours attack.

He despised the Air Officer Commanding and his immediate subordinates with a white-hot passion. In his opinion, they were worse than stupid. The AOC and his senior staff were obstinate as well. In a shooting war, that combination of traits at the top of the chain of command can be fatal to the people who have to fight it. In a siege like the RAF base was facing, it could take down everyone—history was shot through with examples.

RAF Habbaniya and the surrounding area were getting ready to be as hot as a war can get in about forty-five minutes.

Maj. John Randal arrived as Squadron Leader Dudgeon was taking a short breather in his office before giving his pilots their final instructions prior to launching the first air strike against the Iraqi positions on the escarpment.

"All available aircraft have been divided into three so-called *squadrons*, a word we use loosely," Squadron Leader Dudgeon explained to Major Randal as he sipped a piping hot cup of tea with his feet up on his desk.

"The Audaxes are divided into two dive-bomber squadrons under the overall command of Larry Ling. The first … ah …. *squadron* consisting of the twelve machines that can carry the 250-pound bombs will be commanded by Wing Commander John Hawtrey—you met him."

Major Randal said, "Good man."

"The second squadron of Audaxes only capable of carrying the eight twenty-pound bombs will be commanded by Wg. Cdr. Glynn Seyln-Roberts. He is really an engineer but also a pilot and we roped him in. The third and fourth wing commanders flying are Paul Holder and Pete Paige, Mandy's father. Both of them have been given roving commissions to fly Audaxes for anybody."

"Mandy's father is flying combat?"

"One of three pilots we were able to wrangle out of the AOC's office. Volunteered straight away. The rest of the staff who are pilots have all come up with some yellow-livered excuse or another."

"There's a lot of staff officers at AHQ," Major Randal said, "wearing wings."

"Bunch of bloody cowards, Major. A national disgrace; never would have believed it of Englishmen."

"We need every man fighting," Major Randal said. "Civilians are pitching in—girls."

Squadron Leader Dudgeon said, "Rank has its privileges."

"The Audaxes will be flying from the polo pitch. That means five wing commanders will be commanding twenty-three airplanes. All taking off and landing from the polo pitch auxiliary field—conveniently out of sight of the Iraqis.

"Meanwhile, I soldier on here with forty-three aircraft outside the wire in plain view of the enemy troops a few hundred yards away on the escarpment. My guess is the rebels will not sit idly by watching us take off and land to refuel and rearm so we can bomb the hell out of them some more."

"You command the airfield?" Major Randal said. "The largest military installation—those wing commanders outrank you, Tony."

"The fourth and largest squadron commanded by me," Squadron Leader Dudgeon said, "consisting of both fighters and bombers of three different types will operate from here at the airfield."

"Forty-three," Major Randal said, "You said there are only thirty-nine pilots for both airstrips?"

"'Tis a strange tale," Lieutenant Dudgeon said, "but true. Those are the numbers."

"Feel like you've been hung out to dry, Tony?"

"Mine is not to reason why," Squadron Leader Dudgeon said. "I am simply giving you a report, Major, as a courtesy RAF flunky to Strike Force commander.

"The Butcher has set up a small operations center here in one of the hangars, but he has no direct command function other than to assign target priorities based on pilot after-action reports."

"Never much gold braid on the sharp end," Major Randal said, lighting a cigarette. "What's your plan?"

"Maximum delegation at all times," Lieutenant Dudgeon said. "I split my machines into three *flights*—again, a word used loosely.

"The largest flight under my personal command will consist of twenty-seven Oxford bombers. The next flight, seven Gordon bombers, will be commanded by Flight Lieutenant David "Horse" Evans—used to be a jockey before the war.

"Last and least will be our ancient museum piece fighter squadron consisting of nine bi-wing Gladiators commanded by Flight Lieutenant Dicky Cleaver. We are in real trouble if they have to defend against the Royal Iraqi Air Force's fighter pilots.

"Dicky's boys will be blown out of the sky—followed shortly by mine."

"Pam told me there's a Flying Officer Featherstone on base," Major Randal said. "Fighter pilot. He one of yours?"

"You mean Bunny?" Lieutenant Dudgeon said. "Man has not drawn a sober breath since he arrived. Understand he was in Abyssinia—sent here to dry out by the South Africans. Not currently on flight status."

"Shot down nearly the entire Regia Aeronautica single-handedly," Major Randal said. "Put him in a fighter, and he'll kill something."

"If you say so, Major; in my opinion, Bunny is a degenerate drunk," Lieutenant Dudgeon said. "On second thought, why bloody not! We are fair and truly desperate—we need every pilot we can scrape up. Who am I to judge? The Desert Air Force marooned me here for a rest cure—I'm washed out, they say."

"How many pilots do you have flying, Tony?"

"Counting Bunny, nineteen."

"That's a lot of your aircraft sidelined," Major Randal said. "Not fighting."

"Use them all before this is over," Squadron Leader Dudgeon said. "Maintenance is going to be critical in this battle. Most of our hoary air fleet would not pass a normal flight inspection. Our fitters are barely able to keep the planes flyable under training conditions—combat is going to be a stretch.

"Now if you will excuse me, Major, I have a war to go fight."

"I need copies of your latest photos of the extreme left flank of the Iraqi positions," Major Randal said. "Reason I stopped by. And, I need you to take pictures of the Iraqi armored cars stationed there at last light when you do your final photo reconnaissance sweep of the day."

"No problem," Lieutenant Dudgeon said, standing up from behind his desk. "You are already in possession of the latest. Mandy's Pony Express girl hand-carried every recent photo we have to your Strike Force Operations Center about two hours ago.

"I shall see to it the pictures I shoot at sundown are developed first, in duplicate, and rush delivered to you—take about an hour. No reason for your photo club people to concern themselves with processing tonight."

"That'll be perfect," Major Randal said.

"Easy enough to whiz over and snap the armored cars on the Iraqi left if they are of particular interest ..."

Major Randal said. "Anything Strike Force can do for you, Tony, consider it done."

"I shall hold you to that," Squadron Leader Dudgeon said. "How is the vacation, by the way?"

"I had hoped to get in a little shooting," Major Randal said.

"Bet it works out for you."

MAJ. JOHN RANDAL RETURNED TO HIS OPERATIONS CENTER. Things were quiet in the large tent. Nothing much happening at this hour.

Red was not going to come on duty for another thirty minutes. The glamorous Clipper Girl had been briefed on all planned Strike Force activities. She was a very capable woman, and Major Randal did not expect there to be any slacking of efficiency.

Clipper Girl slots on BOAC are hard to come by. Six or seven hundred applicants from the stewardesses flying other flights apply for each rare opening on the plush Flying Clipper ships. Those chosen are selected for their beauty, poise and ability to function under stress while exuding that fabulous "Clipper Girl Charm" demanded of them at all times.

Red had recently been recruited by MI-6—the British Secret Service.

Major Randal did not have a need to know that. He thought she worked for the Inner-Allied Service Bureau—one of the cover names

Special Operations Executive operated under in Egypt. In fact, Red thought that too. She had been employed under a "false flag."

Red was in such deep cover she did not have a "Need to Know" who actually employed her.

In Kenya, Red had been part of a counterintelligence operation to locate and eliminate the Italian master spy in Nairobi who put the invasion of Italian East Africa at risk. She, Brandy, Lt. Pamala Plum-Martin, Lt. Penelope Honeycutt-Parker and Capt. the Lady Jane Seaborn had formed a team that shadowed the suspected enemy agent until his untimely death at the hands of his fiancée's current husband. At least that is what Red and the prosecutor's office in Kenya thought. The jilted husband had been arrested for the crime.

In fact, Major Randal shot the spy on a dark country road late one night.

Seeing that all was well, Major Randal went into his red-and-white-striped CP tent, put a few items in a canvas parachute bag, snapped it shut, then walked to the base water tower a few blocks away.

The sky was beginning to lighten. Old desert hands knew there would be a period of early morning dawn thirty minutes before things could be distinguished at any distance.

Aircraft engines cranking up could be heard coming from the airfield and the polo pitch. The Iraqis had to be wondering what that was about.

It was already hot.

Mandy and Mr. Twinning were waiting for Major Randal at the water tower. He had not been expecting them to be there.

"Major," Mr. Twinning said. "The Boys Anti-Tank Rifle is mounted on the rail. I have inspected the improvised traversing mechanism. It is simple and functional. You should find it satisfactory.

"Several lightweight folding chairs have been placed up on the tower. There is a spotting scope too, courtesy of the Rod and Gun Club. A water cooler and cups—someone will refill it at noon. Several sets of ear protection are up there as well.

"We mounted a power winch in order for you to bring up additional .55-caliber ammunition or anything else you might need from time to time.

"The phone company ran a private line to the Operations Center. The telephone is installed up top.

"Anything else you can think of, sir?"

"You've outdone yourself, Mr. Twinning," Major Randal said.

"In that case I shall be getting back to my desk," Mr. Twinning said. "Things should hot up after the bombers go in. Once it starts we are in for incoming artillery or possibly the Iraqis will put in a ground attack … who knows?

"Snipe a few for me, Major."

"Mandy," Major Randal said when they were alone. "What do you think you're doing here?"

"I'm your assistant gunner, John."

"No, you're not," Major Randal said. "You're the captain of the Pony Express. Go do your job."

"My girls are all in position, waiting for the balloon to go up," Mandy said. "I put myself on the second shift at the airfield with Tony. There probably will not be much to do until he makes the bomb damage assessment of the initial attack later this morning.

"Besides, I want to see the show."

"Ah, hell," Major Randal said, as he started climbing the steel ladder with Mandy right behind. "And I thought I was going to have a nice quiet morning all to myself.

"You ever shoot a Boys?"

"Actually, no," Mandy said. "But I did see one fired at a demonstration put on by one of the Levies companies. The A-T squad demonstrated firing it off hand."

"How'd that go?"

"Knocked the gunner down," Mandy said. "Gave him a bloody nose. Dislocated his shoulder. Father told me the .55-caliber AP round is not capable of penetrating any known armor."

"Works good on people," Major Randal said.

15

DAWN PATROL

SQN. LDR. TONY DUDGEON WAS RUNNING AROUND LIKE A man possessed. He was a veteran air commander, with fifty combat missions under his belt as a squadron leader in the Desert Air Force. Predawn takeoffs were nothing new to him.

However, today was something different from anything Squadron Leader Dudgeon had ever imagined. He was commanding three "flights" of three different makes of airplanes of two types, fighters and bombers. The planes were obsolete. The pilots were either not current, recently graduated from the No. 4 Service Training School or burn-out cases.

One was a drunk.

The morning's target was only a few hundred yards away. Even armed with inert bombs, student pilots had never been allowed to fly training missions in as near a proximity to the cantonment as these enemy lines. Deemed too hazardous, and rightly so. One slight miscalculation and a bomb could be bouncing down the runway or punching through a hangar.

When the Oxford flight carrying 250-pound bombs attacked the Iraqi forward positions, the target would be DANGER CLOSE. RAF Habbaniya was going to take shrapnel from the blast. The plan called for the bombers flying off the airfield to bring air strikes in virtually on top of their own base in a preplanned blue-on-blue.

The situation was that desperate.

Even though Squadron Leader Dudgeon was medically classified as battle fatigued, he had no complaint about being placed in command of the bulk of RAF aircraft—in fact he preferred it. He was a take-charge, do what works, get the job done kind of battle leader.

Not being able to take the steps needed to best prepare No. 4 Service Training School for active combat operations the past few weeks and having to go through an out-of-touch-with-reality chain of command rooted in denial and hoping for better days ahead had been more stressful for him than flying the fifty combat missions that had caused him to be battle fatigued.

Squadron Leader Dudgeon characterized the run-up to the morning's mission as "order, counter-order and disorder."

Now that he was taking charge of tactical operations at the airfield, that nonsense was going to stop. He intended to follow orders that made sense and ignore orders that did not. And if anyone on the AOC's staff had any objections, well—you could not blame him—he was a burned-out case … it was on his record.

The thinking at No. 4 Service Training School had been that the advanced student pilots could be pressed into service to fly against the insurgents since quite a few of their training hours had been spent circling over the plateau the Iraqi Army was now occupying while making touch-and-goes at the airfield. That hope went out the window when a predawn strike was called for. None of the students had ever taken off in the dark.

No one really wanted to be responsible for ordering them to attempt it on their first combat mission in an airplane loaded with bombs. Not even Squadron Leader Dudgeon, who was willing to try almost anything.

That left him nineteen pilots present and ready to fight on the first strike. Some of them were members of the Royal Hellenic Air Force—at RAF Habbaniya on a training course—who could not speak English.

Guided by hooded torches held by the ground crew, the airplanes were snuck out of their hangars one at a time and lined up for takeoff. "Snuck" being a relative description—the rebels could hear their engines.

Having issued AVM Harry "Reggie" Smart the ultimatum that if the school flew its aircraft the base would be shelled, the Iraqi rebels had to be wondering what was going on.

In his Oxford with one of the only two qualified bomb-aimers stationed at RAF Habbaniya on board, Squadron Leader Dudgeon led the way in the dark. There were no flare path or navigation lights activated. He taxied for takeoff, picked up speed and as soon as the heavily-loaded bomber lifted off, having avoided the casuarinas and pepper trees at the end of the runway, he pointed the nose to the right of the escarpment where the Iraqi positions had to be and opened the throttle up all the way.

The ten Wellington heavy bombers flying out of Basra were on station, orbiting over RAF Habbaniya. Squadron Leader Dudgeon's mixed "squadron" of Oxfords, Gordons and the Gladiator fighters from the airfield linked up with the Audax bomber "squadrons" from the polo pitch, and then No. 4 Service Flying Training School rendezvoused with the Wellingtons. The RAF air armada gradually reduced itself into a whirlpool of deadly machines flying directly above the Iraqi Army.

There were now forty-nine airplanes of five different models race tracking at different altitudes and cruising speeds, over an area the size of a medium-sized golf course, doing their best not to have a mid-air collision.

The first bomb went down at 0500 hours.

MAJ. JOHN RANDAL WAS SITTING ON A FOLDING chair sixty feet up on the RAF Habbaniya water tower. Mandy was sitting in a chair next to him. They were waiting for enough daylight to begin engaging the Iraqis bivouacked on the escarpment. The Boys .55 Anti-Tank Rifle was mounted on the metal pipe railing that ran around the walkway encircling the tower.

The sky turned pale gray-green.

The sound of the airplanes at the airfield and the polo pitch queuing up and taking off had died away. Time was standing still. Major Randal glanced at his Rolex watch to see if it was broken.

Waiting was always like this.

Mandy said, "Are you a really great sniper, John?"

"I'm not even a good one," Major Randal said, squinting through the No. 32 scope mounted on the Boys Anti-Tank Rifle, "compared to the Lovat Scouts we have in Raiding Forces."

"Then what makes you think you can hit anything as far away as the Iraqi position—has to be 700 to 1,000 yards away?"

"The .55-caliber round is capable of tagging a man-sized target out to one mile, maybe more," Major Randal said. "Bolted down like this, all I have to do is identify the target, place the cross-hairs on it, tighten the tension wheel to fix the Boys in place and touch it off."

"Will you be trying for head shots?"

"Negative," Major Randal said. "Kill an enemy soldier, all you've got is a dead bad guy."

"That *is* the point of shooting one," Mandy said, "to kill him—right?"

"Not always," Major Randal said. "If you only nick 'em, you create a casualty situation. The opposition has to provide aid, move the man back to a safe place for more medical treatment, and then evacuate him to a hospital. Ties up a lot of people, takes up a lot of time, not great for enemy troop morale to see one of their own shot up, and that's always good, militarily."

"Shoot to wound," Mandy said. "So, how do you plan on doing that with a .55-caliber projectile the size of a cigar made out of solid homogenous steel traveling at almost 3,000 feet per second?"

"I'm just going to blaze away," Major Randal said, "and see what happens."

SQN. LDR. TONY DUDGEON LED THE RAF HABBANIYA contingent, boldly christened the "Air Striking Force," in his Oxford trainer-turned-attack-bomber even though it was still painted bright yellow. The air fleet of Wellingtons, Oxfords, Gordons, Audaxes and

Gladiators made one more turn of the aerial wheel. There was just enough light to begin the attack as ordered.

As he came around for the last time, banked over the plateau with his flight of Oxfords lining up in trail behind him looking like a string of yellow bumblebees, Squadron Leader Dudgeon mentally reviewed the sequence of attack. The Oxfords would attack first from 1,000 feet.

Their strike was the signal for the high formation of desert-camouflaged Wellingtons to toggle their bombs from 5,000 feet.

The silver Audaxes and Gordons were dive-bombers, and once the first bombs exploded, they would be cleared to go in right down on the deck to virtually zero altitude before pickling their bomb load.

High overhead, circling like elderly eagles, were the bi-winged Gladiator fighters providing what passed for a combat air patrol.

AVM Harry "Reggie" Smart had convinced himself that three hours of bombing would send the Iraqi Army back to Baghdad with its tail between its legs. If, in fact, he truly thought that, he was the only person on three continents who did. Air Vice Marshal Smart had made the classic military mistake of holding his enemy in contempt, and everyone knew it.

The Iraqi Army on the escarpment consisted of three brigades, one of which was artillery. The artillery brigade was at full strength. One of its battalions consisted of 20 mm anti-aircraft artillery. There was another battalion of light antiaircraft made up of a combination of .30-caliber Lewis and .50-caliber Browning machine guns mounted on antiaircraft tripods. The third battalion consisted of mixed batteries of 18-pounders and 4.5-inch howitzers.

The disposition of the enemy forces had managed to evade the asleep-at-the-wheel intelligence department at RAF Habbaniya. Unknown to the Air Striking Force, it was going against a heavy umbrella of anti-aircraft weaponry. And, while the Iraqi Army was not there expecting to fight, it was not planning to run away.

Squadron Leader Dudgeon banked over his initial target. In the back, his bomb-aimer Sgt. Arthur Prickett, spoke into the gosport speaking tube. "Bombs away, sir."

The time was dead on 0500 hours.

The rest of the Oxford flight pickled when they saw the lead jettison its bomb load—a plan that had taken into consideration that not one of the other bomb-aimers were trained men. Sgt. Prickett's aiming point had been pre-selected with a mass bomb drop following his release in mind.

The Wellingtons began unloading their bombs; when they cleared the area, the Audaxes and Gordons went in. Going straight down almost vertical—hell diving. When they did, they were met by a blizzard of incoming antiaircraft fire coming up at them.

One Audax took fifty-two rounds through the fuselage—incredibly not one struck the pilot.

The first strike lasted less than ten minutes from takeoff to landing back at the airfield. One Oxford was shot down in flames over the target. There were no parachutes.

The Iraqi troops were taken by surprise, but they recovered quickly and fought back hard. In addition to putting up a blizzard of antiaircraft fire, the 18-pound artillery and the 4.5 howitzers immediately began shelling the cantonment. One of the first rounds detonated in the square and killed two D Company troopers of the King's Own Royal Regiment.

The Wellington bombers were big, slow targets, and 5,000 feet is not very high altitude. They all took multiple hits. One spiraled down to the airfield and managed to make an emergency landing.

The crew immediately exited the airplane under fire from every Iraqi gun that could be brought to bear. The airfield thundered with the *CRUUUMPH, CRUUUMPH, CRUUUMPH* of incoming rounds. The airmen sprinted for the safety of a slit trench dug on the edge of the landing strip. Miraculously, none were hit.

The airfield ground crew had no proper equipment, such as a tow-bar, to move the abandoned Wellington. But within minutes, a tractor was racing (in tractor terms) toward the bomber through intense machine gun and pom-pom fire. The driver pulled up to the aircraft, bravely jumped off the tractor and hitched a thick rope to the tail wheel.

Jumping back on the tractor, he put the machine in gear, but before he could take up the slack, a salvo bracketed the Wellington. The next volley slammed in seconds later and set the airplane on fire. It also knocked out the tractor.

A Rolls Royce from No. 1 Armored Car Company with "Intrepid" emblazoned on the side dashed up and—in true cavalry style—rescued the tractor operator. The driver was unscathed, but he did admit to being "a bit deaf" when they hauled him inside the armored car.

Intrepid was halfway back to comparative safety when the crew found out what the airmen, who were buried as deep as they could worm themselves in the slit trench, had not had time to tell anyone. The burning plane had a full bomb load on board, having been shot up before it could make its attack run.

The Wellington blew sky high.

After he landed from the first mission, Squadron Leader Dudgeon raced to Grp. Capt. William "Butcher" Saville's operations center located in a corner of one of the hangars, to make his first after-action report while his bomb-aimer and rear gunner re-armed the Oxford.

"You can tell the AOC to expect the Iraqis to be on the run in three hours right enough, sir," he said to the Butcher. "Hauling up more ammunition."

MAJ. JOHN RANDAL WAS FIRING STEADILY. HE WAS ENJOYING what is sometimes described in military circles as a target-rich environment. Iraqis were thick on the leading edge of the escarpment.

Some were crewing unmasked antiaircraft weapons, some manning artillery pieces, while others stood up and fired their individual weapons at the airplanes swarming overhead. Major Randal's intention was to inflict as many casualties as possible in this first shoot. He wanted to give the Iraqis something to think about when they added up the numbers at the end of the day.

Time to work over the thin-skinned vehicles later when the troops realized they had to go to ground. No rush. The Iraqis could not hide them from view on the open desert. Not from him in the tower. The big Boys .55 round was death on cars and trucks. The rebels had a lot of them—one brigade was mechanized, which meant the troops were all transported in unarmored wheeled vehicles.

He was having a turkey shoot.

Mandy was spotting through the 20X spotting scope. She would identify a target and then describe it using a simple method Major Randal had taught her while they waited for daylight. The way it worked, the escarpment was like the face of a clock with twelve o'clock being straight ahead.

"Man in the open firing a rifle two fingers left of the tank at two o'clock."

BOOOOMMMM!

"Antiaircraft gunner, John, one finger left of the command car at the bottom of the escarpment at eleven o'clock."

BOOOOMMMM!

"Two men manning a heavy machine gun three fingers right of the target you just took out."

BOOOOMMMM!

"Looks like an officer with his command party in the open," Mandy said. "One finger right of the plume of smoke from the airplane burning on the airfield at nine o'clock.

BOOOOMMMM! BOOOOMMMM! BOOOOMMMM!

Major Randal and Mandy had been at it over two hours. It was clear the battle was not going well. Planes were spiraling down and crashing. Some were being blown up on the airfield after they landed. Iraqi artillery was peppering the field continuously. The rest of the base was being shelled intermittently. Fires were burning, and sirens wailing as emergency vehicles rushed here and there on their missions.

Rebel aircraft flew over from time to time and dropped bombs.

The base was fighting. The blockhouses engaged the Iraqis with their Lewis guns. Rod and Gun Club snipers were in action all along the front of the base. The RAF was race tracking, unloading their bombs on the enemy positions, then landing immediately to refuel, rearm and immediately take off to make another attack run. The number of RAF planes doing the attacking was declining with every circuit.

The only good news was that the Iraqis had not put in an immediate ground attack the minute the battle started.

Every fifteen minutes, Major Randal took a break to let the Boys' barrel cool down. The anti-tank rifle was not designed for continuous firing. It was normally a one- or two-shot weapon. In combat that was as long as a Boys gunner usually lasted.

"Get the newspaper publisher on the phone," Major Randal ordered. "Tell him to get over here."

"On the way," Mandy said, putting down the phone.

"Call Squadron Leader Page," Major Randal said. "Have him re-up our Boys .55 ammunition locker."

Before she could make the call, Mr. Thymes arrived, got out of his car and started climbing up the ladder to the tower. He was huffing and puffing when he arrived at the top. The newspaper man was clearly disturbed by the height.

A tearing sound, *WHICCCCCHA, WHICCCCCHA, WHICCCCCHA,* then an artillery shell came screaming past and exploded somewhere behind them. *KABOOM.*

"Are they shooting at us on the water tower," Mr. Thymes demanded, "with cannons?"

"Been doing it all morning," Mandy said. "Rotten shots."

"How are you coming with your plan, Mr. Thymes," Major Randal said.

"Plan?"

"To make the Iraqis go away."

"Not particularly well," Mr. Thymes said. "My editorial staff has been looking into superstitions and religious beliefs. So far we have failed to hit upon anything we think might be effective ..."

"You ever play that parlor game where someone gives you a word," Major Randal asked, "and then you expand on it and turn it into a story?"

"Actually," Mr. Thymes said. "I *have* played that game."

"Let's give it a try," Major Randal said.

"You want to play a word game in the middle of a shooting war?" Mr. Thymes asked.

"Squirrel," Major Randal said.

"Squirrel?"

"Yeah, painted orange."

"Squirrel," Mr. Thymes said looking at Mandy for help, "painted orange ..."

"Any squirrels on Habbaniya?" Major Randal asked.

"There are," Mandy said. "Lots."

"Let me help you get started," Major Randal said. "Have a contest to trap squirrels. I need as many as you can get by tonight."

"A contest," Mr. Thymes said. "What kind?"

"How about a kissing contest," Major Randal said. "Mandy gives out kisses—that ought to work. OK with you, Mandy?"

"Love to, John," Mandy said.

"Major, if Mandy awards a kiss to everyone who catches a squirrel, every boy over the age of five and man under ninety will be out trapping. Result in the extinction of the entire squirrel population on Habbaniya," Mr. Thymes said.

"We have a few over in the base zoo, come to think of it."

"Now you're getting into the spirit," Major Randal said.

"I suppose you want me to paint the squirrels orange."

"Roger that."

"Then what do I do?"

"Put each one in a little wicker cage," Major Randal said. "I'll arrange for Squadron Leader Dudgeon to give you parachutes that he'll take off aerial flares and you can strap 'em on the baskets."

"Tonight, Pam will drop 'em in over the escarpment."

"You want to parachute orange squirrels on the Iraqis?"

"Affirmative," Major Randal said. "The squirrels will chew their way out of the cages and pretty soon they'll be running around inside the Iraqi lines."

"And why would we want to have orange squirrels running around inside the Iraqi lines?" Mr. Thymes asked.

"How the hell would I know?" Major Randal said.

"That's your job, Thymes. Come up with a story. Print up leaflets explaining the whole deal to the Iraqis so they won't have to figure it out for themselves. Have 'em ready for Pam to scatter over the plateau tomorrow night when she puts in the second wave of squirrels."

"Now move out."

After the newspaper publisher departed, Mandy said, "Mr. Thymes does not seem like he is very good at games."

"I bet," Major Randal said, "he surprises us."

16

THE AIRFIELD

TAKEOFFS AND LANDINGS AT THE AIRFIELD AFTER DAYLIGHT had to be made in full view of the Iraqi gunners. The pilots were flying a constant round-robin—take off, circle over the plateau, identify a target, bomb it, return to the airfield, land, rearm and refuel if necessary, then take off again. Flights lasted only a few minutes.

Sqn. Ldr. Tony Dudgeon completed his Oxford's cockpit check inside the shelter of the hangar, out of sight of the Iraqis on the escarpment who were looking down over the open sights of their heavy artillery. The airfield was a shooting gallery. The rebel gunners opened every time a plane took off or landed. He glanced at the airman who was posted in the door of the hanger—off to one side out of sight of the Iraqis, but in a position to see the landing strip.

The airman had the tricky assignment of watching for incoming RAF aircraft, then signaling the ready pilot in the hangar when it was safe to take off.

After completing a mission and landing in full view of the enemy, the inbound planes were taking fire, swerving around the side of the hangar, then scooting inside to get out of the Iraqis' sight.

Not the school solution technique for parking an airplane in a hangar, but under the exigencies of the day—standard operating procedure (SOP).

The trick was for a pilot *inside* the hangar wanting to take off not to go hightailing it out the door on to the airfield just as another *outside* was wheeling in.

The lookout gave the all clear. Juggling the throttles and brakes, Squadron Leader Dudgeon swept out of the hangar into full sight of the enemy, engines going flat out. The hollow *CRUUUMPH* of incoming artillery rounds immediately began detonating. He shot through the opening in the camp fence and was going 30 mph before he even hit the edge of the airfield outside the wire.

The instant Squadron Leader Dudgeon made it through the gate onto the airfield and built up enough flying speed, he dragged the Oxford off the ground, dropped a wing, pulled around *away* from the escarpment in the steepest turn he dared, came back on the throttle, retracted his wheels, then climbed out to bombing altitude at 1,000 feet. All the while, every Iraqi on the main-line-of-resistance (MLR) who possessed a weapon from a pistol to a howitzer was blazing away at the yellow bomber at point-blank range.

Landings were worse. That gave Squadron Leader Dudgeon something to think about. He would be back in a few minutes.

MAJ. JOHN RANDAL SAID, "WHAT TIME DO YOU GO ON DUTY?"

"I assigned myself the noon to 1600 shift," Mandy said. "Red has you penciled in to be sleeping at that time so I am free to take my turn at the airfield."

Major Randal was having second thoughts about stationing the Pony Express riders at the airfield or the polo pitch. Both locations were taking fire—the airfield under more or less constant attack. The last thing he wanted was a dead teenage horse girl.

The battle of RAF Habbaniya was "Victory or Death." Exactly like

Col. William B. Travis signed his last communiqué from the Alamo not long before the Mexican Army breached the walls, overran the fort and killed everyone inside. If the Iraqi Army overran the cantonment, the *lucky* girls would be the ones who were dead. Everyone had to pull their weight. Still ...

The phone clattered.

"Tony for you," Mandy said.

Sqn. Ldr. Tony Dudgeon did not mince words. "We are in serious trouble. This battle is not going according to plan. Larry Ling is in the hospital seriously wounded. Wing Commander Paul Holder has been shot down, but he made it back, and then got shot down a second time. Made it home again and is still flying; that's the way it's been. Another Wing Commander had to have an emergency appendectomy today, of all days.

"The Iraqis shelling the airfield are going to destroy every one of my planes on the ground unless we do something about it. Can you send the Strike Force armored cars so we can use them to drive along beside the aircraft to screen them from the shrapnel when they taxi?"

"Polo pitch need cars too?" Major Randal asked.

"No doubt."

"On the way, I'll bring a platoon to the airfield," Major Randal said. "We'll send another to the polo pitch. Be there in fifteen minutes, Tony, maybe less."

"Thanks, John."

"Mandy," Major Randal said, racking the bolt to unload the .55 round in the chamber of the Boys Anti-Tank rifle, "get Squadron Leader Page on the horn. Tell him to have two armored car platoons ready to move out by the time we get there—five minutes max."

Before they made it down the ladder, Major Randal and Mandy could hear the sirens on the armored cars wailing as they raced to the Operations Center. When the two came to the small tent city that had sprung up on the grounds of the BOQ, they passed Cpl. Basil James and a group of Boy Scouts roasting a goat on a spit over an open fire. One of the chefs from the club restaurant was on hand to guarantee a successful result.

"Good work, men," Major Randal called. "Shoot another one tonight."

Mandy suppressed a giggle and gave the Scouts a Miss America-quality wave as they strolled by.

Sqn. Ldr. John Page was standing-by. Major Randal issued him his orders, "You stay on top the situation here at the Ops Center with your remaining platoon in reserve."

"Yes, sir."

"The Iraqis are going to test our perimeter sooner rather than later. When they do, you hit back hard and fast. Don't wait for orders."

"Sir!"

"Have the ammo locker at the water tower re-up'd," Major Randal said.

"Sir?"

"About out."

"Major," Squadron Leader Page said. "That was our *entire* stock of .55 ammunition. We stored it at the water tower to have all our AT in one location. Sir, how much do you have left?"

Major Randal looked at Mandy. "Eight or ten bullets," she said in a little girl voice.

"You fired over *two hundred* rounds of AT!"

Major Randal said, "I wasn't counting."

"The Levies only have two Boys AT rifles, we have one per platoon in the cars. My guess, sir, is that there is less than 25 rounds of .55 armor-piercing ammunition left on Habbaniya now."

"Uh-oh!"

"Somebody should have advised me," Major Randal said. "We're going to need more .55."

"My mistake, sir."

"Mandy, ask Mr. Zargo to meet me at the airstrip. Find Pam—have her link up with us there."

Major Randal went into his CP tent and retrieved his Zeiss scoped M-1903 A-1 Springfield wildcat 7 mm-06 and a bandoleer of ammunition.

"What model of armored cars are these?" he asked, handing the No. 1 ACC commander an 8 x10 photo when he came back out.

"Crossleys," Squadron Leader Page said, sounding bitter. "Our government gave them to the Iraqis. Light-years more modern than my Rolls Royces."

"No. 1 ACC have people who know how to drive 'em?"

"We do, sir," Squadron Leader Page said. "My company trained Col. Fahmi Said's Independent Mechanized Brigade in armored cavalry tactics, using their Crossleys—stationed up there on the escarpment as we speak."

"I need two drivers for a hazardous mission," Major Randal said. "Report to Red at 1800 hours."

"Yes, sir," Squadron Leader Page said. "Am I permitted to volunteer?"

"Negative," Major Randal said, climbing into the platoon leader's command car. "I need you doing what you're doing. Don't worry, you'll see plenty of action before this fight is over."

Squadron Leader Page watched as the two platoons of antique Silver Spirit Rolls Royce armored cars rolled out on their first combat mission. "The Major fired over 200 rounds of AT in one morning. That is impossible. Do you think he hit anything, Mandy?"

"Almost never missed."

"Weapon is a piece of rubbish," Squadron Leader Page said. "We only kept a limited supply of .55-caliber ammunition on the station because it is so hopeless. The round is incapable of piercing armor."

"Works good on people," Mandy said.

THE AIRFIELD WAS A BEATEN ZONE. ARTILLERY ROUNDS were coming in every time an airplane landed or took off. Since the pilots were race tracking—taking off, circling over the Iraqi Army to drop their bombs, immediately landing to rearm, then taking off for another run –the incoming fire was almost nonstop. It seemed very foolish to be running air operations out in the open in full sight of the enemy—only a few hundred yards away in some cases—*felt* foolish, too.

Maj. John Randal surveyed the scene as the platoon of armored cars arrived at the hangar complex.

The skeletal remains of a wrecked Wellington bomber burning on the field complicated takeoff and landings. Black geysers caused by incoming artillery rounds detonating were spiking up everywhere he looked. The blockhouses were manned by the Levies who were engaging with their machine guns. And there was the steady crack of gunfire from the Rod and Gun Club Big Bore Rifle Team stationed along the outer edge of the perimeter.

The battle was raging.

Inside a hangar, Sqn. Ldr. Tony Dudgeon briefed the platoon leader from No. 1 Armored Car Company while his Oxford was being rearmed. "What I want you to do, Lieutenant, is to keep a pair of your cars stationed out on the landing strip at all times. When an aircraft comes in to land, have the cars race up on both sides of the plane as it touches down, then escort it all the way to the hangar."

"Sir!"

"Keep the rest of your cars here at the hangars," Squadron Leader Dudgeon said. "Have two flank each plane taxiing out for takeoff. Stay alongside the entire way until they become airborne."

"Require some high speed driving, sir," the platoon leader said. "Our cup of tea."

"In the event the Iraqis attack the perimeter," Major Randal said, "we may have to pull the cars off duty here temporarily to take part in the counterattack."

"Understood," Squadron Leader Dudgeon said.

Mr. Zargo arrived as the armored cars were driving off to take up their duty stations. He had Lt. Pamala Plum-Martin with him.

Major Randal said, "Tony, what say we take the fight to the bad guys?"

"What do you have in mind?"

"The Iraqi Air Force has been flying missions against us all morning," Major Randal said. "Why don't you brief Mr. Zargo and Lieutenant Plum-Martin on the enemy airports you think they're flying from. Tonight we'll pick one out and get Pam to fly a few of us over there in her Seagull, land on their airstrip so we can get out and shoot up as many parked planes as we can."

"Fly to a hostile military airfield and land," Squadron Leader Dudgeon said. "Are you nuts?"

"That's how you do it," Major Randal said.

"Has to be more to it that that!"

"Arrive in the dark of night—unannounced and unexpected," Major Randal said. "Shoot up the place, come home. The Iraqis know you don't have any night-flying capabilities. They'll drop their guard once the sun goes down."

Mr. Zargo fiddled with his pipe. Lieutenant Plum-Martin gave Major Randal a dazzling smile. Squadron Leader Dudgeon said, "You people are serious."

"Be a big help," Major Randal said, "if you could make a photo-recon flight over the targets before last light."

"Nothing I would rather do," Squadron Leader Dudgeon said, "if it will help."

"Time spent on reconnaissance," Major Randal said, "is rarely wasted."

"So I have heard," Squadron Leader Dudgeon said. "Certainly not, if you take out as much as a single Iraqi attack aircraft. Habbaniya does not have an early warning system. Without advance notice, our Gladiator pilots have not been able to scramble and intercept the intruders. That, we need to stop."

Flt. Off. Gasper "Bunny" Featherstone, DFC, was standing beside his Gloster Gladiator at the far end of the hangar. Armors were reloading the little bi-winged fighter's four Browning .303-caliber machine guns. When no one was looking, the former member of the legendary (and virtually extinct) Millionaires Squadron took a nip from the silver flask he never left home without.

Major Randal walked over to have a word with him while Squadron Leader Dudgeon, Mr. Zargo and Lieutenant Plum-Martin repaired to the operations office to select a list of suitable candidates for the night's raid on an Iraqi airfield.

"Hello, Major," Flying Officer Featherstone said. "What brings you to sunny Habbaniya?"

"Vacation," Major Randal said. "You?"

"Here to dry out," Flying Officer Featherstone said. "Being marooned on this Devil's Island of a prison camp is enough to drive a man to drink even more."

"How's it going, Bunny?"

"The lads are flying hard," Flying Officer Featherstone said. "Not making a dent in the bloody Iraqis though; too many of them. The opposition may have been taken by surprise initially, but they are heavily armed and fighting for all it's worth now.

"Degrading our air fleet pretty fast."

"All done, Bunny," one of the armors called.

Flight Officer Featherstone climbed into the seat of the fighter, revved the engine, and without waiting for armored cars to screen his takeoff, taxied out the door. Everyone at No. 4 Service Flying Training School stopped to watch. Takeoff and landings were always cliffhangers.

The Gladiator was going wide open by the time it shot through the gate to the airfield. Flying Officer Featherstone immediately came right and started his takeoff run. Artillery rounds began impacting the strip as the little bi-winged fighter leapt into the air.

Standard Operating Procedure was to turn away from the escarpment and pile on altitude as soon as a pilot was airborne. Flying Officer Featherstone paid no attention to SOP. What he did do was to turn *toward* the plateau as soon as he lifted off and rolled in, guns blazing. The former Millionaire Squadron pilot and scourge of the Regia Aeronautica in Abyssinia wiggled the rudder back and forth as he raced the length of the Iraqi position at virtual zero altitude strafing the startled enemy at haircut level with his four Browning .303 machine guns.

A cheer went up from the airfield.

Flying Officer Featherstone made a single showy pass—hammer down—firing up all his ammunition. He came around, landed and made a mad dash for the hangar amid a thunderstorm of incoming artillery rounds. His flight was the shortest combat mission of the day—three minutes from start to finish.

Everyone agreed it was the gutsiest move they had ever seen.

17

TROOPING THE LINE

MAJ. JOHN RANDAL AND MR. WALTER STANBERRY, THE captain of the Big Bore Rifle Team, started at the far left flank of the airfield and worked their way all the way up the length of the landing strip. They were under fire from time to time. The leading edge of the front line of the Iraqi Army, also known as the Main Line of Resistance (MLR), was a pistol shot away. They inspected each of the positions the civilian marksmen had chosen. Some were semi-concealed sandbagged hides, and others were located on top of the two-story concrete bunkers spaced every 300 yards along the perimeter.

The Iraqi artillery was firing primarily on two targets: aircraft and the concrete bunkers. It was a poor decision by the rebel artillery commander. The airplanes constantly landing and taking off were moving targets and hard to hit. The bunkers were reinforced concrete, and while they took hits from time to time and suffered damage, the incoming rounds were not able to knock them out of action.

The Rod and Gun Club riflemen were middle-aged and older, and they took their skill with a rifle seriously. They were fighting as hard as men can fight. All had wives, children, and in some cases, grandchildren in the cantonment. No one was under any illusion about what would happen if the Iraqis overran the base.

The marksmen were methodically carrying out a cold-blooded execution of their enemy. They worked in two-man teams—shooter and spotter. Each shooter fired ten rounds and then rotated jobs with the spotter. The range was from 500 to 1,000 yards.

Unlike formal target matches, the riflemen did not have to place their rounds in the black to score points. They did not have to achieve small groups. All they had to do was to "get on paper." All hits counted the same. Compared to competition combat, scoring was easy.

The big difference—paper targets did not shoot back. The Iraqis were, but it was intermittent fire and inaccurate. Mostly the rebels shot at the airplanes.

The drill was the same at every post Major Randal and Mr. Stanberry visited. The Strike Force commander was not paying a social call, and the men did not need any morale boost. Mostly they ignored him. He inspected the site and observed the shooting. Then he assumed a firing position with his modified 7 mm-06 M-1903 A-1 Springfield and took a few shots.

There were plenty of targets. The Iraqi troops never seemed to understand that they could not show themselves. When an airplane took off or landed, the rebels would stand up fully exposed and fire at it with their individual weapons.

For that indiscretion, they paid a price.

When Major Randal had a suggestion, he made it to Mr. Stanberry. A few of the men expressed interest in the wildcat 7 mm-06 A-1 Springfield. Like all long-range competition target shooters, the Rod and Gun Club men were perfectionists—tightly focused, busy; while friendly, they did not welcome interruptions.

Major Randal was careful not to interrupt them.

"We are going to have our hands full reloading tonight," Mr. Stanberry said. "Underestimated the amount of ammunition we would need."

"Unless the bad guys get their act together and assault," Major Randal said. "My guess is you can expect tomorrow to be pretty much the same as today."

"We shall be better prepared," Mr. Stanberry said. "May run short of ammunition today before we lose shooting light."

"If I were you, Mr. Stanberry," Major Randal said, "I'd move my people off the exposed tops of the bunkers. Drawing too much fire up there."

"With your permission I shall rotate them to new positions straight away," Mr. Stanberry said. "Already had three men wounded."

"Tell your men they're doing good work," Major Randal said. "Probably taking out more bad guys than the RAF."

"There was someone firing a heavy rifle from the water tower," Mr. Stanberry said. "Made a rather impressive crack when it came over. Rebels simply exploded.

"Was that you perchance, Major? First-rate marksmanship, but it ceased."

"It's easy when your weapon is bolted down," Major Randal said, "and you're shooting a .55 round that travels as straight as a beam of light out to about a mile."

"You should be up there right now," Mr. Stanberry said. "Or, I can supply a qualified man if you have other pressing duties."

"Ran out of ammo," Major Randal said. "You wouldn't be able to reload .55 Boys by any chance?"

"Afraid not."

"It was good while it lasted."

MAJ. JOHN RANDAL WAS ON HIS COT IN THE RED-AND-white-striped Command Post tent. A busy night was ahead, and he had to rest when possible. He was asleep, but it would not have been a good idea to try to sneak up on him. Flanigan, the police guard, was on duty. Red had issued firm instructions that Major Randal was not to be interrupted.

Outside in the street could be heard the clatter of one of the Pony Express girls on the way to the Operations Center with a message. An incoming artillery shell screamed in *CRUUUUUMPH*. A horse shrieked in agony. People shouted.

Major Randal was up and running out the gate into the street.

Mandy was laying crumpled, unconscious on the pavement. Her Arab pony was disemboweled. The horribly-wounded animal was kicking spasmodically. One of the animal's steel shod hooves barely missed the girl's head.

Major Randal shot the horse with his Colt .38 Super.

Red ran up, followed by Flanigan.

"Get a doctor," Major Randal ordered. He picked Mandy up and carried her to the cot in the CP. For a minute he thought she was dead.

That was a bad minute.

The doctor arrived almost immediately. Major Randal waited outside the tent with Red and the policeman. They were chain smoking.

"Girls are tougher than they look," Red said.

"I don't think so," Major Randal said.

The doctor came to the flap of the tent. He was all business. "She is awake. No symptoms of concussion. No signs of broken bones."

"See, John," Red said. "Mandy is going to be fine."

"Bed rest," the doctor said. "Aspirin as needed. Have a headache for a day or two. Do not let Mandy go to sleep for a couple of hours. Keep her talking.

"Now, I have other patients."

Major Randal went in and sat in a canvas chair next to the cot. Mandy gave him a weak smile. "How is Blackie?"

"Blackie, huh? He didn't make it."

Mandy started to sob. Major Randal felt about as bad as he could ever remember feeling in his life.

"My mule got killed in Abyssinia," Major Randal said. "I really hated that."

"Your *mule*?" Mandy wailed. "Blackie was a purebred Arabian."

"Well, I liked Parachute."

"What happened to him?"

"Pyro Percy blew him up," Major Randal said. "You'll meet Captain Stirling one day when this is all over. Don't be anywhere in the area if he's ever going to do any demolitions."

"Pam told me you kept two slave girls when you were in Abyssinia," Mandy said. "She said they were beautiful."

"Rita and Lana," Major Randal said. "The girls weren't my slaves. I ... well, ah ... shot their owner and inherited them. Way it works out there."

"They're Zar Cult priestesses."

"You had a pair of priestesses as your personal body slaves?"

"No, Mandy, they weren't my slaves. In fact, the girls wouldn't even talk to me."

"They talked to Pam," Mandy said, "and to Parker."

"They've joined the Royal Marines," Major Randal said. "Work for Lady Jane now. They talk to her too, not me."

"Tell me about her," Mandy said. "Everyone says Lady Jane is drop-dead gorgeous and crazy mad in love with you."

"Well ..."

"Pam said you rescued her husband from the Nazis. How is that working out, John?"

"It's a little complicated ..."

"Parker told me the reason they brought you here to Habbaniya was to spirit you out of Cairo to keep you away from a scorching Norwegian blonde who wanted you to phone her. Lady Jane's husband's mistress—I would not make that call if I were you, John."

"Don't you have a boyfriend we can talk about?"

"I did," Mandy said. "A fighter pilot. In the Regia Aeronautica—stationed in Italian East Africa. You probably shot him too."

Outside, the sound of people scattering could be heard as a horse and rider came sailing over the wall surrounding the BOQ grounds.

"Mother's here," Mandy said.

Major Randal stepped to the tent flap in time to see a tanned woman in white t-shirt, jodhpurs and riding boots bring her horse around short of the pool, dismount and throw the reins to the startled policeman. It was clear where Mandy got her looks.

He walked outside.

"John Randal."

"Veronica Paige," the woman said. "Mandy mentioned you, Major—I thought you would be bigger.

"She inside?"

Veronica brushed past without waiting for an answer.

"Saw the doctor, Mandy," Veronica said. "Said you bumped your head. It's a foot from your heart. Thirty minutes' bed rest, then you need to go back on duty, girl."

"Yes, mother."

"Major, if Mandy is not up to riding, I shall fill in for the rest of her shift," Veronica said.

"Not a problem," Major Randal said. "We already have a replacement at the airfield."

"In that case, I shall be off," Veronica said. "Artillery is frightening the horses."

"Mother is in charge of the base stables," Mandy said, "Governor of the women's equestrian clubs."

"I see," Major Randal said, which meant he did not have a clue.

"Thirty minutes, Mandy."

Major Randal walked Veronica out of the tent and held her horse as she mounted. "Your husband is Wing Commander Paige—flying Audaxes off the polo pitch?"

"That's right."

"How would you like a job?"

"MR. TWINNING, WE NEED TO PUT A STOP TO THIS IRAQI artillery," Maj. John Randal said.

"I agree," Mr. Twinning said. "Anything I can do to help?"

"Know anything about magic?"

"Cannot say that I do, Major."

"Do you have any magicians here on Habbaniya?"

"None that I can think of."

"Put out a call," Major Randal said. "We need anyone who knows anything about magic or illusions. Have 'em report here in the next thirty minutes."

"We can do that," Mr. Twinning said. "Radio public service announcements and sound trucks should do the trick. If that does not bring results, I can mobilize a door-to-door campaign, but that will take considerably longer."

"Do whatever it takes," Major Randal said.

"It might help," Mr. Twinning said, "if I knew why we want magicians or illusionists."

"There are two ways to deal with the Iraqi artillery … well, actually three," Major Randal said. "Go out, kill the gunners and blow up the guns—that's one way. But we can't do that in broad daylight. Or, we can get the Iraqi artillery to target some place we want them to hit and let them have at it."

"Like what, Major?"

"Well, an empty field or an isolated building that's not of military value," Major Randal said. "Draw fire—better than having 'em shoot at the hospital or ammo dump."

"Makes sense," Mr. Twinning said. "Trick the Iraqis into firing on a worthless target. How do we go about doing that?"

"That's what we need the magician for," Major Randal said.

"Capital idea," Mr. Twinning said. "I shall oversee this project personally. You said there were three ways to stop the artillery. What is the third?"

"The RAF could knock the guns out," Major Randal said. "But I wouldn't count on it."

"Why not, if you do not mind my asking?"

"They've been bombing nonstop since sunrise," Major Randal said. "Noticed any drop off in incoming?"

"No," Mr. Twinning said. "Seems to be picking up in intensity, actually."

"Roger that," Major Randal said. "We need some magic."

MAJ. JOHN RANDAL AND MR. ZARGO WERE IN THE Operations Center tent looking at the mosaic of aerial photos of the Iraqi positions. There was a swirl of activity around them as people were going about their appointed tasks. A lot was happening.

"Take a look at this," Major Randal said, pointing to the map. "Bad guys inched up pretty close to our wire on the left flank."

Mr. Zargo clenched his cold pipe in his teeth and studied the area Major Randal pointed out. "Some infantry and two armored cars at the crossroads west of the bend in the Euphrates."

"How far out do you estimate?"

"Appears to be about half a kilometer, Major. Five hundred yards."

"I had the civilian marksmen avoid that stretch of the perimeter," Major Randal said. "We don't want the Iraqis abandoning the crossroads."

"Why?" Mr. Zargo said. "The overall objective is to get the Iraqis to pull their troops back, is it not?"

"Not there," Major Randal said. "Tonight I'm going to take a couple of drivers, go out and capture those two Crossleys. I need a language man from Z Patrol to go with us."

"That would be King," Mr. Zargo said. "What about the raid on Baqubah Airfield Lt. Plum-Martin and I have been planning? We were expecting you to lead it."

"I'll hit those two cars at 0200," Major Randal said. "We'll drive them in the gate at the corner of the base—take five minutes max.

"Schedule the departure time for the raid to be 0230," Major Randal said. King and I will link up with you and the rest of Z Patrol prior to that."

"That will work."

Major Randal took out a Player's and lit it with his hard service Zippo. "Mr. Zargo, what are your duties here at Habbaniya? No one ever said, exactly."

"Counterintelligence, for the most part," Mr. Zargo said. "You may have noticed there are a large number of Iraqi and Indian civilians living on the base. They have to be vetted. Then it is necessary to keep our eye on them to make sure they stay loyal."

"You ever work with Captain Sandstorm, Chief of Counterintelligence in Cairo?"

"Sawed-off, sandy-haired fellow, toothbrush moustache, expatriate Englishman—his family sells insurance out here in the Middle East—likes to mix it up with his fists when he makes arrests?" Mr. Zargo said.

"Yeah."

"Never heard of him."

18

WAR MAGIC

MAJ. JOHN RANDAL WAS IN HIS CP TENT. RED AND MANDY were present. Mr. Thymes, the publisher, passed out single sheets of paper for them to read.

The girls started giggling immediately.

IRAQI SOLDIERS BEWARE
YOUR PENIS IS AT RISK!

ROGUE ELEMENTS LED BY THE NOTORIOUS BRITISH
SPECIAL FORCES ASSASSIN, MAJOR JOHN RANDAL, HAVE
SEIZED CONTROL OF MILITARY OPERATIONS ON RAF
HABBANIYA.

ON HIS ORDERS SQUIRRELS SATURATED WITH
TARTRAZINE (YELLOW #5) THAT TURNED THEM
YELLOW AND ORANGE HAVE BEEN PARACHUTED ON
YOUR POSITIONS. MORE WILL BE DROPPED EVERY
NIGHT.

DO NOT BREATHE THE AIR WITHIN ONE-HALF MILE
OF THE YELLOW SQUIRRELS. ORANGE SQUIRRELS ARE
MORE TOXIC — RUN AWAY IF YOU SEE ONE.

YELLOW #5 WILL CAUSE YOUR PENIS TO SHRINK, ROT,
AND IN MANY CASES FALL OFF.

SYMPTOMS INCLUDE, BUT ARE NOT LIMITED TO,
FEELING HOT, ITCHING AND BLURRED VISION.

YOU HAVE BEEN WARNED.

The warning was printed in English on one side of the paper and in Arabic on the other.

"I don't see any reason why you have to bring me into this," Major Randal said.

"We have mobilized women from the Indian contingent of the Habbaniya civilian population to weave straw basket cages," Mr. Thymes said. "The life expectancy of one of the squirrels is zero once they chew their way out and escape. With no trees around, jackals will get them quick.

"Consulted on the subject with the base veterinarian. He came up with the idea to make a small incision in the squirrel's neck and insert a capsule of rat poison, then stitch it back up. The jackals will bite the squirrel, taste the poison, possibly die – but in any case, not *eat* it.

"Oh, that's good," Major Randal said.

"Iraqis will see live orange squirrels, dead orange squirrels and possibly a few dead jackals with orange squirrels in their mouths," Mr. Thymes said.

"We do this in two phases—drop the squirrels, then before sunrise, paper the Iraqis with thousands of these leaflets.

"Repeat as needed."

"Sounds like a plan," Major Randal said. "How many squirrels can you have ready?"

"Approximately fifty tonight," Mr. Thymes said. "More tomorrow night. The lads are trapping their hearts out. Remember the contest, Mandy?"

"Outstanding," Major Randal said. "How'd you come up with this memo?"

"Editorial Board," Mr. Thymes said. "The paper is essentially a volunteer operation. My writers are mostly journalism students. You have to watch them like a hawk—revel in this kind of devilry."

"Iraqis are chauvinists," Red said. "You played on their worst fears, Mr. Thymes. No way for them to ignore this message—it's perfect."

"The symptoms are brilliant. Hot and itchy," Mandy said. "We are in the middle of a *desert*."

"Roger that," Major Randal said. "I got blurry vision reading the flyer."

MAJ. JOHN RANDAL AND THE Z OPERATOR, KING, LINKED UP to make a Leader's Reconnaissance for the night's mission to capture the two Crossley armored cars stationed on the far left flank of the Iraqi position.

A Leader's Reconnaissance is an integral part of patrol preparation. However, exactly how to go about performing one is often either misunderstood, deemed too risky to be feasible, or simply not done. Experienced combat veterans know ignoring the Leader's Reconnaissance places the troops going on the mission at peril.

A simple map study may be all a patrol leader can do under certain circumstances. But the best Leader's Recon is to put eyes on the target either by aerial reconnaissance or walking the ground. Air is not always possible, and it is dangerous to take all the element leaders of a patrol out together to scout the objective ahead of time, which is what they teach in most military schools.

If the leaders are killed, wounded or captured while conducting the Leader's Reconnaissance, the mission ends before it even gets started.

Today's was simple. All Major Randal and King had to do was go to the Levies bunker on the extreme left flank. The Crossley armored cars were in plain sight 500 yards away up on the escarpment.

The two men climbed up on the second-story roof of the bunker. This was possibly the quietest sector of the front. No firing was going on at the moment.

Major Randal studied the rebel position through his Zeiss binoculars and then handed them to King. The merc was very thorough in his observation. The mark of a professional soldier is that he does not get in a hurry unless he has to.

"What route do you intend to take tonight, Major?"

"We'll be coming in the back door," Major Randal said, lighting a Player's with his U.S. 26th Cavalry Regiment Zippo. "Tonight the two Crossley wheel men, you and I will fly out to a yacht we have in the middle of the lake with a patrol of the King's Own stationed on board.

"We'll take small boats to the shore. Come in overland—about two miles. Time it to hit the target at 0200 hours."

King studied the objective. "Major, we are not able to see the entire route from the target to the lake from here. Mind if I offer a suggestion?"

"Let's hear it."

"Why don't I patrol out after dark, reconnoiter the target up close, scout the route all the way to the lake, then rendezvous with your team at the shore when you come in?"

"By yourself?"

"I like to work alone," King said. "No witnesses."

"You got it," Major Randal said. "Anything else we need to discuss before we go down and coordinate our entry of friendly lines tonight with the NCO in charge of the bunker?"

"I'm a blade man," King said. "Interested in how you like your Fairbairn, Major."

"You know F/Ss?"

"Heard they were good weapons," King said, "designed for silent killing."

"I have a spare," Major Randal said. "Take it along tonight and see how it works."

"I would like that."

"Sharp," Major Randal said. "Don't cut yourself."

MR. TWINNING WAS WAITING FOR MAJ. JOHN RANDAL WHEN he walked into the Operations Center. He had a skinny teenage boy sitting at his desk who looked to be about fifteen years old. He was wearing big thick glasses that looked like the bottoms of Coke bottles.

"Major," Mr. Twinning said. "I would like you to meet Teddy. Our local, and as it turns out, only, expert on the black arts."

Major Randal said, "We need someone who can advise us on creating military illusions. Are you the man, Teddy?"

"Yes sir, Major."

"Teddy has already come up with an ambitious catalogue of ideas," Mr. Twinning said. "Time being of the essence, we pared them down. Thought you might want to hear what we have decided on."

Major Randal said. "Run it down for me, Teddy."

Mandy came into the Op Center, saw Major Randal, walked over and stood by his chair. The Strike Force commander knew the girl was there to remind him of a meeting scheduled with his two senior infantry troop commanders in five minutes. She did not interrupt.

"The secret of creating an illusion is to make the audience look where you want them to," Teddy said, not unmindful of Mandy. Sounding as if he were quoting from a conjurer's handbook, he continued, "The great magicians accomplish this by performing their trick where the audience expects them to, knowing that people will resist looking where they *think* you want them to, when they know in advance you are going to try to trick them."

"I see," Major Randal said.

"Mr. Twinning says the goal is to persuade the Iraqis to concentrate their artillery fire on a worthless target."

"Roger that," Major Randal said. "How're we going to do it?"

"Simple, sir," Teddy said. "All we have to do is make the Iraqis believe their artillery has already hit a valuable target, caused damage and that they need to concentrate their fire to destroy it."

"Very good," Major Randal said. "How do you make that happen?"

"Oil drums, sir," Teddy said. "Our first task is to create thick smoke columns the enemy can see from the escarpment with the naked eye to make them think they have hit one of our fuel storage areas. Later it will be necessary to create more elaborate mock targets. Erect tents, or maybe incorporate old buildings Mr. Twinning says we can destroy into the subterfuge."

"And why would we want to do that?" Major Randal said.

"Eventually Iraqi rebel pilots will fly over to see what their artillery hit," Teddy said. "We would not want them reporting back it was a vacant field with some burning oil cans in it."

"That's a good answer," Major Randal said. "You've got the concept of military magic down, Teddy."

"Major, there is no such thing as magic," Teddy said. "It's all illusion. The art is in designing and setting up the mechanics of the trick and the showmanship. Once you understand that, there's no difference in fooling one person, a thousand or the Iraqi Army."

"We need the deception to work day and night," Major Randal said. "Can you do that?"

"Nighttime will be a snap," Teddy said. "Pretty easy to make the Iraqis see what they want to see in the dark."

"I have a crew out procuring the materials for our first effort," Mr. Twinning said. "Teddy will supervise. Hope to have his first decoy in operation within the hour."

"What do you plan on being when you grow up, Ted?" Major Randal asked.

"Magician."

"Done many shows?"

"No, sir." Teddy said. "Today will be my first public performance."

"Make it a good one," Major Randal said. "This is your chance to be a hero."

"CAPTAINS FABIAN AND SMITH ARE STANDING BY FOR A briefing, per your orders," Mandy said.

"*Mother* is in your Command Post waiting to see you."

Major Randal waved at the officers. "Mandy, tell Fabian and Smith I'll be right with them."

He walked over to his red-and-white-striped CP tent next door.

Veronica was sitting in a canvas chair with her booted legs crossed.

Major Randal said, "We stationed Pony Express girls at the airfield and the polo pitch to deliver messages in the event the phone lines were knocked down. Also to hand-carry the latest developed aerial photos of the Iraqi positions."

"Mandy's club will make reliable messengers," Veronica said, taking out a cigarette.

Major Randal lit it with his battered Zippo. "Yeah, well, I've pulled the girls off that. We haven't been getting emergency calls from the airfield or the polo pitch. If they need us to do something, they can walk over here and tell us what they want in person.

"The pilots at the polo pitch are not making after-action reports because it's too much trouble, and Group Captain Saville is not accommodative."

"The Butcher is a pig-headed fool," Veronica said. "Always go by the book. Even if we lose the war in the process."

"What I need, Veronica," Major Randal said, "is for you to take charge of getting the after-action reports from the pilots at the polo pitch and dealing with Saville. Recruit whoever you need to help."

"I can do that, Major," Veronica said. "Did Mandy's horse being killed have anything to do with your decision to pull the Pony Express riders from the airfield and polo pitch?"

Major Randal said. "I never endanger my people for no gain."

"You do understand what is going to happen to the girls," Veronica said, "when the Iraqis grow weary of being bombed and realize all they have to do to make it stop is overrun the cantonment."

"I have some idea," Major Randal said.

"Smart attacked on the Muslim holy day," Veronica said. "The Grand Mufti is furious. He was on Radio Baghdad within the hour declaring a Jihad against Habbaniya. A Holy War means Allah has conveniently forgiven in advance any crimes the 'Soldiers-of-God' happen to commit."

"I didn't know about that."

"Now the Iraqi rebels have a free pass to murder, pillage and rape," Veronica said. "They will."

Major Randal said, "Yes, they will."

"You need to quit worrying about Mandy's girls and get on with doing what you do best—killing enemies of the state," Veronica said. "I hear you are quite accomplished at it."

"Right," Major Randal said. "Can you handle a pistol?"

"Of course."

"Buckle this on," Major Randal said, as he selected one of the holstered .9 mm Polish Radoms hanging off the end of his cot by its web belt, seized when they boarded the mother ship. "It's loaded."

"Is that a blood stain?"

"Ah ..."

"No bother," Veronica said. "Cold water will remove it."

MANDY WANTED TO SPEAK TO MAJ. JOHN RANDAL BEFORE his meeting with his two infantry troop commanders. He huddled with her in a corner of the Ops Center.

"John," she said. "Are you taking our situation seriously?"

"Seriously?"

"Those Iraqi rebels are planning to do really depraved things to me," Mandy said. "They will not be kind to anyone who has a book out saying 'Kill 'em all and let Allah sort 'em out.' Agreed?"

"Yeah," Major Randal said. "Probably won't be too happy about that."

"In that case," Mandy said, "why are you treating this whole thing like a joke?"

"What?"

"Painting squirrels orange and letting Teddy do magic tricks," Mandy said. "That is so sophomoric."

"Psychological warfare," Major Randal said. "Smartest guys in the world invented it, not me."

"Come on, John."

"No … it's true," Major Randal said. "In England, Political Warfare Executive—an organization so secret they would probably put me in the Tower for telling you its name—has a whole division that makes fake pornographic photos of high-ranking Germans, and then sends them to their mothers, wives and girlfriends."

"You are jesting!"

"In Abyssinia, Capt. Hawthorne Merryweather, Raiding Forces PWE officer, won a battle single-handedly by hanging out of an airplane with a loudspeaker and telling the defenders of an Italian fort they were being attacked by cannibals with 'Wop liver on the menu.'

"Out of Seaborn House we used to drop dead pigeons with fake messages strapped on their legs to a nonexistent German Resistance movement on Enemy Occupied France. And parachutes weighted down with blocks of ice."

"Did any of those tricks work?"

"They all did," Major Randal said. "Pam's going to be dropping parachutes weighted by blocks of ice tonight. The ice melts and all the Iraqis will find is an empty parachute—now that's a problem for them. Where did the guy in it go?"

"Sounds silly to me, John."

"The crazier the story, the better it seems to work," Major Randal said. "Someday, ask me about Operation Blue Boot—you'll never believe that one."

"I had no idea the military was involved in psychological warfare," Mandy said. "Interesting! Thanks for telling me, even if it is classified. I was concerned maybe you had gone off your rocker—battle fatigue."

"Now that I've told you," Major Randal said. "I have to kill you."

"*You* … shoot a woman?" Mandy said laughing. "Give me a break."

19

WARNING ORDER

MAJ. JOHN RANDAL BRIEFED CAPT. VALENTINE FABIAN AND
Capt. John Smith on the night patrols. They were looking at the giant
mosaic map made from the most recent aerial photos of the Iraqi
positions. The two-mile enemy front line was sectioned off into twenty-
four more or less equal sectors that were marked by blue knitting thread
that Red had pinned on the map.

The idea was to "Keep it Short and Simple" as dictated in Raiding
Forces Rules for Raiding. Major Randal tried to give the appearance of
calm, cool military professionalism, but in fact he had serious reservations.
Twenty-four individual patrols going out in such a concentrated area was
a lot. On paper it looked like a training mission, and in a way it was.

The King's Own Royal Rifles was an infantry battalion. Not the
Commandos or the Royal Marines trained in the art of night patrolling.
The Levies Company was composed of men whose loyalty might be in
question, and they were primarily intended to be a static defense unit.

Except for today's incoming artillery, none of the troops going out
tonight had ever been under fire.

The two companies were being tasked to break down into small patrols, go out and conduct individual night raids. Every military unit has to have its baptism of fire. What Major Randal had planned for tonight was asking quite a bit for a starter operation.

The working definition of a raid is a small-scale military operation of short duration, executed with extreme violence and with a preplanned withdrawal. They are more difficult to carry off than they sound on paper.

"*MISSION*," Major Randal said.

"Tonight Strike Force will be conducting 'Contact Patrols.' Each patrol will move into their sector and advance on the Iraqi positions by a route of the Patrol Leader's choosing, staying within their lane, until they make contact. Then they will withdraw and return to base.

"Contact will be defined as locating an enemy position and firing on it.

"We have broken the front into twenty-four sectors," Major Randal said. "For simplicity we lettered them from left to right A thorough X, same as your patrols are named. Patrols will operate in the sector named for them.

"Y Patrol, commanded by Lieutenant Kidd, will be operating against the Iraqi rear. My personal Z Patrol will be carrying out a raid on the extreme left flank of the Iraqi position.

"I want your lieutenants going on patrols—they know that already. The men need to see their officers in the field, leading from the front.

"What are your questions?"

"What is our timeline, sir?" Captain Fabian asked.

"Get with Red on that," Major Randal said. "We want the latest aerial photos available before you brief your patrol leaders, so time will be dictated by when we have them. Conduct patrol leader briefings individually. Then I'll give the Strike Force Patrol Order to the combined group so that they will have the big picture.

"Have the patrols draw ammunition and test fire their weapons prior to the briefings so that they have that detail out of the way. Then, after you brief your patrol leaders, they can plan their patrol, issue their Patrol Order and carry out rehearsals.

"Best to do that while it's still light if we can."

"How do you want to handle the final inspections, sir?" Captain Smith asked.

"You two men and your platoon leaders will have to do that tonight," Major Randal said. "I will be out with Z Patrol.

"Captain Smith, I will brief you separately later on what I want your A Patrol to do tonight. We need to coordinate their scheme-of-maneuver with Z Patrol's raid."

"Yes, sir."

Major Randal took out a cigarette. The captains did the same. He studied his two infantry company commanders. They were eager but inexperienced. This might not end well.

"Tonight," Major Randal said, "can only be described as short-range patrols—a few hundred yards out, make contact and back. Emphasize to your patrol leaders the importance of putting out as great a volume of fire, as fast as possible, then immediately breaking contact and withdrawing. No going in with the bayonet or hand-to-hand combat. I don't want anyone getting into a prolonged firefight.

"Is that clear?"

"Clear, sir," the two captains chorused.

There was a lot more Major Randal wanted to say, but he did not say it.

RED AND MAJ. JOHN RANDAL WERE SITTING IN HIS COMMAND Post tent. The Clipper Girl was one of those rare redheads who tanned but did not freckle. Major Randal had it on good authority from her boyfriend, Maj. Sir Terry "Zorro" Stone, that she did not have a single freckle on her entire body. He tried not to think about that.

Red was very capable, able to deal with stress and manage multiple tasks with no visible frustration—used to dealing with an airplane full of passengers who all thought they were very important people. That said, beneath her calm exterior was the heart of a full-blooded hell raiser.

She was giving Major Randal a status report on everything Strike Force was currently doing or in the process of planning to do. The list was long and covered a wide range of military subjects. Initially set up as a quick reaction force, they had picked up a number of other projects along the way.

It almost took a scorecard to keep up.

Major Randal kept his own counsel, but he knew that everything the Strike Force and its ancillary units combined were doing did not add up to a good-sized pinprick when stacked up against the overwhelming numbers and firepower the Iraqi rebels up on the escarpment enjoyed. The siege of RAF Habbaniya was a worse situation than the one he found when he landed at Calais. At least then, Swamp Fox Force had been made up of troops from the Rifle Brigade and the King's Royal Rifles, two of the finest regiments in the British Army.

And, it was highly mobile—not trapped in a wire enclosure with a river on three sides, an enemy army to its front, thousands of women and children in the mix and less than four days rations left to feed them.

Mandy stuck her head in the tent, "Captain Sorrels is here to see you, John."

"Sorrels?"

"Commands the provisional combined mortar battery," Mandy said. "You sent for him."

"I'll be with the Captain in zero five," Major Randal said.

"Veronica has reported from the polo pitch," Red said. "Wanted you to know you were right. The pilots are not reporting to Group Captain Saville after each of their missions. Not to worry, she will have every one debriefed the moment he lands."

"Where's Pam?"

"Not sure."

"Find her," Major Randal ordered. "I want Pam getting eight hours sleep from now on. "Move her into the Pony Express quarters. Make sure she has her own room and have the guard at the door. Instruct the girls when they come in off duty not to disturb her."

"Pam may not want to cooperate," Red said. "She likes to be in the thick of things."

"I'll have Flanigan handcuff her to the bed if necessary. Tell her I said that," Major Randal said. "She's going to be flying all night—needs her rest."

"I shall make sure Pam is fully informed of your orders, John."

"Red, I'm not getting any enemy intelligence," Major Randal said. "Talk to Mr. Zargo. Between the two of you, try to come up with some way to get me information on who's up there on the escarpment. All I know is three brigades of Iraqi rebels and that there's about 10,000 of 'em."

"We are not getting guidance of any kind from the AOC's office," Red said. "Like a black hole over there, completely dysfunctional. Hopefully Mr. Zargo will have a suggestion."

"What are you carrying?" Major Randal said.

Red looked at him, "Baby Colt .22. My issue weapon—it's in my purse."

"Buckle this on," Major Randal ordered, handing her one of the web belts containing a holstered 9 mm Polish Radom.

"Pistol's loaded," Major Randal said, "chamber's empty.

"Don't let me see you without it."

CAPT. RICHARD SORRELS WAS A LEVIES OFFICER SECONDED from the North Staffordshire Regiment. He had experience with mortars, having commanded a section of three-inch infantry mortars as a lieutenant serving in the West Kent Regiment. The one thing the Levies Companies had going for them was that their British officers were all handpicked volunteers seconded to it for a two-year tour of duty. They brought with them a rich and varied range of experience.

Maj. John Randal said, "I want a Time-on-Target fired on this position at approximately 0200 hours."

He tapped the map, "We'll be conducting a raid starting at 0200. The signal for you to commence firing to cover our withdrawal will be two green flares—likely at 0205 or thereabouts.

"Have an observer stationed in the Levies' bunker directly across from the objective to watch for the flares. Make sure he's in landline communication with your battery. In the event the phone line is knocked out, a Pony Express rider will be standing by to hand carry the message to your mortars to open."

"Two green flares," Captain Sorrels said. "I understand, sir."

"After that," Major Randal said, "You're cleared to fire H&I missions until sunrise. Do a map study, or maybe you can hitch a ride with Squadron Leader Dudgeon at the airfield to identify targets you can register on tonight. Knocking out their artillery would be a good thing. However, your primary mission is to keep the Iraqis awake and scared.

"Work over the whole rebel position from end to end," Major Randal said.

"The Time-on-Target as a screen for your raid is simple enough," Captain Sorrels said. "My men are pretty much rank amateurs when it comes to mortars, sir. Pinpoint targets like a battery of artillery may be beyond their capabilities."

"Understood," Major Randal said. "Keep the bad guys up at night and give 'em something to think about—enough for me."

"Quite right, sir," Captain Sorrels said. "You have given me a fire mission my people can deliver. We have a tremendous supply of mortar ammunition laid in. You will not be disappointed."

"We're going to have patrols out across the front tonight," Major Randal said. "You or your designated representative need to be at the Patrol Leaders Order to make sure you know where they'll be operating and plan your fires accordingly."

"Yes, sir," Captain Sorrels said. "Enough troubles without a blue-on-blue."

MANDY SAID, "COLONEL ROBERTS IS IN YOUR CP TENT TO see you. And Mr. Twinning wants you to meet him at the water tower to observe Teddy's first efforts at decoying the Iraqi artillery."

Col. Ouvry Roberts was chatting with Red when Maj. John Randal arrived.

"Major Everett is planning a daylight raid," Colonel Roberts said. "His plan is to have one company mounted on lorries sally forth at the Iraqis across from the airfield. The idea is to race straight at the escarpment, dismount and climb it. Attack the Iraqis, then climb back down, re-board the vehicles and return to the containment.

"I want your professional opinion, Major," Colonel Roberts said, "on his chances of success. Off the record, naturally."

"Let's go take a look at the map, sir," Major Randal said.

They walked to the Operations Center tent. Colonel Roberts pointed out the proposed location of the raid.

"Sir," Major Randal said, studying the pictomap, "we have no artillery. I was just in a meeting with the commander of our provisional mortar battery—they're not capable of providing close fire support due to the low skill level of the mortar crew.

"I have the Strike Force broken down into twenty-five patrols, all of which will be carrying out raids tonight. We're not available to go to the rescue if Major Everett gets pinned down.

"And, I will not order Squadron Leader Page to provide armored car support—they'd be going in right down the mouths of an estimated fifty Iraqi cannon. We have to save No. 1 ACC until the time when we do commit the cars / the gain is worth the risk."

"Afraid you were going to say that," Colonel Roberts said. "Ted's a fine officer. Wants to have at the enemy, as do I. But nothing is gained by a forlorn hope attack that stands no chance of success, and wastes lives and precious resources."

"We're going to have to tackle the Iraqis head-on sooner rather than later," Major Randal said. "Ted's not wrong about that, but today is not the day, sir."

"I shall order him to stand down," Colonel Brown said.

"Why not suggest he hitch a ride with Squadron Leader Dudgeon," Major Randal said. "Visual recon of the objective. Ted will make the decision to abort the operation once he sees firsthand what he's going up against."

"Excellent," Colonel Roberts said. "No need to dampen anyone's martial spirit."

"Roger that," Major Randal said. "It's about all we've got going for us around here, sir."

MAJ. JOHN RANDAL, MANDY AND THE POLICE OFFICER, Flanigan, walked to the water tower. In the distance, a column of thick black smoke was rising. Teddy was carrying out his first-ever public magic illusion.

Leaving Flanigan at the foot of the ladder, Major Randal and Mandy climbed up to the catwalk at the top. Mr. Twinning was there studying developments through a pair of binoculars. The smoke was beginning to kick in. The oily black column towered over the cantonment.

Within minutes a single artillery shell swished over, sounding a lot like a freight train as it went by and exploded in the general vicinity of the source of the smoke. A second round followed. Then sporadically, other artillery pieces targeted the smoke.

The Iraqi artillery was firing free gun. They were not conducting battery fire. The effect was an intermittent but constant rain of artillery shells on the base.

"A round that lands out in that empty open area," Mr. Twinning said, "is one that does not hit a valuable target. This may work, Major. I confess … I had my doubts.

"I intend to post an observer up here to log the fall of the shells the decoys draw off. Provide us a way to judge which diversion is most effective."

"Every little bit helps," Major Randal said. "Good job, Mr. Twinning."

"Teddy did it," Mandy said, looking through Major Randal's Zeiss binoculars. "Who would have ever believed? Not me, that's for sure."

More and more Iraqi guns began registering on the smoke column.

While the group on the tower watched, a massive secondary explosion erupted, sending up an even greater mushroom cloud of black smoke. This resulted in a frenzy of artillery rounds fired at the decoy target.

"Iraqis are really miserable shots," Mandy said. "Actually believe they hit something, the fools. Unbelievable."

"Yeah," Major Randal said. "That fake secondary of Teddy's was a really nice touch."

20

DAY ONE DONE

MAJ. JOHN RANDAL DISPATCHED RED TO REPRESENT THE
Strike Force at AVM Harry "Reggie" Smart's evening briefing. Since
Mandy was sleeping, ahead of what promised to be a long eventful night,
Red invited Veronica Paige to accompany her. Military briefings cover a
lot of details, and two heads are better than one.

She did not want to miss anything.

As it turned out, there was not much to miss. Air Vice Marshal Smart
did not attend. When Col. Ouvry Roberts took the chair, a hush settled
in. RAF Habbaniya was a Royal Air Force Base. For the Air Officer
Commanding to delegate responsibility for the most important briefing
in the history of the cantonment to an Army officer was telling.

Red knew that it was one thing for a subordinate commander like
Major Randal to send a representative to a briefing because of other
pressing duties, but it is quite another for the senior officer commanding
to fail to attend his own briefing. Everyone present was aware that
something was badly wrong, but what?

"Unbelievable," Veronica whispered. "The Ambassador's wife must be spot-on."

"What?"

"Tell you later."

When Grp. Capt. William "Butcher" Saville gave his report on the status of the provisional squadrons of No. 4 Service Flying Training School, the somber mood in the briefing turned to open despair. Losses had been catastrophic. Of sixty-four irreplaceable aircraft, twenty-two were out of commission, having been shot down, burned out, damaged by antiaircraft fire, hit by artillery on the ground, damaged in bad landings, etc.

Thirty-nine pilots (all there were) had participated in the fourteen-hour air campaign. At the end of the flying day, ten of them were dead or seriously wounded, unable to continue. More than a few of those pilots still flying had been wounded but continued to fight ... some more than once.

Ten Wellington heavy bombers had flown in support of the initial morning air attack on the Iraqi positions. One was shot up before dropping a single bomb, made a forced landing on the RAF Habbaniya airfield (which was too short for them to operate off of) and exploded. All nine of the other heavy bombers were so damaged by rebel anti-aircraft fire that they were grounded when they returned to their base and did not participate in the afternoon's air campaign.

All the losses were for no discernable gain.

The Iraqi Army had not abandoned its position in three hours like Air Vice Marshal Smart had prophesied. Enemy artillery fire was increasing in volume. And there were signs that rebel morale was improving as the Royal Iraqi Air Force ramped up the number of missions they flew against RAF Habbaniya toward the end of the day.

The squadrons of No. 4 Service Flying Training School were fighting hard, but their losses were shattering. At this rate, RAF Habbaniya would be defenseless in two more days. The senior air staff appeared disoriented. And there was no command guidance because the commanding officer had absented himself.

There was a sense of impending doom.

The unasked question looming over the assemblage was: "What was keeping the Iraqi Army from launching a ground attack?" No one knew the answer.

The briefing was over almost as soon as it started.

On the way out, Sqn. Ldr. Tony Dudgeon said to Red, "Not wasting time attending another one of these cock-ups."

Translated, this meant that now *everyone* was fighting his own private war. No. 4 Service Flying Training School, Levies, King's Own Royal Rifles and Strike Force—all operating freelance with no central command and control. It is not uncommon for different branches of service like the Army and Air Force not to be on the same page in a campaign. However, when the RAF fighting squadrons decide to ignore the RAF Headquarters staff that is supposed to command them—that is a military meltdown.

"I was talking earlier with the Ambassador's wife. She evacuated Baghdad last month to take shelter in Habbaniya with the other 250 or so women and children from the Embassy, thinking it would be safer here," Veronica said, when she and Red were alone outside.

"She disclosed to me privately that Reggie had gone off his rocker this afternoon. Claimed he was ranting and raving, blaming Field Marshal Wavell for our predicament. Said the doctor had to give him a shot—a sedative to knock him out."

"What to say to John?" Red said. "Pretty awful in there."

"He needs to hear from you exactly what transpired. No sugar-coating it," Veronica said. "Then I shall tell him the Ambassador's wife's story.

"Major Randal is capable of drawing his own conclusions. The Major requires facts and information with all the details. Our duty is to see that he stays fully informed at all times. "

Red asked, "Have you ever heard of a more desperate situation than the one we are facing?

"No," Veronica said. "Not ever—this is the worst. We are isolated, surrounded, fighting a Holy War, running out of food, no artillery of our own, a quarter of our pilots lost in a single day, our commanding officer has been sedated and the clock is ticking."

Red said, "So much for Habbaniya being a paradise in the desert."

Veronica said, "Best swimming pool in the service."

MAJ. JOHN RANDAL WAS IN A CANVAS CHAIR IN HIS COMMAND
Post tent, having completed the evening's inspection of the Boy Scouts
and the Annie Oakleys. He was listening to Red and Veronica's recital
of the Air Officer Commanding's evening briefing, which the AOC had
failed to attend. He did not seem alarmed to learn the extent of the day's
losses in pilots and aircraft. The story about AVM Harry "Reggie" Smart
being sedated failed to draw much of a reaction.

Strike Force had its own briefing scheduled in five minutes.

"Good clear report," Major Randal said, when the two women
concluded their recital. "OK, Red, make sure you brief friendly losses, but
there's no reason to mention the AOC—his condition is not confirmed."

"Understood."

Col. Ouvry Roberts ducked into the back of the Operations Center
tent just in time to hear someone at the front call, "ATTENTION!"

Since many of the people in the packed tent were civilians and this
was the first Strike Force evening briefing, there was some confusion over
exactly what they were supposed to do. Eventually, everyone stood up.

Major Randal walked in, accompanied by Veronica and a skinny
teenager wearing Coke-bottle glasses, "The Great Teddy."

He immediately ordered, "As you were."

The three took their seats next to Mr. Twinning, center front row.

Red began with a recital of the day's events, concluding with the
battle damage and casualty report from the Royal Air Force. The Clipper
Girl was so glamorous that some of the men in the audience were having
trouble concentrating.

She was followed by Sqn. Ldr. John Page who gave a report on No. 1
Armored Car Company operations at the airfield and polo pitch, followed
by the commander of the RAF Habbaniya Motorcycle Patrol (Colonel
Roberts had heard the motorcycles making their rounds all day but did
not know what they were), followed by the sergeant advising the Annie
Oakleys, who was followed by the sergeant advising the Boy Scouts.

Veronica provided a detailed report on the state of affairs at the
airfield and the polo pitch, to include the steps she had taken to ensure
Strike Force had post-mission intelligence on Iraqi dispositions from all
pilots after each and every mission.

Colonel Roberts grasped for the first time exactly how dysfunctional the communications between the RAF's different elements had become. Not only were the fighting squadrons ignoring higher headquarters, they were not reporting all the missions they flew or providing after-action reports following each sortie to Grp. Capt. William "Butcher" Saville.

Mandy gave a rundown on the status of the Pony Express. She concluded with, "One of our horses, Blackie, was killed in action, but the Pony Express always gets through. Our riders will press on with the mission, regardless. "

To a man, the troops—and more than a few of the civilians—in the room stood up cheering, catcalling and wolf whistling—it was a sure bet they were not thinking about poor Blackie.

Mr. Twinning reported on the state of the base's civil affairs. Then, each of his department heads came up and gave an account of their individual area of responsibility. Even the base meteorologist ventured a prediction that the following day would be, "clear and hot with zero percent likelihood of precipitation," which drew a laugh from the audience.

The president of the photography club gave a short explanation of how the photos for the pictomap were developed on site at the airfield before being delivered to the Strike Force Operations Center.

The captain of the Rod & Gun Club Big Bore Rifle Team provided an astonishing claim of 467 Iraqi personnel shot at and hit. The riflemen could only report hits or misses. They had no way to confirm kills.

Colonel Roberts was struck by how involved people were. This briefing was the exact opposite of the one put on by the AOC's staff. The men and women in the Operation Center tent had sky-high morale. Everyone was contributing.

Conspicuously missing, however, was any enemy intelligence.

Captains Fabian and Smith briefed the night's planned patrols. Strike Force had an ambitious series of small-scale raids planned all along the Iraqi MLR.

Lt. Pamala Plum-Martin briefed the night's special air operations:

1). Dropping empty beer bottles from high altitude—the bottles would whistle on the way down, making the same sound as falling bombs to keep the Iraqis awake.

2). Dropping parachutes weighted down with ice blocks that would melt and leave empty parachutes along the flanks and rear of the Iraqi positions to give the rebels something to think about in the morning.

3). Parachuting squirrels behind Iraqi lines as part of a Psychological Warfare Operation to put psychological pressure on the rebel troops.

As Mr. Thymes was explaining the "Orange Squirrel Special Warfare Program," Mandy and Red passed out copies of the skull-and-crossbones warning to be dropped with the squirrels. Everyone in the room was cracking up as they read the paper.

Reading his copy, Colonel Roberts smiled for the first time in a while and realized he felt better. Why? He had no confidence the orange squirrel scheme was anything more than a military dirty trick—pretty funny. Might not hurt enemy morale, but it sure raised that of the Strike Force.

Major Randal briefed the night's snatch mission to capture the two Iraqi Crossley armored cars, planned for 0200 hours. He left out any reference to the existence of a ship on Lake Habbaniyah with Strike Force troops stationed on board.

No mention was made of the raid to be carried out later that night on the Royal Iraqi Air Force field at Baqubah by Z Patrol—Classified.

"And now," Major Randal said, changing subjects, "I want to introduce a real stud. Strike Force's war magician, 'The Great Teddy.'This afternoon, he set up a decoy fuel installation. A hoax designed to draw the Iraqi artillery away from firing at targets the bad guys want to take out and trick 'em into shooting at what *we* want 'em to—which means nothing of military value.

"Step up here, Ted," Major Randal ordered. "Give us a report on your current military magic operation and future plans."

Colonel Roberts was riveted. This was the first he had heard of the deception program. What caught his attention was the time, support and resources Major Randal and Mr. Twinning seemed willing to invest in a fifteen-year-old boy in the middle of a fight to the death.

Teddy explained how he had set up burning oil drums in a vacant area of the base to create the illusion the Iraqi artillery had damaged a fuel storage depot in order to draw down more rebel cannon fire.

Mr. Twinning interrupted, "We stationed an observer on the water tower to log the fall of all incoming artillery. From the time we started counting, approximately one third of all enemy rounds have been aimed at Teddy's fake installation."

The pronouncement was met with applause and cheering from the audience but no wolf whistles or catcalls.

"Tonight," Teddy continued, peering out from behind his thick glasses, "My plan is to introduce fireworks to the illusion. With the airfield being shut down after dark not occupying the rebel gunner's attention, the goal is to dupe them to concentrate full time on blowing up our decoy fuel storage area.

"*Abracadabra—hey, presto!*"

Colonel Roberts left the tent without having announced himself. He was impressed. At the same time, he knew everything the Strike Force was doing was mostly for show.

All the Iraqi Army had to do was advance forward on line for 500 yards. It would be all over in minutes. There was nothing anyone on RAF Habbaniya could do to stop them.

Even so, his morale was lifted—orange squirrels?

MAJ. JOHN RANDAL CONDUCTED A BRIEFING AFTER THE briefing. It was a "Frag Order," meaning a fragment of the Patrol Order—covering just the paragraphs he wanted to discuss. Present were Capt. Valentine Fabian; Capt. John Smith; Capt. Richard Sorrels, the commander of the mortar battery, and the twenty-four patrol leaders, each wearing a violet patrol leader cord laced on his left epaulette. Red and Mandy had rearranged the Operations Center so that the men were seated in folding chairs facing the large pictomap.

Mr. Zargo was leaning against one of the tent poles, observing.

"*SITUATION,*" Major Randal said.

"The bad guys are out there. We're in here."

The men laughed, breaking the tension, which was thick in the room. Tonight, the patrol leaders were going to lead their first combat mission.

This was, for them, the night every military leader from corporal to field marshal sweats bullets over, sometimes for years and years, until it finally happens—initiation into the closed society of those who have commanded in battle.

You can only become a veteran combat leader by traveling to a combat zone, going on a mission and participating in combat at a command level. Putting that behind them is a big deal to military leaders of all grades. Tonight, the Strike Force patrol leaders not only wanted to get the experience over with, they wanted to perform well.

There was a very real chance not everyone in the briefing would be coming back. The men understood that. It kept them in tight focus.

"*MISSION*," Major Randal said, scanning his audience, making eye contact with each man. "This is a contact mission—a raid by fire. You will advance down a narrow lane until you come into contact with the Iraqi MLR. Your mission is to fire on the enemy, inflict casualties, break contact and return, staying within the confines of the lane you have been assigned."

"*EXECUTION*," Major Randal said.

"Line of Departure time is 0200 hours. Move your patrols at your own speed. As you can see from the photos, the Iraqi lines are almost unbroken along our front. However, in some places the bad guys are closer to our wire than others. We are not trying to time this with any precision, but I expect you should all have made contact by 0230 hours.

"You need to be pulling out by then, because starting at that time the three-inch mortar battery under Captain Sorrels will commence Harassment & Interdiction fire missions. Best to be well away from the area when that happens."

"*CONCEPT OF THE OPERATION*," Major Randal said.

"We want to surprise the Iraqis with our aggressiveness, to inflict casualties and motivate them to pull their lines back from Habbaniya.

"Each patrol is armed with one submachine gun, either a Thompson or MP-18, and at least one shotgun. Put those weapons at the front of your patrol, with orders to empty them as fast as they can in the event of a meeting engagement. Have the rest of your men who are armed with rifles carry extra hand grenades and designate 'em as grenadiers. I want 'em throwing grenades with both hands when you exercise your raid, then break contact and come home. Shoot 'em up and get the hell out of Dodge.

"Is that clear?"

"CLEAR, SIR!"

"My guess is that tomorrow night when you go out, no one will be carrying their Enfield—they'll all want shotguns. That's fine. Let your troops decide for themselves what weapon they prefer. Learn from experience and make adjustments. For these kinds of patrols, grenades are the main things, so use 'em—a lot of 'em.

"In Raiding Forces we call it the 'P-for-Plenty Formula.'"

The men laughed.

Major Randal looked at his patrol leaders. There was a lot he wanted to say. What he said was, "Good luck and good hunting."

Veronica was waiting to speak to him in the CP tent.

"You don't believe we have a chance, do you?" She said. "There is no hope for Habbaniya—tell me the truth."

"No," Major Randal said. "The Iraqis hold all the cards. We can't defeat the rebels. Breaking out is impossible. There's no rescue coming."

"Thank you for being honest, Major."

"I've made arrangements for Mandy to fly out with Pam when the Iraqis launch their assault. You be on the plane too."

"That is thoughtful," Veronica said. "I could never abandon my husband."

"Be on the plane," Major Randal ordered. "Tell the Wing Commander your plans. That way when the time comes, he can fly himself out without having to worry about you and Mandy."

"Quite right," Veronica said, "He shall be relieved."

"Can Mandy handle a handgun?"

"Naturally," Veronica said. "She was on her school pentathlon team— her events were riding, skiing, swimming, fencing and pistol shooting. The Swiss favor military sports.

"Why do you ask?"

"You might want to have a talk with her," Major Randal said. "Being captured is not an option."

"I understand," Veronica said, "in the event she fails to make it to Pam's plane. What about you—what is your plan?"

"I'm on vacation," Major Randal said.

MANDY WALKED INTO THE CP TENT. MAJ. JOHN RANDAL HAD the canvas chair pulled up next to the cot, checking his equipment laid out there. Attention to detail with his weapons and personal gear was a passion.

It promised to be a busy night.

"Mother said you wanted to see me."

"I do," Major Randal said. "Got something for you, Mandy."

He reached down into his trunk and pulled out the two pearl-handled Saur 38 (H) pocket pistols that Mr. Zargo had found in the Iraqi Air Marshal's safes. The weapons were fully engraved—a gift from Field Marshal Hermann Goering.

"Put one in your purse and buckle the other on," Major Randal said. "Don't let me see you without it."

"These are beautiful," Mandy said. "I love them!"

"Been meaning to give you the Saurs," Major Randal said. "Excellent craftsmanship, lightweight, won't get in the way horseback. Not that you'll be doing much more riding now that you're my military aide."

"You noticed," Mandy said. "Parker ordered me to take care of you before she left."

"Yeah, well ..."

"Excellent," Mandy said. "Now I am on the team—officially."

"Why might that be?"

"Because," Mandy said, "You give all your women pistols."

21

MISSION PREP

MAJ. JOHN RANDAL WAS IN THE RED-AND-WHITE-STRIPED CP tent. Outside around the cantonment, a steady drumbeat of incoming could be heard detonating from time to time. Mandy stuck her head in. "Murder Inc. is here."

Major Randal said, "Tell 'em to come on in."

Z Patrol was smiling as they filed in for their mission briefing. The tough soldiers-of-fortune liked Mandy. And, they liked being called "Murder Inc."

Lt. Pamala Plum-Martin arrived. The mercs liked her too. They ogled the Royal Marine like a pack of Doberman pinschers eyeballing a piece of prime rib.

She paid them no more attention than if they were boxes of freight.

Mr. Zargo was last to arrive.

Major Randal stepped outside to have a word with Flanigan. "No one comes inside—or hangs around."

"Rest assured, Major."

"You overhear anything we're talking about," Major Randal said, "you didn't hear it."

"I understand," the policeman said. "Permission to shoot prowlers, sir?" The stress of the unrelenting incoming artillery fire was starting to affect people—everybody wanted to take their frustration out on something or someone ... anyone.

"Negative," Major Randal said. "Just beat 'em around the head and shoulder area."

Mandy returned—Major Randal said, "Not her, Flanigan."

The big policeman grinned.

She said, "What?"

Back inside the CP tent, Major Randal was all business.

"*SITUATION.*"

The Iraqi Air Force outnumbers our Air Force three to one. That was before they killed or wounded twenty-five percent of our pilots and destroyed one-third of our aircraft today.

"The Iraqis' contract aircraft mechanics from the U.S. have departed the country, so maintenance is problematic for them in the short term.

"*MISSION.*"

"Tonight at 0245 hours, Z Patrol, aka Murder Inc., will land at Baqubah Air Base in a Seagull piloted by Lieutenant Plum-Martin. You will exit the aircraft as it taxis down the landing strip and engage the rebel aircraft parked along the runway with individual weapons, destroying or damaging as many as possible.

"*EXECUTION.*"

"Z Patrol will conduct an individual tap out, exiting the aircraft one man at a time as the Seagull rolls down the airstrip. Once on the ground, you will immediately engage as many targets as possible, taking care to aim at the engine cowling where your rounds can inflict the most serious damage.

"Lieutenant Plum-Martin will continue down the airfield dropping people off until the entire team is deployed. She will make a U-turn, pause briefly, then taxi back up the strip. Be prepared to re-board the plane on the roll as the Seagull comes back past. It's a one-shot deal, gentlemen—make it on or be left behind.

"Is that clear?"

"CLEAR, SIR!"

"I'll be first out," Major Randal said, "and last back on board. Mr. Zargo will designate the sequence you men exit during the rehearsal immediately following this briefing.

"*CONCEPT OF THE OPERATION.*"

"Z Patrol's mission is to damage enemy aircraft. It's not necessary to destroy 'em to accomplish our objective.

"To give the impression we're a larger force, load your magazines every second round tracer. Put one entire magazine into each airplane, aiming at the engine. Reload, move on and engage the next target."

"This is a hit-and-run raid of short duration. Everyone who goes in comes out. Shoot 'em up and get the hell out of Dodge.

"What are your questions?"

Murder Inc. consisted of professional soldiers for hire. They knew a good Operations Order when they heard one. There were no questions.

Next up was Lieutenant Plum-Martin. "Tonight you will be flying aboard a Supermarine Seagull pusher-type amphibian configured with interior seats removed. All Z personnel will be sitting on the deck of the aircraft for ease of rapid exiting and re-boarding.

"Five minutes out, I will advise Major Randal we are making our final approach and then give him a one-minute warning to touchdown. The first operators to exit will have to do so at a fairly high clip—I shall try to bring the speed down as quickly as possible.

"Once the last man has exited the aircraft, the Seagull will loop around and pause, as Major Randal explained. After waiting three minutes, the ship will begin taxiing back up the airstrip picking up people one by one.

"Go in, do your mischief, load up fast on the roll-by, and I will fly you out," Lieutenant Plum-Martin said.

"Thank you for choosing Raiding Forces Airlines."

REHEARSALS COMMENCED IMMEDIATELY FOLLOWING THE briefing. Lt. Pamala Plum-Martin had selected a straight stretch of the perimeter road at the far back of the cantonment to use as a secret airstrip.

It was as far away from the Iraqi front lines as possible. The Euphrates River ran along the back of the base, which gave it a little extra security from enemy patrols.

And even in daylight she could take off and land without being in line-of-sight view of the rebel gunners on the heights because eucalyptus trees screened that stretch of the perimeter road.

The special operations missions Lieutenant Plum-Martin would be flying were classified. No good would come of everyone at the airfield or the polo pitch being aware of what Strike Force was doing. The RAF pilots were all subject to being shot down, captured and interrogated. What they did not know they could not reveal.

Lieutenant Plum-Martin had cut her teeth as a combat pilot flying missions into the wilds of Abyssinia. She was used to operating in the dark of night. Making water landings on unknown lakes or improvised landing strips (usually roads) behind enemy lines was business as usual.

Acting on her instructions, Mr. Twinning had assigned a crew to set up fifty-five-gallon steel drums along the improvised landing strip. The barrels were one-third filled with a cocktail of diesel fuel, gasoline and kerosene. A simple signal was developed. When Lieutenant Plum-Martin flew over in the dark and raced her engine, that was the signal for the crew to light off the fuel in the bottom of the steel barrels.

The fire in the drums could only be seen from directly overhead— perfect clandestine landing lights. The Iraqis would never know for sure what was occurring even though they might hear the Seagull's engine. As soon as she landed, the ground crew would place the steel tops on the drums to extinguish the flame and conserve the fuel.

That way the landing lights were always immediately available for reuse.

Z Patrol practiced loading drills. They practiced exiting the plane (only stationary—taxiing the plane up and down the improvised strip would have alerted the Iraqis something was afoot and might have drawn artillery fire). They practiced re-boarding individually.

They practiced. They practiced. And then they practiced.

On a raid, it's the little things that are important—figuring out the best way to position your personal equipment for a given mission, knowing in advance where a handhold is located, or where to put your boot in the dark when you are in a hurry. Details can be the difference between life and death, success or failure. Professionals know that.

Murder Inc. did not complain about the repetitiousness of the training or the simplicity of what they were rehearsing.

In fact, when it was time for Maj. John Randal and King to depart, the remainder of Z Patrol continued to practice walk-through drills of loading and unloading.

"King and I are heading out to make final coordination with the perimeter bunker, where we're going to re-enter friendly lines," Major Randal said to Lieutenant Plum-Martin. "On the way back, I'll link up with Captain Valentine, bring him here, and then you can fly us out to Brandy's yacht."

"Wilco."

"Fabian's going to brief Lieutenant Kidd's men," Major Randal said. "Fly him back here when he's finished."

In the distance, an explosion shook the night and a massive fireball went up. It came from the direction of "The Great Teddy's" decoy fuel dump. Iraqi artillery began slamming in, trying to completely obliterate it.

Naturally, the rebel gunners did not hit a thing.

"Ted's an overachiever," Major Randal said, lighting a cigarette with his battered U.S. 26th Cavalry Regiment Zippo, admiring the fireworks.

"How did you ever find Teddy?" Lieutenant Plum-Martin asked, producing her own Player's, which he lit.

"Same way I found you," Major Randal said. "He just turned up."

MAJ. JOHN RANDAL SHOWED KING ON THE MAP WHERE TO be on the shore of Lake Habbaniyah to rendezvous with his raiding party landing by boat. "Flash your red filtered flashlight out toward the middle of the lake three times. Wait five minutes and repeat until we come in."

"Right, three every five."

"The two drivers and Lt. Kidd will be with me."

"Any more than four," King said, "somebody will get hurt."

Flanigan drove Major Randal and King to the bunker. Incredibly, RAF Habbaniya had not been ordered to go on blackout this first night of the battle. The policeman drove with his lights off anyway.

Final coordination with the NCO in charge only took a few minutes. Signal information was reconfirmed. The password was verified. Tonight, the challenge was "BROADSWORD" and the countersign was "TO THE HILT."

"We'll be coming fast in two Crossley armored cars," Major Randal said. "We're not going to be able to hear any challenge so tell your troops to forget that part—they see my green flares and a pair of armored cars heading this way, open the gate or we'll knock it down."

"Understood, sir."

"Squadron Leader Page of No.1 Armored Car Company will arrive no later than 0100 hours," Major Randal said. "He'll take charge of the two Crossleys.

"Be expecting him, sir."

"King," Major Randal said, "see you on the shore."

"I'll see you first, Major."

THE SEAGULL PURRED THROUGH THE NIGHT, SKIMMING across the surface of Lake Habbaniyah. Coming up fast in the distance was a large yacht—the mother ship operated as a floating patrol base by Brandy Seaborn and Lt. Penelope Honeycutt-Parker. There were no lights showing on the boat. In fact, there were no lights anywhere on the lake. When the Iraqi Army moved in, all boating activity had ceased.

The lake was dead.

That is exactly how Maj. John Randal wanted it. His Lake Patrol was set up to operate with impunity from a No Man's Land. They could come and go under cover of darkness, completely undetected.

The gamble was that the Iraqi Army would never take Lake Habbaniyah into consideration militarily. The rebels had no amphibious capability of their own, and Major Randal was betting that they discounted the idea the Royal Air Force personnel trapped in the cantonment might figure out some way to use the vast body of water to their advantage. The

Iraqis' eyes were fixated straight ahead on their target—Royal Air Force Base Habbaniya.

That was a mistake.

Lt. Pamala Plum-Martin splashed down next to the big yacht. When she taxied up to it, Major Randal climbed out on a float and caught the rope Brandy tossed him to use to tie off. Within minutes they were on all deck.

Capt. Valentine Fabian immediately issued his orders to Lt. Roy Kidd's two corporal Patrol Leaders. Tonight they would be conducting the first Lake Patrol missions. The objectives were high value. Both were raids on artillery positions.

Captain Fabian had aerial photos of the batteries to be attacked. While the assignment was ambitious, the scheme of maneuver was simple. The two patrols would be landed on shore, move overland infiltrating the Iraqi positions, conduct a hand grenade attack on their assigned battery and withdraw.

There was a reasonable possibility that because of the dark and fog of war, the grenades would be mistaken for aerial bombs or incoming mortar fire. The Iraqis knew that RAF Habbaniya did not have any artillery capability of its own but did have mortars.

Success depended on stealth.

After their briefing, the two King's Own corporals departed to draft their individual Patrol Orders to issue to their patrols. Major Randal met with Brandy to show her on the map where he wanted to be dropped off with his team.

As soon as Brandy completed that mission, she and Lieutenant Honeycutt-Parker would begin inserting the King's Own patrols.

Brandy took Major Randal down to the Captain's Suite to show him the safe that the locksmith had opened.

"Mr. Zargo wanted me to take possession of everything inside," Brandy said. "We discovered nothing of military value."

"What was in the safe?" Major Randal asked, as they made their way below.

"Drugs, reels of pornographic movies, a collection of gold jewelry, a pistol and this," Brandy said, producing a small black velvet bag from her handbag.

"What?"

"Diamonds."

"Really?" Major Randal said, pouring the glittering stones out into the palm of his hand. "Valuable? I don't know anything about jewelry."

"Extremely," Brandy said.

Major Randal looked inside the open safe. He picked up the profusely engraved Walther PPK 7.65 pocket pistol—another gift from the commander of the Luftwaffe.

"I'll keep the handgun. You turn the diamonds over to Jane first chance. She'll know what to do. I have no idea what the rules on the spoils of war are when it gets to that level."

"Jane will know," Brandy said. "Or more likely know someone who can advise us. A portion goes to the crown, but in our military system, at least in part, it's finders, keepers—prize money."

"Take charge of the jewelry, Brandy. Found a bunch in the basement suite at the Officers Club too—we're not giving it back to the Iraqis. I don't care what the rules are; you girls can have it."

"What about the pornographic movies?" Brandy said.

"If you can find a movie projector," Major Randal said, "you and Parker watch 'em."

BRANDY SEABORN WAS A WORLD CLASS OPEN-SEA SPEED boat racer. She liked to go fast in a boat. Tonight she was charged with putting Maj. John Randal and his team ashore in absolute stealth. That meant she had to go slow.

For the last half mile, the raiders used paddles.

Brandy was to drop Major Randal off, wait half an hour, then motor back out to the mother ship to help Lt. Penelope Honeycutt-Parker ferry the other two patrols to their dismount points.

Major Randal said, "Follow me."

The men slipped over the gunwale and waded silently ashore. Major Randal was on point with Lt. Roy Kidd in the Number 2 slot, followed by the two drivers from No. 1 Armored Car Company. Right about now the two drivers were having second thoughts about volunteering for this crazy mission.

The patrol moved inland for a short distance, then set up a perimeter. "Wait here," Major Randal ordered Lieutenant Kidd. "I'll be back."

The night was pitch dark. The moon had gone down. It was chilly.

King moved silently up to the edge of the shore. Following instructions, he pointed his red-filtered flashlight out to the middle of the lake and blinked it three times. Nothing happened.

The soldier-of-fortune waited the prescribed five minutes and blinked three times again.

On the third blink, he felt something cold pressed on the back of his neck. Despite being a tough-as-nails mercenary soldier, he could not help shivering. Quickly getting himself under control, he froze dead still.

There was the click of a pistol hammer being cocked, "BROADSWORD."

King panicked momentarily, struggling to remember the countersign, "TO THE HILT."

He was a professional. He was not supposed to have been that afraid or this relieved.

"Didn't really think I was going to land exactly where you expected?" Major Randal said, uncocking his silenced .22 High Standard Military Model D.

Actually, he had.

22

DARK OF NIGHT

KING LED OUT. THE ORDER-OF-MARCH WAS THE MERC, MAJ. John Randal, the two drivers from No. 1 Armored Car Company and Lt. Roy Kidd. The patrol snaked its way silently to the confluence of the Euphrates and Lake Habbaniyah, and then turned back toward their objective, keeping the river on their right flank.

This was the extreme right flank of the Iraqi Army. The rebels had done things by the book, the way they had been taught by their British trainers. The main force was screened on both flanks by detachments of armored cars reinforced with a small infantry element in support.

Major Randal was betting that since they were operating detached, the rebel infantry with the armored cars were simply camping out. The next-to-last thing they would be expecting was to be attacked by the British forces trapped in RAF Habbaniya. The last thing the flank security screen would be expecting was to be attacked from the *rear* by British forces trapped in RAF Habbaniya.

By design, the Crossley armored car position had not been targeted for air strikes or the Rod & Gun Big Bore Rifle Club snipers. The idea was for the rebels in the flank security position to feel like observers to the battle. If the enemy soldiers did not sense they were part of the fight, they might let their guard down.

At least that was Major Randal's plan. His patrol was getting ready to find out if it was a good one.

Patrolling is an art, not a science. The skill can be learned, but it helps if you have natural talent. Major Randal, Lieutenant Kidd and King were masters at silent movement in the dark. The two drivers were stumbling along behind, striving to be quiet but sounding like a herd of elephants to the other three men.

It was good the Iraqis were not on alert.

King led the patrol for approximately a mile and three-quarters, then brought it to a halt. Major Randal moved forward immediately to confer. He could see the dark shapes of the cars dead ahead.

"The infantry is positioned off to the right, hugging the river," King whispered. "Exactly where they are supposed to be—right out of the handbook."

"How many bad guys between us and the cars?" Major Randal asked.

"Only the crews," King said. "Six ... seven men, tops. All sound asleep when I came through earlier."

"Probably not a great idea to try to sneak in," Major Randal said, "with the two drivers making such a racket."

"Affirmative."

Major Randal snapped his fingers twice. Lieutenant Kidd glided forward out of the dark like a phantom.

"Wait here," Major Randal ordered. "If the rebels stir or a shot is fired, charge the position immediately. Kill everyone, grab the cars and head for the base."

"Yes sir."

"I'll be right back. But you take the flare pistol in the event something happens. Pop two greens—that's the drill."

"Can do."

Major Randal moved forward. He found the crews asleep, clustered in groups of three around the Crossley armored cars. No security was posted. The Iraqi commander of this position was guilty of murder.

Just as Major Randal was ready to go to work, King appeared at his side, "You really think I was going to let you do this all by yourself, Major?"

Actually he had.

"I'll take this car," Major Randal said in a whisper. "Can you handle that one?"

"The fools are asleep—no problem."

"Right, move out."

Major Randal swanned over to the Crossley. The rubber soles of his canvas-topped raiding boots made nothing more than a soft rustle in the sand. He could see the forms of the rebel soldiers racked out in their bedrolls.

No one was awake.

Holding his .22 High Standard Military Model D with its silencer at the ready in both hands, Major Randal approached the car and stood next to the small bed of coals which were all that was left from the fire the men had built to keep warm.

Whiiicccch. Whiiicccch. Whiiicccch. The pistol made a sound no louder than a match striking. Point blank. The three enemy troopers no longer posed a threat.

He wished he had brought along a couple of dead orange squirrels— would have been the perfect setup.

Major Randal moved over to the other Crossley in time to see King slit the throat of his second victim. The nickel-plated, double-edged blade of the Fairbairn knife flashed, reflecting the light of their campfire. At Commando Castle, Captain Fairbairn had taught his students that he wanted the last sight an enemy soldier to see before he died was the gleam of his blade in the moonlight.

This enemy soldier was asleep. He did not see a thing and there was no moon … but the good captain would have been proud.

Major Randal shot the third man when he sat up.

When he heard Major Randal clap his hands three times, Lieutenant Kidd led the two drivers forward. The No. 1 ACC men seemed shaken by the sight of the dead enemy soldiers. Avoiding looking directly at the forms, the drivers climbed into the Crossleys and cranked up.

Both cars started on the first try.

The drivers grasped the concept Major Randal had explained to them prior to the mission about the importance of teamwork and "Getting the hell out of Dodge" fast. The No. 1 ACC men did their part. They were ready to move on command.

Major Randal jumped onboard one car and Lieutenant Kidd and King piled in the other.

"Let's go," Major Randal ordered, pulling the Very pistol out of the canvas holster he had slung over his shoulder, after taking the signal gun back from Lieutenant Kidd. He opened its short, stubby barrel, plopped in a green flare round and held a second round ready between the fingers of his left hand like a fat cigar.

"Don't stop for anything."

The Crossley rolled down the slope, quickly gaining speed. When it had traveled 200 yards, Major Randal fired the first green flare, quickly reloaded, and popped the second. He looked back to see the second Crossley right on their tail.

The driver cut right and pulled up on the gravel road running to the gate beside the bunker at the point they were going to cross into the base. Ahead, through the dark and the eerie green illumination of the flares swaying under their tiny parachutes, they could see the fence surrounding RAF Habbaniya. The car was going wide open when they shot through the open gate and slammed on the brakes. The Levies troopers manning the gate slammed it closed behind the second Crossley after it raced through.

Not a single shot had been fired at them. It was possible the Iraqis had still not connected the dots. When they did, some officer charged with screening the right flank was going to have a hard time explaining to his higher commander why he let two irreplaceable Crossley armored cars simply drive into the RAF base. Or how six of his men were dead without a sound.

Major Randal stepped out of the car. Sqn. Ldr. John Page was there with Mandy and Flanigan. All three were sporting happy smiles. The Levies troops manning the bunker were euphoric. Lieutenant Kidd walked over to the group with his MP-18 held down by its pistol grip.

"Nicely done, sir," Squadron Leader Page said. "I shall take these off your hands."

"All yours," Major Randal said. "Your men did good."

Mandy said, "One of the Annie Oakley ambushes engaged about twenty minutes ago."

"Goat?"

"They think not."

"Really?" Major Randal said. "OK, Corporal Jeffers knows what to do. He needs to have the women follow Standard Operating Procedure. Stay in position. No one moves forward to check anything out until sunrise. I'll be back before then."

"That was exciting," Mandy said, mounting her pony. "Bye, Roy."

Lieutenant Kidd said, "See you, Mandy."

"Feel up to some real action, Roy?" Major Randal said, lighting a cigarette.

Lieutenant Kidd said, "What do you have in mind, sir?"

"King, a few of his associates known as Murder Inc. and I are taking off about fifteen minutes from now in Pam's Seagull to raid an Iraqi airfield. Care to tag along?"

"Now, sir, how could I pass on an offer like that?"

"You could just say no."

FLANIGAN DROVE MAJ. JOHN RANDAL, LT. ROY KIDD AND King to the stretch of road Lt. Pamala Plum-Martin had selected as her clandestine airstrip.

Major Randal briefed Lieutenant Kidd as they rode. "According to the latest aerial photos, there are twenty-one Iraqi aircraft parked on the airstrip at Baqubah …"

A ripple of firing broke out in the distance from the direction of the escarpment. The trained ear could detect it was all one way, no return fire. One of the Strike Force patrols had initiated contact.

More firing broke out as other Strike Force patrols engaged. The contacts sounded like small, fierce thunderstorms building in intensity to a violent crescendo—then fading away. Soon the Iraqis were fighting back. Now the crackle took on an entirely different sound.

Firefights sound angry.

Soon all the Strike Force patrols were in action. Firing spread all along the Iraqi Main Line of Resistance. The sheer volume of the rebel fire was spectacular but wildly inaccurate, evidenced by tracers streaking at all angles into the night. Some gunners were even firing up into the sky at imaginary planes.

The men in the car turned to try to get a view.

By the time Flanigan arrived at the improvised airstrip, the Iraqi Army was fighting across its entire two mile front. The rebels were shooting at ghosts. The patrols had all begun withdrawing according to plan.

Strike Force was bearding the tiger—hit and run.

"Hello, Roy," Lieutenant Plum-Martin said, when they stepped out of the car. "Going with us tonight?"

"I am."

"Crank it up, Pam," Major Randal said. "Let's do this."

Murder Inc. began boarding the Seagull. The interior of the airplane was dimly lit by red lights to protect the raider's night vision. Major Randal and Lieutenant Kidd were last on. Mr. Zargo sat directly across from them on the deck of the airplane with his back pressed against the fuselage, holding his MP-18 between his knees.

He had a story to tell.

"You asked Red to inquire if I had any way to provide intelligence on the enemy forces," Mr. Zargo said. "No one in the Habbaniya chain-of-command knows anything other than what you already are aware of. There are three enemy brigades stationed on the plateau outside the station—one infantry, one artillery and the Mechanized Brigade under Colonel Said."

"Roger."

"What the AOC's intelligence section has been unable to provide," Mr. Zargo said, "is which specific infantry brigade, which specific artillery brigade and if the three brigade commanders are operating independently or under the central control of a division commander."

Major Randal said, "Never hurts to know who you're fighting."

"I can fill in a couple of pieces of the puzzle," Mr. Zargo said. "While we were standing by for you to return from your little adventure, three of us went out and grabbed a prisoner—a junior officer.

"He is a member of the 4th Iraqi Infantry Brigade. The lieutenant does not know anything about the artillery but told us his brigade is not part of a division."

"Very good, Mr. Zargo," Major Randal said. "Got bored, huh?"

Z Patrol laughed—the men were following every word of the conversation.

"Here is where the story becomes interesting," Mr. Zargo said, pointing with his pipe stem. "Our prisoner wanted to know why we attacked them since no state of war exists between Great Britain and Iraq.

"He was very upset with us."

"Upset?"

"According to the lieutenant," Mr. Zargo said, "The 4th Infantry Brigade was ordered out on a field training exercise. The troops were instructed to bring live ammunition with them. No one was informed that they were to besiege or attack RAF Station Habbaniya. The air raids this morning caught them on their religious day of the week, during their prayers, and took them by surprise."

"Let me get this straight," Major Randal said. "We attacked people on their equivalent of a Sunday who had not come here to do battle with us?"

"Appears to be the case," Mr. Zargo said.

"So, we're the aggressors?"

"Major, we heard the same story when we rescued Red," Mr. Zargo said.

Major Randal said, "You think the Golden Square failed to get the message to the troops?"

"That would be my guess," Mr. Zargo said.

"Always that ten percent who don't get the word," Major Randal said. "In this case, nobody did. I hate it when that happens. Especially to the bad guys."

Murder Inc. laughed again.

"My assessment," Mr. Zargo said, "We are facing three independent brigades of different branches of the Iraqi Army. The brigade commanders are likely operating independently, under sealed orders from the Golden Circle.

"Probably only a handful of senior officers knew they came here to invest Habbaniya. The junior officers and the troops have no idea what is going on; they are confused and angry."

"Five minutes, John," Lieutenant Plum-Martin called from the pilot's compartment.

Major Randal stood up and leaned in through the door next to her. The Seagull was flying with all its lights extinguished. The Iraqis would not be able to see them coming.

It was widely known that while No. 4 Service Flying Training School had no night-flying capability, the rest of the Royal Air Force had a preference for nocturnal bombing. As a precaution, Baqubah Air Base was blacked out.

The Iraqis did not possess night-flying capability either. There was not much for them to do at night other than maintenance. Standard Operating Procedure was that when flying light was lost at 2000 hours the airfield shut down operations and most personnel went home. A few guards remained on duty to patrol the perimeter at night. The security was intended to prevent petty theft.

No one was expecting a planeload of Strike Force raiders to come calling.

"One minute," Lieutenant Plum-Martin announced.

Major Randal took a last look at the Baqubah airstrip through the windscreen. The rebel planes were tethered along the edge of the field exactly the way they had been in the aerial photos taken by Sqn. Ldr. Tony Dudgeon. He ducked back inside the cabin.

"Lock and load," Major Randal ordered, taking out a thin Italian cigar left over from Abyssinia. "On the ground in zero one—Smoke 'em if you've got 'em, gentlemen.

"We ain't here on a stealth mission."

The announcement caused the atmosphere in the back of the plane to ratchet up. Landing on an unknown strip behind enemy lines with plans to get out and shoot it up is not for the faint of heart. The Z Patrol soldiers of fortune fumbled for cigarettes and cigars of their own.

The sound of the men checking their weapons filled the confines of the Seagull.

Major Randal touch-checked his weapons. First his 9 mm Beretta M-38 submachine gun, then his Colt .38 Supers. The 9 mm Browning P-35 was in its skeletal holster around back under his faded green bush jacket. He reached down and tapped the grenades in his billows pockets.

Each man was carrying four.

His Fairbairn knife was in its place, strapped to the harness of the .22 High Standard Military Model D on his chest. Everything was copasetic, as they liked to say at No. 1 Parachute Training School.

Lieutenant Plum-Martin greased it—a perfect landing. The Seagull hardly made a ripple. Major Randal struggled to his feet and, doing the Airborne Shuffle so as not to trip, scooted his way to the open door Z Patrol was going to exit from. The Seagull had slowed substantially, but it was still traveling fast.

"STAND UP," Major Randal ordered. He realized he was the only one exiting trained to make high-speed landings—parachutes come in hot.

"FOLLOW ME."

When the Seagull rolled past the first parked airplane beside the strip, Major Randal leapt out. He landed on the balls of his feet, twisted, and making certain to keep his elbows well in, almost touching on the stock of his 9mm Beretta M-38 with his chin tucked down on his chest, managed to hit all five points of contact, making a respectable parachute landing fall—minus the parachute. Still, he hit hard.

Lieutenant Kidd, next out after the Seagull had traveled fifty yards, not having the benefits of one million PLFs practiced at No.1 Parachute Training School—pancaked on the hard-packed dirt strip but managed to get up limping. The men of Murder Inc. had it better as the plane had braked substantially by the time they made their individual exits. In less than thirty seconds, the entire team was in action.

Major Randal could not see what anyone else was doing because the moon was down and it was black as pitch. He came abreast of an Iraqi fighter, raised the 9 mm Beretta M-38 to his shoulder and emptied a thirty-round magazine into its engine cowling. With every second round being a tracer, the submachine gun put out an impressive light show.

Out of the corner of his peripheral vision, he could see Lieutenant Kidd engaging his first target. Major Randal reached in his pocket, extracted a grenade, pulled the pin and threw it at the airplane. Then before it detonated, he moved on to his second target. The rebel planes were parked fifteen to twenty yards apart.

By now firing had erupted all down the length of the airstrip.

On the run, he changed magazines and immediately opened on the next aircraft when he came up. It started burning. Even so, he repeated the process of following up with a hand grenade.

Major Randal was firing on his third target when the Seagull began taxiing back up the airstrip. There was little time to get his grenade away before he had to dash to the plane. He barely made it.

Mr. Zargo had to reach out and haul him inside.

"GO, GO, GO!" Major Randal shouted the second he cleared the door.

The Seagull is famous for its short take-offs. Lieutenant Plum-Martin may have set a record with hers.

Nothing is better than the first few minutes after being extracted from a high-risk mission—and that means *nothing*. If Murder Inc. felt any emotion about having pulled off a daring raid, it would not have been possible to tell from their demeanor.

The mercs were models of nonchalance.

"Everybody OK?" Major Randal asked.

Except for minor scrapes and abrasions, there were no injuries. Not one man had seen an Iraqi. By all accounts, not a single round had been fired at the raiding party while they were on the ground.

The element of surprise is a beautiful thing—when it works.

Major Randal was a master of target selection. The secret to small-scale raiding, he had learned by trial and error, is to hit soft targets. Attack an objective not prepared to defend itself and surprise is almost guaranteed, enemy resistance is virtually nonexistent and a small force can accomplish results out of proportion to its size.

In baseball terms, it's called "hitting 'em where they ain't"—and Major Randal had the concept down to an art form.

A quick debrief on board the Seagull as it flew out indicated Z Patrol had damaged or destroyed eighteen Iraqi aircraft. There was no way to determine how much actual destruction had been accomplished in the short time they were on the ground.

One thing was certain. The Royal Iraqi Air Force would never be able to repair or replace the aircraft shot up in time to get them back in the fight at RAF Habbaniya.

As the Seagull purred through the dark, Major Randal finally lit the thin cigar he had clenched in his teeth. He had already turned his thoughts to the casualty report from the Strike Force patrols he knew would be waiting for him.

And Major Randal was beginning to think about what he was going to do next to hit the rebels.

23

STUDS

RED AND MANDY WERE WAITING FOR THE SEAGULL WHEN
it landed. When Maj. John Randal and the Z Patrol soldiers of fortune
stepped off the plane, the first thing they heard was an incoming artillery
round. As they were boarding ground transportation, another artillery
round slammed into the base. It was soon followed by a third.

A crew was standing by to load the Seagull for its next mission.
Wicker cages of the orange spray-painted squirrels were carried on first.
Blocks of ice with parachutes and static lines attached came next. Last
were stacks and stacks of propaganda leaflets warning of the danger posed
by the orange squirrels (and yellow ones—of which there were none.)

Mandy hopped on and sat in the co-pilot's chair. Two volunteer door
kickers from the No. 1 Armored Car Company boarded. Lt. Pamala
Plum-Martin immediately took off.

Lt. Joe Kidd stayed on board the aircraft. Lieutenant Plum-Martin
would drop him off at the mother ship on Lake Habbaniyah before
commencing her first Psychological Warfare mission of the night. On

her second mission, the Seagull would be armed with a combination of real and fake bombs (empty beer bottles).

Red briefed Major Randal in the car as Flanigan drove them back to his Command Post.

"All our patrols have returned. Captains Fabian and Smith are wrapping up their after-action reports following the Patrol Leader debriefings. Mr. Twinning has provided two stenographers to type up the reports for you—available first thing in the morning."

"Casualties?"

"Three men KIA," Red said. "Eleven wounded, four of them seriously—in hospital. The others were treated and released back to their units."

While not light casualties, Major Randal had been prepared for worse. Running as many patrols in as confined a space to maneuver as Strike Force had sent out was inherently risky. Even without the Iraqis shooting at them.

"Any word on the Annie Oakley ambush?"

"The women are following SOP," Red said, "waiting for daylight to investigate. Two of the Boy Scout ambushes have triggered as well."

"Busy night," Major Randal said. "What's the bad news, Red?"

"The Iraqi artillery came alive after the Strike Force raids along the Iraqi MLR," Red said. "Pounding us, John."

"Yeah," Major Randal said. "We stirred 'em up, all right. That was the idea. Hammering us but degrading themselves as well."

"What makes you think that?"

"The Iraqis don't have unlimited ammunition," Major Randal said, "and their troops won't be able to sleep with their own guns in action all night. Only thing worse than trying to sleep during incoming is to try sleeping next to a battery conducting fire missions."

"We're grinding 'em down."

"So, the fact the Iraqis are trying their best to blow us off the face of the map," Red said, "is a good thing?"

"Roger that ..."

"Does not feel wonderful to me," Red said.

"If the Iraqis are going to sit up on that ridge without putting in a ground attack," Major Randal said, "then we're in a slugging match. We'll see who can take it the longest."

"The rebels seem to be doing all the slugging," Red said. "Artillery does grate on one's nerves."

"The bad guys get a free shot during the hours of darkness," Major Randal said. "The RAF will go back to work when the sun comes up."

"Actually," Red said, "the rebels are not hitting much. Teddy has created several more deceptions. Appears his magic illusions are diverting a fair share of the incoming fire."

"Good for him."

"John, you need rest."

"So do you, Red," Major Randal said. "Go to the Pony Express girls' rooms—hit the rack. Safe down there."

"What about you?"

"I'll be in the CP," Major Randal said, "grab a couple hours on my cot before checking out those ambushes at first light—0530 hours."

AS THE SKY WAS BEGINNING TO LIGHTEN, MAJ. JOHN RANDAL was waiting on the perimeter road behind the Annie Oakley ambush party that had engaged earlier during the night. Cpl. Jeffery Jeffers briefed him on events.

"At approximately 0325 hours, the tin cans we tied in the wire rattled. The ladies went on high alert. Shortly they were able to observe a form or forms wiggling under the fence on the goat trail. The woman in charge of this position, Mrs. Watkins, initiated the ambush by firing her individual weapon, a 12-gauge over and under skeet gun.

"The rest of the women followed SOP. Each one emptied her weapon into the killing zone of the ambush, and then reloaded. I was summoned to the scene.

"Again, following SOP I primed an M-36 grenade and threw it into the wire where the goat trail crosses. Following that, the Annie Oakleys stayed in position, on alert where they are now."

"Let's go see what they bagged," Major Randal said, racking a round into the chamber of his 9 mm Beretta M-38 submachine gun.

Major Randal walked toward the perimeter fence in front of where the line of Annie Oakleys could be seen lying in the prone position with their shotguns at the ready—"Standing To." Corporal Jeffers was behind him with his Enfield rifle.

"Ladies," Major Randal said, as he stepped between two of the prone women. "Lock your weapons—ground 'em."

The ambush site was about ten yards from the killing zone where the trail crossed the wire. After taking only a couple of steps, Major Randal was able to see two dead enemy soldiers crumpled in the wire. Both were armed with brand new Thompson submachine guns and bags of grenades.

The men were mangled, riddled with shotgun pellets and shrapnel from the Mills Bomb.

Major Randal did not take any chances, even though the two bad guys were about as dead as anyone can get. Aware that he was setting an example for the women who were observing his every move, he put two short bursts into the downed enemy infiltrators. The message: There is no such thing as overkill.

"Mrs. Watkins," Major Randal called, "bring your party forward. Take a look."

The Annie Oakleys surveyed the scene somberly. The impact of what they had done set in. They were alive, and the enemy who had come to kill them and their families was dead. While not exactly jubilant, the women were not unhappy either.

Beat shooting skeet.

"Doesn't get any better than this," Major Randal said. "You ladies are real studs."

MAJ. JOHN RANDAL WAS STANDING ON THE PERIMETER road behind the Annie Oakleys ambush, waiting for Flanigan. The policeman had dropped him off and driven on to pick up Lt. Pamala Plum-Martin and Mandy after their night of flying. A truck raced past with workmen piled in the back.

"The Great Teddy" was riding in the passenger seat. He peered out the window from behind his Coke-bottle glasses as the truck went by. Major Randal waved. The Strike Force war magician gave him a salute.

Teddy was en route to put a camouflage net over Lieutenant Plum-Martin's Seagull before any Iraqi reconnaissance aircraft overflew RAF Habbaniya. Magicians make things appear and *disappear*.

Major Randal decided that he needed to keep that thought in mind—might come in handy later.

Flanigan pulled up. Lieutenant Plum-Martin and Mandy were in the back seat. Major Randal climbed in the front.

"Drop the ladies off at the O-Club," Major Randal said, "then run me up to the airfield."

"My pleasure, Major."

"Give me a report," Major Randal said, pulling out a cigarette and lighting it with his U.S. 26th Cavalry Regiment Zippo.

"Not much to report," Lieutenant Plum-Martin said. "We dropped the squirrels, the leaflets and the ice-weighted parachutes as planned. On our second mission, we dropped our bombs on Iraqi batteries we could see firing. Pretty sure we scored a couple of hits, John."

"I bombed away with beer bottles," Mandy giggled. "Hope it scared the hell out of the rebels—cannot wait to do it all over again tonight."

"The door kickers tossed out over a hundred hand grenades," Lieutenant Plum-Martin said. "Between their own artillery firing, our massed mortars—we could see the rounds impacting all over the Iraqi positions, my 100-pound bombs, Mandy's beer bottles and the grenades… most likely quite a lot of enemy personnel were awake all night."

"You stayed above 5,000 feet, per your orders?" Major Randal said.

"Except when we glide-bombed the batteries," Lieutenant Plum-Martin said. "I have no idea how to aim a bomb flying straight and level, John."

"Take much fire?"

"Not really," Lieutenant Plum-Martin said. "The Iraqis knew we were up there but they could never see us. Most of their anti-aircraft fire was small and very erratic."

"Nice job," Major Randal said, locking eyes with Lieutenant Plum-Martin in the rearview mirror as they pulled up to the Officers Club complex. "Go in and go to bed. I don't want to see either one of you before the 1200 hours briefing—that's an order."

Flanigan drove Major Randal to the airfield. He intended to troop the line of the Rod and Gun Club Big Bore Rifle Team again. Today he did not bother bringing his scoped 7 mm-06 M-1903 Springfield rifle with him.

The Rod and Gun Club men did not need to see him shoot in order to demonstrate he was leading from the front. Yesterday at times when he did, Major Randal felt like he was getting in the way. All he was going to do today was put in a brief appearance.

As a green 2nd Lieutenant, Major Randal had been tutored in the finer points of leadership by two of the best NCOs in the U.S. Army, when he was in the 26th Cavalry Regiment. He only knew what they taught him, which was to lead by example. However, when working with the two Master Sergeants, Tiger Stripe and Hammerhead, running counterinsurgency operations deep in the Philippine jungles, he had also learned to never interfere with a man who knew his job while he was in the act of performing it.

A quick walk-through to show that the Strike Force commander was interested in what they were doing would suffice—then he would go away and let the Big Bore Rifle Team get on with their mission.

Major Randal wished there was more .55-caliber ammunition. He would have liked to spend the morning back up on the water tower sniping rebels with the Boys Anti-Tank Rifle. There were a lot of thin-skinned vehicles up on the escarpment that needed plinking.

SQN. LDR. TONY DUDGEON HAD NOT GONE TO BED UNTIL after 2400 hours, and he had arrived on the flight line at 0400 hours this morning. Though outranked by several senior men, he was in command of the largest number of aircraft on RAF Habbaniya. In fact, he commanded the airfield. That meant not only did he have to plan the missions and fly operations, Squadron Leader Dudgeon also had to supervise the servicing and arming of the aircraft.

He was also the only pilot on the air station who was qualified to fly photo reconnaissance. So in between bombing missions and at the end of the flying day, Squadron Leader Dudgeon had to go take pictures. That seemed a lot to ask of a pilot who had been assigned to No. 4 Service Flying Training School as a rest cure because he was declared medically unfit for combat flying after a tough fifty-mission combat tour.

Squadron Leader Dudgeon spent most of his time worrying about Frankie, his dachshund. The dog did not like the incoming artillery. So there was only one thing to do—he took Frankie with him in his Oxford on missions.

Frankie curled up on the floor of the airplane and slept virtually the entire time.

Squadron Leader Dudgeon and Frankie had completed their first bombing run of the morning when Maj. John Randal arrived at the airfield. Veronica walked out of Grp. Capt. William "Butcher" Saville's office as Flanigan was parking the car.

She was there collecting the most recent target information the Group Captain had posted on his pictomap. The Butcher did not much care for sharing what he considered *his* intelligence. Nor did he think women should be involved with operational matters during air-combat operations.

Veronica made short work of him.

The three went into Squadron Leader Dudgeon's office.

"How're you doing, Tony?" Major Randal asked.

"We lost about a third of our airplanes and a quarter of our pilots yesterday," Squadron Leader Dudgeon said. "Most of the planes going up today would be written off on any other RAF station—shot to pieces but patched together with baling wire and tape.

"Six or seven of the pilots are stitched up from wounds that would automatically get them grounded, except we have to have them flying."

"The command situation has not improved either," Veronica said. "I took the morning AOC's briefing for Red so she could get some rest. The Air Vice Marshal failed to attend again. No one would talk officially, but rumors abound that Smart has suffered a nervous breakdown, as I told you."

"Who's in charge?" Major Randal asked.

"Colonel Roberts was in the chair for the briefing—the de facto commander."

"That means there is no one in command," Squadron Leader Dudgeon said. "The next senior RAF man should have stepped in immediately. Habbaniya is Royal Air Force. No one is going to take orders from an army colonel. Not with an air campaign on."

"Agreed," Veronica said.

"Maybe we are better off without him," said Squadron Leader Dudgeon.

"His strategy all along has been to pigheadedly ignore the facts or the situation and hope our relationship with the Iraqis will magically get back to normal on its own accord without having to take a stance that might reflect unfavorably on his career. That kind of Colonel Blimp military rationale has caused the British Empire more than its share of debacles.

"I bloody well do not intend to be part of the next one if there is any way to avoid it."

"Agreed," Veronica said.

24

ARMOR ATTACK

MAJ. JOHN RANDAL WAS STANDING IN ONE OF THE ROD &
Gun Club Big Bore Rifle Team positions, looking at the Iraqi lines
through his Zeiss binoculars. The rebels were not displaying themselves
as blatantly as they had yesterday. The enemy troops had thrown up sand
earthworks in some places as protection from direct fire.

"I believe you're right, Mr. Stanberry," Major Randal said. "The bad
guys have pulled their exterior lines in. Your men must have gotten their
attention."

"Not out of range yet," Mr. Stanberry said. "Harder and harder for us
to get a chip shot at the rebels, though."

"Down the road," Major Randal said, "if the Iraqis do move back out
of your effective range, have some of your riflemen switch over to Enfield
.303s loaded with standard-issue, armor-piercing rounds. Start plinking
their thin-skinned vehicles. You don't have to destroy anything, damage
will do just fine."

"My lads fire Military Class competition," Mr. Stanberry said.

"Surplus Lee-Enfield Mark IIIs we have tinkered with a bit. I may get started on your suggestion this afternoon, Major."

"If the Iraqis move their vehicles farther back," Major Randal said, "load the first three rounds or so tracer, fire off a firm rest, get on target, and then pump in the AP."

"The engine compartment of a truck is a big target," Mr. Stanberry said. "The Iraqis will never be able to protect their vehicles from us as long as they remain parked in sight on the escarpment."

A Pony Express girl clattered up on her pony. "Major Randal," she called, "Sir, you are wanted at the Strike Force Operations Center. The Iraqis have launched an armored attack against the perimeter in the vicinity of Blockhouse No. 12."

"Ride to the polo pitch," Major Randal ordered, "and find Mrs. Paige. Tell her I said to dispatch the platoon of No. 1 ACC armored cars stationed there to the Operations Center immediately."

"Yes, sir," the girl said, and was away before Major Randal could say anything else. Mandy was right. Her Pony Express girls could ride like the wind.

Major Randal started running toward the airfield about a half mile away. Flanigan caught up to him in the police car and pulled alongside before he had traveled very far.

"Need a lift, Major, or are you doing your daily constitutional PT?"

"Haul ass, Flanigan," Major Randal ordered, as he piled in.

"Might I ask where I am hauling arse to, sir?"

"First to the armored car platoon leader's position on the airfield, and then to Group Captain Saville's office so I can use his phone. The perimeter is under ground attack."

"Hang on!" Flanigan threw a switch and the car's red light started flashing and the siren wailed.

The Pony Express girl was already out of sight.

MAJ. JOHN RANDAL WAS IN GRP. CPT. WILLIAM "BUTCHER" Saville's office on the phone calling his Operations Center. The Butcher was glaring at him silently, clearly not pleased with the intrusion.

"Major Randal," he said, "who's got the duty?"

Red came on the line summoned by the switchboard operator.

"You're supposed to be asleep," Major Randal said.

"Blockhouse No. 12 is being attacked by an estimated five Crossley armored cars," Red said, ignoring him. "Squadron Leader Page has already launched with the No. 1 ACC Ready Reaction platoon."

"I'll go straight to No. 12 with the airfield armored car platoon," Major Randal said. "Have the No. 1 ACC platoon from the polo pitch head that way the minute they get to your position."

"Veronica phoned," Red said. "She is taking the cars directly to No. 12. They should arrive there any minute."

"Perfect," Major Randal said. "Have the Motorcycle Patrol head that way too. Make all the racket they can."

"I have been in contact with Captain Sorrels," Red said. "He is in the process of dropping a concentration in front of No. 12 as we speak."

"Good job, Red," Major Randal said. He heard the first of the mortar rounds impacting in the distance. "I'm on the way—moving now."

"Do not let them break in, John!"

Running out to the police car, Major Randal spied Flt. Off. Gasper "Bunny" Featherstone taking a sip out of his silver flask while waiting for the ground crew to finish servicing his Gladiator.

"Rebel armor attacking the northeast quadrant, Bunny," Major Randal shouted, "Kill anything that moves in front of the wire."

Flying Officer Featherstone leaped into his Gladiator fighter, with armors and fitters scattering to get out of the way, and was taxiing before Major Randal could climb into Flanigan's car.

With their sirens screaming, the Rolls Royce armored cars fell in behind and followed the police car to Blockhouse No. 12. The position was manned by troops from No. 6 Levies Company. On the way, the convoy raced past an additional platoon from No. 6 Company double-timing to reinforce the bunker.

When Major Randal arrived, sirens were wailing, motorcycles thundering and weapons firing.

The volume of noise was deafening. Sounded like a small army. Unfortunately, it was virtually all nonlethal.

The commander of No.1 Armored Car Company, Sqn. Ldr. John Page, had his cars deployed on line, and they were engaging the Iraqi armor with their .55-caliber Boys Anti-Tank Rifles. There were two problems:

1) Major Randal had shot up nearly all the .55-caliber ammunition;

2) The .55-caliber ammunition No.1 ACC did have would not penetrate the enemy Crossleys—rounds were ricocheting off the rebel vehicles.

Major Randal ran inside Blockhouse No. 12 and up the stairs to the roof. Veronica and the sergeant from No. 6 Company in charge of the position were there observing the Iraqi attack. One quick glance was all the Strike Force commander needed to realize that RAF Habbaniya was about to be overrun.

The Iraqis had three Fiat tanks supporting the armored car column that was rapidly approaching the perimeter. There were more than the five reported Crossley cars.

Mortar rounds were causing no visible effect on the rebel armored attack formation—it would take a direct hit for a mortar to cause any substantial damage, and the odds against that were astronomical. Across the wire, Flying Officer Featherstone was furiously strafing the Iraqi armored column at an altitude of what appeared to be about fifteen feet.

Regrettably, the Gladiator was only armed with four .303 machine guns. Flying Officer Featherstone was not doing any more materiel damage than the mortars or the Boys Anti-Tank Rifle gunners. He was scaring the rebels.

The armored cars and tanks buttoned up.

Now the Iraqis were broiling like lobsters inside their fighting vehicles in the desert sun—but they were still advancing.

"Get Colonel Roberts on the horn," Major Randal ordered the Levies sergeant.

Veronica said, "May I borrow your binoculars, Sergeant?"

The NCO handed her his glasses as he reached to crank the field phone. Instead of looking at the Iraqi armor, she began scanning the sky.

"My husband was rearming his Audax when your message arrived," Veronica said. "He will be on the way here as soon as his plane is serviced.

The Audax is a dive-bomber capable of striking pinpoint targets. Unfortunately, Pete has not flown operationally in about eight months—says he feels somewhat rusty."

"Whatever we're paying you, Veronica," Major Randal said. "It ain't enough."

"Colonel Roberts, sir," the Sergeant said, handing the phone to Major Randal.

"We've got eight Crossleys and three Fiat tanks maneuvering in front of Blockhouse No. 12—there's no supporting infantry, but this is a serious attack," Major Randal said. "The Iraqis are committing half of their known armor."

"What can I do to help?" Colonel Roberts asked.

"Put the rest of the perimeter on high alert," Major Randal said. "Could be a feint; if it is, the Iraqi infantry and the rest of the armor will come in hard somewhere else while we're distracted here."

"Can you keep them out of the wire?" Colonel Roberts asked.

"Negative," Major Randal said. "If the rebels keep coming they'll be inside the cantonment in about three minutes."

"What is your plan?" Colonel Roberts said.

"We'll stand and fight," Major Randal said, "but we can't stop armor."

"Do your best, Randal."

"Call my Operations Center," Major Randal ordered the Levies sergeant.

"Red, have Fabian and Smith assemble their companies and start them this way on the double, bring grenades, bring Molotov cocktails," Major Randal ordered. "Tell Mr. Twinning to rush every bulldozer on the base down here right now. The drivers are going to have to try to knock the Iraqi armored vehicles over with the blades of their dozers.

"Tell him that."

"Are things so desperate, John?" Red inquired.

"Roger that."

Major Randal hung up the phone. He studied the Iraqis through his Zeiss binoculars. This was a major attack. The Iraqi armored column was every bit as threatening to RAF Habbaniya as the 10th Panzer Division had been to Calais.

Maybe worse. At Calais the British Forces had artillery to counter the tanks. RAF Habbaniya's only two cannons were covered in twenty-one layers of paint. Each layer of paint represented a year since the two guns had last fired a live round.

"Veronica," Major Randal ordered, "tell Flanigan to drive you to the Operations Center. Pick up Mandy and Red, and then report directly to the Seagull. Have Pam fly you out, as planned."

"John ..."

"Do it *now!*"

Before Veronica could reach the stairs, three silver Audaxes came screaming straight down, hell-diving from 5,000 feet—one behind the other—targeting on the three Fiat tanks. The dive-bombers pressed home their attack until the planes were only 250 feet off the ground, then one after the other pickled their bombs.

One of the Fiats exploded. Another toppled over, tossed like a child's toy from a near miss. The third ground to a halt.

The three dive-bombers barely pulled out of their dives. One after the other the planes looped up, skimming the surface of the desert floor, blowing sand dust devils in their wake. The Audaxes immediately began climbing to gain altitude for a second pass. This time, the silver trainers were going to make a run on the Crossley armored cars.

They did not have to go to the trouble.

Rebels bailed out of the cars and the surviving tank, abandoning them on the spot. The crews started running back toward their MLR on foot. That was a mistake.

Flying Officer Featherstone, circling in his Gladiator, pounced on the fleeing men with his machine guns chattering. Then the Audaxes came down and peppered them with their organic machine guns. Dead enemy troops littered the desert.

The Iraqi attack was over in the blink of an eye.

Major Randal and Veronica walked downstairs to where a visibly relieved Squadron Leader Page was watching the aerial show with his men. The troops were standing on the hoods of the Rolls Royces waving their caps and cheering until they were hoarse.

"Go get those Crossleys," Major Randal ordered. "Bring the tank back too."

"Was that as near run as I suspect?" Veronica asked.

"Doesn't get any closer," Major Randal said. "We dodged a bullet."

MAJ. JOHN RANDAL WAS LEAFING THROUGH THE TYPED after-action reports from the Strike Forces' night patrols. To the knowledgeable military reader, they told a fascinating story. The Iraqi Army had set up on the ridge in textbook style with listening posts (LPs) out. Most of the contacts last night had been against the lightly held LPs.

Major Randal heard voices behind the Command Post tent. He went around back and found Mandy and Red there smoking. When the girls saw him, they instantly threw their cigarettes on the ground.

"What the hell?" Major Randal said.

"Clipper Girls never smoke in public," Red said.

"Do *not* tell my mother," Mandy said.

Twenty minutes earlier, the Iraqis had been within seconds of breaking into RAF Habbaniya. The two would have been lucky if they had been only killed outright. Now Mandy and Red were concerned about getting caught smoking.

Fair enough. The girls had priorities. Major Randal had his. It's good to know what to worry about and what not to in a war.

"I wasn't here," Major Randal said. "This never happened. We're not having this conversation."

COL. OUVRY ROBERTS AND LT. COL. ALISTAIR BRAWN PULLED Maj. John Randal aside before the Strike Force noon briefing.

"The Iraqis have moved a field piece behind the Burma Bund on the far side of the Euphrates River across from No. 8 (Kurdish) Company's section of the perimeter," Colonel Roberts said. "They are firing it into the station from there."

Lt. Col. Brawn said, "No. 8 is planning a platoon-sized raid on the gun. Normally this would be something for Strike Force to tackle, but my lads are keen to give it a go. Would you care to observe, Randal?"

"What time, sir?"

"1400 hours."

"Mind if Captains Fabian and Smith accompany me?" Major Randal said. "I'd like them to get the experience, sir."

"Invite anyone you like," Colonel Roberts said.

While the personnel were the same, it was a different-looking and acting group that assembled for the noon briefing—which would have normally been at 0600 hours—except that Strike Force was sleeping days and operating nights. The people in the Operations Center tent had all been under fire for the past twenty-four hours.

They were veterans now. RAF Habbaniya had been subjected to incoming machine gun fire, artillery and enemy air strikes. The Patrol Leaders had all led a combat mission—a raid.

While no one was acting the part of a hero, all in the group were secretly pleased with themselves. People had pressed on with their tasks through shot and shell. They had done their jobs, and they would again and again. There was an atmosphere of shared danger and mutual respect in the tent.

Red began the briefing. "Between midnight and 0300, RAF Habbaniya recorded 200 incoming artillery rounds ..."

Major Randal had not heard the number before. More than one round a minute—a lot. He made a mental note to ask how many had been fired at the base after 0300 hours—approximately the time Pam and Mandy had commenced flying their mission.

Mr. Twinning was next up. He announced a mandatory blackout for RAF Habbaniya for the duration of the battle—something AVM Harry "Reggie" Smart should have done first thing.

Capt. Valentine Fabian and Capt. John Smith both briefed the twenty-four contact patrols conducted by the Strike Force.

Veronica Paige briefed the air operations at the airfield and polo pitch. She also gave a rundown of the Iraqi armored attack on Blockhouse No. 12. Cheering broke out when the audience heard her description of the Iraqis fleeing on foot, leaving their priceless armored vehicles behind to be captured.

Lt. Pamala Plum-Martin briefed the raid on Baqubah Airfield. There was a hush as she described the mission step by step. Somehow, the Royal

Marine pilot made flying to an enemy air base north of Baghdad, landing in the middle of the night on an unlit runway, Z Patrol (led by Major Randal) deplaning on the roll and shooting up the Iraqi aircraft parked along the strip, then re-boarding and flying home, seem routine.

The audience stood up clapping, whistling and cheering when Lieutenant Plum-Martin wrapped up her portion of the briefing. Most had seen raids like she outlined in Hollywood movies. None of them had believed they would ever be associated with anyone who actually carried out those operations in real life.

Mandy briefed the air mission the two girls had flown, dropping orange squirrels and parachutes weighted down with blocks of ice. The troops seemed mesmerized by her description of bombing the sleeping Iraqis with empty beer bottles, but then … they had been mesmerized before she even began her briefing.

"The Great Teddy" described the various diversions he had constructed around the station. He discussed his future projects. The youngster was focusing on camouflaging vital installations such as the electricity plant, telephone exchange, etc. He even had a plan for the water tower.

Mr. Stanberry briefed the actions of the Rod & Gun Club's Big Bore Rifle Team. He confirmed that the Iraqi front had pulled back up to a quarter mile from the wire in some places along their Main Line of Resistance. The riflemen were planning to switch their priorities to engaging enemy thin-skinned vehicles with armor-piercing rounds.

After the briefing, Major Randal had a word with Mr. Zargo. "The Kurdish Company is going to conduct a platoon-sized raid on an Iraqi artillery position on the Burma Bund."

"When?"

"About an hour," Major Randal said. "I want you to observe the operation with me."

"A daylight raid—across a swift-flowing river—with troops who are desert people not known for their boating or swimming skills—against a hard target?" Mr. Zargo said, with a raised eyebrow.

"Yeah," Major Randal said, "my thoughts exactly. We may have to take Murder Inc. over later tonight—finish the job for 'em."

"I was afraid," Mr. Zargo said, "you were going to suggest something like that."

25

REVENGE OF THE ORANGE SQUIRRELS

MAJ. JOHN RANDAL, CAPT. VALENTINE FABIAN, CAPT. JOHN
Smith and Mr. Zargowere in Flanigan's police car, preparing to leave for
the Levies No. 8 Company. The Kurds were going to launch a platoon-
sized raid across the Euphrates River against a pair of Iraqi 3.7-mm
howitzers that had been moved into position behind the Burma Bund
and were firing into the base. Mandy showed up at the last second and
demanded to be allowed to go along.

"The Burma Bund is approximately 400 to 500 yards distance from
the river," Captain Smith said. "The Kurd platoon will have to cross the
river, wade through a belt of reed swamp on the opposite bank, then cross
several hundred yards of open desert to reach the Bund. Then scale it and
attack the field guns on the far side. What do you wonder the Iraqis will
be doing the whole time that's taking place?"

"We have the better idea in Strike Force," Captain Fabian said.
"Operate under cover of darkness—utilizing the element of surprise."

"The Kurds in No. 8 Company are generally considered to be the best in the Levies," Captain Smith said. "Still, the men are garrison troops whose mission is to man the Blockhouses.

"While my tour seconded to the Levies has been enjoyable, I shall be happy to return to my regiment for some real soldiering when this is over."

"Sounds like a suicide job," Mandy said. "Why not put a stop to it, John?"

"I'm not in the chain-of-command," Major Randal said. "We're guests. Keep that in mind. We're here to observe. Save your comments until we get back. We'll debrief at that time."

The Strike Force group walked up the stairs at No. 8 Company's HQ Blockhouse. Col. Ouvry Roberts and Lt. Col. Alistair Brawn were there with No. 8's company commander, Capt. Michael Cottingham. The assault platoon was assembled on the bank of the Euphrates. The Kurds had two outboard motor fishing boats to ferry the platoon across the river.

By squeezing everyone in, they could make the trip in a single lift. The boats were dangerously overloaded. When the platoon shoved off, the water was right up to the top of the gunwales.

Everything was going according to plan until one of the boat's motors conked out. The current caught the stalled boat, and it began to drift sideways. The troops in the other boat threw a line to take it under tow.

When the slack went out of the rope, the dead-in-the-water boat began to drag the boat attempting the tow downriver. The troops in both broke out oars, but there were not enough of them to go around. Men paddled with the butts of their Lee-Enfield rifles.

Disaster was averted. However, all the activity had attracted the attention of the Iraqis on the Burma Bund. The rebels engaged the boats with long-range machine gun fire. Fortunately, the enemy howitzers were on the far side of the Bund and unable to depress their muzzles low enough to open.

The boats made it ashore, but they had been swept a quarter mile down the river. The Kurds jumped over the side into a reed swamp composed of silt that oozed up to their knees. Soon the troops were crawling through the slimy mud because they were unable to walk upright in the muck. And they were under fire.

The platoon began to take casualties. The only way to evacuate the wounded was back through the swamp to the boats. To do that, troops who should have been part of the assault were forced to drag wounded men through the mud and reeds with bullets kicking up all around them.

When the wounded were finally assembled for the return trip, the boat's motors would not start.

At this point, the assault platoon had made it to the far edge of the swamp but was pinned down by heavy machine gun fire. More dead and wounded were piling up awaiting evacuation, meaning being dragged through the muddy sludge back to the boats.

That effort proved to be a lot more difficult than anyone had imagined. The medical evacuation began siphoning off more and more men from the attacking element.

The injured who had already made it back to the riverbank were waiting in the boats while desperate boat drivers tried to start the outboard motors. No luck. Eventually both the ropes used to crank the engines snapped.

Now the only way back across the Euphrates was to paddle against the swift current. To have any hope of making it, the boats would need additional men to serve as oarsmen, which further degraded the assault element.

The No. 8 Company platoon commander called off the attack.

The Kurds low-crawled back through the swamp, bringing the rest of their dead and wounded with them. The platoon managed to load in the two boats under fire and started paddling for their lives. For a time it appeared as if the boats were going to broach in the river, get swept downstream in the swift current, capsize and be lost.

Luck was with them. Both boats made it back.

The survivors straggled ashore and fell exhausted on the bank. The troops were covered from head to toe in thick, greyish muck. The Kurds did not look like soldiers … or even men.

When the platoon leader made his report to Captain Cottingham, he claimed thirty Iraqis killed by "long-range rifle fire."

On the way back to the Operations Center, it was quiet in the car.

Mandy said, "A Royal Marine lieutenant I went out with told me that opposed river crossings are one of the most, if not *the* most, difficult of all military operations. Is that true, John?"

"I wouldn't know," Major Randal said. "I've never tried to make one."

"Well, that one certainly looked awkward."

MAJ. JOHN RANDAL TOLD FLANIGAN TO STAND BY TO DRIVE him to the airfield. He took Capt. Valentine Fabian and Capt. John Smith into his CP tent.

"Forget the debrief," Major Randal said. "'Poor prior planning produces poor results.'The two master sergeants on my team, when I was a 2nd Lieutenant operating against insurgents with the Filipino Scouts, hammered that into me every single day. Don't you forget it."

"Sir!"

"Tonight," Major Randal said, "combine your patrols and cut the number in half. Put your best Patrol Leaders in command no matter who's the ranking man.

"Plan raids on fixed targets with a priority to artillery, tank, armored car and truck parks. If you can identify an enemy HQ, hit it. Coordinate the targets with Lieutenant Plum-Martin—don't want her bombing an objective your men just overran.

"What are your questions?"

"Can we take out patrols, sir?" Captain Fabian asked. "I used to be a rather good infantry platoon leader."

"Negative," Major Randal said. "You'll get your chance. I have something in mind for tomorrow night that should interest both of you."

MANDY WAS PETTING FRANKIE, SQN. LDR. TONY DUDGEON'S dachshund. Frankiewas a criminal dog. Lately he had been stowing away on combat missions. The pooch could not stand all the incoming artillery and became panic-stricken while his master was flying—which was nonstop. So Squadron Leader Dudgeon took him along, in clear violation of Royal Air Force regulations prohibiting pets in aircraft.

What was the RAF going to do—court-martial Frankie?

After agreeing to do a photo recon over the Burma Bund at the end of the day to take shots of the two Iraqi 3.7 mm howitzers, Squadron Leader Dudgeon briefed Maj. John Randal on the current state of No. 4 Service Flying Training School's operations.

The situation was bleak and getting worse. The loss rate in pilots and aircraft had continued at the same rapid pace as in the first day's battle. That meant by the end of flying light, No. 4 SFTS would have suffered over fifty percent casualties in two days.

There were no replacements.

"I used to envy the Audax pilots," Squadron Leader Dudgeon said. "Thought they had the more desirable assignment dive-bombing down on the deck while my Oxfords have to fly straight and level, bombing from altitude.

"Saw 'em in action," Major Randal said, "do good work."

"True, but our Audaxes have been quite literally shot to pieces," Squadron Leader Dudgeon said. "Most of the pilots are flying with stitched-up wounds that would have required hospitalization under peacetime conditions. We are about out of pilots. At the current rate we are losing dive-bombers, No. 4 SFTS will not have any left by noon tomorrow."

"There were still women and children refugees from the Embassy in camp, and we had to get them out somehow. This morning, 31 Squadron flew in from India in their DC-2s to do the job. Wng. Cdr. John Hawtrey had his Audax squadron standing by to put down a covering attack on the Iraqi antiaircraft positions when the transports came in.

"Armored cars screened the DC-2s as they landed and taxied into the hangars. Only a couple were damaged. None of the aircrew were injured. Veronica Paige was here supervising the civilians. She loaded the passengers in record time, and they were away and gone before the Iraqis could react.

"Had all the elements of a proper tragedy. Visions of dead women and children littered all across the landscape were dancing in my head if the Iraqis shot down one of the DC-2s. I do not mind admitting, I was scared to death until the transports flew out of sight."

"See how you would be," Major Randal said.

"Reggie Smart went with them," Squadron Leader Dudgeon said. "He commandeered one DC-2 entirely for himself. Sat in a chair in front of the locked crew compartment with a submachine gun on his lap."

"The AOC deserted?" Major Randal said.

"There are several versions of the story as to why," Squadron Leader Dudgeon said. "Who knows the truth? They all end with Reggie being long gone."

"Who's in command?"

"Why Reggie, of course," Squadron Leader Dudgeon said. "We are in the middle of a shooting war, our commander has quit his post, and the senior air staff is conducting a full-fledged cover-up. We are not to tell anyone that Air Vice Marshal Smart has departed Habbaniya."

"You told me.'

"No, I did not."

"Do you have any good news?"

"Actually, yes," Squadron Leader Dudgeon said. "Perchance you heard that sound of bombing in the distance, early on last night?"

"Roger—about 2200 hours."

"That was the Iraqi Royal Air Force mistakenly hammering their own positions at Ramadi."

"Got confused," Major Randal said, lighting a Player's with his old battered Zippo. "Bombed themselves—night navigation can be a little tricky."

"One other item of interest," Squadron Leader Dudgeon said. "We sent our Gladiators out at first light to raid the airfield at Baqubah, north of Baghdad. Caught twenty-one Iraqi fighters on the ground."

"Really," Major Randal said, "knocked 'em all out, huh?"

Mandy looked up from petting Frankie. Major Randal winked at her. She kept her silence. Apparently, Squadron Leader Dudgeon had never been informed that Z Patrol had executed a raid on Baqubah.

That is what happens when different branches of the military are fighting their own private war and not communicating with each other.

"Lined up like wooden ducks in a shooting gallery," Squadron Leader Dudgeon said. "Parked along the edge of the airstrip. Only three of the rebel planes even made an attempt to get off the ground. Story of my life—I miss all the good ops."

"Maybe not."

Mandy said, "Tell Tony the truth, John. Everyone expects that from you."

"The truth?" Squadron Leader Dudgeon said.

Major Randal said, "You do it."

"Pam flew Murder Inc. to Baqubah last night. She landed on the airfield, and John and the mercs got out and shot up eighteen aircraft parked along the strip."

"No way," Squadron Leader Dudgeon said.

"We briefed it," Mandy said. "You should have been there so you would know what is going on around here, Tony. The only RAF officer in the tent was the commander of No. 1 Armored Car Company, and he's part of the Strike Force.

GRP. CAPT. WILLIAM "BUTCHER" SAVILLE CAME OUT OF HIS office, something he almost never did, and looked around. "Major Randal, the airfield has received a priority request from an inbound aircraft to have you meet it here when they land in the next few minutes."

"Any idea who, sir," Maj. John Randal said.

"No," Group Captain Saville said. "The aircraft is a Hudson. We were instructed to use a code word identifier not in our signal's book—*frogspawn*. The pilot plans a quick turnaround. Requests you, Lieutenant Honeycutt-Parker and Lieutenant Plum-Martin be standing by when it lands."

Major Randal had been wondering what had happened to James "Baldie" Taylor and Sqn. Ldr. Paddy Wilcox.

The Hudson came in low and slow, making its final approach. The instant it touched down, the Iraqi gunners on the heights opened on it. Clouds of black smoke from incoming artillery rounds mushroomed down the airstrip as the plane touched down.

Ground crew signaled frantically for the pilot to taxi between hangars, then around back and inside.

No one could explain why the gunners quit firing when they could no longer see their target. They could have kept shelling the hangars. For some reason, the Iraqi artillery never did.

When a set of stairs was rolled up against the door, a Royal Artillery lieutenant and two other ranks were the first to deplane. The men were carrying metal boxes of tools.

"Lt. Kit Wilson, sir," the officer introduced himself. "Can you direct me to the 18-pounders?"

"Eighteen pounders?" Major Randal said.

"The ceremonial cannon," Lieutenant Wilson said, "supposed to be a pair of them on Habbaniya. We are here to put them right."

"In that case," Major Randal said, "you'll find a police car parked right outside the hangar. Tell Officer Flanigan I said to run you over to the Air House."

"Very kind of you, sir."

"Welcome to Habbaniya, Lieutenant."

"There are three pallets of 4.5-inch High Explosive ammunition on board the Hudson. Would it be possible for you to arrange for someone to load the rounds on a truck and have it delivered to where the cannons are located, sir?"

"I'll see that it gets there, Wilson."

Jim Taylor and Squadron Leader Wilcox exited the aircraft.

"Enjoying your vacation, Major?" Jim called as he was coming down the stairs.

"You should think about becoming a travel agent after the war, General," Major Randal said. "Got a real talent for picking hot spots."

"Surely you do not believe I knew anything about the Golden Square laying Habbaniya to siege in advance of our trip," Jim said.

"I only found out the Iraqi Army had blockaded the air station when Paddy came on board the day we first landed."

"Bad timing," Major Randal said, "a lot of that going around."

"We had to fly up to Baghdad to get some of our … ah … friends out of the Embassy," Jim said. "After we flew them to a secure location, we received a signal to pick up some Boys Anti-Tank rounds. Seems there is a desperate shortage at Habbaniya.

"Then before we could fly the ammunition in, we were diverted to India to get Lieutenant Wilson and his team of artificers."

"The General's spot-on," Squadron Leader Wilcox said. "I explained the situation to him the minute you and Parker stepped off the plane."

"Where are Parker and Plum-Martin?" Jim asked. "You three are coming with us as soon as the ground crew can off-load our cargo and service the Hudson. We are headed down to Palestine to organize a relief column to break the siege."

"Parker and Brandy are on a yacht in the middle of Lake Habbaniyah," Major Randal said. "We have a clandestine floating patrol base out on the lake operating against the Iraqi rear."

"Brandy Seaborn is here at Habbaniya?"

"Affirmative," Major Randal said. "Heard we were here and flew in to join the party."

"Oh no!" Jim said. "Any way for us to ..."

"Negative," Major Randal said. "And I'm commanding the Habbaniya Strike Force. Pam is flying special ops. We won't be coming with you, General."

"Do not do this to me, Major," Jim said. "Please, can you imagine what Lady Seaborn's reaction is going to be when she finds out you are surrounded here? Do not force me to go through that again."

"Maybe you can get us relieved before Jane finds out," Major Randal said. "If you don't, well, we only have a couple of days' food left—can't stay mad for long."

"Can you two excuse us," Jim said, turning to Sqn. Ldr. Tony Dudgeon and Mandy.

"Stand fast, Mandy," Major Randal ordered. "Mandy's my aide, in addition to being in charge of our mounted messenger service.

"I've got Boy Scouts and the Women's Skeet Team with a couple of grandmothers on it pulling night ambushes. A fifteen-year-old magician is my Chief of Deceptions. Like I said, Brandy and Parker are behind Iraqi lines operating a floating patrol base that carries out raids every night.

"This fight is the Battle of the Alamo and Custer's Last Stand rolled into one, and everyone knows it. I don't have any secrets. Just don't tell us anything you don't want the rebels to know."

"All right," Jim said. "Mandy, do not repeat a word of what I am about to say to anyone. Do you understand?

"Perfectly."

"I have been activated to take charge of certain matters in Iraq since we do not have any other assets on the ground," Jim said. "A relief column is being organized in Palestine—*that* much you already know.

"What you do *not* know is that none of the troops have assembled yet, and some of the units, like the Lounge Lizards, are over 1,000 miles away across trackless desert from the assembly area, which is 500 miles from Habbaniya. It will be days before the column can get organized and move out. When the relief force does launch, it will be lorried infantry with some armored cars.

"There is no guarantee the column can win through—it will not have any air support. Field Marshal Wavell only gives the relief of Habbaniya a 50-50 chance of success. Says he 'believes' they can pull it off. There is a betting line at the Gezira Club on how long the station can hold out.

"That said, you people must have been putting up a pretty stiff fight here. Y-Service, our signals intelligence, has intercepted Iraqi radio messages that the 11th Infantry Brigade stationed on the plateau is refusing to stay in the line. The entire unit is having to be relieved by the 4th Infantry Brigade brought down from Baghdad."

"When?" Major Randal said.

"The movement was in process when we flew over," Jim said. "The Iraqis have a traffic jam developing at the bridge over the Euphrates. The 11th is streaming back to their barracks.

"A fresh artillery brigade is having to be rotated in also—same problem."

"Any idea why the rebels don't want to stand and fight?" Major Randal said.

"The intercepts, which are not any big secret since the fools are transmitting in the clear, report the Iraqi Army on the escarpment is being subjected to 'constant sniping, aerial bombing, ground attacks at all hours of the night and intense *psychological pressure*,'" Jim said. "What the hell is going on here, Major?"

Mandy started giggling.

"Show him," Major Randal said.

The girl produced a copy of the skull and bones Yellow #5 handbill out of her purse.

"My God, they will be studying this leaflet in psychological warfare schools for the next hundred years," Jim said, reading the flyer and then passing it to Squadron Leader Wilcox.

"Gone out yet?"

"Pam and I dropped the orange squirrels on the Iraqi positions late last night," Mandy said. "We only had orange—there were no yellow ones."

"The orange squirrels are the worst," Squadron Leader Wilcox said, studying the flimsy.

"How did you manage to dream this up?" Jim asked.

"Local journalism students," Major Randal said. "Smart teenagers with a license to kill."

"Drove a nail in the Iraqis' morale," Jim said. "Intense psychological pressure—you sure those Yellow #5 squirrels are *not* dangerous?"

"We could tell you, Jim," Mandy quipped. "But then we would have to ..."

"Major," Jim said, "you have become a bad influence."

26
MISS UCLA

SQN. LDR. TONY DUDGEON ORGANIZED A RAPID RESPONSE to Jim "Baldie" Taylor's report. He ordered every Oxford, Gordon and Gladiator being serviced at the airfield to the bridge as soon as they could take off. Veronica Paige was notified, and she passed the information to the Audax pilots stationed at the polo pitch. Those dive-bombers on the ground being rearmed and refueled were rerouted to the area as soon as they were topped off.

In short order, the Iraqi 4th Infantry Brigade and its replacement 11th Infantry Brigade were under a constant round-robin of high- and low-altitude aerial attack. The RAF pilots only had a few hours of flying light left, and they made the most of it.

The Oxfords and Gordons flew over, pickled their bombs and returned to base to rearm as fast as new bombs could be fitted. Audaxes pressed their hell-diving attacks suicidally low. Gladiators swooped in, strafing from inches off the ground.

There was no way to do a comprehensive bomb damage assessment with night coming on. However, what was clear to everyone flying was that the road leading up to and away from the bridge was littered with burning vehicles.

Since the battle had begun, No. 4 Service Flying Training School had suffered crushing losses in the flying and fighting. However, as the sun went down on Day Two, pilot morale was the highest it had been since the start of hostilities. For the first time, the fliers could see concrete results.

Still, the number of No. 4 SFTS serviceable aircraft, the number of pilots physically able to fly (two pilots even had to be grounded for combat fatigue) and the total number of combat sorties flown had fallen off dramatically.

The RAF was being shot to pieces.

AT LAST LIGHT, MAJ. JOHN RANDAL MADE A QUICK TOUR OF the Rod & Gun Club Big Bore Rifle Team positions along the edge of the airfield before returning to the Strike Force to begin preparing for the night's operations.

The riflemen had been on the firing line all day. The Iraqi infantry had pulled their forward positions back well up on the escarpment, which had created a "No Man's Land." Most of the shots the marksmen were getting now were at considerably longer range.

That was a good news/bad news development. The good news was that the shooters were driving the Iraqis back. The bad news was that they were not taking down as many rebel soldiers as before.

The members of the Big Bore Rifle Team liked to run up a high score.

Major Randal walked to a position and quietly gathered the men around. "We're not having this conversation—is that clear?"

The men did not relish the interruption. Pep talks were for youngsters. The marksmen were worn out from a long day in the sun, but an introduction like that made them more inclined to listen to what was coming next.

"Clear."

"The Iraqi 4th Infantry Brigade has quit the field and is being replaced by a fresh unit from Bagdad, the 11th Infantry Brigade. One of the reasons is the constant sniping. They can't take it.

"Pour it on, boys," Major Randal said. "Let's see if you can send the 11th Brigade packing too."

At every position, he left tired, happy, stone-cold, middle-aged killers.

"Drop by any time, Major, we always look forward to your visits."

Sure they did.

WHILE MAJ. JOHN RANDAL PERFORMED HIS ROUTINE inspection of the Boy Scouts and the Annie Oakleys, Murder Inc. was huddled in his Command Post tent with Lt. Pamala Plum-Martin, planning the night's raid on the two Iraqi howitzers behind the Burma Bund. Mandy delivered the latest aerial photos Sqn. Ldr. Tony Dudgeon had taken of the position.

The photos showed two 3.7 mm howitzers. The guns had been firing into RAF Habbaniya all day long. A platoon of rebel infantry secured the area.

Most likely the troops with the guns were feeling pretty good about themselves. Hidden behind the Bund, they were protected from direct fire from the base. And, they had beaten off an attack by a superior force earlier in the day.

Z Patrol intended to go over and kill them tonight.

Mr. Zargo and his men worked through every aspect of the operation—ran every possible combination of options. The idea was to cross the Euphrates, march far out into the desert, swing around behind, come back and hit the guns from the rear. The Iraqis would never expect something like that at 0200 hours.

"The day was for fighting, the night was for sleeping."

The seven men of Z Patrol, counting Major Randal, armed with automatic weapons firing all tracers, should be enough to deal with a drowsy platoon of Iraqi infantry. It was decided that Lieutenant Plum-Martin would drop a pair of 250-pound bombs on the two howitzers at precisely 0200 hours. That would be the signal for the waiting patrol to go in, kill the rebels and blow up the guns.

Charges were prepared to carry out the demolitions.

Every detail of the raid was carefully thought out, every move choreographed step by step. Each man knew exactly what his duties were, what he was responsible for and when he was supposed to do it. The mercs were good at planning missions that they would then go and carry out.

The only problem was getting across the Euphrates and back.

Major Randal arrived.

Mr. Zargo briefed him on the plan.

"How do you intend to cross the river?"

"That is the difficulty we have to resolve," Mr. Zargo said. "The patrol can go by boat, but then it would have to traverse the belt of swampy land. We saw how that worked out this morning. Besides, an Iraqi patrol might stumble upon the boat and be waiting in ambush when we return."

"Any of you men parachute-qualified?" Major Randal asked. "Didn't think so."

"Pam, can you land the Seagull on this straight stretch of road in the dark?" Major Randal asked, pointing to the pictomap with the tip of his Fairbairn Commando knife.

"John, what you are asking is not the same as putting down on a big wide regulation military airfield the way we did at Baqubah," Lieutenant Plum-Martin said. "I can land on the road, but it would need to be marked with landing lights."

"What's the minimum number of markers?" Major Randal said.

"Three per side," Lieutenant Plum-Martin said, "200-yard spacing."

"OK," Major Randal said. "Mandy, round up a half dozen five-gallon cans. Need to have metal tops. Pam, you show her how to mix up the oil and kerosene concoction. Fill the cans up a quarter of the way, tape the lids on tight and put them in a canvas duffel bag.

"I'll jump in and set up the landing lights."

"Parachute onto the Burma Bund all alone at night?" Lieutenant Plum-Martin said. "Are you serious?"

"Have a better idea?"

"Sounds like the worst plan since the 'Gunfight at the Blue Duck,'" Lieutenant Plum-Martin said.

"Your idea, as I recall," Major said. "'How hard can it be …?'"

"I never should have spoken those words," Lieutenant Plum-Martin said. "Ended with a Nazi bullet in your chest less than an inch from your heart."

"John has a heart?" Mandy said. "I thought a lion ate it."

THE EVENING BRIEFING AT THE STRIKE FORCE OPERATIONS Center was widely attended. Word had gotten around that if you wanted to be in the loop at the end of the day, Maj. John Randal's briefing was the place to be. Even Sqn. Ldr. Tony Dudgeon turned up—possibly because he did not want to miss knowing about any more raids on enemy airfields or possibly because he was a hard-drinking, woman-chasing combat pilot and knew Red and Lt. Pamala Plum-Martin would be in attendance.

Red prevailed on him to brief on the state of air operations.

Lt. Kit Wilson advised that the two eighteen-pound cannons would be repaired by the next day.

Lt. Col. Alistair Brawn briefed on the river crossing attack by the Kurds of No. 8 Company. While he did not categorize the mission as a failure, the commander of the Levies battalion made it clear that it had only had "limited" success.

Mr. Stanberry reported that the Iraqis had pulled their forward positions back on the plateau. The Rod & Gun Club shooters claimed another 348 rebels sniped. The marksmen had fired armor-piercing, small arms rounds into 213 Iraqi thin-skinned vehicles.

"The Great Teddy" reported the astonishing news that by actual count, sixty-three percent of all incoming artillery fire had been directed at one or another of his decoy targets. When a murmur of skepticism came from the audience, Mr. Twinning verified the number. One of his staff had the responsibility for plotting the fall of enemy artillery. Teddy was only quoting the numbers provided him.

The boy concluded his portion of the briefing with the statement, "The key idea of camouflage is deception." Not one person in the audience had the faintest idea what he was talking about but that was not important—it was only necessary for Teddy to understand and keep distracting the Iraqi artillery.

The Boy Scouts and the Annie Oakleys sergeants explained the ambushes they had conducted, killing two Iraqi infiltrators and three more goats.

Capt. Valentine Fabian and Capt. John Smith briefed the Strike Force raids planned for the night.

No mention was made of the upcoming Z Patrol operation.

Then the briefing turned to civil affairs. When it drew to a conclusion, everyone present had a reasonable idea of what had gone on all over RAF Habbaniya that day and what was planned in the way of evening combat operations. Attendees knew how many air strikes had been flown, how many artillery rounds had been logged incoming, how many people on base, both military and civilian, had been killed and wounded. They knew how many road repairs had been made, how many bandages had been rolled, etc. Knew more than anyone had a reasonable need to know, but having the knowledge made for cohesion.

People left understanding exactly where they fit into the big picture, feeling like they were part of a team. Everyone was contributing. Not simply sitting around waiting to be overrun.

Immediately afterward, Lieutenant Plum-Martin flew Captain Fabian out to the mother ship to issue Lake Patrol their orders. She had instructions to bring back Lt. Roy Kidd.

He was going with Z Patrol to raid the rebel 3.7 mm howitzers on Burma Bund.

Z PATROL HAD ITS FINAL BRIEFING. MAJ. JOHN RANDAL briefed. He had intended to bring in Lt. Joe Kidd as his wingman. However, Mr. Zargo informed him that King wanted to partner with him again tonight.

"King's our best point man. He specifically asked to work with you, Major, and since you are going to be the Patrol Leader you will want to be at the front."

"King, huh," Major Randal said. "He's a good man. Fine with me."

"Lieutenant Kidd can pair off with me," Mr. Zargo said. "Rear security."

The men test-fired their weapons. Everyone on Z Patrol except Major Randal was armed with a 9 mm Bergmann MP-18 submachine gun with a 32-round "snail" magazine. He was carrying his 9 mm Beretta M-38 SMG with its 30-round stick magazine affixed.

Murder Inc. was armed with a wide variety of exotic side arms. Every man carried at least one pistol they admitted to. The mercs all had a hideaway.

Lieutenant Kidd was wearing both his Luger P-08 automatics.

For the assault on the guns, every soldier on Z Patrol would have one special 32-round drum magazine loaded all tracer. The men would be attacking out of the night, utilizing the element of surprise. The idea was to make it look like there were a lot more of them than there actually were.

Major Randal always found the test firing and final weapons check (there was a joke that he would be checking his weapons right up until the minute the final assault went in) to be reassuring. If there were going to be a problem, it was best to find it out now before the mission. The weapons check also gave him a chance to observe the men going on the mission—evaluate them.

Finally, Major Randal called a patrol formation with the men, including Lieutenant Kidd and Mr. Zargo in the single rank. Taking his time, he went down the line and inspected every man. Each member of Z Patrol was ordered to jump up and down. If anything rattled, it would have to be adjusted so that it would not make any noise on the patrol.

Nothing rattled.

Major Randal inspected every visible weapon. He exchanged a few words with the troops, but mostly the men stared straight ahead in a position of relaxed attention as he went about his business. It was a hands-on inspection. He would grab each man's web gear and shake him.

The mercs did not resent the manhandling. In fact, they enjoyed the process. They were professional soldiers. The way they saw it, they got a chance to evaluate Major Randal—see if he knew his stuff.

The final inspection was totally unnecessary. Except that it demonstrated Major Randal's command authority, it showed that he was paying attention to detail and that he knew what he was doing. And, it gave him a chance to interact briefly one on one with each man.

Then Z Patrol moved to the Seagull's airstrip on the road. The mercs were not doing a lot of talking. There was some quiet laughter. Every man was wrapped up in his own thoughts.

Major Randal chuted up. Since he was the only paratrooper, there was no jumpmaster inspection for the simple reason there was no jumpmaster. Not that it mattered—he had done this before.

Then it was hurry up and wait. He did what he always did prior to a mission. He sat down, leaned back against his parachute, tried to relax and rehearsed the mission in his mind.

Major Randal became aware that Mandy was sitting close in the dark, touching him. It took him a minute to realize the girl was scared. He could feel her heart hammering like a runaway gun.

What was this?

"John," she said, "tell me about you and Lady Jane."

"Like what?"

"Pam said that when you two met, it was love at first sight."

"Well, I don't know about that, exactly."

"What was it like when you were first getting to know each other?"

"Jane was always laughing at me," Major Randal said, "only I didn't realize it at the time."

"Laughing at you?"

"Yeah, I used to tease her that she reminded me of my *old* high school teacher," Major Randal said. "Jane went along with it—only I didn't know that she knew all along that my student teacher was Miss UCLA—the best-looking beach bunny in California."

"So, how did that work out for you, John?"

"Just swell," Major Randal said. "Mandy, what the hell are you worried about?"

"I am afraid of what could happen to you tonight," Mandy said, fighting a sob. "You are always getting involved in something reckless."

"All I'm going to do is fly over to an empty spot in the desert," Major Randal said, "and jump out of an airplane."

What could possibly go wrong?

27

CHARGING THE GUNS

THE PLAN WAS SIMPLE. MAJ. JOHN RANDAL RAN OVER IT IN his head for the millionth time. Lt. Pamala Plum-Martin was going to drop him on a deserted stretch of road on the Burma Bund. He was going to set up six landing light markers improvised out of five-gallon cans.

While he was setting up the markers, Lieutenant Plum-Martin would fly back to RAF Habbaniya and pick up Z Patrol, augmented by Lt. Roy Kidd. Then she would fly back to the Burma Bund and land on the marked strip.

Z Patrol would disembark and move out on an azimuth for two miles into the desert. Lieutenant Plum-Martin would take off and return to RAF Habbaniya again, to have a pair of 250-pound bombs mounted on the Seagull. She would stay on the ground until 0145 hours, then take off and fly to the target area where the two Iraqi 3.7 mm howitzers were located.

At 0200 hours, Lieutenant Plum-Martin would drop her bombs

on the Iraqi position. As soon as they detonated, Z Patrol (waiting in concealment in the desert nearby) would immediately launch a ground assault on the Iraqi howitzers. Demolition charges would be placed on both guns.

Immediately upon destroying the 3.7s, Z Patrol would move out on the double, down the Burma Bund back to the improvised landing strip. The Seagull would land. The Strike Force troops would board and be extracted back to RAF Habbaniya.

The plan followed Raiding Forces "Rules for Raiding" down to the ground.

MAJ. JOHN RANDAL GLANCED AT HIS ROLEX. THE LIME green hands pointed at 2355 hours. Time to saddle up. As usual, every time he looked at his watch, he thought about Lady Jane. Usually he wondered what she was doing, but this time he knew.

Lady Jane was in England working things out with her husband, Cdr. Mallory Seaborn, RN. With his Norwegian snow princess, Rocky, now out of the picture in Cairo, that one was easy to figure.

The Seagull's engine wheezed, backfired, and finally, almost in slow motion turned over. Then it caught.

Z Patrol gathered around.

"I'll see you on the ground in a few minutes," Major Randal said. "Be ready to move out as soon as you step off the plane—King, then me, Joker, Queen, Ace, Jack, Lieutenant Kidd and Mr. Zargo. Let's do this."

Lt. Joe Kidd carried the duffel bag containing the five-gallon cans. It was attached to Major Randal's left ankle by a sixteen-foot lowering line. The two walked to the Seagull.

Major Randal sat in the open door dangling his canvas-topped raiding boots outside. He hooked the snap hook on his static line to a D-ring that had been bolted inside the fuselage. A sharp tug on the yellow static line cord made sure the hook was set and that the D-ring would not tear loose.

The field-expedient device had not been properly tested—probably worked.

Lieutenant Kidd handed him the duffel bag. Major Randal clenched it between his knees. He was going to exit the Seagull from the sitting position.

The door he was exiting was well forward toward the cockpit. Since the Seagull was a pusher-type aircraft with the engine positioned high, above and behind, the location of the door was not a problem. He would be able to communicate directly with Lt. Pamala Plum-Martin by leaning back and shouting.

The Seagull had never been intended as a paratroop dropper. Lady Jane had jumped one in Abyssinia. Tonight should work fine.

"Prepare for takeoff, John," Lieutenant Plum-Martin called.

The Seagull ran down the strip and lifted into the air. Lieutenant Plum-Martin kept it down low until they crossed the Euphrates. The swiftly flowing river sparkled in the moonlight.

Major Randal was going to be exiting from 1,000 feet. Normally, combat jumps are at half that altitude—the idea being to get down quick. Coming in hot was not a good idea tonight since he was jumping all alone.

The extra height would make for a softer landing.

When the Seagull climbed to altitude, Mandy unbuckled her safety belt and came back and knelt down beside him. Her job was to haul in the static line after he had jumped. In the event that Major Randal became entangled and "towed" behind the airplane, she had a razor-sharp knife strapped to her leg.

Plan B for the contingency of a towed parachutist was for Lieutenant Plum-Martin to fly back out over the river and Mandy to cut the line towing him. The chance of surviving was zero, but it was the only option they had. There was no way to drag Major Randal back inside the airplane and landing with him being towed behind was a no-go. He did not have a reserve parachute.

There are certain risks in jumping from an aircraft in flight.

"Anytime," Lieutenant Plum-Martin called, "go when ready."

"Don't you dare get towed," Mandy cried, feeling the full weight of her responsibility. "War really is hell, John!"

"Yeah," Major Randal said, giving her a wink. "But we still have to win it."

"Please be careful."

"Stop worrying," Major Randal said. "I'm a professional."

He threw the duffel bag straight out and followed it. Since he was shoving the bag, he did not get his hands down to lift off. The big canvas bag hit a wheel well and bounced back. Instead of lifting up and out, like slipping into a swimming pool, Major Randal hung up on the lip of the door and tipped forward.

He crashed into the rebounding canvas duffel bag, which knocked him backward, causing his head to clip the side of the Seagull. Naturally, Major Randal was not wearing a helmet—there was not a single jump helmet on RAF Habbaniya.

When he regained his senses, he was laying face-down, spread-eagled on top of the canopy of his semi-deployed parachute. That was impossible but true. The duffle bag attached to the sixteen-foot lowering line tied to his left boot was dangling down over the side of the canopy. He seemed to be floating on a magic carpet, but Major Randal knew that was an illusion.

In fact, he was burning in.

Major Randal struggled to his feet and, with the silk billowing up almost to his knees, ran three steps across the canopy and dove head first off the far side, following his duffel bag. Somehow he had to get jumper, parachute, and the equipment bag in some semblance of the right attitude before they came down.

When Major Randal went over the side, the parachute turned inside out—a malfunction known as an inverted canopy. One of the lines wrapped around his right ankle, then whipped across the top of the canopy, taking up the slack until he was jerked up short, causing a second malfunction known as a Mae West.

At this point, Major Randal was suspended upside down under the inverted canopy. A second major malfunction—created by the line wrapped around his ankle running across and over the top of the parachute—had developed, causing it to have two small silk domes instead of one big silk dome. It now looked like Mae West's brassiere. He was hanging by one ankle, while the duffle bag was dangling down from the other leg, swinging in the breeze—exactly where it was supposed to be.

In Airborne Forces jargon, his situation was "not good."

Your face is not one of the requisite five points of contact incidental to a parachute landing fall (PLF).

Hanging upside down did afford Major Randal an excellent view of his drop zone (DZ). That was when he got the bad news. There were people on the ground.

They were not part of the plan.

There are nomadic scavengers in the desert who do not belong to any organized sect or clan, who do not recognize boundaries or national governments. They steal for a living. The nomads view everyone else as their enemy and have no compulsion about slitting a throat or two in the course of their business—which is crime.

To them the war was an opportunity.

The men standing on the road (Major Randal's DZ) were hoping to find a way to recover a few of the brass shell casings from the Iraqis' 3.7 mm howitzers battery firing on RAF Habbaniya. Since the Iraqi Army routinely shot at them when they came around, the scavengers were keeping their distance while waiting their chance.

When the Seagull flew over, the men were surprised to see something detach itself and float down to earth. Not one of them had ever seen a parachute before. They had no idea a man was attached to it.

When Major Randal smoked in, he managed to duck his head before slamming into the ground and actually hit four of his five points of contact—only in *reverse* sequence. That he lived through the PLF was a testament to his training at No. 1 British Parachute School.

Major Randal was semi-paralyzed by the impact. All the wind was knocked out of him. The parachute came straight down and landed on top of him. One of the nomads ran over and pounced on the silk.

Allah had sent a present.

When Major Randal regained his senses, he was entangled in the canopy. Someone had picked him up and was attempting to carry him off. His arms were pinned against his sides and he could not reach his submachine gun or any of his pistols.

The one weapon he could lay hands on was his Fairbairn Commando knife. Major Randal managed to slide it out of its sheath. Unable to see anything, he stabbed at his abductor through the cloth of the parachute.

The 7 1/2-inch double-edged blade struck something solid and went in halfway to its hilt.

A loud shriek was his reward. Major Randal hit the ground again hard when the startled scavenger dropped him. When he fought free from the silk, he saw a screaming man lying on the ground, holding his bloody thigh with the nickel-plated handle of the F/S knife sticking out. A small group of men were running in his direction out of the dark.

The mob appeared to be armed with clubs and sticks ... maybe swords. They were on him. Major Randal rolled over on his back, brought up his 9 mm Beretta M-38 submachine gun.

Brrraaaap. Brrrraaap. Brrrraaap. The attackers went down in a pile.

Major Randal struggled to his feet. He limped over to the man with his Fairbairn knife stabbed in his thigh. The wounded scavenger looked up, screeching in horror. *Brrrraaaap.*

So much for slipping in unannounced.

THE SEAGULL LANDED ON ITS PRIVATE STRIP ON THE BACK road at RAF Habbaniya. Mr. Zargo had Z Patrol formed up and ready to board. The troops were in line in the reverse sequence in which they would disembark. Mandy jumped out, "Go, Go, Go."

The mercs shuffled on board. They took up positions sitting on the deck of the Seagull, with their backs against the fuselage. King was by the door ready to lead the patrol off. Mr. Zargo, serving in the role of Assistant Patrol Leader, would be last man.

Lt. Roy Kidd was sitting next to him with his 9 mm MP-18 between his knees. "You guys do ops like this much?"

"Not as often," Mr. Zargo said, "as we would have people believe."

The Seagull lifted off. Lt. Pamala Plum-Martin made a beeline straight for where they had dropped Maj. John Randal. She was not expecting him to be able to set up the lights this quickly, but if he managed to, the last thing she wanted was him sitting alone in the desert with signal fires burning.

The Royal Marine was also worried.

Mandy had reported that she thought Major Randal had struck the side of the airplane when he exited.

As soon as Lieutenant Plum-Martin climbed to altitude, she saw the clandestine landing lights glowing in the bottoms of the cans. Major Randal was OK! He had worked fast.

"Stand-by to land."

Lieutenant Plum-Martin brought the Seagull around hard, causing her passengers to hang on. This was not a commercial flight. She wanted to put down fast.

King trotted off the Seagull. Major Randal was standing in the middle of the road, holding his 9 mm Beretta M-38 submachine gun with the butt on his hip. There was a pile of dead men littering the landing strip.

"You do that, Major?"

"Yeah," Major Randal said. "Check 'em out to make sure they're all KIA."

Mr. Zargo came up to the front of the column when it halted.

"Shots have been fired," Major Randal said. "Didn't have any choice."

"Only yours?"

"Four short bursts—last one probably wasn't necessary."

"Nothing to concern yourself about," Mr. Zargo said. "Random firing is heard in the desert at night. No one pays attention unless there is an exchange of gunfire."

"All clear," King said, when he returned. "Ready when you are, Major."

"Move out," Major Randal said. He glanced at his Panerai wrist compass to confirm line-of-march and indicated the direction to his point man. "Send up the pace count every half mile, Mr. Zargo."

"Wilco."

The patrol snaked out into the desert, moving fast. As they disappeared into the dark, the Seagull ran down the road and took off back to RAF Habbaniya to rearm with a pair of 250-pound fragmentation bombs. As soon as everyone was gone, a pair of hyenas slunk up on the road and began to nose around the dead nomads.

Land navigation in a flat, featureless desert at night can be problematic. However, tonight Major Randal was aided by the Iraqis firing their howitzers at RAF Habbaniya every fifteen minutes or so. All he had to do was to keep the guns on his right and move two miles.

On the azimuth they were traveling, when they reached their Objective Rally Point (ORP), Z Patrol would be directly behind the Iraqi gun battery a quarter mile out in the dark. The plan was that at 0145 hours, the patrol would leave the ORP and move up to within approximately 200 yards of the rebel position. Lieutenant Plum-Martin would be on station and toggle both her bombs at 0200 hours.

Except for the fact that Major Randal was in more pain than he cared to admit, the movement to the ORP was like a training exercise. Lesson learned: in the desert, people can be expected to be encountered on roads, at waterholes or other prominent terrain features, even in the middle of the night.

Z Patrol arrived at the ORP at 0115 hours. The patrol set up a small perimeter. After coordinating with Mr. Zargo, Major Randal and King moved out silently on a reconnaissance of the Iraqi gun battery. They were specifically scouting for rebel listening posts (LP).

King was disappointed. The Iraqis did not have any LPs out. Neutralizing sentries was his specialty.

Major Randal was not disappointed. He did not want to run any chance of alerting the rebel security platoon of their presence. There are no guarantees when eliminating an armed sentry, no matter the skill level of the person doing the takedown.

Z Patrol closed in on the Iraqi guns. The patrol was on line. Major Randal and King moved to the center of the formation so that when the men went in firing he would be in the best position to exercise command and control over the assault.

The Iraqis had no idea what was about to happen.

The pair of 250-pound bombs going off almost simultaneously created a massive end-of-the-world type explosion. The blast seemed to lift Z Patrol off the ground. Everyone was blinded and deafened by the tremendous flash. The mercs all felt like they had been body-slammed.

The concussion from the detonation was a lot worse than Major Randal anticipated. They may have inched forward closer than 200 yards. If it was this bad for Z Patrol, he wondered how the rebels were doing. Time to find out.

"FOLLOW ME!" Major Randal shouted, as he stood up firing his weapon. "LIGHT 'EM UP—YEEEEEHAAAAAAA!"

Z Patrol stepped off as one, even though their ears were ringing and they were still staggered from the tremendous bomb blast. The mercs were screaming, they were firing short, controlled bursts from their 9 mm Bergmann MP-18s, and they were not stopping for anything. The stream of tracers streaking from the eight submachine guns converging on the battery lit up the target.

In the dark—considering the gigantic explosion and the element of surprise—it must have seemed to the rebels like a battalion attacking. Z Patrol did not have numbers on their side, but they did have speed of attack and violence of action. Their execution was textbook flawless.

Grenades were exploding. Mercs were cursing and yelling. Automatic weapons were blazing. Panicked Iraqis were running and shouting in confusion. The patrol swept into their camp, firing on the move, chopping rebels down left and right.

The two 3.7 mm guns swam into view out of the dark and smoke. Designated demolitions men broke off and slapped their prepared charges into the breech of both guns.

"FIRE IN THE HOLE, FIRE IN THE HOLE."

The assault line did not waver or take cover. As ordered, the mercs kept moving forward, guns chattering. Magazines were being changed and weapons recharged—the firing never slacked. Z Patrol swept completely through the rebel camp.

Whuuuuump. Whuuuuump. The charges went off behind them.

"Clear, sir. Clear, sir. Clear, sir," mercs were calling as they secured their assigned sectors of the enemy position.

Resistance was almost nonexistent. Return fire was light, and what there was of it was wild. Most of the enemy troops had been asleep when the 250-pound bombs slammed in. Those rebels not killed or wounded by the bomb blast or the walking fire of the Z Patrol assault abandoned the battery and fled into the desert in all directions—many without their boots or their weapons.

No one fought back.

"Casualty report?" Major Randal said, looking around the objective.

Dead rebels littered the ground like rag dolls. Only a few could have escaped. The howitzers were twisted metal.

"None on our side, Major," Mr. Zargo said.

"Weapons recovered?" Z Patrol was going to secure any automatic weapons captured and take them back.

"Two Bren guns, Major," Mr. Zargo reported. "Six Thompsons."

"Let's go, King," Major Randal ordered. "No sense hanging around here to see if any bad guys get their courage up."

"Moving now, Major."

Z Patrol double-timed down the Burma Bund straight back to where the Seagull had landed the team. The landing markers were re-lit. Lieutenant Plum-Martin was orbiting overhead and touched down before the last flare flickered on.

Z Patrol filed on quickly. The Seagull taxied for takeoff and was airborne in a matter of minutes. The mood onboard the aircraft was controlled exhilaration. Attacking a gun battery is one of the toughest military operations in the book to accomplish.

The mercs had known that going in.

Major Randal, the only raider to receive a scratch tonight, was sitting in the door of the Seagull, with his boots dangling out when it lifted off. One of his last Italian cigars from Abyssinia was clenched in his teeth, unlit. He watched the soft glow of the landing lights in the five-gallon cans down below disappear as the Seagull banked around hard and headed for home.

Mission accomplished. The lime green hands on the Rolex said 0235 hours—ahead of schedule.

Major Randal wondered what Lady Jane was doing right about now.

SITUATION REPORT: NUMBER 1

MAY 1940 ASSESSMENT BY GENERAL ARCHIBALD WAVELL, Commander-in-Chief Middle East Command: Why oil is important to Great Britain.

1. Oil, shipping, air power and sea power are the keys to this war, and they are interdependent.

> Air power and naval power cannot function without oil.

> Oil, except in very limited quantities, cannot be brought to its destination without shipping.

> Shipping requires the protection of naval power and air power.

2. We have access to practically all the world's supplies of oil.

> We have most of the shipping.

> We have naval power.

> We have potentially the greatest air power, when fully developed.

THEREFORE, WE ARE BOUND TO WIN THE WAR.

SITUATION REPORT:
NUMBER 2

MAY 1940 ASSESSMENT BY GENERAL ARCHIBALD WAVELL, Commander-in-Chief Middle East Command: Why oil is important to Germany.

1. Germany is very short of oil and has access only to very limited quantities.
2. Germany's shipping is practically confined to the Baltic.
3. Germany's naval power is small.
4. Germany's air power is great but is a diminishing asset.

THEREFORE, GERMANY IS BOUND TO LOSE THE WAR.

SITUATION REPORT:
NUMBER 3

APRIL 1941 ASSESSMENT BY PRIME MINISTER WINSTON
Churchill: Why is Iraq strategically important?

1. There is a lot of oil in Iraq.*
2. Should Germany gain control of the Iraqi oil fields, the conclusions in
Situation Reports 1 & 2 by General Wavell will be invalidated.

THEREFORE, WHOEVER CONTROLS IRAQ WINS THE WAR.

*Iraq produces enough oil to supply Germany's annual military needs.

SITUATION REPORT:
NUMBER 4

HAND DELIVERED MOST SECRET EYES ONLY PRIME MINISTER
Ultra Order of Battle Intercept:

The German 22nd Air-Landing Division placed on alert for immediate deployment to Iraq.

BURN AFTER READING

1
WOLF'S TEETH

"ARE YOU PREPARED TO RECEIVE A WARNING ORDER," MAJ. John Randal DSO, MC said. It was not really a question. No answer was expected.

Capt. Valentine Fabian; Capt. John Smith; Sqn. Ldr. John Page; Sqn. Ldr. Paddy Wilcox DSO, OBE, MC, DFC; Sqn. Ldr. Tony Dudgeon; Lt. Pamala Plum-Martin OBE; Lt. Roy Kidd; Lt. Kit Wilson and Mr. Zargo were sitting in folding chairs in the small private briefing area of Major Randal's red-and-white-striped Command Post tent. The formal statement alerted them that a mission was imminent. And, that they would be playing key roles in it.

Tension ratcheted up.

"*SITUATION.*"

Col. Ouvrey Roberts and a tall broad-shouldered civilian in a cream-colored suit and round steel-rimmed glasses came in at the back of the tent.

"Colonel," Major Randal said. "This is a classified briefing."

"Quite right, Major. I think in this case we can make an exception."

"Sir ..."

"Jimmy has been touring the Middle East on official business and arrived here at RAF Habbaniya this morning in the capacity of a neutral observer," Colonel Roberts said. "Among other things, he is a captain in the United States Marine Corps.

"I am confident you can count on his complete discretion."

Squadron Leader Wilcox made eye contact with Major Randal and gave him a small nod.

Major Randal said, "Situation: The Iraqi Army in division strength occupies the escarpment between RAF Habbaniya and the lake two miles distant. The rebels have been subjected to intensive bombing, an aggressive night raiding program and a psychological warfare campaign that caused the Golden Square to have to replace 4th Infantry Brigade and bring in a fresh artillery brigade after only two days of action because their troops quit fighting.

"*MISSION.* Tonight at 0200 hours, Strike Force will conduct a raid on the village of Sin ad Dhibban—Wolf's Teeth."

Major Randal flipped the cloth covering over the back of the tripod revealing a diagram map of the objective.

"*EXECUTION.*"

Captain Smith, No. 4 Levies Company, will move down the road to attack the right flank of the Wolf's Teeth with his Levies Company. Captain Fabian, A Company, King's Own Royal Rifles, guided by Mr. Zargo's Z Patrol, will scale the escarpment, infiltrate 'round the left flank and attack simultaneously with No. 4.

"Squadron Leader Page will follow Captain Smith's company with No.1 Armored Car Company. Once contact is made, the armored cars will pass through No.4 Levies Company and spearhead the final assault.

"Lt. Roy Kidd will land his patrol from the lake, move overland and conduct a demonstration to the rear of Wolf's Teeth, five minutes prior to the main attack.

"All three Strike Force companies will attack on signal and consolidate on the objective. Once Wolf's Teeth has been secured, we will return to RAF Habbaniya. Order of return march will be Levies, King's Own and

No. 1 ACC.

"CONCEPT OF THE OPERATION."

"Murder Inc. will supply guides to lead the companies to their Final Objective Lines.

"Squadron Leader Wilcox, flying a Gordon bomber, and Lt. Plum-Martin in her Seagull, will drop a pair of 250-lb. bombs on Wolf's Teeth at 0200 hours, which will be the signal to A Company, King's Own and No. 4 Company Levies to launch the ground assault. No. 1 Armored Car Company will pass through No. 4 and drive home the final attack.

"Squadron Leader Dudgeon will lead an element of Oxford bombers flying from the airfield to carry out suppression missions in the event the Iraqi artillery attempts to engage. Sqn. Ldr. Dudgeon's flight will also interdict any mechanized or infantry reinforcements should they attempt to respond to counter the Strike Force raid.

"Lieutenant Wilson will support the withdrawal phase with the two 4.5 guns that have been outside Air Headquarters; his fitters have serviced and certified them cleared for action.

"This is a raid of short duration. Execute it with speed and violence of action. Consolidate on the objective. On command, be prepared to pull out and return to base.

"Tomorrow at 1000 hours, Maj. Ted Everett will launch a follow-up three-company attack on Wolf's Teeth with B Company of the King's Own under command of Captain Clayton, and C Company commanded by Major Gibbons. No. 1 ACC will be attached.

"Major Everett's mission is to mop up the remaining Iraqis in the vicinity—drive 'em out of the Wolf's Teeth.

"COMMAND AND SIGNAL."

"I command the Strike Force raid. The chain of command is me, Captain Fabian, Captain Smith, then Squadron Leader Page. The Operations Order is scheduled for 1400 hours. Line of Departure (LD) time is 0115 hours for the King's Own, 0130 for the Levies. No. 1 ACC will follow the Levies Company across the LD.

"The signal to attack will be the airstrike on the objective at 0200 hours.

"The signal to withdraw will be three green flares.

"ADMINISTRATION AND SUPPLY."

"Make sure every man has a double basic load of ammunition with one magazine loaded all tracers for the initial assault and four frag grenades.

"Questions?"

VERONICA PAIGE AND HER DAUGHTER MANDY CAME INTO the CP tent when the Warning Order was concluded. After everyone cleared out, Major Randal sat perched on the edge of his desk.

"Take your blouse off, Major," Veronica commanded.

Maj. John Randal started unbuttoning his faded green jungle jacket. He noted that Jimmy had not left the tent.

Getting the jacket off was not easy. Major Randal was wrapped in bandages from his armpits to the bottom of his ribs, some of which were probably cracked. He grimaced in pain.

Mandy started cutting through the bandages with a pair of scissors. Major Randal was black and blue, with brilliant patches of violet, dark purple and green mixed in. Jimmy's eyes squinted when he saw the scars beneath the bruises. An experienced African big game hunter, he knew they were too large to be a leopard—lion?

Major Randal said, "United States Marines?"

"James J. Roosevelt," Capt. Roosevelt said.

"Really," Major Randal said.

"My father, *President* Franklin D. Roosevelt, sent me on an around-the-world tour to let certain interested parties know that it will only be a matter of time before the U.S. enters the war. I am out here doing exactly that. Winding up my tour."

"Welcome to scenic Habbaniya," said Major Randal."

"You are on my short list of people to talk to," Captain Roosevelt said. "James Taylor told me this was where I would find you."

"James Taylor?"

Captain Roosevelt looked at Major Randal, "I flew in with him this morning. Baldie said you would probably play it this way—*frogspawn*."

Major Randal lit a cigarette with his battered Zippo lighter with the crossed sabers of the U.S. 26th Cavalry Regiment on the front.

Veronica had wrapped a clean bandage around his chest and was tying it off.

"Finish up, Mrs. Paige," Major Randal ordered. "You're not a doctor."

"Nor a veterinarian," Veronica said. "Mandy, make the Major soak one hour in the pool, starting right now, then rewrap him with fresh bandages."

"Yes, Mother," Mandy said. "I am going to go change into my swimsuit. Be ready for the pool when I get back, John—do not give me a hard time."

"On your way out," Major Randal said. "Tell Flanigan not to let anyone in here."

When they were alone, Captain Roosevelt said, "After I conclude my business in the Middle East, my next assignment will be in the office of the Coordinator of Information. Col. "Wild Bill" Donovan's my new boss. He tried to see you when he was out here a few months ago, but you were behind the lines in Abyssinia."

"Fighting 69th," Major Randal said. "Medal of Honor?"

"That's him," Captain Roosevelt said. "He asked me to evaluate British Commando training and operations, with an eye to setting up Marine Raider Battalions in the future. Your name came up as being an authority on small-scale raiding. In addition, Baldie says you are the most experienced guerrilla commander in Africa.

"Both raiding and guerrilla operations are of great interest to Colonel Donovan."

"I see," said Major Randal, which meant he did not have a clue what the Marine was talking about.

"The Colonel asked me to inform you that when the U.S. enters the war he intends to offer you a job."

"And what might that be?"

"I have no idea," Captain Roosevelt said. "It is my understanding that Colonel Donovan is working out a joint operating agreement with one of the British Intelligence agencies where the U.K. and the U.S. cooperate on certain activities, both overt and covert. Would you be interested in something of that nature—direct action?"

"Captain," Major Randal said. "The Iraqi Army can stroll down that ridge they're sitting on and overrun this base in five minutes anytime they decide to get up and do it. I'm not thinking any farther out than that."

"You are not opposed to the idea, in principle—I can report to the Colonel?"

"If the United States comes in, Colonel Donovan can count on me to serve where needed," Major Randal said. "Best check back later, though. There's 10,000 bad guys out there on that hill, and we're planning to make 'em really mad tonight."

"Yes, you are," Captain Roosevelt said. "A bold plan in the extreme—some might call it suicidal."

"When I arrived, Habbaniya had four days' rations for the civilians," Major Randal said. "*This* is day four."

"Read your book, *Jump on Bela*," Captain Roosevelt said. "Didn't know what to expect when I finally got around to meeting you. Never imagined to find the legendary commander of the Strategic Raiding Forces being bullied by a couple of women."

"Yeah," Major Randal said. "Kind of a let-down, wasn't it?"

MAJ. JOHN RANDAL WAS SOAKING IN THE SHALLOW END OF the pool said to be the best in the Royal Air Force. Mandy was sunning on a lounge chair, watching him over the top of a three-month-old movie star magazine. He was in a lot of pain.

Intermittently, an incoming artillery round detonated somewhere on the base. Most were aimed at one decoy installation or another designed by fifteen-year-old magician "The Great Teddy," doing very little material damage. The explosions had become commonplace at this point in the siege.

Unless, that is, one landed close by.

Mr. Zargo was giving Capt. James J. Roosevelt a tour of the Strike Force and its auxiliary operations.

Capt. Valentine Vivian Fabian, Capt. John Smith and Sqn. Ldr. John Page were at their company command posts, issuing Warning Orders to their platoon leaders—the two Strike Force infantry companies had both been reconstituted back to their original table of organization for the raid.

Sqn. Ldr. Paddy Wilcox and Lieutenant Pamala-Plum Martin were making preparations for the night's mission. The Gordon bomber was flown down and landed on the stretch of road that Lieutenant Plum-Martin used for her nocturnal operations in the Seagull. After it was covered up by field-expedient camouflage netting developed by "The Great Teddy" out of fishing nets, Squadron Leader Wilcox entertained himself counting the patched-up bullet holes and shrapnel splinters in the airplane.

He gave up when the number reached seventy-two.

Major Randal was lying on the steps in the shallow end of the pool, soaking his battered ribs and reading a pocket-sized training pamphlet authored by a Col. G.A. Wade, MC, titled, *The Fighting Patrol.*

The colonel listed six of what he described as "CHARACTERISTICS: Determination, Skill, Ability, Instinctive Reaction, Simple Movements and Confidence.

"These are the six principal characteristics we should aim to produce in our fighting patrols."

Major Randal thought that sounded good.

1. Determination to attack any enemy quickly and bloodthirstily.

2. Skill in handling weapons.

3. Ability to move quietly, inconspicuously and *quickly* across the landscape.

4. Instinctive reaction to attack.

5. Power to carry out simple, well-synchronized pincer and other movements.

6. Confidence in the Patrol Leaders.

Major Randal went back and re-read the list of "Characteristics" and verified that they did not match the second "six principal characteristics." Hmmmm?

Nevertheless, *Fighting Patrol* was a neat little handbook with a wealth of good advice for how to prepare for, and conduct, a fighting patrol. Major Randal thought it would be an excellent tool for training Patrol Leaders.

Colonel Wade was clearly keen to get at the enemy. His introduction to the art of training "Fighting Patrol Leaders" on the flyleaf concluded with, "And then, when the Great Moment comes for you to lead your fighting patrol against the invading Huns, KEEP YOUR MEN TOGETHER, KEEP YOUR MOMENTUM, and you will find yourself enjoying the FINEST SPORT ON EARTH!"

No invading Huns here, but Major Randal believed the colonel's advice was tailor-made for the nights raid on Wolf's Teeth—concentrate Strike Force's companies and drive hard on the objective, fast.

Overhead, a single Wellington bomber had detached itself from a formation of five that was on its way to bomb the Iraqi airfield at Fallujah. It did a flyover of the converted polo pitch/golf course airstrip at about 1,000 feet. Three tiny specks detached from the aircraft, parachutes billowing out, looking like swimming octopuses as their static lines deployed them. The crack of each individual canopy popping open was distinct.

Mandy looked up and shaded her eyes with her hand. "Wonder who would be mad enough to parachute into a place surrounded by homicidal Iraqis?"

"Tanning while standing-by to be overrun by 'em," Major Randal said, going back to his reading. "And, you think someone *else* isn't playing with a full deck?"

Presently, a staff car pulled up at the gate to the Officers' Club. Capt. the Lady Jane Seaborn, RM Lana Turner and RM Rita Hayworth stepped out.

Major Randal said to Mandy, "Here comes trouble."

ABOUT THE AUTHOR

PHIL WARD IS A DECORATED COMBAT VETERAN COMMISSIONED at age nineteen. A former instructor at the Army Ranger School, he has had a lifelong interest in small unit tactics and special operations. He lives on a mountain overlooking Lake Austin with his beautiful wife, Lindy, whose father was the lieutenant governor to both Ann Richards and George W. Bush.

Other books in the Raiding Forces Series:

Those Who Dare

Dead Eagles

Blood Wings

Roman Candle

Guerrilla Command

Necessary Force

Private Army

Visit **www.raidingforces.com** and **www.facebook.com/raidingforces** to read more about the Raiding Forces Series.

Made in the USA
San Bernardino, CA
23 June 2014